The Gl

Mink Elliott is a hard-working writer, ridiculously proud dog-owner and completely knackered mother. She mainly writes about the funny side of life, if she can find it.

Also by Mink Elliott

Annie Beaton's Year of Positive Thinking
The Glory Years

THE
GLORY
YEARS

MINK ELLIOTT

hera

First published in the United Kingdom in 2022 by

Hera Books
Unit 9 (Canelo), 5th Floor
Cargo Works, 1-2 Hatfields
London, SE1 9PG
United Kingdom

A CIP catalogue record for this book is available from the British Library.

Print ISBN 978 1 80436 178 8
Ebook ISBN 978 1 80436 177 1

Cover design by Rose Cooper

Look for more great books at www.herabooks.com

Printed and bound in Great Britain by Clays Ltd, Elcograf S.p.A.

1

To Sam and Max, the sunshines of my life

We shall not cease from exploration
And the end of all our exploring
Will be to arrive where we started
And know the place for the first time

Four Quartets, T. S. Eliot (no relation!)

'And menopause can fuck right the fuck off.' Kate sniffed. 'I mean, who gets pimples on their wrinkles? And wrinkles on their bloody cankles?!'

Portia laughed at this – with rather a lot of unexpected force as it turned out because, at exactly the same time, she also farted.

Gallantly, neither Seamus nor Kevin batted an eyelid. Kate, however, snorted in delight and chuckled hard – so much so, her pelvic floor let her down, as per, and she crossed her legs, cursing herself for not putting a Tena Lady in her knickers earlier.

Once you hit *uncertain age*, she thought, it's either flatulence or incontinence that'll get you. Often both. Simultaneously.

She loved how incongruous it was, though: the gorgeous, sophisticated, goddess-like Portia letting rip like that. Just goes to show, she thought, you can take the ladette out of the Nineties, but you can't take the Nineties out of the ladette.

Confident Portia slapped her (slim, shapely) thigh and laughed along, but the two men seated at the table now swapped nervous glances. Was it okay to laugh? Would that render them insensitive? Pathetic incels?? Sexist pigs? Raving misogynists? And what the hell were cankles, anyway? They nodded slowly at each other, as if to give each other the go-ahead and haw-haw'd cautiously, shrugging their shoulders and pouring more wine into their own glasses.

Kate continued to cackle, safe in the knowledge that while, yes, she was indeed in possession of calves as thick as Doric columns, there were, as yet, no wrinkles on them.

Earlier that day, she had spotted a line encircling each cankle and had been suitably mortified. But she was quickly relieved to discover they were merely marks left by the too-tight trainer socks she'd been wearing as she tried to tackle that old Davina McCall exercise DVD in her front room again.

But at least with the cankles remark, she'd managed to totally trounce the competition in the Who's Looking Oldest? game. Although, to be honest (as Kate always tried to be these days, what with trying to be a good role model for the kids and all), it was never really much of a contest.

Everyone knew that Kate, with a penchant for anything with astronomical levels of fat, sugar and salt and two kids under her undo-up-able belt had always looked way more haggard and older than her best friend, childless Portia.

Kate tilted her head, looking fondly at her, remembering how the pair had fared so differently nearly twenty years ago now when they both read *French Women Don't Get Fat* and adopted its cool approach to eating and drinking.

It had been written by the impossibly suave female CEO of Veuve Clicquot who advocated walking everywhere, turning the TV off, quaffing expensive French (Veuve Clicquot anyone?) champagne, taking a few bites of buttery croissants and popping a couple of squares of dark organic chocolate into a perfectly lipsticked mouth every now and again.

It was all about being sophisticated and indulging your desires every so often, pushing the pleasure principle, the idea that a *little* bit of what you fancy does you good.

Of course, Portia, who already looked like a French noir movie star by the time she was three years old, had no trouble staying slim and looking all leggy and louche and glamorous whatever she did. The French woman diet involved very little change for her, being blessed as she was with lustrous hair, porcelain skin, legs up to her armpits and an award-winning, gold medal pout.

Kate, though? *Quel catastrophe!* Just a few centimetres shorter than Declan, her twelve-year-old son, she had always been a total stranger to such alien concepts as 'moderation', 'control' and 'self-restraint'. And she just didn't *like* dark chocolate – give her a family block of Fruit & Nut, a packet of Tunnock's tea cakes and a couple of Kit Kat Chunkys any day – but bitter, tooth-breaking dark chocolate? What was the bloody point?

An image of her chubby arm with its fat fingers opening a battered old fridge full of Veuve Clicquot and KitKats flashed into Kate's head. All the French woman diet ever made her was drunk and fat. And overdrawn.

'Podgy, pissed and poor,' she muttered to herself, as if she were introducing three new, lesser-known dwarves to Snow White.

'Who?' Declan sauntered into the room, rubbing his eyes, bloodshot and bleary from too many hours glued to the Xbox.

'Hmm?' Kate un-cocked her head, de-glazed her eyes and sat up straight in her chair. 'What are you doing down here?'

'I couldn't sleep,' Declan put on a baby voice.

'Bollocks,' Seamus piped up. 'You've been throwing that bloody Xbox controller around your room in a rage for hours.'

'Have not!' Declan squeaked.

'Have too!' Seamus boomed back.

'Have not!' Declan squealed again.

'Have too!'

'Have not!'

'Have TOO!'

'Have NOT!'

'Have—'

'Oh, for fu—' Kate groaned. 'Grow up, the pair of you.'

Seamus and Declan glared at her and responded in perfect harmony: 'YOU grow up!'

Kate shot Portia a defeated, look-what-I-have-to-put-up-with glance and eyed the wine bottle hungrily. Her bottom lip quivered ever so slightly and she knocked back the dregs of her tepid Pepsi Max.

'Decko, honey,' Portia said, her voice deep and warm from the wine, 'why can't you sleep?'

Declan immediately softened. He loved Portia, his godmother, who had always been there for him when his mum was otherwise occupied. There was something safe and patient and totally loving about her. He wandered over to her and pouted.

'Phoebe says Grannie's coming to live with us.'

Seamus spat out his mouthful of Pinot Noir and gasped. 'What?'

'Over-reaction, much?' Portia scoffed.

'Phoebe says a lot of things,' Kate muttered, rolling her eyes to the ceiling and almost shouting. 'She thinks she knows everything, but really, she's only fifteen – she hasn't got a Scooby, sweetheart.'

'I don't want her to come here,' Declan went on. 'She's mean and creepy and always says horrible things.'

'Only because she was gaslighted—' Portia began.

'GASLIT!' came Phoebe's voice from upstairs.

'...by George for all those years. He really was a bit of a prick, it has to be said.'

'Porsh!' Kate shot her a filthy look. 'That's my dad you're talking about!'

'Oh, come on! Just because she didn't want to have sex with him after she'd had you and Steve, he went off and had a gazillion affairs – and then convinced her she was crazy for being suspicious! Dictionary definition gaslighted.'

'Why wasn't I consulted about this, Kate?' Seamus looked wounded.

'Ah, she'll never come, don't worry. I asked her, but she insists on staying in that crumbly old house like Miss Havisham – just with more cobwebs and even more bitter.'

'I love Jenny!' Portia butted in. 'She's sharp and funny and she needs you now more than ever, now that... George has... and Steve never...'

A silence fell over the table, all eyes on Kate. Kate took a deep breath in through her nose, closed her eyes and slowly let the breath out.

'Back to bed.' Seamus took a ginormous swig of Pinot Noir to replace the lost, spat-out one.

Kate opened her eyes and watched her husband scoop up her son, throwing him over his shoulder, heroic fireman's-lift style. She bit her bottom lip, something strange stirring within her, confusing the very core of her being. She felt hot all of a sudden and wondered what the hell was going on.

Was it lust?

Couldn't be, she thought to herself, answering her own question. The sexual part of her life was well and truly over. Had been for yonks. After all, it had been twelve years, nine months, seventeen hours and exactly twenty-three minutes since the last time she'd had sex. With Shay. IRL, as the kids would say. Not that she was counting. Much.

It had always bothered her, their lack of sexual contact after they'd conceived Declan – and it had driven Seamus quite mad. But there was always something more pressing to do – like sleep. And she was always so self-conscious about her body, the thought of anyone touching it or seeing the cellulite-y rolls in all their fleshy glory killed any desire she might have ever felt stone dead.

'Let's go, Big Man,' Seamus chuckled as Declan struggled valiantly in mock protest.

Kate's fingertips tingled as a tsunami of lava crashed and roared up from her feet to her forehead. Of course it wasn't lust! The thought of sex? With Shay?! She'd rather drink nuclear waste!

No, this was just another in a series of infuriating, ill-timed and absolutely boiling hot flushes. She huffed as she watched them go.

It's funny, really, Seamus thought to himself as he trudged up the stairs: he never thought he'd see the day when he'd voluntarily leave a party to see to the kids. And carrying one of them like this? With *his* aching back?

Like all the old mates he never saw any more, it had taken him quite some time to come round to the whole kid/family thing. If he was being honest, he'd never really wanted kids at all. He knew they'd put a major crimp in his social life. His home life hadn't fared much better, either. And don't even mention sex.

Kate had changed so much since Declan and Phoebe came along, she was barely recognisable these days – and not just looks-wise. Sure, she'd put on a few pounds, padded out a bit more – who hadn't? And who cared? It was more the way she ignored him that really got his goat. The way she seemed permanently pissed off with him, like *he* was responsible for ruining *her* life or something!

She was a million miles away from the fun, free spirit he fell in love with all those years ago. These days, he wasn't sure he even *liked* her very much anymore, let alone loved her. Maybe they should get divorced. Or at least be apart for a while – a trial separation, perhaps.

He felt the hairs on his nose prickle as though he was about to cry when he realised, for the umpteenth time that week that their marriage was over and there was no way they would never return to those easy, child-free, happy times.

Speaking of happy times, he perked up a bit when he got to the top step when he remembered he was due to tee off at nine. He'd better knock it on the head soon, if he was going to be any cop on the golf course tomorrow. Or chatting up his favourite barmaid at the nineteenth hole afterwards.

—

Kate fanned her face and tried to compose herself. But she just couldn't get comfortable, however she arranged herself on the dining chair.

'Sorry about that, Kevin. Kids, eh?' She smiled weakly as a bead of sweat raced down her nose and leaped off the end of it, like a ski jumper.

Kevin glanced over at Portia, who looked away quickly, her eyes studying the slightly nauseating orange/brown/beige swirly mess of a carpet to her right. For a strong, smart, fiercely independent and still spectacular-looking woman in her mid-fifties, she suddenly seemed vulnerable and fragile. Even the tiniest bit anxious.

But only to the well-trained eye. Only Kate would have noticed those flickers of fragility in Portia, because she'd known her for what sometimes felt like forever. They'd been best friends practically since the moment they first met, a hundred years ago in Reception.

As they got older, they only seemed to get closer – and now they could read each other like a favourite, well-thumbed, decidedly dog-eared (in Kate's case) book.

'Nope.' Grinned Kevin. 'Well… none that I know of, anyway.'

Portia looked up and smiled at him, her relief obvious. Kevin took this as major encouragement and beamed back.

Kate got up to open a window.

'Is it just me or is it hot in here?' she asked.

'It's just you,' replied Portia. 'It's only the beginning of June, remember. And one mild evening does not a summer make. No need to break out the Pimm's just yet. Although…'

A wicked smile crept across Portia's full, scarlet-lipstick-drenched mouth and she half winked at Kevin across the dining table.

Kate watched Kevin's Adam's apple bob up and down as he swallowed hard. He'd barely been able to take his eyes off Portia all night and now he looked not only smitten and mesmerised, but really quite nervous, too.

'Now there's an idea,' Kevin said in the Sean Connery as James Bond voice he used when he was desperately trying to sound cool. 'Why don't I wander down the High Street and get some? You girls see if you can rustle up some mint, cucumber and oranges and I'll be back in a jiffy.'

Kate raised an eyebrow at Kevin's (quite frankly rubbish) Scottish accent – as well as being referred to as a 'girl'. Because in less than a month's time she would turn fifty-five. Fifty-fucking-five?! How the actual fark did *that* happen?

When exactly did she stop being the fun one? When did she stop being the one who never said no to a laugh, a quick ciggie and a cheeky pint with Portia on a school night? At precisely what moment did she get so old and boring? When did she and Seamus cease to be love's young(ish) dream and morph into this barely recognisable, barely talking twosome – like those old couples you see out at restaurants on Valentine's Night, just going through the motions, nothing left to say, nothing left to give a toss about?

Oh god, she thought to herself. If only she'd noticed things were heading south at the time, she could've stopped her rapid descent into middle age! If only she'd known how things were going to turn out when she was busy larking about in London with Portia, she'd have done so many things differently.

For starters, she told herself, she'd marry the real love of her life, the original Mr Right, her ex, Tom. She'd go back to work quickly after she'd had kids, too. And soon after that, she'd start up her own mega-successful advertising agency. She smiled and nodded to herself knowing that if she could turn back time, she'd change… just about everything.

2

'Fresh mint?' Kate's muffled voice came from somewhere deep inside a kitchen cabinet.

'He'll be lucky. Closest we've got to fresh mint is a new tube of Colgate upstairs. Ooh – hang on – do you think this… ah, dried basil,' she squinted, bringing the Aldi jar up to her eyes, 'ah… best before March… 2018 will do?'

She clambered down from the kitchen chair and looked in the fridge, yanking open the crisper drawer. She let out a gasp when she spied half a tomato wrapped in cling film, a few curled-up outer leaves of a long-gone iceberg lettuce, something yellow, shrivelled and furry and one small but perfectly formed cucumber.

'Well, looky here!' she crowed. 'I'll just chop this little beauty up and we'll feel like we're front row at Centre Court any minute now!' She grasped the cucumber with her right hand, and its jellied mush oozed forth between her fingers.

'In a *jiffy*, you mean,' Portia beamed as she glided in, putting the near-empty pasta bowl on the kitchen table and twirling to face Kate as though it was all part of a carefully choreographed ballet – The Dance of the Fifties Housewife or something.

'Yeah,' Kate snorted, chucking the liquefied cucumber mess into the bin where it landed with an unexpectedly heavy thud.

'It's just like the old days, this,' Portia went on as she pirouetted and plié-ed, gently placing three empty wine bottles in the recycling. 'You know, getting drunk together—'

'Speak for yourself! I haven't touched a drop for years!' Kate protested.

'...not a care in the world, fancying the new lad, hoping to get a snog...'

Portia broke off as Kate silenced her with a hand and a 'shoosh!'.

'What? They're not babies any more, you know,' Portia pointed out.

'I thought I heard... I'd better go and—'

'No, no,' Portia grabbed her by the elbow. 'Let Shay deal with it. And besides, when was the last time you and I had a good old chat, just us two, no husband, no annoying kids?'

'Can't remember,' sighed Kate and plonked herself down into a kitchen chair.

'Exactly.'

'God, they really were the good old days, weren't they? Young, free, able to do what you wanted when you wanted... when you didn't have to arrange a spontaneous night out three months in advance and you'd spend hours 'avin' it large, with loads of mates... when you only had the one chin—'

'That you didn't have to shave!' Portia piped up.

'I told you that in strict confidence!'

Portia mouthed the word 'sorry', pouted and hung her head in shame.

'I can't afford to get my 'tache lasered – not when Shay's out of a job and I can't even bloody hold onto one! I told you the Co-Op sacked me, didn't I?'

12

'Couldn't get the hang of the till?'

'I kept forgetting how to work it! And the twelve year olds working there couldn't explain it, either. They all lost patience with me in the end.'

'You're too analogue, that's your problem.'

'And too old… and too short.'

Portia nodded in agreement. 'So how are things with you and Shay?'

'Still shit,' Kate said. 'No sex, no affection, no interest. Same as it ever was.'

'Objection!' Portia, ever the 'on' barrister, couldn't resist taking the piss a bit. 'That's not even true! Once upon a time you two really were a dream couple if I recall correctly. M'lud.'

'A million years ago, maybe,' Kate conceded. 'It's all so boring and mundane now, though. I mean, talk about separate lives. Where's that giddy feeling, that sudden rush of intoxicating blood to the head? The butterflies in your tummy? Whatever happened to feeling like if you didn't see them soon, you'd just die?'

'That's only for fifteen-year-old kids. Or twenty-somethings.'

Kate slumped back, contemplating the frightening prospect of never experiencing those dizzy, heart-popping feelings of being madly in love ever again.

A sneaky smile scudded across Portia's face.

'Or fifty-four year olds…'

But Kate didn't hear Portia, she was too busy remembering what it felt like when she was twenty-nine and hopelessly, crazily in love with her boyfriend at the time, Tom.

She hadn't seen him in the flesh for a hundred years (approximately), but she hooked up with him regularly

13

in her dreams – about three or four times a week, these days. Sometimes she'd tell herself that this made her officially Mrs Normal, three times a week being the national average and all.

She would wake up all flushed and breathless, bursting with energy and good vibes – even if it was 2:35 a.m. and her desperate need to wee had wrenched her out of the best, raunchiest sex of her life.

To be honest, she couldn't really remember what sex with Tom had actually been like, all those years ago. For all she knew it might have been rubbish. And not even that regular. But Kate maintained they were tearing each other's clothes off at every available opportunity back in the day and that the resultant shag was always magnificent. So that's how it was. Fact.

'Earth to Kate O'Reilly, come in, Kate,' Portia said into her cupped hand, making her voice sound as though it was coming through a Tannoy.

'Sorry,' Kate apologised, 'I was miles away.'

'No change there, then,' Portia sighed. 'Yet another trip down memory lane, I'll bet. You've got to stop living in the past, darling. What's done is done. You can't change it. I believe it was Eleanor Roosevelt who said something like yesterday is history, tomorrow is a mystery, but today is a gift, which is why it's called the present.'

Portia looked pleased with herself. Kate looked nonplussed.

'In other words, be here now, as Oasis might say.'

'Right,' said Kate.

'Not being funny, but you don't want to wind up all bitter and twisted like your mum, do you? And you don't want to miss all the good stuff in the here and now – your gorgeous kids, your wonderful husband. You're so lucky, you know. I'd give anything to have what you've got.'

'Really?'

'In a heartbeat!'

'But you've got it all!' Kate tried to jump out of her seat, but her bum was a bit too firmly wedged into it. 'You've still got a waist! And a fab career! God, I wish I'd never stopped working – oh, to be in an office again! The goss, the drama, the banter, the money…'

'Ach,' Portia dismissed Kate with her elegant hand. 'Too much bloody drama, mind-numbingly prurient banter and nowhere near enough money. Work isn't like it used to be, you know. Now it's just endless uncertainty. Some whippersnapper's going to come along and steal your job from you any minute, you have to keep on training and everyone thinks you're a ball-breaking bitch who is so selfish she chose career over kids. It was sexist before, but now it's off-the-scale misogynistic. And all I want is a little contentment: the house, the husband, the kids—'

'The handbrakes, you mean.'

'Yes!'

'But it's so arse-achingly boring!'

'Give me boring any day,' tutted Portia.

'Whaaat? You'd swap your amazing Marylebone mansion flat for a crappy Thirties semi in the arse-end of Reading? With all the cracked lino, the net curtains and skanky Seventies carpets?'

'Well obviously I'd Farrow & Ball the walls into submission, bin the nets, put up some plantation shutters, rip out those gruesome carpets, put oak floors down—'

'How very dare you?!' Kate put her palm to her chest in mock offence.

Portia grinned and the two friends looked around the room, their mouths slowly turning down as their eyes landed on a large Aldi plastic bag filled with other plastic bags spilling out onto the heavily crevassed lino floor.

'Where's Kev?' Seamus whispered as he peered around the kitchen door jamb.

Kate and Portia were singing along to 'Disco 2000' by Pulp on Glory Years FM (The Greatest Hits of All Time, All The Time, Anytime At All!) softly playing on Alexa, and gestured for him to join them.

But he was rooted to the spot.

Kate swayed over to him in a cack-handed attempt to appear – exactly what, she wasn't sure. Sexy? Seductive? Light-hearted? Attractive in some way?

Whatever she was going for, it fell flatter than a gluten-free vegan pancake.

'Any beer left?' Seamus sniffed, brushing past her.

Kate checked to see if Portia had clocked this rejection. Which of course she had.

'Even the music was so much better in the Nineties,' Kate broke into the awkwardness. 'God, I miss the good old days!'

'I don't,' Portia stared off into the middle distance, her grin fading fast.

Kate felt a stab of sadness as she watched a sorrowful shadow cast itself over Portia's face.

Seamus must have picked up on it too, because he suddenly got all excited.

'Now you're talking,' he said a little too enthusiastically, slapping Portia awkwardly on the back. 'Oasis, Britpop, fantasy football—'

Just then the doorbell rang.

'Oh, shoosh!' said Kate, her mummy reflex rearing its irritable head.

'You're shooshing the *doorbell* now?' Seamus tutted, rolling his eyes as he went to answer the door.

'I'll bring the rest of the stuff in,' Portia said, darting off after Seamus, suddenly delighted.

Soon Kate could hear Seamus, Portia and Kevin talking and laughing as she carried on clearing up in the kitchen. Amazingly, she managed to resist going into the dining room and asking them to keep it down. But only because she couldn't move, paralysed as she was by a heavy sense of dread.

Had both she and the kids been younger, she would have relished these few precious moments alone while they slept the sleep of the innocent upstairs. But as it was, here, on her own, in the shitty old kitchen that would cost more than one hundred times their paltry savings to renovate, she felt like someone was pushing an anvil down on her shoulders. She suddenly felt old. And brittle. And so horribly, terribly lonely.

Just as she was welling up, Portia reappeared with two tall glasses of Pimm's.

'Screw the oranges and mint – all you need's a bit of lemonade and this stuff's simply divine!' Portia declared.

Kate stood up straight, threw her shoulders back, and imagined she was shaking off the crushing weight of that anvil.

'Go on, then.' She didn't even bother to take off her Marigolds – she simply grabbed the Fuller glass and downed it in one gargantuan gulp. She didn't even wince at her first taste of booze for ten years.

'Finally she drinks again!' Portia giggled.

Kate wiped her mouth with the back of the pink rubber glove and didn't even bother to stifle a burp.

'Atta girl,' Portia said proudly.

Kate beamed at her best friend.

Having people round for dinner was so much more fun than falling asleep on the couch only five minutes (max) into a new Netflix series, she thought to herself. What with Brexit, then Covid, then a catastrophic cost of living crisis where millions of people had to choose between heating and eating, it was nice to just forget about it all and let your hair down a bit. And it felt good to have Portia here, so happy, so full of beans. On a school night!

Kate couldn't remember the last time she'd thrown caution to the wind. Ever since she'd had the kids, she'd done what was best for them first, Seamus second and herself last. If she'd featured in the consideration equation at all.

She knew it was the same for all her selfless old mummy friends – the ones she never heard from again once the kids had started secondary school. And in the unlikely event that any of them ever did call, there was no way she'd ever admit that sometimes she wished she only had herself to think about and look after. Not all the time, of course, just most of the time.

Still, that's what she had her healthy addiction to nostalgia for – those times when she wanted to escape but couldn't, tied to the house and kids as she was. And it's not like there was anything wrong with it. Was there? It didn't hurt anyone's feelings, it didn't give her a hangover, she didn't need expensive Past Life Regression therapy or embarrassing stints in rehab – and it was free.

Her obsession with the past was now her safety harness, her private, non-chemical Prozac, her coping mechanism of choice. Because when being a wife and mother got too much, making her feel trapped and overwhelmed, all Kate had to do was take a quick journey back through her personal history to where the music was way better, her social circle way wider, her self-esteem way higher and her waist way, way smaller... *et voilà!* All was right with her world again.

Or at least it would be if only she could shake off the nagging feeling that she made some seriously bad decisions back then – including marrying the wrong guy. Talk about gutted. To add insult to injury, she had to deal with the inevitable flatlining, the depressing come down when Kate 'came to' only to realise that there wasn't a damn thing she could do to change it. Not IRL at any rate.

'So what do you think of Kevin, then?' Portia asked. 'Cute or what?'

'Or what!' Kate nearly choked. 'You need to go to Specsavers, Porsh.'

'You can talk,' sniffed Portia. 'Shay's not exactly giving George Clooney a run for his money, is he?'

'True,' Kate nodded.

If he hadn't clumsily caused an unholy commotion – due to his unfortunate propensity for tripping over himself at every turn – she probably wouldn't even have noticed Seamus when she first met him. He was so vanilla, camouflaged completely by his beigeness, blending into his background like a speccy, geeky chameleon. Especially when he was next to out-fucking-standing Mr Charisma himself, super-lad Tom.

Portia waved a hand in front of Kate's face.

'Hello? HE-LLOOO!'

'Sorry.' Kate snapped out of it. 'So, um, yeah. Not particularly cute, no. I've got to be honest. He's not some kind of grotesque gargoyle or anything, but he's no Bradley Cooper, either.'

'Whatever.' Portia turned her attention back to her Pimm's.

'Don't get me wrong, he's a perfectly nice guy. Knows a buttload about IT according to Shay...'

Portia looked hurt.

'But he's just so not your type!' Kate blurted out.

'And what exactly is my type?' Portia spat. 'Total and utter bastard?'

'Erm...'

'Well not any more it isn't! Kev's sweet and smart, he's the right age, he's single, he hasn't got kids, he's not bad-looking... And correct me if I'm wrong, but I think he might fancy me!'

'Of COURSE he fancies you! He's only human—'

'So I'm going for it. This could be it, you know. My last shot at happiness in this life!'

'Now THAT was a good show.' Kate went misty-eyed again.

'What?'

'*This Life!* Miles. Phwoar! Remember?'

Portia pursed her lips, shook her head and untangled her endless legs in a huff. She stomped off into the living room, leaving Kate to bite her bottom lip and smile to herself, lost in the hazy memory of a sexy fictional character in a popular TV series from the last century.

3

'Oh, you're more than e-bloody-nough, lady,' Kate muttered as she schlepped up to the bathroom mirror and saw *I AM ENOUGH* lipsticked on it. Portia had written that there yonks ago, to remind her that she was worthy of love and respect, even if she felt invisible and incompetent and totally at odds with the modern world. Portia was full of good advice and positive affirmations like that.

Kate stared at her reflection.

'Face like a Picasso portrait, eye bags that could carry the weekly shop and a belly like a blancmange. No wonder you haven't seen your feet for over a decade.'

It was always a shock, seeing herself like this. Seeing herself at all, actually, was a bit of a surprise. Over the past ten years or so, she'd slowly stopped looking. She'd grown accustomed to avoiding her image wherever she could – shop windows on the High Street, all mirrors, black computer screens – she steadfastly refused to glance at any reflective surface, lest she catch an accidental glimpse of her portly, ageing self.

She scraped her ever-thinning Bill Bailey-esque bob back into a small, split-ended ponytail and almost smiled at the thought of the one thing she looked forward to about getting older and going bald: wearing a wig. At least then her hair would do exactly what she wanted it to do – neither rain nor humidity – not even gale force winds would mess up her 'do'. And what joy that would be! What sweet relief.

She brushed her teeth. At least they were all still her own – a fact she often cheered herself up with when she found herself on yet another search for the silver lining. They could really do with some atomic bleaching though, she thought, to erase all those years of red-wine-glugging, enthusiastic smoking and tea slurping she'd done before she'd had kids and become sensible. Or became, as Shay had said once, mid-row, *boring*.

'Takes one to know one!' Kate had yelled back.

She shook her head at the memory and wondered how the hell she and Shay had come to this – barely speaking to each other, practically unable to look each other in the eye, Kate thinking her bits must have grown over, thanks to a distinct lack of action and Shay, by stark contrast, suffering RSI of the wrist thanks to his 'secret' PornHub Premium subscription.

Not exactly the happy home life she'd always dreamed of.

She looked at herself in the mirror, jutted her chin out and inspected it, remembering how Tom used to say she reminded him of Reese Witherspoon, so strong was her jaw line when she was younger.

'More Bruce Bloody Forsyth these days,' she mumbled, when she noticed that overnight one or two (OK, OK, six or seven) new thick black hag hairs had sprung forth and some of the older ones had turned white.

'God, you're looking old.' She sighed.

She imagined herself on a half-day coach trip with all the other OAPs, stopping at the nearest Wetherspoons for lunch.

I'll have a lukewarm, milky Horlicks, a glass of Steradent and a large bowl of salt and vinegar regret on the side, please.

She leaned on the sink and knocked Seamus' disposable Bic onto the floor. She stared at it. She looked up and spied the shaving foam sitting on the basin, next to the tap. She looked at the Bic again. Back to the foam. To the Bic, to the foam. The Bic, the foam, the Bic, the foam, Bic, foam, Bic, foam, Bic, foam—

'Ah, fuck it,' she said.

She pulled her dressing gown tie tight around what she imagined might be her waist, girded her Barbie Doll loins, took a deep breath and proceeded to cut her chin and upper lip to ribbons.

—

'No, YOU'RE a dickhead!' Declan squealed, his face red, eyes bulging out of their sockets.

Kate stood in the kitchen doorway.

'Charming,' she said as though this insult was aimed at her. Which it probably was, let's face it. Or at least it would be soon enough.

She assumed what she hoped was an authoritative air as she walked into the kitchen, pressing little bits of torn loo paper onto the bleeding cuts on her face.

Phoebe, sitting opposite Declan at the kitchen table, smirked and put her head down, lost in her phone once more.

Kate asked Alexa to play the radio as she made herself a coffee and put some porridge on. She wandered over to the table and fired up her laptop. First stop? Facebook.

Honestly, she thought to herself, where do these people come from? All those Facebook friends of hers posting pictures of their idyllic holidays in rustic France, their photogenic, photoshopped, ridiculously beautiful kids with their Boden floral dresses tucked into their knickers trying to catch tadpoles in sun-dappled streams while they themselves, all impossibly young and good looking, sip wine and laugh easily, relaxing under the shade of nearby willow trees in shabby-but-effortlessly-chic straw hats.

'I mean,' she said aloud, 'are they for fucking real?!'

'You're obsessed with Facebook and Twitter,' Phoebe said, not looking up from her phone. 'Time you gave your social media addiction a rest.'

'You can talk!' Declan came to his mum's rescue through a mouthful of Crunchy Nut.

'Well *you* can't,' Phoebe deadpanned. 'Too busy stuffing your face.'

'YOU'RE a face!' came his considered reply.

'No wonder you haven't got any friends.' Phoebe shot daggers at him for a second, then went back to TikTok.

'I wish you'd wait till I've made the porridge, Decko,' Kate said. 'Much better for you than that crap. I could put some date syrup in it? Or some maple syrup? Sweeten it up in a good vegan, non-processed, palm oil and sugar-free almond milky kind of way!'

Kate got up from the laptop on the kitchen table and shuffled over to the stove in her pink bunny slippers, the ear of one chewed completely off by Rafferty when he was a puppy.

Kate thought about what Phoebe had just said. Was she addicted to Facebook and Twitter? Nah. Surely not. Not her. She could stop any time she wanted! She just didn't fancy stopping right now, that's all.

'Mum?' Declan asked calmly. 'Can women have penises?'

'Hmm?' hummed Kate over her shoulder. 'Shouldn't it be penii?'

'No, it shouldn't,' growled Phoebe. 'I'm the one doing Latin GCSE, I know my plurals and it's "penises".'

Well that told her. Kate often deferred to Phoebe's superior knowledge of, well, everything, so she nodded, suitably chastened, and brought the wooden spoon up to her lips to taste the porridge.

'And in answer your question, Declan,' Phoebe continued, 'as to whether women can have penises, the answer is – obviously – yes.'

Kate nearly choked on her porridge as Seamus popped his head around the door frame. Kate jerked her head towards the steamy window through which you could see rain cascading like a waterfall down the neighbour's red-brick wall, their well-tended hedge swaying violently in the wind.

'It's blowing a hurricane out there,' she said to Seamus.

'Typical,' tutted Seamus. 'Just as I'm about to tee off.'

'You can't play golf in this weather!' Kate shrieked. 'It's positively torrential!'

'Watch me,' he sneered, bending down to kiss Phoebe on the cheek and ruffle Declan's hair. 'Or rather, don't. Why break the habit of a lifetime?'

It was true. Kate couldn't bear golf – either playing or watching it.

'When will you be back, then?' Kate felt helpless.

'When I'm back.' He turned on his heel. 'And, by the way, we need to talk.'

This made Kate wince. The last time she'd heard that phrase was… Well, she couldn't remember exactly. When

Tom had dumped her? When she'd been sacked from the Co-op? It never prefaced any good news, like an all-expenses-paid trip to Disneyland or a major lottery win, did it? No. She shook her head. No, it bloody well didn't.

'Laters!' Seamus called out a little too cheerily and slammed the door.

Kate was sure there was a pointed finality to the sound of the front door slamming. It certainly was a big, fat audible full stop. Maybe even an exclamation mark. In bold. And it had created a new unsightly crack in the kitchen wall to boot.

She stood there in her dowdy dressing gown in her humid kitchen and wondered whether this was how her mother had felt when she used to have those horrible fights with her dad when Kate was a kid. George would stride over to their front door while Jenny called after him, 'Where are you going?' George would always reply by shouting, 'OUT!' Then the door would slam and he would be gone for hours. Sometimes even days.

Kate would have burst into tears at this memory – if she hadn't been on Sertraline since forever and, as a result, unable to cry.

Rafferty sensed something was wrong – or maybe he was just frightened of the thunder roaring outside – so he nuzzled up against her.

She got down on her hands and knees and buried her head in the cupboard under the sink, looking for some long-forgotten dog food that might be lurking up the back. 'So have you paid for my trip to Zermatt yet?' Phoebe said, making Kate smack her head on the underside of the sink.

'Ow!' Kate backed out and stood up, rubbing her head. 'Bloody... dog!'

'How is she allowed to go to Zermatt when you won't even let me go online?' Declan piped up.

'She isn't,' Kate said, retrieving some left-over lasagne from the back of the fridge and slopping it into Rafferty's bowl. 'We can't afford skiing trips at the moment, you'll just have to wait—'

'I NEVER get to do ANYTHING!' Phoebe huffed.

'YOU don't?' Declan whined. 'What about ME?'

'Christ on a bike,' Kate muttered under her breath as 'Once In A Lifetime' by the Talking Heads started playing.

'Ooh, I love this song,' she said, dashing over to the kitchen bench so she could turn Alexa up.

She steadied herself, leaning both arms on the kitchen sink and closed her eyes. She listened to David Byrne singing about how this wasn't his beautiful house and nor, indeed, was this his beautiful wife. Too bloody right, Dave, she thought as she bobbed her head in time to the music, too bloody right.

As she warbled along with the song, the kids groaned and rolled their eyes at her slightly pitchy, out-of-tune voice. But Kate didn't care – she was in her element.

So immersed was she, she very nearly missed the unmistakeable plinky-plonky piano beginning to that Baddiel and Skinner Euro 96 classic, 'Three Lions', once the Talking Heads had finished. But when she they started singing/chanting, she felt a rush of excitement whoosh through her veins. She shut her eyes and broke into a grin. Her head tingled and her heart sang. Better than her voice, to be honest.

'CHOOON!' She forgot herself and pointed her finger to the leaky ceiling, pogoing off the cracked floor a bit with the sheer glee of it all.

Her mobile looked like it was imitating her, mocking her when it started to vibrate so much, it chucked itself off the table and fell onto the lino, jumping about with joy. Or maybe terror. It was Kate's mum calling, after all.

'MUM!' Declan shouted.

Kate opened her eyes and saw her son pointing to her phone on the floor. She picked it up, put her mum on speakerphone and wandered into the pantry.

'Hi, Mum,' she sighed.

'Don't you "Hi, Mum" me, young lady!'

The kids sniggered.

'Not when you've given my number to all those bastard care home predators! Now, listen carefully! For the umpteenth time, I am NOT going into a home! And I'm not going into YOUR home, either. Buggered if I'll ever leave this house – they'll have to carry me out in a coffin first!' Jenny went on.

Rafferty, who hated confrontation of any sort, started barking in protest.

'I'm well,' Kate called out. 'Thanks for asking.'

'What?' Jenny crackled. 'You'll have to speak up, I can hardly hear you! Some cacophony or other going on somewhere – this line is dreadful!'

A roll of thunder rumbled into the kitchen and the lights flickered on and off, making Rafferty bark even more dementedly.

'I mean, really!' Jenny prattled on. 'The least you could do is show some spine, some decency, some TRUE bloody GRIT for goddamn sake as your father used to—'

The smoke alarm started bleating its insistent beep, cutting Jenny off, and when Kate looked over her shoulder at the stove, she saw the porridge pan smoking like crazy.

'I've burnt the bloody porridge!' she shrieked.

'Again,' the kids groaned in unison.

A jagged shard of lightning split the sky outside and cut across the kitchen. The kids screamed, Rafferty ran into the pantry and leaped up at Kate, his paws landing on her chest, knocking her to the floor.

It went all echoey and slo-mo as she shut her eyes tight, imagining her head bouncing repeatedly off the rotten floorboards, her cheeks and lips flubbering about most unflatteringly over her teeth. She wondered whether a nuclear bomb had gone off and whether she, the kids, Rafferty and her phone would shortly be flung against the melting walls by the sheer force of the blast and fried alive by the accompanying intense heat.

But all those photos of the kids on her phone that she'd never got round to downloading! And what about her bank details? Her whole stupid, boring, pointless life was on that phone – oh, the humanity! Mind you, she thought, at least it would shut Jenny up. Every cloud…

But of course not even a nuclear bomb could shut Jenny up because Kate could still hear her banging on – albeit fading into the distance. She also heard the muffled screams of the kids getting further and further away as if they were retreating with the thunder itself.

Suddenly she got a strong whiff of perfume. She knew it wasn't her Air Wick plug-in air-freshener thingy – that had run out yonks ago. And it's not like the kids or Seamus would ever take it upon themselves to change it. Ha! Are you quite mad?

No, this was an altogether posher, more expensive smell than any supermarket air freshener could give off.

There was a different feeling in the air, too – and, although not remotely cold, Kate felt a shiver run up and down her spine.

She flipped her eyes open. At once she saw a vase full of deep, vibrant red and orange gerberas in front of a spotless window which looked out over blue, sunny skies.

A gleaming tap looked down on a bright-white ceramic double Belfast sink and a stainless-steel Zanussi dishwasher (sans grubby finger marks) sparkled to the left of her. She looked back up to the window and squinted, focusing on the Roberts radio/CD sound system.

'Way-HEY!' she heard Chris Evans say, seconds before he started wittering on about football over the end of 'Three Lions'. When, finally, the fast-talking DJ took a breath, so did Kate.

But panic caught in her throat – the kids! Where were the kids? She sat up and turned around, frantically searching the spookily familiar room expecting to see Phoebe, Declan and Rafferty all huddled together in the corner, shaking with fear and crying 'Mummy! Where are you? Come back, all is forgiven!' The kids, that is – Rafferty would just be barking and whimpering a bit, obviously.

But instead of her brood, she saw a fresh-faced, Cristalle-scented Portia sitting down at the small, round kitchen table.

'I'm just saying that once a woman has a baby, her career's over,' she said matter of factly. 'Simple as that.'

'Oh do wake up and smell the skinny cap, Porshie,' grinned Steve as he poured a gigantic portion of Crunchy Nut Corn Flakes into a bowl.

Steve! Steve? STEVE! What the actual fu—?

'It's nineteen *ninety*-six – not nineteen-*fifty*-six! Right, Katie?'

Steve and Portia both looked down at Kate sitting on the floor.

Kate stared back at them. Portia looked even more gorgeous than she did in her old photos – and Steve! He looked wonderful – all young and smiley and happy and full of potential. Just the way he always was in her mind's eye.

But here he was, in the flesh! Here, now, with her! She thought she might hyperventilate.

She scratched her head and began to entertain the possibility that she'd had – or was having – a stroke. Or maybe she'd contracted late on-set narcolepsy and this was all one big, crazy dream.

She felt something in her hair. She pulled at it and out came two tiny bits of loo paper with one dot of blood in the middle of each.

'Whaaaaaaaat?'

She flicked the shreds from her fingers as her eyes darted all over the place, trying to process everything, take it all in. Where was she? Why was she… *how?*

'Am I… *dead?*' she asked, voice wavering as she grasped the table leg and felt her forehead prickle with sweat.

She must have died, she thought – died of exhaustion from trying to be the perfect wife and mother, probably. Yes, that was it! She'd died and gone to Heaven. Not that she was even remotely religious, but being here with two of her favourite people in the world ever would be her idea of Heaven, wouldn't it? Bit of a surprise that she didn't end up in Hell, though… Or maybe that's where she'd been all this time before now! Doing time in suburban, boring, middle-class, middle-aged hell.

'Oh, come on.' Portia rolled her eyes. 'It wasn't that big a night. Get up off the floor, you lightweight!'

Kate pulled herself up, holding onto the table edge and marvelled at how easily she moved, how light she felt.

'It was only a couple of gentle Sunday drinks, nothing more nefarious than that. Now get a shift on or we'll be late for work,' Portia tutted.

'Uh… erm… ah,' Kate stammered.

She tried to put her hands on her hips, but there was nothing there. She gasped when she looked down – her Marie Antoinette side-shelves had all but disappeared and her nipped-in waist had come back! She saw her legs encased in khaki combats and a flat belly exposed by her favourite Miss Selfridge long-sleeved crop-top with a pink-and-white tie-dyed love heart on the front. Her boobs were proud and perky. Her bingo wings no more.

Her hands darted up to her throat and she felt for her chins. But there was only one! With not even a *hint* of stubble on it! And her neck felt soft and smooth, too.

Kate laughed the kind of nervous laugh you come out with when you're on a roller coaster – when you're scared witless, but exhilarated at the same time.

'Oh. My. GOD!' Kate's breaths were getting shorter and shallower with every word. 'Is it? Is it really 1996?'

'Take some brotherly advice, Katie my love, and lay off the Es,' Steve said as he crunched on a, by all reports, ludicrously tasty mouthful of Crunchy Nut Corn Flakes and nodded towards a Take That calendar on the kitchen wall.

Sure enough, beneath a picture of the lads larking about, it said:

JUNE 1996

Kate put her soft, callus-free hands over her mouth to stifle a yelp.

And then she fainted.

4

'Kate? Kate!' Portia fell to her knees next to her best friend's prone body.

Steve joined her on the kitchen floor and slapped his sister's face. Not too hard, of course – but with just enough force to leave a small, reddening patch.

Regardless, Kate lay motionless.

'Kate? I'm sorry, sweetie. This hurts me more than it hurts you, believe me. Here goes...' This time Steve slapped Kate really hard.

'OWWWW!' Kate sat up. 'What the actual *fuck*?'

'That's what they do in old movies! I'm sorry, babes, but you fainted—'

'And we didn't know what else to do!' Portia chimed in. 'Are you OK? How do you feel? You all right?'

'I'm fine,' Kate said, slowly unknitting her brow. 'Fine. Just a bit, erm, woozy.'

Portia and Steve helped her up and walked her into the living room, plonking her onto the perfectly shop-distressed leather couch.

'Gave us a bit of a fright there,' said Steve, relief spreading itself all over his handsome face. 'Don't do it again.'

'Hey!' Portia said as she rubbed Kate's arm. 'You're not pregnant too, are you?'

'What?' Kate mumbled, her cheek sore, her head muzzy, the cogs of her brain cranking up slowly.

'Typical,' Portia sniggered. 'Always stealing my thunder. Tell me at lunch, yeah?'

Kate didn't have a clue what Portia was chuntering on about, so just sat there.

'Come on, let's go!'

'Hang on,' Kate said slowly, her eyes drawn to the Jenga blocks lying about casually on the coffee table and the coir carpet underneath it.

She was about to say, in her best authoritative voice that was always duly ignored, 'Clear up those blocks before I count to ten!', but then she remembered her kids were nowhere to be seen and the rest of this flat was spotless. The kind of spotless you have when you don't have children – *professional-cleaner-once-a-week* spotless.

Spotless the way their shared flat was in West Hampstead in the Nineties.

The penny started its long, winding drop. Had she really been transported back in time? Simply because she had wished for it so hard and for so long? But she'd tried asking the universe for stuff loads of times and it never seemed to work, so why now? Why her? Why—

Her speeding heart thudded in her chest and she gripped the edge of the couch.

'Where are the kids? And what about Shay?'

Portia and Steve blinked at her blankly.

'I've changed my mind!' Kate yelled at the ceiling.

She hadn't really ever wanted to be without them, not really. And she hadn't meant all those horrible things she'd said and secretly thought about them in the heat of too many moments to mention. Sure, she'd clung on to her child-free past in her head, wouldn't let it go, because sometimes it seriously felt like if she did, she'd have nothing. Nothing good or fun or nice or fulfilling in her life. Nowt. Nada. Nil all.

So she went on a bit much about the good old days and how much better everything was back then. So what? That didn't mean she actually, physically, *literally* wanted to go back in time to when she was young, free and single.

Did it?

No! She loved her family to bits – what would she do without them? She heard the blood whooshing around her ears as she thought about Phoebe and Declan. Even Shay. Of course they were all capable of being thoroughly annoying sometimes – who wasn't? And yes, they could be right royal pains in the arse, not to put too fine a point on it. But they were *her* pains in *her* arse. So to speak.

She hugged herself, rubbing her arms in an effort to provide some much-needed comfort, as Seamus used to do in the old days. And just at that moment, when she was on the verge of screaming, she realised she could nearly completely close her fingers around the top of her arms.

Which totally stopped her in her tracks.

She was shocked. She was stunned. She did it again and again, her French-manicured fingers showing absolutely zero signs of arthritis as they almost met her thumbs on both hands. Her eyes nearly popped out of her skull – she couldn't believe what she was seeing. It was simply too amazing!

'Ha!' she shrieked at her flatmates, 'Check *this* out!'

'What?' Steve and Portia chorused.

She opened and closed her fingers around her arms, wild-eyed, mouth agape.

Nothing.

'Look how thin my arms are!' Kate looked at them herself by way of encouragement.

Tumbleweeds.

Suddenly Kate felt weightless. And not just because she'd obviously just shed four stone, but also because no one was hanging off her, depending on her, burdening her with bum-numbingly thankless, relentless responsibility. No one was making constant, unreasonable demands on her time and goodwill, expecting her to drive them everywhere, be the whipping boy whenever they felt like lashing out, take the blame for everything that's gone wrong ever in the history of epic mummy fails… She was finally free!

But how long was she going to be in 1996 for? Would she ever return to 2022? Had she ever really *been* in 2022? Maybe that had all been one long, weird dream (or nightmare, depending on her mood swings) and she'd never actually ever left the Nineties.

Oh god! How would she ever understand the quantum physics involved in time travel when she was so crap at maths she had to take her shoes off if she was ever counting past ten?

Maybe she was doomed to roam different space/time continuums — continua? Where was Phoebe when she needed her? — surf different dimensions for the rest of her suddenly rather exciting life.

'Like Dr Who,' she said breathlessly, as it dawned on her that it didn't matter how she had got here, the important thing was that she *was* here. And here was her chance to put everything right. This — right here, right now — was her dream coming true. Talk about the present being a gift — all her Christmases had come at once!

At that precise instant, she made the snap decision to make the most of it and enjoy it. And change all those things that desperately needed changing – like her husband. God knows when she'd be flung back to the future, never to return. Portia was right, she'd better get a shift on!

She set her Witherspoon jaw to 'determined', grabbed the size 10 cropped, faded blue denim jacket off the back of the couch and slipped it effortlessly over the upper arms formerly known as bingo wings.

'Listen, lady,' said Steve, wagging his index finger at Kate, 'I'm the unhinged one in this family – don't even think about pissing on my chips. OK?'

'Yeah,' said Portia, looking worried. 'Why on earth are you banging on about Dr Who?'

'No reason,' beamed Kate. She stood up a little too quickly and felt the blood drain from her head and rush madly to her platform Spice Girls sneakered feet.

'Let's go.' She swayed a bit while she got her balance. 'I may not have much time!'

5

DING!

Kate felt a vaguely familiar flutter in her heart as the lift doors opened on the ground floor of PGT&B, the magazine publishing house where she used to work.

The owners of PGT&B thought it was hilarious to say those four initials stood for the company's core values: Profit, Good Times and Banter. But seriously, they would say, slowly taking their red noses off and folding up their floppy shoes, it was actually the initials of The Four Horsemen – as the founding fathers often referred to themselves – Peter, Glenn, Todd and Ben.

As soon as Kate stepped into the mirrored lift with the bright-red, squeaky nylon carpet she had to steady herself, grabbing hold of the stainless-steel bar that went all the way around the reflective walls at rib-cage height. She stole a glance and forgot to exhale when she saw how slim, young and pretty she was. Used to be. Whatever.

And here she was back in The Lift. This crazy lift! THE lift! This was where it all happened – or at least where you got the goss about everything that happened. Especially on Monday mornings when the excited gaggle of Sales, Editorial and PR would huddle together, squeezing into the tiny box as Friday-night exploits, debacles and degradations were discussed.

She remembered the icy stab of hurt she'd endured, for four slow, clunking floors the time she heard that little tart, Tamsin, bray about stealing Tom away from her at her own birthday party! Kate had been the first one to get into the lift that fateful Monday morning and as it filled up with weary workers beginning yet another week at the grindstone she'd got buried right up at the back in a corner, squashed and unseen by the clear-skinned, loud-voiced Tamsin who forced her way into the already packed-to-capacity lift just as the doors were closing.

'I tell you,' Tamsin had bellowed at Lucy, the receptionist on the PR floor, 'he was like an animal! Honestly, it was like he hadn't had it for *months*! Bit sore, actually – but phwoar, he is so gorgeous, I just couldn't help myself.'

'Doesn't he have a girlfriend?' Lucy was practically whispering by comparison.

'Shhhhh!' Tamsin sprayed spit all over everyone. '*Had* a girlfriend you mean. But keep it under your hat – she works here. In PR or something sad.'

Before they'd got to the fourth floor, Tamsin had waxed lyrical and loud about how fantastically real-looking Tom had said her breasts were, how wonderful her flat stomach was, how gorgeous and slender her long legs were, how charming and amusing she was and how her face had that innocent yet 'slutty' quality that both he and the punters loved. When the lift finally went DING! and the doors opened at the fourth floor, Tamsin stepped out, saying, 'He's going to get me some glamour work in *Lashed*. Says I'm every schoolboy's dream. Wet dream, more like!'

She teetered off in her platform boots and the lift doors closed, but Kate had been unable to move after hearing all that gubbins. In fact, she'd stayed stuck to the spot and was forced to go up nine more floors, then down to the basement, then languish about, slumped in the corner for a while before her boss, Archie, rolled in, eyes rheumy, hair reeking of booze and birds and really bad bunk-ups.

'All right, Kate?' he'd said cheerfully. 'Kate?'

'Hmm?' she dragged her wild eyes up from the hideous carpet and met his.

'Bit late this morn – soz! It's those *Lashed* lads – no clue what a swift Sunday avvie bev actually means, eh?' Archie chuckled.

Amazing, she thought to herself. She could so easily recall the details of that excruciatingly painful morning as though it was yesterday. She'd re-lived that moment so many times over the past few decades so it was really no wonder, she supposed – but as she stood in The Lift now, she thought it remarkable that she physically felt exactly the same as she'd felt all those years ago.

Of course, in her nearly fifty-five-year-old mind, she cringed when she remembered that her boyfriend, the Ladmaster General, the man she thought was The Love of Her Life, The One That Got Away, her Mr Right was responsible, as editor of uber lad mag *Lashed* for making it OK – nay, making it de rigeur, a mark of true manhood for young boys to openly ogle scantily clad women while saying things like: 'Cor! Out of ten, I'd give her one! Har har har!'

Imagine Phoebe at the mercy of that kind of attitude! Imagine Declan cockily saying, 'Grab yer coat, love – you've pulled,' to some poor girl in a smoky, leery pub. She felt decidedly uneasy at the thought.

On the other liver-spot-less hand, she reminded herself, back in those heady days, before Instagram and Twitter and Youtube and influencers and all that social media stuff, back when lad culture reigned supreme and being brash, busty and able to drink your own body weight in Boddington's was as good a way as any to spend a Saturday night. And being in a lads' mag or in *Big Brother* was a sure-fire way to get famous – what was wrong with that? No one got hurt and everyone had a good time. Right?

Sure, the men held all the power and the patriarchy was having a whale of a time, keeping women down, objectifying them for their own pleasure... And yes, lads' mags like *Lashed* were like bibles for the beery, sweary, mad-fer-it masses before #metoo came and tore their playhouse down.

There was a lot of untoward, predatory behaviour about in those days that wouldn't stand muster back in 2022 and yet... And yet Tom was so bloody charismatic! So quick-witted, so handsome! And it wasn't her fault that she'd simply been caught up in the madness of those crazy days like everybody else – swept away on the tide of being sort of close to the thick of it; almost where it was at, on the outer rim of the in-crowd, the warmer bit of the Cool Britannia set. Yes, yes, she was ashamed to admit, she'd been as star-struck as all the other liggers.

That was the only feasible excuse she could offer herself for turning a blind eye to the misogynistic, boorish bad behaviour of her boyfriend and his cronies.

She couldn't have gone along with all their sexist shenanigans because she thought it was all a bit of harmless fun, a bit of old-fashioned seaside postcard kind of a giggle, could she?

Well, yes, she conceded as she looked around The Lift in wonder, she could have. Which made her shudder.

But that was her then and this was her now. Or, rather, that was her then and this was her then, too! God, this timeslip business was confusing – and she'd only been back in June 1996 (according to her Take That kitchen calendar) for five minutes.

She bucked up when she told herself that this was her chance to set the record straight on the old sexism score; put things right and strike a blow for feminists everywhere, from all decades – for the suffragettes that were and the fantastic females to be!

Just as soon as she'd slept with Tom again.

'WHAT?' Kate's inner Germaine Greer sat bolt upright and glared at her.

'Oh, come on!' Kate tried to reason with her. 'What harm could it do? Turn the tables and use the *man*, for once, I say. And Seamus won't know – nor will the kids. It might even be *good* for me to reawaken that long-forgotten part of myself. I mean, I haven't had sex for so long, I can't even tell the difference between feeling saucy, having a hot flush and being pissed for christ's sake!'

'Fair point,' said her inner Germaine and lay back down again.

And at that, Kate thrust her nose in the air and confidently strode out onto the fourth floor.

Lucy looked up from the magazine propped up on the switchboard, stopped twirling her hair and smiled.

'Are you Kate?' she asked, all bright-eyed.

'Of course I am! You know me—' Kate stopped herself when she remembered Lucy had only started in June of that fateful year. Maybe today was even her first day.

'Yes,' she said, regaining her composure. 'Some guy's been calling for you all morning... Tom? From the third floor? Here,' she said as she handed Kate five slips of paper with *While you were out...* written at the top in red.

Kate felt herself blush. She felt excited, proud – even a little smug. Because even though the receptionist didn't know who Tom was just yet, she would soon. And she, like most of the other girls at PGT&B, would be as envious as all hell of Kate. He was a real trophy boyfriend. Lucky Kate.

'Ooh, lucky me!' Kate giggled.

'And there's something for you on your desk, too.' Lucy motioned to a sea of carrels, people bustling about, glass offices and... Tamsin.

'Lucky me,' said Kate again, suddenly deadpan.

She walked over to her desk, dropped her tiny rucksack on the floor, hung her denim jacket on the back of her chair and gasped when she saw the spray – nay, shower, storm, *typhoon* – of lilies virtually taking up her whole desk.

She plucked the card out from the flowers. It read:

> *Say you will – please, please, PLEASE say you will.*
> *Oh go on – you know you want to.*
> *T xxx.*

Kate surmised that the florist – for reasons known only to them – must have put that full stop after the kisses. Because Tom would *never* have dictated that – he was a stickler for grammar and punctuation, you see, and would often correct Kate on her, by comparison, more casual approach to detail: things like apostrophes in the wrong place, an over-liberal use of exclamation marks and other faux pas of the pen. At first Kate thought it endearing – something pernickety about the man who seemed so comfortable and cool with everything being lackadaisical – or lax-a-daisical, as Kate once said, only to be reprimanded sharply by Tom.

She smiled to herself, secure in the knowledge that this time around, if he tried to correct her the next time she said 'pacific' when she meant 'specific' – even if accompanied by his famously sexy, disarming grin – she would surely lamp him.

Tom wanted Kate to move in with him – he'd been asking her for months. But even though she wanted to – really, badly wanted to – two things were holding her back.

Since her brother, Steve, had split up with his long-time girlfriend and lost his job, he'd been living with her and Portia, with Kate basically paying his way. Until he got his act together, Kate felt as though she couldn't leave him – and she was pretty sure Tom wouldn't want them to move in as a job lot. So she was kind of stuck there.

She was also a bit hesitant because… actually, she could never put her finger on why, really. The first time round, she called it instinct and intuition – like she had some sort of sixth sense that something wasn't quite right about them living together and that she would somehow, most likely have her heart smashed to smithereens by Tom. Naturally, she now *knew* he was a cad and bounder of the highest order and, if her calculations were correct (iffy at the best of times, not much of a chance with time travel added into the mix), in about a month's time, at her twenty-ninth birthday do, Tamsin and Tom would run off together and Kate would have to relive that horrible lift scene all over again.

But wait, thought Kate – that's it! That's why he took off with Tamsin – because she refused to move in with him! Maybe if Kate agreed and they *did* move in together, maybe Tom would be faithful and they could live happily ever after. Or even just for a little while, to give her some closure on the relationship that had haunted her for years. And to have sex with him in the flesh – not just in her dreams? Well, that would be great! Wouldn't it?

A picture of Phoebe, Declan, Seamus and Rafferty – the one on her iPhone wallpaper – all tumbling over each other and mugging for the camera, suddenly flashed in front of her mind's eye, as if she suddenly remembered she had a husband, a couple of kids, a delinquent dog and a whole other life.

She heard a strange ringing in her ears – a brutal, masculine sound that she couldn't quite place. It wasn't the gentle harp sound of her iPhone (a sound that she often never heard, actually, it being far too soft and serene to penetrate the ear-splitting chaos usually surrounding her) – nor was it a tinny, irritating ringtone – like some hideously awful novelty pop song involving an Ibiza backing track and a maniacal frog on a motorbike or something. It was just her ordinary work phone, buried somewhere beneath all those flowers.

6

'He's dumped me!' cried Portia as soon as Kate picked up the receiver.

'What?' replied Kate. 'Who?'

'SIMON!' Portia shouted back, followed by some small coughs, signalling the beginning of a hysterical sob session.

Ah, sighed Kate inwardly, *Simon*. Kate knew this was going to happen because:

Simon was always making passes at any female who moved (including Kate) as though the seriously gorgeous Portia wasn't enough for him and he could do better. Ha! As if! And she'd already lived through the whole episode once before, twenty-six years ago, so she knew *exactly* what was going to happen. And that's when it really hit her – this slightly strange feeling that she was cheating or something – like she had insider knowledge or a secret super power. Which she sort of did.

'Shh, shh. Come on, shh. Calm down, now, sweetheart,' Kate soothed, sounding like her mother. No, hang on a sec! She sounded just like herself, her *real* self – her 2022 self. Kate looked around and wondered whether anyone had heard her. But of course they hadn't – they were all still too busy throwing spit balls up onto the ceiling, having sword fights and 'bantering' loudly to be

46

heard over the banging tunes that were blasting from the office CD player.

There was silence for a second on the end of the line, though – Portia was shocked by the motherly, warm, comforting tones of her best friend. Not that Kate didn't show *potential* to be like that – she would be a great mum one day, everyone knew that – it was just that Portia never really gave Kate much opportunity to hone her sweet mothering skills.

Portia was normally so in control, so fearless, so unfazed, that merely hearing her cry, imagining her all small and vulnerable, made Kate want to climb down the phone line, draw Portia close to her (not-so-mumsy and ample now) bosom, stroke her hair, tell her everything was going to be all right, make her some pink milk, settle her down with a duvet in front of the telly, get the old lady from next door to watch her, get in the car, hunt that Simon down, yell at him until he cried and promptly disembowel him on the spot.

'I mean, how COULD he?' continued Portia. 'In my condition! And you wanna know the worst bit?'

Portia didn't wait for Kate to answer.

'He did it by fax. He sent me a fucking *fax*! My secretary brought it to me – so she read it, and has probably photocopied it and stuck it up in the staff room by now and… oh, Kate! What am I going to *do*?'

'What did it say?' Kate said.

'What does it matter? I can't bear to read it again – especially not over the phone. Can you get out? Can you meet me somewhere?'

Kate scraped pens, papers and coffee mugs off her A5 desk diary and was surprised to see a pretty packed schedule. She'd become so accustomed to keeping all the kids' appointments in her head or on the backs of envelopes stuck to the fridge, she panicked a tiny bit when she could see no mention of D (for Decko), P (for Phoebe) or S (yes, yes, for Seamus) and dentists, doctors, playdates, concerts, practice yada yada yada.

She was so used to the days drifting in and out with no shape or form to them – apart from, of course, distinctly kid-shaped form. She was so used to putting the kids first, she couldn't even remember the last time she'd actually had an appointment anywhere for herself. An appointment, a meeting – even an organised (months in advance) cup of tea in a nice cafe – never happened for Kate. Now more than ever, it was clear that she came last on her list of priorities.

But not today. Not on Monday the third of June, 1996. Nope, today she was back at (paid) work!

She shook her (thick, beautifully, professionally highlighted, with not a single wisp of grey) Rachel-from-*Friends* hairdo and ran her index finger down the diary page.

'Can we meet up after work?' Kate asked, putting on her best business voice, which meant she sounded distant and cold all of a sudden. 'It's just that I've got a meeting with Archie right now – ooh, ten minutes ago, actually – then I've got a client lunch and then, straight after that, I have to go to a launch… the launch of some teen soap or something—'

'You're so important, yeah, yeah, I get it,' sniffed Portia. 'I might actually call it a day here, cry off with a migraine. I can defo feel some soul-searching on the Southbank coming on.'

Kate imagined Portia looking all wistful and contemplative, sitting on one of those benches, staring out at the river, a well-thumbed old Virginia Woolf paperback classic in her lap, her hands pulling her coat collar up around her ears as black storm clouds gathered overhead.

'Ha! All dark and dramatic? Doesn't sound like you,' Kate snorted.

'It's the perfect day for it!' said Portia, suddenly getting excited.

Kate looked out one of the windows to see a duck egg blue sky, the weak sun valiantly trying to break through some light cloud cover.

'So where's this launch on, then? I could do with a drink or ten. Specially if it's free.'

Kate told her where it was and what time she would be there.

'You just hang on in there,' Kate said, all soft and mum-like again. 'We'll sort this out soon – don't do anything stupid until you see me. Understand?'

'Then can I do something stupid?'

'Absolutely,' Kate said matter-of-factly and hung up.

She grabbed her diary, found a pen and walked (with ease, despite the hollow plastic heels of her Spice Girls sneakers) over to Archie, the head of PR at PGT&B. He was in his glass office (or cage or cell as he sometimes referred to it), sitting on his big leather swivel chair behind an oversized desk, as if to physically emphasise, through office furniture, how big and crucial to the company he was.

'Ah! Young Kate,' he said by way of greeting.

How sweet those words sounded.

Kate gurned back at Archie. She got on well with him, always had, from the moment she'd met him at her interview for the job. They'd hit it off straight away and had made it a priority to try to always see the funny side of any situation, always have a laugh together. Kate trusted and respected Archie and, even though he was a good five years older than her, she sometimes nearly felt *equal* to him, in a professional capacity, if not an earning capacity – she was, after all, constantly bumping her head on the glass ceiling at PGB&T. But Archie had often told her that her ideas were as good as his – usually much better, in fact – and he needed her to make him look good.

He was almost attractive, she thought. There was nothing particularly handsome about his face – but neither was there anything hideous or offensive. His eyes twinkled when he smiled and his Scouse accent really was very cute – nearly sexy, even. But looking at him now, swamped by the chair and desk (he was only five seven – at a push), she felt not the sudden, hot rush of sexual desire, more the slow, warm, gooey spread of maternal feeling: all she wanted to do to Archie was wipe his nose, smooth his hair down and kiss his cheek.

'Good weekend?' he asked her.

Kate didn't have the faintest idea.

'Yeah, yeah,' she said, trying to sound confident. 'You?'

'Well bladdered. Started Friday afternoon, as you know, and just went nuts from there. I've said it before and no doubt I'll say it again – that feller of yours is an insane party machine!'

'I know!' She grinned.

'But he's gone and got himself and his mag in a bit of bother, now, Kate – and I want you to help me fix it. It's damage-limitation time and we need to work fast.'

'Why? What's happened?'

'Nothing we can't handle – just some strumpet from a small feminist publishing outfit called Medea Media having a go at him, saying he's to blame for the poor self-esteem young girls are supposedly suffering from these days. Poor body image blah-de-blah-de-blah...'

'What? You mean *my* boyfriend? The one at the vanguard of the new lad revolution, propagating the absurdly sexist myth that the only thing women have to offer the world is a cracking set of boobs? Or nothing at all if they are flat, can't afford surgery, plain or – imagine! – interested in other things apart from male attention/objectification?'

Kate crossed her arms over her chest, widened her eyes, interrogating cop-style and, chuffed with herself for calling it exactly as she saw it, waited for Archie to close his mouth and take that stunned look off his face.

'Erm, no. Not exactly,' he eventually managed. 'Oh, come on, Kate! Whose side are you on?'

But just as Kate opened her mouth to speak, she was silenced by the tower of boxes outside Archie's office falling to the floor with the almighty crash and scream of glass bottles breaking.

'Oops!' a tall, lanky, speccy young man bent over and tried to pick up bits of shattered brown bottle now being carried down the corridor on a frothy tide of room temperature beer. 'Sorry, I—'

'There goes breakfast,' Archie grimaced.

Kate furrowed her brow and stared at the scene of devastation. There was something eerily familiar about this hapless guy: his awkward presence, as though he was too big for himself. It was as if occupying any amount of space was too much for him and this made her cock her head to one side, like a dog trying to understand what a human was saying. The fact that he'd drawn a whole office's attention to himself and his clumsiness made him appear all the more uncomfortable in his own skin.

Kate could tell by his body language that he wanted to run and hide, wanted the ground to swallow him up whole, to instantly disappear. And when he looked up, ever so briefly, mumbling apologies, coughing nervously and smiling twitchily, she got it.

It was Seamus!

Kate couldn't help herself and jumped out of her seat a bit, letting out a squeal. She quickly composed herself, putting a hand over her mouth, and shook her head affectionately.

'It's all right, Kate,' laughed Archie, 'there's plenty more in the fridge.'

Kate couldn't take her eyes off Seamus. He actually had hair — thick, jet-black hair. After all the years they'd spent together, Kate always pictured Seamus with a could-have-been-hot-in-his-day bald pate — she'd forgotten that he used to be quite hirsute. His coke-bottle-bottomed John Lennon glasses still did absolutely nothing for him — she'd been right to insist he bin those soon after they got together, and she congratulated herself on her once-wise fashion advice.

'Dress sense of a total dork,' she used to say to him — and, once again, as she could quite plainly see now, she had been right. He was wearing a cagoule over a Liverpool shirt, jeans that were way too tight (leaving little to the imagination) and all-black trainers.

It's not that that, in and of itself, was even so bad, really — it was just that amidst the sea of designer-label-wearing, uber-trendy men who worked at PGT&B, Seamus really stood out. And not in a good way.

God! How on earth did you *ever* get together, Kate asked herself. He was so not your type!

'Hello? Hello!' Archie lifted himself out of his seat by his short arms in a bid to regain Kate's attention.

'Sorry, Archie,' said Kate, turning around to face him again. 'But shouldn't we help Seamus?'

'Who?' said Archie, pulling his chin into his neck and frowning.

Kate gulped. She shouldn't know what this geeky guy's name is.

'Ah, that's me,' said Seamus, standing up, but somehow staying hunched over, as if he was trying to minimise himself and pushing his glasses up with his finger. 'There's no need, I can do it myself. I... I... I just came up here to introduce myself. You're Archie? Is that right?'

Both Kate and Archie nodded fast in an effort to encourage Seamus to hurry up.

'Ah, well, I am, as the lady said, Seamus,' he shot a quick glance down at Kate and blushed. 'And I'm heading up PGT&B's new IT Department. Which is... actually... made up of only me at the moment. But I just wanted to say hi and give you my extension, so if you have any computer problems – or any machine-related problems – anything at all, just, ah, give me a ring.'

'Right,' said Archie, standing up and shaking Seamus' hand. 'And this is Kate, my senior PR adviser and guru of all things grey-matter related.'

Kate stood up in slow motion, giving the moment the time and gravitas she knew it deserved. She imagined herself in black and white, in Forties garb, at a steamy railway station like in *Brief Encounter*. At exactly the same time as she stepped up on tippy-toes and craned her neck in an attempt to look deep into Seamus' eyes, as if she was being filmed in close-up, all Bambi-eyed and inno-cent yet blessed with a knockout, sexy, full, pout, Seamus also bent down quickly, muttering something about too many wires left lying loose on the carpet and the very real tripping dangers they posed.

CRUNCH!

Seamus' forehead collided with Kate's nose in a head-butt of epic proportions.

'YOW!' Kate cried.

'Oh, god! I'm so sorry,' Seamus said, sounding like he was on the verge of tears himself. 'Ah, um – where's the first-aid box?'

Archie ran out of the office and came back in seconds flat, brandishing a load of ice wrapped up in a tea towel.

'There you go, Kate, put that on your face. You'll be all right.'

'Mmmmfff,' Kate grunted.

After flapping around for a few minutes, virtually tripping over himself with 'sorries' and 'oh my gods', Seamus made his exit from the scene, leaving Archie and Kate alone in the office once more.

'I'll be fine,' said Kate. 'I don't think it's broken. With any luck, I won't look too horrendous for my client lunch later.'

Or for my first meeting with Tom, she thought. He must be roaming these corridors somewhere, prowling like a panther, ready to stealthily come up behind her seated at her desk and put his hands on her shoulders to massage them masterfully, as he always used to.

'Right, right,' said Archie as he watched Kate lost in thought. 'Just take it easy for a while – you might have a bit of concussion. I'll get Lucy to cancel all your meetings – you can't go looking like that – nose plastered all over your face like Barbra bloody Streisand! Just take it easy, please, Kate. I'll bring you a tea, you go back to your desk and don't force anything, just casually come up with something brilliant to shut those bloody feminists up.'

'Thanks, Archie,' she said, wondering whether she would have, if she'd been in his shoes, offered her his reclining seat, pulled down the blinds and told her to rest for a while in his quiet office.

As she got up to walk back to her desk, Archie close behind her, heading for the kitchen, he added:

'Oh! And your teen mag? It's in freefall, dying a fookin' fast-paced death. If we can't pull something big out of the bag fast, it's going to have to fold. Sad, but you know. Business is business. So. Two sugars or twelve?'

7

Kate leaned back on her chair, closed her eyes and dabbed at the bridge of her nose with the tea towel that was really just a soggy cloth with a tiny bit of blood on it now. Her top had caught most of the water, mainly on her chest.

'Phwoar!' she heard behind her as she suddenly felt two big hands on each of her breasts. 'Guaranteed first place in any wet t-shirt contest!'

That voice... Those sleazy coming-from-anyone-else-but-dead-sexy coming from him words... Those hands...

Kate got ready for her knees to go weak at this point and she imagined her pins looking like wibbly-wobbly jelly on a plate.

Typical, she thought. Bloody typical! You spend twenty-six years mooning over some man and when you get to see him again, finally, in real life, not just in your desperately bored housewifey fantasies, you've got a black eye, a throbbing, bloody nose and a splitting headache!

It was always the way, she reminded herself. Like, when you've got to get to the shops for some milk, but you've got the flu and you feel lousy and you can only find a pair of battleship grey, grubby trackie bottoms to wear and your hair's pulled back off your wrinkly and simul-taneously spotty face in a greasy ponytail and who decides to start working behind the till at your local corner shop without telling anyone? Only Brad Bloody Pitt!

The radio, with impeccable timing, struck up those distinct few chords of Alanis Morrisette's 'Ironic' and Kate had to agree. *Yes, it is ironic, Alanis. It actually, most certainly is.*

She took a deep breath and opened her eyes. Kate suddenly realised that Tom's touch was *anything* but masterful – he was actually hurting her. As he brought his hands up to her shoulders and kneaded her neck and (oh so satisfyingly hollow, protruding) collar bones, all she wanted to do was wriggle away, get out from under his ham fists.

'Well, *technically*, Alanis,' Tom took his right hand off Kate's (grateful because it was now quite sore) shoulder and she imagined him wagging a finger at the radio, 'it *isn't*. All those things you list aren't ironic at all – the rain on your wedding day, the free ride when you've already paid – they're merely slightly annoying. I think you'll find, my dear, that, in typically American style, you just don't *get* irony. All those things you're banging on about are, quite frankly, just a bit of a pisser.'

Someone, somewhere, laughed – an admiring, brown-nosing kind of a laugh. More of a giggle, really. It was probably Tamsin.

Spurred on by his audience's appreciation, Tom took his left hand off Kate's other poor shoulder and took a bow.

'Thankyou, m'lud,' he said. 'Case closed, I believe.'

Kate felt a little sick. But not because of Tamsin making a show of herself (or Tom, for that matter, making a show of *him*self), but because the downright hugeness of this moment was overwhelming her – with disappointment. For so long she'd planned and prepared what she would be wearing, what she would say, how she would dazzle

Tom with her brilliance when they would meet next –, but when it came to the crunch, she couldn't think of a single witty thing to say.

Even though she'd rehearsed thousands of hilarious opening lines and perfected her air of nonchalance and aloofness and means-nothing-to-me-either-way-ness to a tee over the years, here in her 'office', sat at her pathetic little cubicle, she could barely breathe, let alone be fabulous.

She forced a smile. A twitchy, nervous, constipated-looking smile, but a smile nonetheless.

'All right, lover?' Tom's hot breath filled her ear as he swivelled her chair around to face him.

She gasped.

Tom was just as gorgeous as she remembered – if not more so. And he was so young! So baby-faced! She felt a jolt of shame, as though she was guilty of robbing the cradle, but it passed as quickly as it appeared. And it was replaced, with lightning speed, by a tingling sensation. An all-over body tingling, that was rather pleasant, truth be told, and getting hotter with every second. Definitely *not* a hot flush, she thought to herself.

Tom completed the chair's twirl by putting his hands on her knees, now in front of him. He pushed his right knee roughly between Kate's tightly crossed legs, nudging them apart.

'Tom!' shrieked Kate, shooting glances to first her left and then her right.

'Sorry, babes – just can't help myself around you – you make me so – oi! What happened to your face?'

Bugger. He'd obviously spotted her wrinkles. But then she remembered.

58

'Oh, this?' she put her hand up to her blackening eye. 'Nothing, nothing – just a bit of an accident, that's all. Bumped heads with the new IT guy.'

'I see. What you might call a close encounter... of the *nerd* kind,' he said, looking over in Tamsin's direction, his tongue planted firmly, smugly in his cheek.

Tamsin duly brayed like a donkey.

'Thanks for the flowers,' Kate said, still embarrassed by his insistent knee between hers. She wasn't used to such public displays of... these blatant shows of... of what, exactly? Sensuality? A deep affection and really close connection between two consenting adults? *Ownership?*

She was suddenly confused. Well, not *suddenly* at all, really – she'd been completely dazed and discombobulated ever since she arrived back in 1996, a few hours ago. But now she was feeling as though a rug had been pulled out from under her, Tom-wise. She hadn't remembered him as being such a caricature, such a stereotypical *lad*. Nor did she remember him as being such a crap masseur, either. And she was surprised how, after years of nursing a broken heart, she'd made Tom less handsome in her memory than he was in real life. Because surely when you were as obsessive as she was about the past and the people in it (particularly the ones who'd made her cry) – you'd accentuate, really exaggerate the good stuff.

Perhaps it was a coping mechanism, and the only way she could handle the rejection was to make him plainer in her mind, more anonymous, more everyday, less special.

And then *again*, she smiled looking up at him, maybe she was so intoxicated during their time together (both literally and figuratively), that actually, she had very little clue what he was really like.

'Oh well, how about tonight?' Tom cooed. 'You, me, the moonlight... couple of packs of Marlboro Lights. Drop of champagne. Or a gallon if you're a woman after my own heart. Which I know you are, doll-face. Kensington Roof Gardens. Six of the clock. It's a date. Be there then. See what I did there? Oasis? Be here now? Oh, forget it.'

And god! Did he really used to talk like that? Kate couldn't tell whether she found it offputting or beguiling and quite charming, in a schoolboy, affected kind of a way.

She settled on nonplussed in the end.

'Ah!' she eventually said. 'I can't! I've got to meet Porsh. She's having a bit of a rough time and... well, I need to talk her down, I suppose.'

'Bring with, my love,' he purred, lifting an eyebrow as he looked down at her.

'Oh, no – she needs some serious one-on-one—'

'Girl-on-girl action?' he leered.

'No.'

'Like it! Come on, it'll be fun! Just you, me, Porsh, most of the *Lashed* lads, Archie, probably – come one, come all. With any luck!'

He actually winked then.

'Hmf,' Kate scoffed. 'Intimate.'

'It's a party for a new champagne called... I dunno, some or other bullshit about bubbles... but who cares? It's Monday night! And besides... we are young, dee-doo-dee, something 'bout teeth, nice and clean...' he sang the last bit from that Supergrass song, 'Alright'.

'We'll see,' she said, pursing her lips and sounding like a parent considering whether or not to let their child have any ice cream.

As soon as the words left her lips, she felt like a fraud. Mind you, she'd always felt a tad fraudulent at work, never fully believing that she could get paid quite well just to have fun and think up daft ways of promoting things and planning parties. But now she felt like a total impostor; mutton in lamb's clothing – a beige, non-descript old bag squeezing herself into bright young Miss Selfridge designs.

Honestly, she thought to herself, it wasn't easy flitting about between the past and the future. She was starting to feel like she had a split personality or something, what with one minute being all young and firm and full of future potential and a sexiness she never even *knew* she'd once had – and the next minute falling into the all-too-familiar territory of feeling fat, frumpy and in her fucking fifties!

It was getting bloody hard, actually.

She tried to correct her slightly authoritarian, scolding tone with what she thought might be a coquettish smile. She wasn't 100 per cent sure how to go about this – having never really been a naturally gifted flirt – but she gave it a go anyway, slowly raising the left hand side of her mouth up to greet her nice, sharp cheekbones and looking up at him with her watery eyes from behind her furiously batting lashes. And instead of Tom asking her whether she was all right and did she need a blanket and a good lie down, as if she was having a stroke, it worked.

'You little MINX!' he growled playfully and touched her cheek in a surprisingly tender gesture before he turned around and sauntered off.

Kate swivelled back to face the flowers, puffed her cheeks out to exhale and closed her one good eye to match the other puffy black one.

8

'Thought you'd never get here!' slurred an already sloshed Portia.

'Couldn't get a taxi for love nor money,' replied Kate. 'Didn't wait for me, then, before you got stuck in?'

Portia handed her one of the two balloons of red wine she was holding – the one with the least liquid in it – and the friends clinked glasses as they surveyed the scene.

The launch for *Por Favor!*, an expat teen soap set in Ibiza, was well underway in an all-white warehouse-y loft, up the dodgier end of the Caledonian Road in North London. The usual suspects were there – the scribes from rival magazines, PR people from TV stations, the young unknown actors themselves and a handful of blaggers and liggers, hangers-on who had no obvious connection to the soap or, indeed, any reason to be there apart from the free bar and the off-chance that they might get to rub shoulders with someone famous off the telly.

'Oh thanks, love,' Portia said as she raised her glass to the twelve-year-old waiter who'd just filled it to the brim. 'Got any Pringles?'

The boy, who was probably frightened out of his wits by this Amazonian woman actually looking him in the eye and paying him some attention, pointed, silently, to a long table in front of a big projector.

The table was a veritable smorgasbord; cocktail sausages, crisps (Wotsits, Pringles, Walkers – you name 'em), sausage rolls, prawns, tzatziki, tuna pâté, houmous, a selection of both white (hardly any left) and wholemeal (tons left) M&S mini pitta breads, small boxes of New York-style Chinese takeaway noodles, half-sized spring rolls, dinky won tons and a humungous bowl of Smarties. It was a spread so scrummy that, in 2022, it wouldn't have lasted five minutes before Kate had hoovered up every last morsel ('I just hate waste and can't bring myself to throw all this food out!' she was fond of saying – especially when it came to her kids' leftovers and they'd had fish and chips for dinner). But here and now, she felt happier and more in control (diet-wise) by giving the scoff a swerve and concentrating on the wine.

She looked down at her flat tummy and couldn't resist running her right hand across it, as though she still couldn't quite believe it was hers and there wasn't more to it. There was a slight roundness – what one might call a sensual swell if they were so inclined – but nothing even vaguely resembling the deflated, stretch-marked bag of skin hanging over her pubic bone that it would one day become. And just underneath the waistband of her combats was the spot where one day a caesarean scar would languish, getting redder and thicker and more jagged with the second baby. Kate continued to stroke her own belly, making the most of how tight and taut and *young* it felt to her touch.

'Could we have some shoosh please, ladies and gentlemen?' came the plea from a strawberry-blond guy near the projector, accompanied by three short handclaps.

The buzz of the crowd slowly died down, much to the surprise and immense pleasure of the young man.

'Great! Thanks! Um, right. First off, we'd like to say thank you all so much for coming – we know it's Monday and you'd probably all much rather be sat at your desks clock-watching till six tonight...' He paused to give people time to get the joke and politely guffaw, 'but we figured we'd give you a break from all that strenuous paper shuffling, get you out for a civilised drink or two—'

Portia raised her hand high in the air at this and went, 'Way-hey!' garnering titters from the young waiters and a slightly concerned look from the MC.

'Before the football – yay! – gets underway this weekend and, er, give you the chance to win a trip to the party capital of the Balearics, the one and only beautiful island of Ibiza! Where, as you will soon see, there's so much more to life as an expat teen than just pills and parties.'

Everyone milled about taking their seats in front of the huge cloth screen up against the opposite wall. Even Kate, who knew this poor soap was going to barely see its first series through before it was taken off air, if she remembered correctly, felt quite excited to see the first episode again. It was as though she was really embracing all the promise and potential, the courage to fail and the enthusiasm to succeed that being young (again) gave you automatically. As far as Kate could see at this very moment, *that* was what youth was all about.

She shuffled her tiny bum back into the seat next to Portia and held her wine glass at its base in her lap.

'Oh! And stick around for a little bit afterwards, people, there'll be the chance to win a trip to Ibiza for you and a friend if you do. Now, is everybody sitting comfortably? Yes? Roll 'em, then!'

The show was neither great nor dismal – not that Kate got to see much of it. After approximately just three minutes of flimsy sets and dodgy Spanish accents, Portia nudged Kate hard in the ribs, demanding she join her in the next room for a chat and a much-needed fag.

Kate bent over as she walked and apologised repeatedly in a whisper for causing a black shadow against the dry, dusty countryside on the projector screen.

Portia didn't bother with any of that. Instead, she stopped halfway, looked to the screen, waved at it with both hands, fingers splayed and said, 'How do you do a shadow bunny again? Or a fox – yeah! How do you do a fox?'

Kate grabbed her by the elbow, got her into the smaller adjoining room and opened the windows while Portia grabbed two chairs, virtually throwing them at the wall underneath.

'I don't remember you being so rubbish at holding your liquor,' Kate mused out loud.

'Me? Rubbish? How dare you?!' Portia frowned back at her, looking seriously offended. 'For your information, I've been drinking since I got off the phone to you this morning and I think I'm handling it all pretty well, actually, thangvermuch!'

'But what about the baby?' Kate asked, trying not to show any judgement towards a pregnant woman knocking it back like a sailor on shore leave.

'Yeah, well,' Kate said, sparking up a cigarette.

It was all Kate could do not to grab it out of Portia's mouth, throw it out the window and say: 'That's QUITE enough, young lady! Now go to your room and THINK about what you've done until I say it's time to come out!'

'I've been thinking about that. And if Simon doesn't want it – or me – then I don't want it, either. So consider it gone!' Portia let her cigarette dangle out of the corner of her mouth and slapped her hands together, like she was finished with the whole ugly business.

'You mean, you—'

'Yep, that's right! I've booked myself in at a clinic for two weeks' time and that's the end of it.'

'Marie Stopes?' Kate offered.

'Something like that, yeah, whatevs,' Portia drawled.

Kate was shocked to see her best friend so hard-hearted, so laissez-faire. Kate had always firmly believed it was a woman's right to choose (her own mum had always left her dog-eared copy of *Our Bodies, Our Selves* lying around when Kate was a kid, after all) but in this instance, she knew something Portia didn't and she simply *had* to stop her.

'Porshie, I think – no, I *know* – you're making a mistake. A huge mistake. Don't go to wherever you're going. I know it's not Marie Stopes and I know you'll regret it bitterly. Cancel the appointment, please. Hmm? Will you?'

'No need. I know what I want – my brilliant career. And Simon. I can't have those if I have a baby, so something's got to go. And, besides, I'm far too young for nappies and sleepless nights. I DO NOT want this baby. Why can't you get it through your thick head?'

'Can we at least talk about it? When you're, you know, not feeling quite so raw? You only just split from Simon a few hours ago!'

'No point!' Portia said, taking another ma-hoosive slug of wine. 'No discussion, no debate, no explanation, no apology. What's it to you, anyway?'

66

Kate looked out of the window at the rows of North London chimney pots and pressed her lips together, exhaling through her nose.

How could she possibly tell Portia the truth? How on earth could she explain to her that if she didn't go to Marie Stopes, she would be scarred for life and never – even with extensive operations and painful, heart-breaking and eye-wateringly expensive IVF treatment – be able to get pregnant again.

She couldn't, she decided. Not without giving herself away as a traveller from another time in the future. And, obviously, insane. Portia probably wouldn't believe that, anyway. God knows, Kate was having a hard time getting to grips with it herself.

She'd have to come up with something sneaky, some-thing that Portia, who was as smart as a whip (but who made increasingly dumb choices when it came to men) wouldn't suspect. And it had to be something that Portia thought was all her own idea. Somehow, Kate would have to plant the seed of doubt in Portia's mind and let her think that she decided to go to Marie Stopes all by herself.

She needed to think. And she needed to think fast. She looked at Portia French drawing a large amount of smoke up her nose.

Kate hadn't smoked for… ooh, about a million years, since she first found out she was pregnant with Phoebe. But she had missed it from time to time. And she had never quite managed to disabuse herself of the idea that it made you look cool and helped you concentrate.

'Gimme one of those, will you?' she growled, while simultaneously pulling one of Portia's cigarettes out of its flip-top pack.

'Got a light?' She looked up at Portia.

'Of course,' smiled Portia. 'And even though you never have any fags or lighters on you at the beginning of a night, what's the bet you end up with several lighters and a full pack of Marlies in your bag by tomorrow morning?'

It was true, Kate giggled, remembering their old ritual. Every morning after a big night, the two friends would go through their pockets and handbags for evidence – clues to help them piece their evening together.

Kate inhaled deeply. Then spluttered. Then coughed up a lung. And then, amid a whirlwind of hacking and barking, as though she was in the throes of a particularly nasty case of croup, she vomited. All over the loft's recently lime-washed floor boards.

'Oh dear!' Kate heard someone say. 'Looks like everyone's a critic!'

Kate looked up, wiping her mouth on the back of her hand. That voice belonged to the strawberry-blond MC guy, who, by now, had attached a big Cheshire Cat kind of a grin to his face, just above his ginger goatee.

Portia, who'd moved behind Kate and was holding her hair back off her face (in the way that only true best friends will do in times of crises like these), said, 'Sorry about this. She's not usually so, um, she's not normally this delicate.'

All three of them studied the pool of shame at Kate's feet.

'Ah.' The MC dragged his eyes away from the floor, briefly shut them and gulped hard. He spoke and pointed at the door to the larger room. 'Er, in there, we've been busy watching the first episode and drawing the winner out of a hat for the trip to Ibiza.'

He said the 'z' as a 'th' and opened his eyes, raising his chin high in an attempt to make sure even his peripheral vision didn't clock Kate's humiliating puddle.

'And someone called Kate Henderson from PGT&B is the lucky girl. Would either of you two be—'

'Way-hey!' cheered Portia, letting go of Kate's hair, raising her hands high like she'd just scored a goal 'Look at you, sweetie – one eye all bloodshot and watery, the other a deep purplish shade of black – you *need* this holiday! And so do I! When do we depart, my good man?'

'Whenever you want – as long as it's the fourteenth to the sixteenth of this month. I've got all the details in here, if you want to take a look…'

'Great,' sniffed Kate. 'That's brilliant – thanks so much!'

Portia hooked her arm into Kate's, pulled her along back into the other room and gasped in horror when she saw that the crowd had halved – and what was left of it, was fast making for the door.

'Oh!' she whined, adding a small stamp of her foot to complete the overall picture of a tantrumming three year old. 'We can't leave! We can't go home yet – not now we've got some serious celebrating to do! Where to next, Katie?'

'Well,' said Kate, straightening herself up after signing some travel documents on the buffet table. 'I really don't feel very much like going on anywhere, to be honest. I've got a splitting headache and look at me!'

Portia laughed.

'Don't be silly – you look great! And anyway. What else are you going to do? Go home, microwave a meal for one and settle down to a boring night in troughing Hob Nobs, watching *Question Time* and sipping Horlicks?'

Kate sighed. That was *exactly* what she wanted to do. What a great idea, she thought – the perfect evening, in fact. She pictured herself, snuggled up on one of the leather couches at their flat, a throw over her legs, biscuit crumbs in her tea – and the gentle buzz of the telly the only noise in the place. She couldn't help but wistfully stare into the middle distance as she imagined the scene; no kids running up and down stairs, having sword fights and dead arm competitions, no absent husbands coming home pissed and sleeping on the couch, no washing-up to do, leftovers to eat, clothes to sort for the next day…

'Earth to Kate… Kate? KATE!' Portia yelled in her ear. 'You all right?'

'Oh, yeah, sorry. Just knackered, really, that's all. Tom wanted me to bring you to some do at the Kensington Roof Gardens, but I'm just not up for it tonight, Porshie, sorry. I'm ab-so-*lutely* shattered.'

'Awww, poor you,' Portia said, almost sounding sympathetic and able to see sense, ready to call it a night. 'Luckily, I've got a little something here in my purse that can help with that. Come on, I'll show you when we get to the loos at the Roof Gardens. We'll easily get a cab from here…'

'What?' asked Kate, unable to figure out what her best friend was on about. Portia grasped the shoulder of Kate's crop-top and dragged her to the warehouse exit.

'To Kensington!' Portia cried. 'And don't spare the horses!'

9

Kate opened one (albeit a bit bleary) eye on Tuesday morning to the sound of an old tramp with emphysema squeaking and wheezing away somewhere in her room.

She lifted her head and peered under her duvet, even though she didn't really think she would find anything there, and then very slowly, very gently, lowered her throbbing head back down onto her pillow.

'Ooh,' she winced. 'Ow, ow, ow!'

Upon realising that the invisible old man with chronic lung disease was actually *her*, she reached an arm across to the bedside table for her Ventolin.

A few puffs later, she could breathe again.

'Guess that's another reason I don't smoke any more,' she muttered.

Propping herself up on her hand, she looked over at her bedside table and almost fainted with relief when she spied (eventually, that is – it took a while for her eye to focus) a pint glass filled to the brim with cool, clear water.

Kate licked her lips, sat up and grasped the glass. Slowly bringing it to her mouth, she closed her eye, anticipating the delicious, almost sweet, taste of the water and savouring this, her last moment of dry, cracked dehydration.

One gargantuan gulp later and both her eyes shot open – even the puffy, bruised black one. She scanned the room in seconds flat for a halfway decent receptacle, found none and so was forced to spit a whole mouthful of neat vodka out onto the coir carpet next to her bed.

Luckily, she didn't then throw up for real – diced carrots and specks of mini party food being absolute murder to get out of those deep carpet crevices and grooves.

'ARGH!' she croaked.

It took her a while to calm down, but when she did, she was horrified.

What on earth had she been playing at last night? Who did she think she was?

In her head, she sounded like her own mother, telling her off the first time she drank too much Babycham when she was fifteen and was sick all over her bedroom. Her mum had been pretty cool about it after that, encouraging Kate to have a small glass of wine with her evening meal, in an effort to a) not make drinking such a big deal to the young girl and b) keep her at home and not out on the town with the 'rougher elements' of Bayswater.

I could really do with Mum, now, thought Kate. She would love to hold her mum close, snuggle in to her warm, soft chest and hear her soothing voice offering her brown bread and honey sandwiches, as if they alone could cure the world of all its ills.

But Jenny hadn't been warm and mumsy like that for yonks. Or at least since she gave up her academic career and became a full-time, at-home carer for Kate's dad, old skirt-chasing, philandering George.

Then, when her beloved boy, Steve, went missing, Jenny really collapsed. Not on the outside so that anyone would know, but on the inside where her own bitterness and bile began slowly eating away at her, like acid on flesh.

God, she missed them. George had died before Kate had ever got the chance to tell him she loved him and forgave him for all the crappy things he'd done. She would have finally got closure.

And although her mum was still around, she was so far removed from the lovely, doting woman she used to be, Kate dreaded seeing her or talking to her on the phone. Even getting a text message from Jenny was like having the Grim Reaper drop in on you. Only with fewer laughs.

When Kate started having kids, at the ripe old age of thirty-eight, she'd really wished her mum had been there for her. Everyone else seemed to have motherly advice coming out of their ears, wherever they turned – their own mothers, their partner's mothers – everyone else seemed to be lousy with mothers.

But not her. For Kate, there was no one she could ask for help when she had Phoebe. Even Seamus' mum was a non-starter – she'd left her husband and Seamus when he was five – and no one had heard from her since. Then, with the advent of Decko nearly four years later, when Kate desperately needed to know how to divide your attention between two kids equally, so as to avoid any jealous rages, she would often find herself screaming, wanting to jump into the gaping black hole of uncertainty that presented itself in front of her daily. Or, in the absence of a black hole, the pantry.

If only she could...

Kate sat up, stiff as a board, mouth agape.

'OW!' she groaned, rubbing her head. 'It's 1996, for god's sake. 199-fucking-6!'

'Shut up!' came the chorus from the other bedrooms in the flat.

73

But Kate didn't hear them – she was like a woman possessed.

She leaped out of bed, ignoring all the protestations coming from her head, heart, forearms (for some unknown reason), legs (particularly her calves) and back. She flung her bedroom door open, raced towards the kitchen, backtracked immediately to get her slippers (that coir stuff can be really rough on your toes, you know) and positively crashed into the phone on the kitchen bench.

'Number, number – what's their bloody number?' Kate mumbled frantically. 'GOD! You'd think it would be indelibly printed on my brain, it being the number we grew up with, the first set of numbers I ever managed to memorise when I was six, oh, for the love of—'

She stopped herself faffing about and coolly, calmly sat on the stool by the kitchen bench. She exhaled slowly, deliberately and picked up the receiver.

'Now think. Think!'

She stared at the phone for a few seconds and then noticed the red light flashing on the small, black box next to it.

'Ha,' she laughed softly. 'Answering machine! God – remember when your phone and answering machine were two different things?'

'Yeah,' said Steve, shuffling into the kitchen with his trademark sleepy drawl. 'Like it was yesterday. Because – der – it *was*?'

'Oh, Steve! What's our number? I mean at home,' she pleaded with her brother. 'Quick! What's Jenny and George's number?'

'Mum and Dad, you mean?' Steve's voice was muffled as he peered into the fridge.

He made a point of not calling them by their first names. He resented their 'me' generation ideals and blamed them and their laissez-faire attitude towards parenting (by which he meant *him*) for all his problems.

'Oh, bollocks,' he sighed wearily as he emerged from the fridge, pulling himself up to his full height. 'Plenty of full-fat, but not a drop of skimmed left.'

'Bet there's no unsweetened almond milk, either,' Kate chimed in.

Steve ignored her.

'Typical, I suppose. I blame the parents, you know.'

'Yes, I *do* know,' smiled Kate.

'Well, it's true!' he grinned back at her. 'They never taught us to plan ahead, to make provision for the future… and now look at us! Scrounging a living, foraging around in the steaming rubbish dumps of West Hampstead, never knowing where our next trip to Ibiza is coming from…'

'Go to the shop, you lazy bugger!,' Kate threw one of her slippers at him and felt the merest twinge of recollection in the pit of her stomach.

As she watched Steve lollop out of the kitchen, the twinge grew larger until Kate could actually decipher it. She frowned when she remembered that it always used to nark her somewhat that Steve was so blasé about Jenny and George. And always so spoiled, as though having his university fees, his rent and food, his *life*, pretty much, paid for him by Kate and her parents was his God-given right and nothing to be thankful for or appreciative of. He never even looked as though he was trying to pull himself out of the doldrums he'd been languishing in for ages.

She half expected some all-seeing, all-knowing, pesky 1996 radio to start playing 'Driftwood' by Travis at this point – the song that always made her think of Steve and his aimlessness.

Then she made a mental note to make sure she remembered to thank her parents for all they'd ever done for her, all they'd ever given her and everything they ever were to her and her brother, the second she got them on the end of the line.

'Now, what was… 0208 something – no, hang on! It was still 0181 in 1996! Well remembered, Katie – even with the mother of all hangovers, you've still got it! Now wait, hold on, it's coming back to me, it's coming, it's coming…'

The radio seemed to spring to life all of a sudden, even though it must've been on all night, and Kate felt as though she was going to burst with happiness when she heard Frank Skinner and David Baddiel singing 'Three Lions' again. Whenever she heard it, in either 2022, 1996 or even if she lived to hear it in 2096, she would always immediately feel the unbridled optimism, excitement and enthusiasm of that one month when Euro 96 was a national obsession. Even *she* had been into it, despite never really giving a toss about football in her life before. It seemed like everyone became a football fan that June and England really *did* seem like they were going to win it.

If only poor old—

Oops, she stopped her train of thought. *Better not spoil it for anyone. There'll be plenty of time for crying into our beers later.*

Kate shook her head, as if to force herself to re-focus and concentrate on more pressing matters.

She shut her eyes tight and tried to picture the numbers and after a while, they appeared, as if by magic. She hastily punched them into the phone's keypad, her fingers trembling ever-so-slightly.

It rang.

And rang.

And rang.

Don't be out! You *can't* be out! It's only eight in the morning! Oh, please, please! Don't be out *now*! Come on… come on!

'Eight five zero two,' a voice, not unlike Joanna Lumley's, came on the line.

'MUM!' Kate cried.

'DARLING!' Jenny replied. 'Good. You got my message, then?'

'What? No – what was it?'

'To give me a ring, of course. I called your flat hundreds of times last night, but Steven kept answering, so I had to hang up every time. I left a message for you at work yesterday afternoon, because you were out, *all afternoon*, so I imagine that's where you are now, hmm? At work?'

'No, no – I'm ah, still at home—'

'Oh dear, sweetheart,' said Jenny.

Kate had forgotten that her mum was always so full-on about work – as though Kate was lucky to have a job, and that she shouldn't take it for granted or take the mickey in any way. Jenny never failed to understand, though, that as a salesperson at PGT&B, it actually *was* Kate's job to go to alcohol-fuelled lunches and launches with clients and colleagues. Kate could never make her see that her job – and the magazines she publicised – depended upon her schmoozing and boozing: getting paid to become a total and utter lush.

'What was it this time, hmm? Another client lunch, I suppose?'

'Well that, yes – and the launch for a new teen soap, where I won a trip to Ibiza,' said Kate proudly.

'How? By drinking your own body weight in tequila, I bet. And after that? I must say, honey bunny – you sound awfully rough. Have you got any Alka-Seltzer? Beroccas?'

Kate looked around the kitchen and saw an overflowing ashtray on the table surrounded by several cans and bottles which had contained European beer. Four, actually. Four overflowing ashtrays and a cagoule lying on the floor.

'Four ashtrays and a cagoule,' she unintentionally said out loud, her head really pounding at the sight of all this undeniable debauchery. 'Ha! Sounds like a good name for a movie!'

'I see,' Jenny said. 'Well, regardless of your social life, we really need to talk. About Steven. Can you come to the house – no, no – I'll come and meet you. In Covent Garden somewhere. Can you meet me at Carluccio's tomorrow at, say, one?'

It seemed like forever to wait.

'Not today?' Kate sounded disappointed.

'No, no – I forgot, Ickenham Residents' Association meeting. I simply have to be there, otherwise they'll have me de-frocked or something.'

'Ooh-er, missus!' said Kate, keen to keep her mum on the line.

'Tomorrow at one, then? And don't tell your brother – he can't know I'm seeing you and not him. Understand?'

'Yes, Mum.'

'Until tomorrow, then. Now get some rest, sweetheart – and take some of that echinacea I gave you. Fantastic at warding off colds, apparently.'

And with that, she hung up.

Just like that. One *click* and she was gone again.

But only momentarily. Kate would see her mother again tomorrow – if she wasn't propelled back to 2022 in the next few hours – and she bit her lip in an effort to stop herself screaming with delight.

A few minutes later, Kate made her way to the kitchen table to make a start on clearing up. Even though the mere sight of all those dog ends and overturned cans of lager made her want to heave, she figured someone had to do it – and she was used to clearing up after people, anyway. What was one more disgusting bombsite of a mess to contend with when you had two kids, one dog and a booze-hound husband?

'Two kids and a husband – another good name for a movie!' she said.

'Or not,' said a groggy Portia behind her. 'Urgh. Somebody shoot me. Please.'

'Por Favor, you mean!' chirruped Kate, trying to hide the fact that she, too, felt like death warmed up. Without the warmed-up bit.

'Oh, GOD! Why did I ever let you drag me to Kensington?' said Portia, slumping down at the kitchen table, her head resting on her outstretched arm.

'*Me* drag *you*? I think it was the other way around, lady! And what did you spike my drinks with?'

'Nothing,' said Portia, sitting up. 'Although you were a veritable Hoover in the toilets, if you know what I mean…'

'No, I— Oh, Porsh! Please say it isn't so – not drugs! I haven't done anything like that for a million years – I HATE it!'

'You've got a funny way of showing it! Made Lee look like Mary Whitehouse!'

'What?'

'You went berserk! Mind you, it was quite funny. And I think Lee quite fancies you, actually.'

'Lee who?'

'Blimey, Kate! You really don't remember? Callahan! Lee Callahan! Lead singer of massive guitar band Mirage?!'

'Lee Callahan was there? Last night?'

'Der! You got on like a house on fire, you did. Not that Tom was too pleased about it. Mind you, I think he was probably miffed that it wasn't *him* making Lee laugh all night – not merely that you were talking to him, getting all cosy and stuff.'

'We were?'

'Yeah, looked like a fun couple for a little while, there. Before you got us kicked out—'

'Typical,' Kate mumbled. 'The one time I get close enough to Lee Callahan to actually have a chat, I can't remember a single thing about it!'

'I wouldn't worry about it, Katie,' Portia closed her eyes and yawned so wide, her mouth looked like the entrance to the Blackwall Tunnel. 'It's hardly like he would've said anything particularly erudite, is it?'

'You're probably right. So how did I get us booted out, then?'

'Busting your best *Dirty Dancing* moves on Lee,' Portia smirked, smacking her lips and shaking the packet of Crunchy Nut Cornflakes into a bowl. Kate eyed Portia's breakfast enviously and started to salivate. But there was no way she would ever allow herself any of that carby, sugary treat – why, her hips would never forgive her! Or her back fat.

'Was that all?' Kate said, hoping this would be her cue to feel relieved. Because there was never any harm in dancing, was there? It's not like they lived in that town in *Footloose*, where dancing was banned and the work of the devil or whatever.

'In the gents,' Portia added.

Kate groaned. She wasn't sure she wanted to hear any more. No, no, scratch that – she was. She *was* sure she didn't want to hear any more.

Imagine if Seamus and the kids had seen her! Imagine if Jenny and George had seen her! She was mortified.

'In fact,' Portia went on, 'Lee asked me to take you home – he was quite chivalrous, come to think of it. Seemed more protective of you rather than wanting to take advantage of you or anything. Which was rather unexpected, I must say.'

'Oh, great,' Kate moaned, burying her head in her hands. 'Was it… was I… were we *always* like this?'

'Like what?'

'You know, ridiculously embarrassing. And grotty. And out of control.'

'You mean out there, up for it and always on the lash?'

'Yes… I think…?'

'Dunno. But I think Tom's really led *you* astray. Things have really ratcheted up a few notches since you started going out with him, that's for sure. You've always been a bad influence on me, though. Ever since we started at school together. That's what my mother always says, anyway.'

Kate didn't remember being the ringleader of their exploits, the instigator of their mischief. But now that Portia mentioned it, maybe she was sometimes guilty of egging her best friend on, goading her into doing things she wasn't one hundred per cent sure were the 'right' or the 'good' thing to do.

'Hey! That's not entirely fair.' She grappled with the moral high ground that was fast disappearing beneath her feet. 'You were the one who got me so wasted last night I can't remember any of it! And it involved Lee Callahan?! You've robbed me of my one decent memory of probably the closest brush with fame I'll ever have!'

'You weren't exactly a shrinking violet when it came to Neil Morrissey, either, you know...'

'WHAT?'

'You kept poncing ciggies off him. Not that he minded – he just kept nicking Clunesy's packets.'

Neil Morrissey? *Clunesy*? This was worse – a hundred times worse than Kate first thought.

'STOP! I don't want to hear any more. Let's just forget it ever happened and we'll never mention it again. OK?'

'Mention what again?'

'Atta girl,' said Kate, brushing the hair off her face and shaking her head as though she could erase any remaining memory she might have of the previous evening with a few short, sharp tosses of her mane.

'That's it for me,' she continued, refreshed. 'Never again.'

Portia snorted as though she'd heard this refrain many times before – which she had, not least from her own lips. But unbeknownst to Portia, Kate really *did* mean it this time and would, in an unprecedented move, actually stick to her vow. She'd forgotten how hopeless she was at taking the emotional battering and horrendous embarrassment their mornings-after would invariably bring. And since she'd had the kids, the biggest a night got was usually one family block of Cadbury's Dairy Milk too many in front of *Bridgerton*. Dancing with pop stars and smoking with celebrities was nothing but a dim, distant memory now she was a mother. Or at least it would be if she could remember any of it.

And so now, with her muzzy head quite a bit clearer (her twenty-eight-year-old self's hangover lasting only a few hours in the morning), she sat opposite Portia and looked longingly at her friend's bowl of cereal once more.

'Oh, sod it,' she said, grabbing the packet and filling a bowl to the brim with its crunchy, carby tastiness. She splashed on lashings of creamy, cold, fantastically full-fat and outrageously ideologically unsound cow's milk.

'Do you remember whose that is?' Portia jerked her head towards the rogue cagoule on the floor.

'Of course I don't,' Kate said through a mouthful of sheer bliss.

'God, you really are absolutely dreadful,' said Portia. 'When we got kicked out of the Roof Gardens, we tried to get a taxi home, but couldn't. Then we bumped into some technical guy from your office who was just driving past on his way home from work — must've been about eleven or so — and he rather gallantly put it over your shoulders. You said it felt weird having your fat mummy tummy exposed and he wanted to help keep you warm. As well as preserve what little was left of your dignity, I suppose.'

'Really?' said Kate. 'What was his name?'

'I can't remember. He was quite a nice guy, though — gave us a lift home in his Skoda. Came in for a quick drink our way of saying thank you.'

'Was it… was his name Seamus?'

'That's the fella!'

'And he only came in for a quick drink, did he? I mean, I didn't try to snog him or drag him into the loos or…'

'No, no — not that I'm aware of.'

'Thank god for that,' said Kate, rolling her eyes to the ceiling. She wanted to make sure she remembered getting together with Shay this time around. At this, Portia arched an eyebrow and looked just past Kate's shoulder. Kate turned to look behind her just as an impossibly tall, lanky guy in a Liverpool shirt hopped into the kitchen from Portia's room, pulling on his black trainers.

'I can give you a lift to work too, Kate, if you can be ready in the next ten minutes,' coughed Seamus, his face reddening as he studied his shoelaces.

84

10

She hadn't felt jealous – really jealous – when it came to Seamus and another woman, for— God! Come to think of it, Kate didn't know if she'd *ever* thought that Seamus might have fancied someone else.

But sitting here in his Skoda, the floor littered with empty (she'd checked) Quavers packets and various unidentifiable wires and plugs, she felt herself turning a most unattractive shade of green.

'So,' she said, breaking the silence that had hung heavily in the air between them since they bade Portia farewell. 'I see you're getting to know not only your colleagues at work better, but getting to know their best friends even better!'

Seamus stole a lightning fast glance at his passenger.

'Hmm?' he hummed as he negotiated the morning traffic.

'Portia,' Kate hissed. 'My best mate? The woman with whom you shared a *bed* with last night with?'

Kate momentarily panicked about whether she'd used 'whom' correctly and overdone the 'withs' in that last sentence. She'd never said 'whom' before in actual, real-life speech and half-expected Tom to pop up from the back seat, telling her how wrong she'd got it and how she had, quite unnecessarily, doubled – trebled, even, the 'withs'.

'Who?' asked Seamus, concentrating hard on the road ahead. '*Me?*'

'Well, I don't see any other dirty stop-out here!'

Kate heard herself for the first time that morning and swallowed hard. Trying to rein herself in, she gave herself a brief but strict talking to.

Steady on! He doesn't know he's married to you in the future – barely even knows who you are, yet! You'll scare him off if you carry on like this, so go easy with the wounded wife routine, will you?

'But I didn't! I slept on her floor,' said Seamus.

'Details, details.' Kate couldn't help herself.

'Look,' Seamus said, yanking on the handbrake at a set of red traffic lights. 'I don't know what you're suggesting – or why it matters to you so much, but, just for the record, Portia tried to kiss *me* last night. I declined with thanks, fending off her advances in the most gentlemanly way I knew how.'

Kate stared back at him, her jaw hitting the floor.

'Well,' he went on, 'we'd all had too much to drink and I barely know either of you and it didn't feel all that romantic to me and I know it sounds strange and you'll probably think I'm a real prat, but—'

'Yes?' Kate folded her arms across her chest.

'…I'm just not that sort of guy.'

'Yeah, right!' scoffed Kate. 'You mean human?'

Kate couldn't imagine there was a man alive who wouldn't be bowled over by Portia's beauty. She believed that every man who ever saw her wanted to bed her (as was commensurate with what she'd seen over the years) and couldn't quite comprehend what Seamus was saying.

She felt confused. This was not how it had been the first time round, had it? All straight men were crazy about

Portia, weren't they? And all men were only ever after one thing, weren't they? She felt as though she were blindly weaving her way through a veritable rabbit warren of reality versus perception, fact v fiction, making her feel more like Alice in Wonderland than ever.

'I am sorry about your eye, you know,' he said wearily, as though he'd already said it a thousand times.

Kate grunted.

The lights turned green and Seamus jerked the car into first gear and bunny hopped for a few metres before he spoke again.

'So are you watching the match on Saturday?'

'What match?' asked Kate.

'Ha! Good one,' laughed Seamus.

'No, really – which one?'

'England v Switzerland, of course!' laughed Seamus. 'Where have you been?'

Kate felt her hackles rising. She felt exactly as she did when the kids were little and Seamus would come home from work and, finding the house in a right state with dirty plates and clothes strewn everywhere and kids running riot, and/or bawling their eyes out, say: 'What exactly do you *do* all day?'

'Well, how am I supposed to know?' Kate felt like answering him. 'I've only been back in 1996 for a day! You try to remember a football tournament's schedule from twenty-six years ago on top of every bloody thing else!'

But she didn't. She let her annoyance pass, quickly, and then a wave of excitement washed over her.

'Is it the first one? What do you think of our chances?'

As soon as she'd asked this question, she regretted it. Not because she knew exactly how it all turned out, so it was kind of irrelevant to her, but because she knew that once you got any guy banging on about football, they couldn't shut up. It was as though there was no room left in their heads for feelings and emotions – their brains were packed to capacity with boring stats and 'interesting' facts.

Note to self: remember to never even get him started on Fantasy Football league tables.

'Hmm,' she said, trying to sound as though she'd been listening. 'Still, I wouldn't ever discount the Germans. Best for us to not get complacent and keep on our toes at all times, give it our all no matter who we're playing.'

Seamus looked at her as though she were mad (a look she knew very well) and said:

'Do you like football?'

'Yeah, I suppose so.' She thought of Portia, whose idiot ex, Simon, was so obsessed with football, Portia regularly denounced it as 'a sickness' – and pronounced their sex life at weekends, as a result, DOA. 'But this time it's special, really, isn't it? I mean, a chance like this only comes once in a lifetime.'

Seamus shot her an admiring glance and smiled, nodding his head in agreement.

Kate leaned over and turned up the radio, which was, oddly enough, playing *Once In A Lifetime*.

'Curiouser and curiouser,' Kate said as she sat back and began to enjoy the ride.

'So, Kate,' Archie yelled out across the office. 'Got anywhere with Medea? Or that, um, other matter we spoke about yesterday?'

'Hang on a sec,' Kate called back, organising her bag and hanging her optimistically lightweight trench coat over the back of her chair.

In all the flurry of debauched activity yesterday, she'd clean forgotten all about the media storm brewing between Medea and *Lashed*. And as for *Mad Fer It!*, well, she didn't have a clue how to reverse her favourite teen mag's fortunes.

Kate looked at the phone. She was one of the lucky ones, Archie had told her, to be getting a new whizz-bang machine that was an answering machine and phone in one. State-of-the-art technology, she believed it was called.

But she hadn't received it yet – she imagined Seamus would deliver it to her, hook it up, tell her how it worked and then somehow fall over in some way that would make her other eye black, too. A matching pair.

There were some hand-written messages sitting next to the phone and she looked up to see Lucy, the receptionist, smiling politely at yet another person walking in who looked past her, totally ignoring her, too important to take the time to say hi.

Kate told herself off for not having formally introduced herself to Lucy. It wasn't like her, she thought. Because she'd always made a point of being nice to everyone. Not in a 'you never know who'll you'll bump into on the way down' way, but just because she was generally, overall, for the most part, actually quite a nice person.

She picked up the messages and strode over to reception.

'Hi there,' she breezed, holding out her hand. 'I'm Kate. I don't think we've been properly introduced.'

'No, I, ah, hi! I'm Lucy,' the girl said, shaking Kate's hand. 'Have I done something wrong?'

'No, not at all,' laughed Kate. 'I just wanted to thank you for taking these messages for me.'

Lucy looked puzzled. Then embarrassed. 'Just doing my job,' she said, warily.

'And doing it well, too. Thanks again, Lucy. I'll see you later.' Kate turned around and, immensely pleased with herself, headed back towards her desk.

'Oh, Kate?' Lucy called after her. 'The guy who called this morning – you're holding the message in your hand – was that Lee Callahan? It sounded like him, but is it really *the* Lee Callahan? From Mirage?'

'I very much doubt it,' scoffed Kate as she looked down at her hand. 'When did this... this Lee call?'

'At about 8:30, I think. I wrote it on the paper there, see?'

Kate did see.

> 8:25 a.m. Tuesday June 4
> *When can I see you again? Call me on my*
> *paging service – I gave you the number last night!*
> *Lee Xxx*

'Oh, come ON!' Kate said aloud, looking frantically at the ceiling. 'This has GOT to be a dream. I mean, as IF!'

'I know!' squealed Lucy. 'I thought the same thing! It can't be the real one – he doesn't get up before two in the afternoon!'

Kate stared at Lucy.

'Or... at least... that's what they say in this fortnight's *Mad Fer It!*,' she said, sounding slightly scared and holding up her copy of the magazine, fairly festooned with pictures of Mr Callahan. 'It's a special edition... um... their We Love Lee issue...'

'Yeah,' Kate nodded, calming down a bit. 'Just a joke, I expect.'

She slumped down in her chair and looked crossly at the message.

'What paging service number?' she muttered as she picked her mini black leather rucksack off the floor and rummaged through it.

Kate marvelled momentarily at how little there was in there – save for a few lighters, lots of loose tobacco and broken cigarettes, her purse, her puffer, her favourite Rimmel Raspberry Fool lipstick, Shiseido wet/dry compact, a packet of Extra (sugar-free) chewing gum, a small, travel-sized perfume bottle and, as always, her keys in the special secret zipped compartment. It was really light.

These were the days, she thought – when her handbag wasn't overflowing with wipes, sultanas (both in and out of their box), iPhones (both real and toy), car keys, house keys, crayons, markers, random bits of dog-eared paper with shopping lists and notes to herself scribbled on them, unused but grubby and suspect-looking tissues (she always grabbed four upon leaving the house, contributing to the mini mountain of Kleenex growing daily in her bag), spare pairs of pants (for the kids), tampons and pads (for her), big jars of Vaseline, smashed about tubes of Savlon, half-eaten lollipops stuck to the cloth lining, long-forgotten receipts...

Kate tutted, thinking of all the rubbish she carted about with her back in 2022 – the problem with always trying to be prepared for every eventuality and emergency while constantly being blindsided by the completely unexpected. She sighed. And immediately felt like crying.

Could it be that she was missing the noise and clutter of home? Missing the kids' cute faces? She wanted to hold them all close to her right now, vowing that she'd never, ever, EVER shout at them again, ever. Even if she'd had no sleep and Declan wouldn't get off his Xbox and Phoebs was stuck to her phone like glue... Nope, not her. The second she got back to them – hoping, now, that it would be soon – she would become the perfect mum; unflappable, in control but not stern, warm and funny, stylish and slim – she would really be the kind of mum she'd always wanted to be and everything, as a direct result, would be fantastic.

Kate felt the need to slope off to the toilets for a quiet little power weep. Then she would get back to putting the magazine world to rights.

But as she pulled her hand out of her rucksack, a beer coaster came flying out as well, a soggy corner hitting her square in her bruised eye.

'Oof!' she exclaimed as she bent down to pick the coaster up off the floor. She turned it over and read what had been scrawled on the back in thick pinky-red (Raspberry Fool, anyone?) lipstick:

LC
6781235 #6660
X

She flipped the coaster over and over again so many times, she looked as if she were fanning herself.

'Hey, Hot Stuff!' she heard Tom's confident desert-booted swagger approaching. 'Where did you get to last night? I was looking for you everywhere!'

Out of the corner of her eye, Kate clocked Tamsin's head popping up out of her cubicle, like a meerkat coming up from underground and standing to attention on a mound of dirt, its sharp eyes, excellent ears and cute button nose sensing predators.

'Oh,' she laughed nervously, stuffing the coaster back in her rucksack. 'Ah, nowhere. I mean, home. I was in no fit state to be seen in public, I'm sure you'll agree.'

Weirdly enough, Tom, who rarely noticed how anyone else was looking or behaving, his focus usually being solely on himself, did agree.

'Too big a sesh for such a little girl, eh?' he said, perching his bum on the side of Kate's desk and stroking her hair.

How *did* he get away with being so patronising, Kate wondered, as she started to melt under his touch, annoyed with herself for being such a cliché and fancying him like mad despite his reprehensible behaviour.

'Now, listen, Reese,' he said, crooking his index finger and gently holding it under Kate's chin, as if her head was a budgie and it was sitting on his finger. 'I'm in some hot water with some slappers at Medea – can you sort it out for me? I'm up to my nuts in it this week and just haven't got the time. Yeah?'

Kate nodded.

'Archie's already briefed me,' she said softly.

'Good. Great. Excellent!' Tom said, slapping his hands on his thighs and standing up. 'I've got to check out some flats tomorrow. Round lunchtime. Come with?'

He got up, backed out of the office and pointed finger pistols at her as he winked and made a *nyick, nyick* clicking sound with his tongue.

Kate pondered the Tom question. Just how did he do it? How did he manage to be so creepy and downright sleazy and still so damned sexy? And how did he still look so good, so GQ model-esque when the only working out he ever did was the occasional shag (after which he would always give himself a mark out of ten – usually eleven

– as though he was both Olympic gymnast and judge) and 'taking care of himself' meant he was… what was the office radio playing now? That Pulp song… yes, yes, that's it. How did Tom look so hot when taking care of himself merely meant that he was always sorted for Es and whizz?

Kate heard Tamsin swoon. Or was that her?

She shook her head and got down to work, drafting a document to fax to Medea and flicking through the latest copy of *Lashed* on her desk for inspiration.

She laughed at a few of the magazine's jokes – and when she felt she had the kernel of an idea, she started writing, stream-of-consciousness-style, on her Apple Mac.

She went on and on about how, contrary to Medea's first impressions, *Lashed* is, in actual fact, a celebration of womanhood. And how far from being a tacky skin mag, *Lashed* is ironic and leading the way for women to be taken seriously and loved for all the things they are (sexy *and* smart) in an increasingly man's world. It's tongue-in-cheek, she wrote, and aimed at the intelligent young male, featuring only equally intelligent females in their 'Thinking Man's Crumpet' pages (where a scantily clad TV celebrity would pose, sprawling about on a round bed, her glossy-lipped mouth about to tuck into a jam-covered crumpet. A small Q&A would accompany the pictorial, with such edifying questions as: Which do you prefer – blueberry or strawberry jam? And: thongs or your boyfriend's boxers?).

Kate couldn't believe she was coming out with such drivel. But once she started, she couldn't seem to stop. She pointed out that, contrary to Medea's accusations, *Lashed* loved women – all women – in all their wonderful forms – which is why they often featured women who were shorter than five eleven – and sometimes models who had real boobs! They were not shy about inter-viewing powerful non-pin-up women occasionally, too (even though Kate couldn't find any examples) which was more than many women's magazines were doing, virtually ignoring their local sisters in favour of their Hollywood, perma-tanned, perma-vacuous counterparts.

Yes, *Lashed* was pro-women. From her beautiful body, whatever its shape or size (unlike teen and women's mags who foisted hideously unrealistic-looking girls on their reading public and had the audacity, the chutzpah, to call them role models – now that was anti-women! That was internalised misogyny in action right there!) to her sharp, fascinating mind, to her cracking sense of humour, *Lashed* was on our side (and our front and our back) – and all about equality. And, in the end, wasn't that what Medea Media was all about, too?

The more she went on, the more she almost started to believe it. Maybe the lads at *Lashed* were feminists in the patriarchy's clothing, after all – doing a great job of high-lighting the inequality of the sexes, bringing the struggle up to date and shoving it into the spotlight. Hmm. *Maybe*.

Of course she knew this was complete and utter bull-shit and that Medea was completely correct about *Lashed* – but she also knew that because of its overt misogyny, it wouldn't be around for too much longer, either. Still, it was fascinating to see first-hand for the second time how in this heady, intoxicating atmosphere of New Labour and spin and summer and football and foreign lager, how *male*, how full-on bloke-centred it all was. She'd nearly forgotten how immersed in lad culture she'd been back then – how seductive it had been to be seen as 'one of the boys'.

Jenny's face landed with a thud at the front of Kate's mind. A bony finger wagged at her and her mum looked disapproving. She said: 'You don't get to be equal to men by *acting* like them, darling. We need to be tough, not rough. Drinking like a demented schoolboy and having sex with people whose names you don't even know is not the way to fight for our rights. It might be a double standard – and a lot of fun – but, my dear, it's our minds that will win the war in our favour in the end. So think, don't drink! Think, don't drink!'

Kate blinked her mother's image out of her head and stared at her document. Was it convincing? Would they buy it?

Kate thought hard and, in her final paragraph, promised Medea Media free advertising for their titles (including the worthy, serious *That's Ms To You!* and the softer, more mass-market *Millie* – a reference to the old 'rad fem' Viz cartoon character, Millie Tant) for a year, as a gesture of goodwill, should they decide not to take matters any further.

She was sure they'd go for it – Medea was small and, word had it, about to go bust any second now. Free advertising in the nation's number one men's magazine which, statistics proved, was read by more women than the leading women's magazine? And where a quarter of a page of advertising space would set them back a thousand pounds? They would definitely go for it.

She ran it by Archie, who read it fast and then, with a wry smile, said, 'So glad I asked you to do this. You know what Tom wanted to say? He wanted to ask them whether they needed a good seeing-to, because if they did – the whole of Medea Media – he knew just the mag to give it to them.'

Kate shook her head in mock disbelief because, of course she believed it, it was starting to become all-too-clear what Tom's true colours were, what was on his unevolved mind 24/7.

'Please don't ever leave me – you make me look too good!' Archie said, handing the document back to her.

She smiled at him, but her lips were tight and she sucked on them through her teeth.

Standing at the fax machine, Kate wondered why she just didn't feel as chuffed with herself as she would have done twenty-six years ago upon hearing Archie's fulsome praise. In fact, she rubbed her tummy, wincing, she felt a bit seedy – even grottier than when she'd first awoken this morning.

When she'd finished, she took herself off to the loo and studied herself in the mirror.

Had she really decamped to the other side? The dark side? Was she fast becoming a traitor to the cause, a traitor to her sex? She felt disappointment seeping through her (tightly closed, dewy, youthful, really rather beautiful) pores. Was this really tearing the lads' playhouse down, as she promised herself she would do only yesterday?

Oh, bollocks! This was all getting too much! The Nineties were too hard, far too much responsibility – it was like having the family without the fun – what sort of a break from reality was this?

She wished she was stuck somewhere in the Eighties, her hair super-sized, her waist tiny in an ankle-length white tube skirt, bobby socks and a belted XL white shirt over a t-shirt with big black capital letters saying CHOOSE LIFE on it, dancing to WHAM!

'That should be me,' she muttered to herself, realising that however hard she tried, the corners of her mouth just wouldn't turn down.

'Too much elasticity still in the skin, I expect,' she said, turning her head this way and that, trying to locate the loose stuff, the jowls that she constantly self-lifted in her bathroom mirror back home in 2022 whenever she was passing. 'Smooth, unlined, no wrinkles, no adult acne scars, no hag hairs, no moles or skin tags – you never knew you had it so good, did you? And those bright-blue eyes with their whole life ahead of them.'

She found some stray elastic bands next to the basin and pulled her hair up into two high pigtails over her ears.

'Bit too Baby Spice?'

She heard a toilet flush, which made her jump – she thought she'd been in there alone. One of the cubicle doors opened and Tamsin walked out, smoothing her sprayed-on pencil skirt down over her non-existent hips. She looked like a smug, corporate Pamela Anderson.

'Don't forget your kookiness and your oh-so-pretty chin, Reese,' she giggled, washing her hands and pouting at herself.

Kate felt her temperature escalate rapidly. She was acutely embarrassed and watched, agog, as a deeply unflattering shade of crimson crept up her face, starting from her perky décolletage and going all the way to her line-free forehead.

Tamsin smiled sweetly at Kate as she turned tail and left the loos. And although Kate was mortified her rival had heard her, she managed to spot a rather nasty crop of whiteheads, like a clutch of mini mushrooms, making itself at home just to the left of Tamsin's tiny button nose.

Which cheered her up no end.

11

'So much for the sisterhood,' Jenny said, when Kate told her all about Medea the next day at lunch.

'I know, I know,' said Kate. 'But what can I do? It's my job to put a positive spin on these things.'

'I understand that,' said Jenny, licking the chocolatey froth off her cappuccino spoon, 'but you don't have to go quite so over the top, do you? I mean, surely they'll see through all your claptrap and want to use such a high-profile, controversial magazine like *Lashed* to highlight their plight, illustrate their point.'

'They could do that in a negative way, of course,' said Kate. 'But these days, where magazines are folding faster than a prison laundry, I think I made them an offer they simply can't afford to refuse.'

'You bribed them?'

'Not exactly. I made it more worth their while to use *Lashed*'s profile to better theirs in a positive way. For Medea to be seen to be in bed – so to speak – with *Lashed*. I think it might work and both parties would benefit.'

'Hmm.' Jenny was unconvinced and peered at the menu over her half-moon glasses.

Kate shrugged her shoulders. She knew her position was fairly indefensible – especially to a die-hard feminist like Jenny – but she was stuck between a rock and a hard place on this one.

And, quite frankly, Kate thought, she didn't give a damn. Not at this particular juncture, anyway, what with her beautiful mother sitting before her, no doubt ready to impart pearl after pearl of wonderful wisdom.

'So where's Dad?' Kate asked, gnawing on a Grissini.

She knew they fought like cat and dog in private, and they'd probably had some heinous fight, but they always put a brave face on it in public. It was just so weird to know that this lovely woman in front of her would one day be so anti-men she'd wilt flowers as she walked past.

'Wanted to stay home, back's playing up again,' Jenny said, without looking up, as though it was no big deal and she wasn't out of her mind with suspicion. 'Said to send you his apologies and oceans of love, though. He expects to see you on Sunday for lunch at ours, of course, but he thought today might be nice, just you and me. He's thoughtful like that.'

Kate nearly choked on the breadstick at this blatant lie.

'Of course, penne alla tonno is always a good choice,' Jenny muttered. 'But why do they have to drown it in pesto sauce? Can't they just keep things simple? Someone should come along and show these ridiculous chefs how to strip food down to its essentials, get back to the basics…'

'Like Jamie Oliver?'

'Who?'

'Oh, no one,' Kate shifted uneasily in her seat, remembering she was in a time slightly before *The Naked Chef* and all the Jamie Oliver hype had hit. 'One day soon someone will come along and do just that, though – you mark my words. And he's going to blow us all away.'

But Jenny wasn't listening, caught up as she was in the Carluccio's conundrum of which dish to order.

God it was good to see her – especially looking so together, not rabid with jealousy or devastated by grief and nowhere near as bitter and twisted as she was in 2022.

'It's *so* good to see you, Mummy!' Kate couldn't resist. *Mummy? Where did that come from?*

'Thank you, dear,' said Jenny, running her index finger down the menu. 'I only saw you last Sunday. Except I don't think you've called me Mummy since you were about seven years old.'

A waiter came and took their order (sea bass for Kate, keen to preserve her svelte figure and carbonara for Jenny, for whom carbs had never been a problem) and a stern, serious look came over Jenny's kindly, not yet care-lined face.

'We need to talk,' she said, clasping her hands in front of her on the table.

'About Kevin?' Kate spluttered.

'Who?' Jenny was getting agitated. 'Honestly, Kate, I can't keep up with all your friends, all those pop stars and TV presenters. I don't know who they are and to be perfectly honest, I—'

'No, no, it's the name of a hugely successful book, which... oh, never mind. I'm sorry. Go on.'

'About Steven,' Jenny sighed. 'Your little brother. What on earth are we going to do about him?'

'Interesting you mention my sibling,' said Kate. 'I've been dying to ask you this for years – just how did you and Dad manage to pay us kids the exact right amount of attention so that we didn't get jealous of each other? How did you guys do the whole parenting thing so well?'

'I – well, thank you, Kate – but I'm not so sure we did.'

'Ah, don't be so modest. You were the perfect mother, everyone can see that!'

'That's sweet of you to say, darling, but I think the proof is always in the pudding. And I'm not sure Steven's worked out so well. Not yet, anyway. Seems we've made mistake after mistake with him and before it goes too far, before he does something stupid we'll all regret, I wanted to sound you out.'

'About what?'

'An intervention.'

'A *what*?'

'An intervention. It's when—'

'I know what an intervention is, I just can't see how that will make Steve any better,' Kate said, dimpling her chin and shaking her head. 'In fact, an intervention might be just the thing to tip him over the edge, prove to him how little you really know him and how completely hopeless and incompetent you really think he is.'

'Well he is!'

'No, he isn't – not in the way you think he is. He just needs to get back on his feet, that's all – he's just a little down at the moment. He might need an encouraging shove in the right direction. He needs a bit of help to get him back on his feet – not Dad's usual temper tantrum about how he's draining the family coffers and spoiling everything for him.'

Jenny shot Kate a look.

'Well, we did something right, I suppose,' said Jenny. 'We always wanted you and Steve to be close, to defend each other and look out for each other. None of us are getting any younger and we won't be around for ever, you know.'

'I know,' said Kate, softly as she watched her mother. It may have been a little unnerving for Jenny, but Kate couldn't waste a single moment of drinking in her mother's lovely presence, as though it were the very elixir of life itself. As opposed to the kiss of death like the 2022 version.

'Darling,' said Jenny through thin, hardly-moving ventriloquist's lips as she glanced swiftly sideways, checking whether anyone else was looking. 'You know you're staring…'

'Hmmm,' Kate replied, unable to tear her eyes away from Jenny, as though she was lost in a trance.

Their main meals arrived and the pair were silent. Jenny pushed her food around her plate, taking small, uninterested bites every now and again and Kate continued to freak her mother out, watching her every move, an unsettling, beatific grin plastered to her face.

'Darling,' Jenny sing-songed, getting annoyed with her daughter.

This prompted Kate to come out from under the spell her mother had unwittingly cast.

She coughed a small 'ahem' and, looking down, smoothed her napkin on her lap.

'I think I might have a way of forcing – gently – Steve to sort himself out,' Kate said after a while.

'You do?' Jenny looked at her expectantly.

'Well, as you know, Tom – you know Tom – Tom is crazy-keen for us to move in together and I know you think it will be a total and utter disaster and I know you think he's a misogynist, an arrogant, chauvinist pig and not even that good-looking…'

Kate paused to give her mother the chance to refute any of the above. But Jenny just nodded, listening intently.

'…but I think I'd regret it for ever if I didn't give it a go.'

Kate waited for Jenny to put her hand onto her chest and gasp, but instead she looked at her pasta and pursed her lips as she always did when she was concentrating hard. When, eventually, Jenny did look her in the eye, Kate grasped the edges of her chair and took a deep breath, as if in preparation for the full force of her acid tongue.

'Darling,' she began softly, making Kate relax her vice-like grip of the chair. 'I think you might be right.'

'What?' said Kate, incredulous.

'I think it's just what you need, in order to see this Tom character for what he really, obviously is. And if you moving in with him forces Steve to get a job and pay his own way in the West Hampstead flat with Portia, he'll have to step up to the mark, won't he?'

'Well, that's what I've been thinking.'

'And you know what else?' continued Jenny. 'I suspect that if you *didn't* move in with Tom, you'd forever blame me for talking you out of it. And you'd somehow resent Steve, too, for needing you too much and thus preventing you from getting on with your own life.'

God, she was good. She was right! *That's* what Kate and Steve had fallen out about all those years ago – Steve's dependence on her and Kate's overgrown responsibility gland getting in the way of her doing exactly what she wanted.

'So you think it's a good idea?' asked Kate, a little perplexed by her mother's reaction.

'As long as you think it'll make you and Steve happy.' She smiled.

At that Kate shook her head and welled up.

'God. What happened to you?' she sniffed.

She'd nearly completely forgotten that her mother used to always put her kids' happiness before her own. And even though her daydreams might paint quite a different picture – fantasies involving old boyfriends, old situations, her old life – Kate's main priority, too, was to be a good mum. Frustratingly, it was an ambition she often felt she would never realise.

'What the actual fark did he do to you?' Kate murmured.

'What was that, sweetheart?' Jenny asked. 'I think my hearing's going, you know.'

Kate girded her loins again. Here we go, here we go, here we go...

'So what are we going to do about you then?' Kate began.

'Me? What do you mean?'

Kate took a deep breath and let her have it.

'I think you should come out of retirement, go back to teaching, get a live-in nurse for Dad and start living your life again.'

She held her breath and waited for a response.

'Don't be ridiculous!' Jenny chortled. 'A live-in nurse? For your father? *Your* father? It'd be like being in an endless Benny Hill episode! No way. No way, for god's sake!'

Kate exhaled. Her mum was right. George couldn't be trusted to keep it in his pants at the best of times – but with an object of lust presented to him on a platter? No chance.

Mind you, she thought, what if he didn't fancy the nurse? What if... Bloody hell!

'But men can be nurses, too, you know, Mum.' She shook her head as if disappointed. 'Never had you pegged for a sexist!'

Jenny snorted.

'Well, yes, that's a good point,' she said. 'But how could we ever afford such a thing?'

'You'll go back to teaching at the university. You never really wanted to take early retirement to look after Dad, so...'

Jenny stared into the middle distance as though she was seriously considering Kate's proposition, remembering the joy she got from the cut and thrust of intellectual debate, the look in her students' eyes when they finally *got* Shakespeare.

'Were you always so good at this, Mummy?'

There was that word again. *Mummy*. Kate couldn't seem to help herself. It was as though she so desperately needed her, so keenly felt the need for connection with her, the first person she'd ever truly loved and trusted and respected, who always had her best interests at heart, that to call her by any other name would merely put more distance between them. And Kate couldn't bear that.

'At what, dear?'

'Being the perfect mum.'

'Oh, come on, darling,' Jenny looked around again, but more as though she was searching the room for someone this time. 'I'm far from perfect.'

'But you are!'

'No I'm not.'

'Are too!'

'No, darling. I really am not.'

'Are too!' Kate said again, thumping her fist down on the table.

Jesus! Take it easy – she doesn't know you haven't seen her like this for years! Rein it in a bit, will you?

'We all have our dark sides, sweetie – the bits we'd rather other people didn't see.'

'But not you!' Kate squeaked.

I said calm down!

'Not yet, anyway.' Kate calmed down.

'Yes, Kate, even me.'

Jenny looked slightly beyond Kate and almost imperceptibly nodded at something in the distance. Not too far in the distance, of course – she could only see about a metre clearly in front of her. Further away than that, and it was all a blur.

'And you should watch that tendency of yours to never take off those rose-coloured glasses, Kate. I've always said it – you're too absolute, too black and white. But life's not like that, sweetheart,' she said, eyes twinkling as she reached over the table to hold Kate's hand.

'There are grey areas, messy problems that can't be fixed, people who'll let you down. And I fear I may be one of those, because at this level of adoration, I can only disappoint you in the end. No one can live up to those lofty ideals you have. Certainly not me! And I don't want to be around when you discover my feet of clay!'

Typical of her mum, thought Kate. Typical of the way she used to be, anyway. Always self-aware, sometimes to the point of being overly critical – and always lecturing Kate about humanity and stuff. God, she missed her!

After a tiramisu (for Jenny) and a black coffee (for Kate), they stood up and put on their near-identical Burberry trench coats. Jenny adjusted the blue and gold Hermès scarf that was permanently attached to her coat's collar and Kate fluffed up her own Baby Spice pigtails.

'You'd better get back to work,' Jenny said, giving Kate the distinct impression that she was being hurried.

'Oh, it's OK, I can take my time.'

'Well, I can't,' Jenny said quickly. 'I've – ah – I've got to get back to Ickenham. There's Residents' Association stuff to deal with and a public lecture to prepare – time waits for no woman!'

Kate felt Jenny's hand on the small of her back as she was chivvied out of the restaurant by her mother.

Standing in front of Carluccio's, Jenny proceeded to shoo Kate away.

'Go on, dear,' she said. 'I'll settle the bill, you go back to work.'

Kate didn't move, so surprised was she that her mother, on this most momentous of occasions – momentous to Kate, at least – seemed to actually want to get rid of her.

'But—'

Jenny tutted and put her hands on Kate's shoulders, kissing her continentally on both cheeks.

'Go on! Away with you now! We'll see you on Sunday!'

Kate reluctantly turned and began to walk back to her office. She'd only gone a couple of steps when she glanced back over her shoulder, just in time to see Jenny taking off her coat, draping it over her arm, fluffing up her hair and smoothing down her trousers (which, as Kate had noted earlier, made her look young and zippy and showed off her model figure nicely). Kate watched, transfixed once more, as her mother pointed her chin to the sky, laughed at something hilariously funny and, with arms outstretched, as though she were greeting a much-loved, long-lost old friend, went skipping lightly straight back in to Carluccio's and the arms of a mysterious silver fox.

12

Kate stood at the doors to The Lift, chewing her lip and making grooves in the carpet with the right toe of her sneakers.

It had been so great to see her mum – she looked so wonderful, full of life and radiant, vitality emanating from her every pore. And even though she'd seemed a bit distracted at the end, Kate had basked in the warm glow Jenny always used to bring to the table.

But she wasn't just a great mum – though that in itself was a major achievement and worthy of constant applause – she was a great *person*. With a lot to offer the world. And a full and satisfying life. Or at least, she *was*, before George had destroyed any confidence she'd had in herself and turned her into an embittered nasty old cow.

She wondered whether she was following her mother's tragic trajectory as an image of her bedraggled self, standing by the kitchen sink in 2022, pilled dressing gown hanging crookedly off her rounded shoulder, porridge in her thin, straggly hair, arse the size of Cuba flashed into her head. What had happened to her? How had she got to be like that?

Had she really become one of those women who had nothing else to get up for other than tending to a couple kids? Not that there was anything wrong with that, *per se*, she reminded herself – Mother being the most noble, true and brave profession she could think of.

It's just that when the kids grew up and moved away (which, Seamus promised her, they would one day), what would they leave behind in their wake? A knackered old woman with no job, that's what. And no idea what had happened in the world while she'd been away, out of every loop going, missing in child-rearing action.

She stopped this tired old train of thought so familiar to her from 2022 and metaphorically slapped her wrist – this was her chance! Her chance to make sure she didn't end up like she had the first time around!

She'd only been back in 1996 for three days and she'd seen nearly everyone she wanted to – and even though there was still a small amount of unfinished business with Tom that needed seeing to, right now, she needed to focus on *her*. Imagine! She took a step back at the ferocity of the realisation. And then started to panic. What if she was going to be teleported back any minute? What if she wasn't? What if she never got back and her life as she knew it ceased to exist? What if the kids were wiped out, erased from family photos like Marty McFly's siblings in *Back To The Future*?! ARGH!

At that moment she gasped when she felt viscerally – possibly for the first time ever – that, god, she missed those kids like crazy! Their cute faces, the funny things they came out with (that she had to restrain herself from boring Portia with), Phoebe's classic mardy adolescent strops and Declan's soft, warm hugs which always made her melt, even when she was about to lose her temper and let fly, shouting and stamping her foot, in that hopelessly ineffectual way she had. It was like, even though now she had the career, the social life and just the one chin that she'd pined after for so long, she knew that being around those kids and watching them grow up into smart, empathetic, well-rounded human beings was pretty great, too – and possibly just as fulfilling.

She even missed Seamus, with his grumpy old man frown and his propensity to choose golf over being with the family at every turn.

She pictured Seamus in a CHOOSE GOLF t-shirt, dancing to *Wake Me Up Before You Go-Go* and giggled. He'd never been much of a dancer. Which was hardly surprising, really, considering the act of putting one foot in front of the other and actually *walking* posed too much of a problem for the hapless Seamus sometimes.

Kate smiled. He may be an awkward, uncoordinated old bugger, but he was *her* awkward, uncoordinated old bugger. Or at least he was in 2022.

'How am I ever going to get back there?' she asked her (rather cute, actually) reflection in the mirrored lift doors.

She straightened up and admired her form for a few seconds before the doors opened with a DING!

'Finally,' Kate muttered as she stepped into The Lift, standing in the opposite corner to the boy already in there.

But that was no ordinary boy standing nervously opposite her – it was the young Seamus!

'Hello there!' she said, buoyed by seeing not only a younger version of herself, but also the gangly baby giraffe that was Seamus, whose face was fast turning red with embarrassment.

But embarrassment at *what*?! Honestly, she thought to herself, he really had to sort that shyness out if he was ever going to get anywhere.

And those clothes! What on earth *did* she ever see in him? How did they ever get together, when he was so… so… so *beige*, he was bordering on the invisible?

Her mind flipped through its mental Facebook page for pictures of parties they'd been to together, their wedding, the births of their kids – but she couldn't seem to locate any.

Oh god. It's just like that bit in Back To The Future *when Marty's family start to disappear in that photo, as though they never existed!*

Not being an expert in quantum physics – or any kind of physics at all, for that matter – Kate started to freak out. How did she get here? How would she get back? Where was her family? Were they disappearing? What were they doing? They couldn't possibly manage without her! Could they?

'Oh, hurry up,' she said, looking at the illuminated numbers above the closed doors. 'Why does this bloody lift always take so bloody long?'

'Actually,' Seamus' small voice piped up, as he pushed his glasses back up to the bridge of his nose with a forefinger, 'it's quite speedy, considering. I mean, *technically* it takes no time at all, when you think about the incredible feat of modern machinery that it is.'

Kate's first impulse was to say: 'Oh, what would you know?' – but she was so stunned that Seamus had actually spoken, her head enjoyed a few seconds of quiet, giving her just enough time to have an idea.

Seamus, IT… Google, that's it! I'll Google time travel and work out a way to get back. Ha! Too easy!

Her fear started to subside at the thought of the internet and a wave of sweet relief washed over her.

But as soon as she dared to feel a little bit relaxed about her situation, she heard the sickening screech of metal scraping against metal, so loud and shrill, she swore it would make her ears bleed.

Kate covered her head and screamed as the sound of slow-grinding, gigantic gears and the cranking of similarly large cogs was followed swiftly by an almighty jolt. The Lift suddenly dropped down and stopped dead, leaving Kate (who must weigh eight, eight-and-a-half-stone, tops) suspended in the air for a few moments before landing back down square on The Lift floor with a satisfyingly small thud.

Seamus rushed over to her and she felt those familiar big arms envelop her. She instinctively turned her head to face his chest and felt the strap of something scratch her cheek.

She opened her eyes to the frightening sound of silence just in time for The Lift's lights to go out.

Seamus' grip tightened around her as she breathed in sharply.

'It's OK,' he said, sounding as though he knew what he was talking about.

'Is it?' asked Kate, who had always doubted Seamus' authority. 'Call Reception or someone – the police? Fire brigade!' Kate said, freeing herself from Seamus' embrace.

'What with?' Seamus replied. 'We only have a handful of mobile telecommunication devices and they're all with management.'

Kate's mind raced as she pictured the first mobile phone she ever bought herself. It had been the size of a house brick and she'd felt acutely self-conscious every time she was on a bus and Portia called her just to tease her about having one. She couldn't remember the ring tone, but it was loud, she knew that. And when it rang, people would tut and stare at her crossly, making her put her hand over the mouthpiece and whisper, so as not to inspire her fellow passengers' wrath any further.

'Of course, of course,' Kate said, feeling her way around The Lift walls. 'There must be a phone in here somewhere, mustn't there? Health and safety and all that... A-ha!'

'Well, I'm not sure it works, wherever it is,' began Seamus as Kate's fingernails jimmied the small metal door open. 'We've been having some problems with the—'

She fumbled for the phone inside, put the handset up to her ear and hissed an exasperated 'shhhh!', waving Seamus and his words away with her left hand in the darkness.

A few seconds passed. Thirty seconds passed. Fifty-eight seconds passed. And then Kate nearly passed... out with frustration.

'ARGH!' she thundered, sounding exactly as she did in 2022 whenever she was dragged away from her Twitter feed by hungry children demanding dinner. So inconsiderate! Or when, in a rare and exhausting fit of domestic goddessery, she'd hoovered the front room only to discover an ancient nest of sultanas taking root in the orangey-brown swirly carpet. 'There's no dial tone. It doesn't bloody work!'

She beat the metal box on the wall with the receiver a couple of times until she felt Seamus' cool hand upon hers.

'That's not going to help anybody,' he said, his voice so thick and deep and controlled, like the guy who does those voiceovers for movies: 'In a world where lifts break down at the most inopportune times, comes the surprise hit of the summer, *Elevator!* Because in a trapped lift, no one can hear you scream…'

Except in an English accent.

Kate very nearly swooned.

She heard Seamus somehow locating the hook and replacing the receiver on it. She heard the metal door close and felt a frisson of desire.

There was something undeniably sexy about the whole situation – even to her moribund sense of sauciness. Here she was, trapped in The Lift with zero visibility and a virtual stranger (who would, one day, be her boring old husband – but she didn't want to think about that right now and risk blunting the sharpest of exciting sensations, dulling the brightest spark of potential pleasure) whose voice was so creamy, it was single-handedly raising her libido from the dead. She felt light and giddy, butterflies flittering about in her tummy as Seamus slipped his hand into hers.

She let out a gasp, taken completely unawares by the strength of this unfamiliar lustful feeling.

She imagined how his back muscles would ripple when he took her in his arms and dipped her as though they were on *Strictly Come Dancing* or an illustrated cover of an old Mills & Boon. She pictured him as the white, floaty-shirted hero in tight breeches and herself as the helpless damsel in distress in dire need of rescuing and, maybe, some quick bodice-ripping if there was time.

This wasn't like her. Or, at least, it wasn't like her in 2022. Maybe it was the raging hormones of the young that meant they constantly saw and smelled and felt sex every-where, in every possible circumstance. Then again, maybe it was the preserve of the middle-aged, bored housewife whose inner life was her *only* life worth speaking of, her fantasies running away with her every time she was doing the washing-up and her eyes glazed over, the drudgery of her real life too tedious to bear.

She was always on at the kids to turn the telly off/stop playing those computer games/give her back her iPhone, so that they could give their imaginations a chance. She worried all the time about how kids today (or tomorrow, depending on which decade she was talking in) had it all laid on, how they didn't even have to *read* any more, for goodness' sake, to escape into another world, a world different from their own. Maybe that was Kate's problem, though – perhaps she could do with a little more Xbox and a little less dreaming about her ex-boyfriends. Maybe then her obsession with the past would fade into the background.

Speaking of, Kate thought to herself, maybe it was her imagination that had been responsible for getting her into this mess in the first place. And, if it was, maybe it could get her out of here, too…

Seamus helped her sit down on the floor of The Lift, lowering her gently.

'We could be here for some time.' Those maple syrup-drenched vocal chords worked their magic once more.

'Yes,' Kate whispered, weakly.

Something big swung down from where she imagined Seamus' waist was and hit her head. It couldn't be that big… could it?

'Oh!' she exclaimed, capable of nothing more.

'Sorry!' Seamus said, his voice going up an octave and sounding more unsure than before as he scrambled to contain the wayward object.

Kate pictured a musket hanging from his belt and fanned herself with her hand, the euphemistic possibilities of such swashbuckling attire making her come over all unnecessary.

But then the lights flickered on and a harsh, badly dressed reality stood above her.

It wasn't a musket or a whip or anything even remotely resembling anything phallic or masterful that had struck her head a few moments ago – of course it wasn't! It was one of those big, square-shaped nylon record bags that guys in the media or the record industry used to wear over one shoulder. A kind of precursor to the smaller, more compact man-bag.

And it was the bag's thick strap that had scratched her face when Seamus had pulled her close to him.

But why was he wearing it? It was so not an accessory that Kate would ever have associated with Seamus.

'It's been hanging around the music mags' offices for ages,' Seamus said apologetically, once he noticed that Kate was staring at his bag. 'I... I didn't think anyone would miss it.'

The banality of her situation came crashing down on her and Kate blinked to put it into focus, to put everything back into perspective.

'Looks good,' she smiled, reaching for his hand so he could help her up. 'Very trendy. But what else are you wearing?'

'Um, just jeans and a football shirt – it's a Liverpool one, see?'

He pulled at the insignia on the left side of his shirt and tried to see it himself, which gave him several chins and made him stick out his big bottom lip like a fish gulping for air.

This was not how a romantic hero should look, Kate thought to herself.

'You know,' she began, 'you'd actually be quite cute if you sorted yourself out.'

'Excuse me?' Seamus blinked at her, all wide-eyed and innocent.

'Sartorially, I mean,' said Kate. 'Quite a catch, in actual fact.'

And in that moment, she got it. She hatched a plan in her head to get back to 2022 as soon as humanly possible – and ensure that a handsome, debonair Seamus was waiting for her when she arrived.

'Who do you go shopping with?' Kate asked, knowing full well what the answer was.

'Just myself,' Seamus replied. 'If I ever go shopping, that is. My mum sometimes sends me stuff from catalogues, though, and—'

'And what do you know about time travel? I mean, is it possible to be transported back into the past? Or is it just a figment of my – I mean, *our* – imagination? Like, can you manipulate the universe, the time/space continuum to go into the future?'

Kate thought she sounded quite knowledgeable herself, saying 'time/space continuum' – a phrase she plucked out of the ether, having never said it before in her whole life.

'Like, you mean get The Lift working again? Like it was a short while ago? In the past?' Seamus struggled to get what Kate was going on about.

'Yeah, well, that'd be a start,' said Kate. 'You're a technical genius, aren't you? Can't you fix it for us?'

'Yes and no,' Seamus smiled. 'Well, no and no, to be really honest. Not a *genius*, anyway. I'm good – but I'm not *that* good!'

Kate met Seamus' grin with her own.

'There's not much I can do from the inside,' Seamus carried on. 'It looks to me that everything's fine here – apart from the phone. It's something on the outside that needs fixing.'

'You said it!' squealed Kate. 'I've got a proposition for you. How's about I help you develop your own stylish wardrobe, tell you what suits you and what girls like to see on guys – and you help me find out all I can about time travel. You're the IT whizz, you can Google up a storm for me!'

'*What* up a storm?'

'Google! T'interweb? You know…?'

But Seamus clearly didn't.

Kate had that sinking feeling again. Just like she'd had a few hours ago when she'd mentioned Jamie Oliver to her mum.

'Oh, don't tell me! It hasn't been invented yet, right?'

'What hasn't? I'm sorry, Kate, I haven't got the faintest idea what you're talking about!' said Seamus, his brow knitting, creating the crease that would one day be so deeply etched in his face, you'd swear he'd been *born* looking pissed off.

'I'm thinking of pitching a new mag to the powers that be,' she said, looking wildly around for inspiration. 'Um, a paranormal, sci-fi one, given the, ah, popularity of *The X-Files* and stuff—'

Another jolt downwards made both Kate and Seamus hang onto the chrome bar in The Lift, terrified of what was going to happen next.

The Lift kept moving for a few seconds until DING!

The doors flew open and the little bell pinged continuously as though there had never been a problem from *its* end, everything had been working just fine all along and now it was impatient to see to its other customers, thank you very much.

Tom, Archie, Tamsin and Lucy whooped in delight (although Tamsin's whoop was more sarcastic than delighted, it has to be said and was accompanied by some bored eye-rolling and a fast exit) as soon as the dinging stopped.

'Way-hey!' boomed Tom. 'I knew my punching the buttons would get things moving again! You all right?'

Kate beamed and he pulled her to him, kissing her.

Now *that's* what a romantic hero should look like, she thought to herself. And that's exactly how one should kiss, too, she added.

She was vaguely aware of Seamus slipping away from the group as she closed her eyes, her body going limp with desire.

And as she melted into Tom's embrace, she heard Seamus saying to someone in the distance: 'Are you sure it's turned on?'

'Quite sure,' Kate mumbled to herself. 'Quite, quite sure.'

13

When Kate, Portia and Steve arrived at O'Flaherty's just before three o'clock for the first match of Euro '96, the atmosphere was electric.

In fact, Oasis' 'She's Electric' was playing loudly while young lads in England shirts sang along and spilled their lagers over each other, due to their slightly over-enthusiastic sideways arm swinging in time to the music.

'What are you drinking?' Steve shouted at Kate.

'WHAT?' she yelled back.

Steve mimed drinking a pint and Kate shook her head.

She grabbed Steve by the lapel. 'JUST A LIME AND SODA FOR ME!' she bellowed into his ear.

'Say it, don't spray it!' he pulled away, wiping imaginary saliva off the side of his face. 'Portia?'

'I'll have whatever you're having,' she said, just as the music stopped. 'On second thoughts, better make it a double.'

A baby-faced, shirtless hooligan (as Kate saw him) caught Portia's eye (Portia saw him more as an excited, ripped football fan, roughly the same age as her) and she smiled lasciviously.

'But what about the baby?' asked Kate, instantly regretting it.

'Oh, for fuh— give it a rest, will you?' Portia said, irritated by Kate's little reminder. 'I'm here to have fun.

And anyway, I'm far too young for that sort of thing – can you imagine giving all this up?'

Portia swept her hand out in front of her as she said 'all this', as if she was presenting a gold dinner service to an audience of aghast onlookers. Kate looked around and sniffed snootily as though she smelled something nasty and pooey.

'Like a shot,' she said.

But even as she uttered those words, she knew she was lying. Because she remembered when she was pregnant with Phoebe, all she ever wanted was to have her old life back for one (or maybe two) nights, just to reiterate how much she was looking forward to and desperately in need of a drastic change.

Then, when Phoebe was born, and Kate was unable to breastfeed, when she was finally free to go out on the town, to drink too much and act like a seven year old on a massive sugar bender, it was always the last thing she felt like doing.

Sleep became her desert island luxury item of choice and had remained thus for the past fifteen years. She longed for the little bit of space, the small amount of breathing time sleep afforded her. And now, looking around her at the rowdy pub, she felt exactly like she used to when she'd pick Phoebe up from nursery school – like she was trapped in a loony bin and couldn't wait to make good her escape.

'You may not want it now – but what about the future? What if for whatever reason you, ah, you find yourself infertile and you can't get pregnant? You don't know how you'll feel five *minutes* down the track, let alone five years!' Kate continued.

'Let it go, Kate,' said Steve as he deposited their drinks down on the soggy coasters adorning the already soaking wet, sticky round table. 'Let's just have a laugh and watch some football, eh?'

Kate nodded, reluctantly agreeing to drop the subject just as 'Three Lions' was cranked up to eleven behind the bar.

The first half of the match was extremely exciting, even Kate had to admit that. And despite the fact that she knew how the whole tournament was going to end, she somehow couldn't help but get swept up in the joy of the moment, the sheer bliss of being a part of it all. The expectation was huge, the bonhomie was palpable (particularly for Portia who would be snogging the shirt-less lad by the time the full-time whistle blew) and the camaraderie was contagious.

It was half-time and Kate could feel herself loosening up. She decided to let herself go with the flow, get with the spirit of things, relax and have a nice time – forget about trying to get back to her family in 2022. Just for this afternoon, of course.

She heaved a sigh, imagining all her worries and anxieties about her parenting style, how her family was actually faring without her and how the hell she was going to get back to 2022 to be little bubbles of air, like you'd find in a mint Aero, carried away on the breath expelled from her lungs.

Time to let the good times roll, thought Kate.

'Oh, go on, then,' she said to Steve. 'I will have that pint, after all.'

'I'll get it,' came a voice, dripping in honey, from behind her.

'Seamus!' she shrieked, nearly giving herself whiplash as she turned around to see who it was. 'What are you doing here?'

'The flyers at work said everyone was welcome, the more the merrier—'

'Of course, of course,' Kate spluttered. 'I didn't mean that how it sounded, I'm just surprised to see your face, that's all.'

And she was. Particularly when he looked so youthful and happy and... and actually quite handsome.

'And you, Portia? What would you like?' Seamus asked, ever the gentleman.

'Oh, you are a sweetie,' said Portia, going all gooey and sickly sweet. 'And a man after my own heart. I'll have a gin and tonic. Double. Mother's ruin, right, Kate?'

Portia laughed and nudged Kate in the ribs. Kate threw her head back and pretended to find this hilarious.

Once Seamus was ensconced at the bar (which was three-deep in punters with raging thirsts), Kate glared at Portia.

'Who *are* you? Coming on to every man you see like that? What's got into you?'

Portia's smile faded and she turned to face Kate.

'Take a chill pill, Kate. And when you've calmed down, would you mind telling me just when you decided to go all po-faced and judgemental and boring on me?' she asked. 'And once you've told me that, would you mind giving me my old best mate back? Please?'

'Sorry,' Kate said, looking sheepish. 'I don't know what's going on, really. Stress at work?'

'Yeah? Well, why don't you talk to me about it rather than wag your finger at me all the time? You're not my mother, you know!'

No, thought Kate, she wasn't. But she was *a* mother and she took her role as mum very seriously. More seriously, indeed, than she'd ever imagined she would, to be honest. She was so used to doing it to the kids, she could no longer help herself with adults. It was like her default setting had been re-calibrated since she'd had children and now it was stuck on 'stern, dull, predictable and prone to being a shouty old bag' where once it had been permanently fixed on 'unapologetic, adventurous, always up for a laugh and prone to largin' it with the lads'.

She simply hadn't realised how difficult it would be to shake off her mumsy persona. She'd always pictured herself slipping straight back into carefree, fun-loving, up-for-whatever mode whenever she was daydreaming about the past and fantasising about feeling unshackled and untethered.

But now her fantasy had become a reality, she was stumped. How should she act in such a bizarre situation? As a mum-of-two, she was well aware of the consequences she would suffer for throwing caution to the wind; horrible hangovers (the physical side of which lasted for four days, the emotional battering lasting for ever), the inevitable weight gain from too many fry-ups and the potential for a knock on the door from Social Services any minute. But as a good-time girl in her late twenties, she was obliged to make the most of her time in the sun and go for it. Even if 'it' was a woolly, nebulous thing, usually involving copious amounts of alcohol and playing tonsil hockey with total strangers.

As soon as Seamus returned with the drinks, much to the threesome's delight, Kate made up her mind.

'I really am sorry,' Kate addressed her best friend. 'Let's forget all about it and get hammered, shall we?'

'That's more like it,' Portia said, putting her arm around Kate's back and singing along with Baddiel and Skinner.

'So where do you stand on the Fuzz versus Mirage battle of the bands debate?' Steve asked Seamus, valiantly trying to make small talk.

'Oh, I don't really,' said Seamus. 'I mean, I like them both. Maybe Mirage slightly more?'

'Is that definitely maybe?' Steve grinned.

'Leave him alone,' said Kate, putting a protective arm around Seamus' rock-hard shoulders.

'Are you in the Mirage camp, Kate?' Seamus asked. 'Seeing that you know Lee Callahan so well...'

'What?'

'You know, the other night. I think you were asleep, but as I drove you home, Portia told me the pair of you were getting to know each other quite well at the Roof Gardens.'

'Much to my chagrin,' Tom laughed, his voice piercing the invisible membrane of budding friendship encasing the table as he bent down to kiss Kate. 'But I took it on the chin. I look at it as though the missus was doing my work for me, buttering him up good and proper, so we can make him our cover star and feature the band in our upcoming Best of British issue.' Tom pulled up a stool and muscled in between Kate and Seamus. 'It's going to be a corker. We've already nearly sold out all the available advertising space and pre-orders are up one hundred and ten per cent.'

'One hundred and ten per cent?' Seamus sounded confused, staring at his coaster. 'I'm pretty sure no such percentage exists. I mean per cent means, literally, by a hundred, and you can't have a hundred and ten in every hundred, can you? No, I think you'll find there really is no such number.'

Oh god, thought Kate. Not now. Not here.

'Who brought Einstein?' Tom chuckled.

'Leave him alone,' Portia said, making Kate narrow her eyes and wonder whether her best mate was going to try to snog her husband-to-be again.

Inside, Kate was also confused. She knew she was going to end up with Seamus, but she still fancied Tom like mad, even if he was, to be frank, a bit of a dick sometimes. What on earth was she going to do?

Sitting there, mulling over her quandary, she pictured herself and Portia and Tom and Seamus playing the starring roles in a *Mad Fer It!* photo love story, all pained expressions, sideways glances, tortured souls and slightly off-centre speech bubbles.

But how long would she have to wait before finding out who was to be The One? Would she have to wait for the next fortnight's issue?

And now with the undeniably sexy Lee Callahan in the frame…

'That's IT!' Kate squealed. 'I think I know how to save *Mad Fer It!*'

'Always talking shop, you lot,' said a disappointed Steve, rolling his eyes to the ceiling and tutting.

'No, wait!' cried Kate. 'What if I asked Lee to be in a photo love story?'

'He'd never do it,' laughed Tom. 'Never in a million years.'

'Yeah,' agreed Seamus. 'You've got more chance of getting Nate Callahan to apologise to Damien from Fuzz for saying he hoped he caught AIDS.'

'You know, Seamus,' Kate said slowly, staring at him as though he'd just recited a poem he'd written for her, the whole pub melting into the background, her focus, her personal spotlight shining only on him. 'I think you've just saved *Mad Fer It!* from folding!'

14

'Daddy!' cried Kate as soon as George opened the front door.

She flung her arms around his neck and nearly knocked him over with the force of her unconfined joy.

'You look exactly the same!' she said, studying his face for a few seconds and then hugging him hard again.

George hugged her back, albeit not quite as enthusiastically.

'Not so tight,' he eventually managed to say. 'Leave some for the other girls… Plenty of me to go round.'

'Sorry,' she giggled, ignoring an obvious reference to his affairs. 'But it's been… oh, it just feels like so long since I last saw you! So much has happened since then, Dad, and I've been desperate to talk to you about Mum and a million things and—'

'It was only last Sunday!' George chuckled. 'Tom. Nice to see you. Do come in.'

George extended his hand for Tom to shake, but Tom didn't see it – his Aviator sunglasses were too dark.

George retracted his hand, placed it on his trim, button-down-shirted tummy and ran his other hand through his thick thatch of grey/white hair.

'Your mother's in the kitchen, where she belongs,' George said, his eyes twinkling. 'Not pregnant, obviously, but no doubt barefoot.'

Tom smiled, Kate tutted.

'I'm going out to the garden. Care to join me, Tom?' George went on.

'Nah, you're all right,' said Tom, chewing furiously on some gum, 'think I'll have a quick chat with your missus, find out what's cooking in your average, middle-class suburban kitchen.'

Tom, who always put on a fake, exaggerated cockney accent when he was nervous or talking to tradesmen, left his sunglasses on and brushed past George and Kate.

'Daddy, you look so well!'

'Hmm?' George looked down at his daughter and he did a double-take as though he'd forgotten she was there and was startled to see her. 'I'm not, as it goes. But let's not dwell on that now. I want to hear all about you. What's been happening with my beautiful daughter?'

Typical Dad, Kate thought. Selfless, loving, caring. God, how she'd missed him!

Kate was gripping George's forearms so tightly, her knuckles had turned white.

She couldn't let go. It was as if her heart was controlling the muscles in her hands and she was holding on for dear life.

Which she kind of was, really. She'd missed her father so badly since he'd died, it had become a physical ache. And even though she'd got to the stage where she had almost accepted he'd gone and she could just about live with her loss in 2022, there was no way she was going to let go of her precious dad now she'd found him again.

Steve ambled up to the front porch and muttered a recalcitrant 'Hey, Dad,' without even looking at his father and slowly lolloped up the stairs, Kate and George feeling the exhausted, heavy-hearted pain of each step.

George jerked his head in the direction of the garden and finally managed to extricate himself from Kate's grip, walking off down the hallway towards the back of the house.

The house. *This* house!

Kate couldn't get the grin off her face.

She held onto the knob at the end of the banister as if to prepare herself for possibly fainting from delirium due to too much happiness and closed her eyes. She inhaled deeply and steadied herself, the nearly intoxicating smell of lamb roasting in the oven, with sprigs of rosemary and garlic inserted into the fleshy bits of the joint, nearly bowling her over. She'd always loved her mother's lamb – so had Steve – even when she went through that 'difficult, rebellious phase' (from the age of nine onwards, her mother would say) and wanted to be with friends and boyfriends more than family, she always made it home for Jenny's Sunday lamb roast. She craved the smell, the taste and that unmistakeable feel of home so much, that even when she went vegetarian and moved into a flat with Portia, she'd still never miss a Sunday lunch at Jenny's.

Apart from when George was away, of course. There was always a sick colleague in Oxford he had to go and see. Or he had to give a paper for fellow academics in Leeds or something. Jenny always cancelled the roast when George was away. Probably used the time to catch up on her reading and writing. She was an intellectual force to be reckoned with herself and even though she'd just taken early retirement to look after George full time, she'd always been a powerhouse in the English Literature department at King's College, London.

Kate frowned and cocked her head to the side, opening her eyes. There had always been something rushed, something so last minute about these little trips away of her dad's – and she couldn't quite put her finger on it, but his reasons never quite seemed to ring true.

Despite the fact that Kate would more often than not console herself with ready-made packaged food from M&S (the houmous, the vine leaves, the lemon pesto tuna linguine! Her mouth started to water at the memory), she always felt an emptiness in the pit of her stomach when the Sunday roast in Ickenham was postponed.

'But it's happening today!' she said out loud, pulling her shoulders back, thrusting her nose in the air and marching towards that heavenly aroma.

'I dunno,' Tom was saying, his accent getting thicker by the minute. 'Maybe it's because—'

'You're a Londoner?' Kate piped up, mocking him and pretending to pull out invisible braces from her chest.

'Nah, nah,' Tom shot Kate a cross glance. 'Me muvver died when I were a nippah and me elder sisters brought me up, didn't they?'

'Really, Tom? I never knew that,' said Jenny. 'It's no wonder then, that you're so in touch with your feminine side and get along with women so well.'

Kate tittered. Her mother's sarcasm never missed its mark.

Jenny turned to put the roast back in the oven and, as she did so, winked at Kate and poked the inside of her cheek with her tongue.

'I didn't know that either, Tom,' said Kate, putting her hand on his shoulder. 'You never said—'

'Well, she didn't exactly *die*,' he said, looking sheepish. 'She left us. Dad took off wiv some tart and Mum did the same. We never 'eard from eiver of 'em again. So they're bof dead to us, me and me sisters. It's like we could only ever depend on each other, so we got very close. And to this day, me sisters are still me best mates.'

Kate gave Tom a kiss on the cheek, even though she was expecting a Sid James laugh any minute now. She knew he was extremely close to his sisters, but had never known exactly how they'd got that way. Could this revelation signal a whole new side to Tom? Was the caring, sensitive part of his personality emerging, leaving the bravado and laddish persona to simply, effortlessly fall away, much like a centrefold's bra might at a *Lashed* photo shoot?

Kate looked past Tom and Jenny and saw her dad standing in the middle of their back lawn, staring off into space.

'You okay, Dad?'

George gave a mini start again, as though he was being woken from a particularly deep sleep.

'Oh, I'm OK. Don't mind me.' he sighed, clutching his chest.

'Dad?' Kate put her arm around her father.

'I'm all right,' he half-smiled. 'No, really – I'm fine. But what are we going to do about that lazy brother of yours, hmmm?'

'I am here, you know,' came Steve's voice from on high.

George and Kate looked up to see Steve leaning out of his old bedroom window, having a cigarette.

'Ahoy there!' said Kate cheerfully, shielding her eyes from the sun's glare with a lazy salute. 'Why don't you come down and join us? Lunch is nearly ready and Tom's regaling Mum with tales of his lost childhood.'

'*Fassss-cinating,*' said Steve, the smoke snaking out of his mouth and back into his nostrils at the long, drawn-out 's' sound.

George and Kate both shrugged their shoulders and sighed simultaneously, exchanging 'what-can-you-do?' glances and walked back into the house.

'So, yeah, it's all gone a little bit tits up – sorry – *Pete Tong* if you know what I mean,' Tom was holding forth.

'No, I'm afraid I don't,' said Jenny. 'Enlighten me.'

'It's like this wild beast that can't be tamed! I lost control of it ages ago. I tell you, it's got a mind of its own and goes where it wants to go. And there's not a damn thing I can do about it!'

'Talking about your shagging technique again, Tom?' Steve smirked, flopping into a chair at the dining table.

Tom didn't skip a beat.

'So what started out as a joke, one big schoolboy prank, has now grown into a multi-million-pound publishing phenomenon. Which is pretty cool, yeah – but my sisters can't stand it and they're threatening to disown me if I don't drastically change it and make it more like, I dunno, *National Geographic* or something. Either that or I have to get another job.'

'You talking about *Lashed*?' asked Kate. 'Wow, so the pressure's really on, eh? How come you've never told me any of this before? Not even a hint of it?'

'Oh, I don't know,' Tom said, sounding more and more like the insecure young man he was fast revealing himself to be. 'Didn't fit with the image of the mag, really. Can you imagine the headlines? *Grubby Mag Ed in Bullying By Feminist Sisters Shocker!*'

'Yeah,' said Kate. '*Filthy Rag Ed Is Big Girl's Blouse!*'

'Or *Porn Mag Ed Beats Chest in Bare Breast Fem-Fest!*' Steve joined in, suddenly brighter and warming to the theme.

'That's not bad,' chuckled Tom. 'I didn't know you had an eye for a good headline, Steve. That one sounds like a double page-pictorial spread, with me the caveman filling in a sexy sex sandwich!'

Kate groaned.

'It's like a *Lashed* editorial meeting in here! Only without the drugs!' Tom beamed.

'So much for your inner feminist sympathiser, new age guy coming to the fore, Tom!' laughed Jenny.

'Yeah – you couldn't keep it up, could you?' Kate smiled.

'Fnarr, fnarr!' said Steve and Tom in unison, nudging each other in the ribs.

Kate shook her head and rolled her eyes, fondly.

'That nice guy is in there somewhere,' Jenny said, tapping Tom's head with her forefinger. 'It's just a matter of teasing it out.'

'Now enough of all that – the lamb is ready. Let's have a civilised lunch, shall we?'

Kate laughed. And wished she'd brought Tom to more Sunday lunches at her parents' place. He was really quite sweet when you got right down to it. Like a lost child.

'OK, OK,' said Tom. 'Just don't let it get out that I have feminist tendencies.'

'I don't know, that mightn't be such a bad idea...' Kate trailed off, wondering what Medea Media had made of her fax. She hadn't heard a peep out of them since she sent it off.

'You carve, George – everyone else help yourself to veg and gravy,' Jenny issued the same instructions as always.

Kate sat back, her hands crossed against her bare tummy (she was wearing another crop-top today – this time a

Top Shop tight red mock football shirt with white piping, short sleeves and a V-neck) and surveyed the scene.

She couldn't help but feel smug, somehow. *This* is what she'd been hankering after all these years – *this* was exactly the feeling she was trying to create with Phoebs, Decks and Seamus at home. Yes, she inwardly grinned, this was the family portrait snapshot that would hang for ever in her mind's gallery.

At this thought, she shifted a little in her seat and sat up straight, her lips pursed in deep concentration. She thought something time-travelly might happen any moment when all sounds around her disappeared, like someone had turned the volume right down or pressed the mute button on a remote.

She watched in silence as Tom, Steve and Jenny tucked heartily into their meals, talking with mouths full and gesticulating wildly as another hilarious story was told. George didn't partake – he just chewed his carrots and peas and stared at the silver gravy boat.

They all had issues, of course – more than Kate had ever realised – a clutch of Pandora's Boxes, wriggling and squirming with secrets a-plenty on the inside: secrets too terrible to unleash.

She never would have noticed any of this the first time round, when she was so much younger and always took everything at face value. And anyway, she was too busy living her hedonistic whirl of a life to stop and read between the lines, consider what might or might not be going on in other people's worlds.

She zoomed in on Steve. He was a viper's nest of complex emotions, that was quite clear. But would his demeanour and outlook be changed, simply because he was going to be forced to fend for himself without the financial help of his family?

And what about Tom?

Oh, bloody men – they were always so confusing! No change there, then, she thought to herself.

But Kate's opinion of Tom *had* changed. She'd really seen a more rounded, three-dimensional version of him today. On the other hand, that didn't mean she had to move in with him, did it? And how could she even *entertain* the thought of sleeping with him? She did remember thinking he was quite the master swordsman when it came to their shenanigans between the sheets the first time round... And she *had* dreamed about this moment for such a long time... so how could she back out now, when her chance to right the wrongs of her past had finally come? How could she *not* see her fantasy through to fruition?

On the other hand, though, she was a happily (ish) married woman! Wouldn't that make her no better than Tom – a philanderer with a heart like a fridge?

But wait – what had Portia said yesterday? Something about Kate taking herself too seriously? And wanting to control everything and everyone around her so much, she'd lost all sense of fun and had become a crashing bore? Or words to that effect?

She felt dizzy. With lust? But what about Seamus? And the kids? It would be like being unfaithful, wouldn't it? Well, no, not technically... because it was, quite literally, all in the past! She could *easily* get away with it – she'd slept with Tom loads of times in the past, way before she'd ever met Seamus, so she wasn't sailing through uncharted waters exactly or doing anything *illegal* in a relationship sense. And now she had the chance to do it all over again, but better – no one need ever know!

Besides, she knew only too well that at her upcoming birthday party, Tom was going to run off with Tamsin – exactly as he did the first time round – so where was the harm in making hay while the sun shone?

And who knows? She might be propelled back to 2022 at any moment – especially considering all sound had completely vanished in a scary, vortex/continuum/quantum mechanics-y kind of way – how would she feel if she woke up back at home in 2022, knowing she'd blown the only chance she was *ever* going to get?

I'm going to go for it. I don't have any other choice!

All at once, someone pressed the mute button and noises were well and truly on again.

'Honestly, we was robbed!' Tom was saying.

'No, we weren't,' Steve countered. 'The score reflected the level of play between the two teams. England was totally on a par with Switzerland. We deserved to draw.'

George jumped and spluttered, like an old jalopy trying to re-start its engine.

'Did someone say par?' he winked at Kate as though she was six years old.

Kate smiled back.

'I'm just saying,' Tom went on, totally ignoring George, 'that we stand a great chance of winning this tournament if we *get the goals*. It's no use playing brilliantly but not scoring – or, worse, playing just as well as everyone else, but not asserting our authority over them, dominating them as they deserve to be dominated. Because, mark my words, the Empire shall rise again and come the end of June, that trophy will be ours!'

'All right, all right,' said Steve, leaning back as though the blast from Tom's mock-jingoistic rant was so strong, it was nearly pushing him off his chair.

'Shall we leave football for a minute or two?' Jenny suggested. 'There must be some other news we'd all be interested in hearing, mustn't there?'

Four faces stared blankly back at her, the three men looking decidedly dumb and even a little bit bovine as they chewed their food and let their eyes droop.

'Kate?' Jenny prodded her daughter. 'Anything you want to tell us? Anything at all?'

'You're not pregnant, are you?' Tom gulped audibly.

'What?' Jenny and Kate chorused.

'Phew!' Tom pretended to wipe sweat from his brow.

Jenny got up and stood behind Steve, pointing at him and giving Kate a look that screamed: 'Say something!'

'Oh, uh, yeah.' Kate coughed. 'Yeah, everyone? Tom and I are moving in together. I figured he's been asking me for so long, I had to agree to do it – even if it's just to get him to shut up!'

In a strange, uncharacteristic move, Jenny clapped her hands together, like an excited schoolgirl.

'Ooh!' she squeaked. 'How simply *wonderful*, Katie!'

'Calm down, *Jenny*,' sneered Steve. 'It's not as if she's marrying royalty or anything!'

'Really?' Tom nearly choked on his mint sauce. 'Are you sure, Kate? I mean, are you really sure you want to?'

Tom sounded unsure of himself. It was as though he'd just won the lottery and couldn't quite believe it. Or he'd scammed a lottery win and was waiting to be found out.

'Of course I'm sure,' said Kate, her voice wavering with obvious uncertainty. She was flattered by Tom's reaction and, feeling strengthened by it, decided to issue a warning from her unprecedented position of power. 'But if you hurt me – even if it's just the once – you won't know what's hit you.'

'But I will,' said George a bit menacingly. 'And it'll be *me*. I'll hunt you down and kill you like the dirty dog you are if you hurt one little hair on that girl's pretty little head.'

Taken aback by George's little promise, everyone fell silent, save for another loud gulp emanating from Tom's throat.

'I hate to be a wet blanket,' Steve began.

'Do you?' Kate put it to him. 'Do you *really*, Steve?'

'You know I do! I just want to be sure that you've really thought this through, considered all your options and taken everyone into account.'

'Portia doesn't know yet,' Kate admitted. 'But she'll be fine with it, I know she will. She'll just have to get another tenant in – there's no way she'd ever move out of that fantastic flat.'

'But what about me?' Steve sounded like the small child now.

'What about you?' Jenny said sternly, but turned away to face the kitchen as soon as she'd said it, lest her family see her chin quivering with emotion.

'Get a goddamned job!' George looked Steve straight in the eye.

'How?' Steve pouted and folded his arms over his chest, slumping down into the back of his chair.

'You'll think of something,' Kate said, trying to sound encouraging. 'And I'll help you – we all will. I'm sorry, Stevie – but there's no way I'll be able to pay your way as well as the rent on our new flat – especially if we're moving to Notting Hill like Tom wants to.'

Steve's bottom lip jutted out so far from his face, he started to look like one of those Yanomamo Indians of the Amazon complete with lip plates. Or like Decko when he didn't get his way. Kate had never noticed the striking resemblance between Steve and Declan before – probably because Steve had disappeared MIA years before the kids were born.

Kate suddenly realised the severity of the situation – her relationship with her brother was on the line here, the stakes so high that if she wasn't careful, she knew she might never see him again.

Everyone except for Steve stood up and started bustling about the table, clearing plates and picking up glasses. Talk slowly turned to football again, then the weather and eventually to how delicious that roast was and whether it was Welsh or New Zealand lamb because it was so melt-in-the-mouth tender, it really was rather incredible—

BANG!

The front door slammed, knocking a row of kitsch but relatively inoffensive figurines off the sideboard. The foursome making themselves busy in the kitchen looked up from what they were doing and swapped wide-eyed, worried glances.

'Steve?' Jenny called.

'STEVE!' shouted Kate, dropping a cup and running for the door.

15

'So where's he gone, then?' Portia had called Kate at the office first thing on Monday morning.

'I don't know,' sniffed Kate. 'But it's all my fault! Just because I wanted to see what it was like to have sex with Tom again! I've been so selfish, blaming Steve for Tom running off with Tamsin—'

At that moment, as if on cue, Tamsin appeared out of the blue, right beside Kate's desk, gurning like the cat who'd got the cream.

'What *are* you banging on about, Kate? You're not making any sense!' Portia said.

'I've, um, got to go – call you later,' she said and swiftly hung up.

'Morning, Kate,' Tamsin said sweetly. 'I was just wondering how things were going with *Lashed* and Medea. Do you need any help handling it? I could really use the experience and to work with you on this one would be a once in a lifetime opportunity.'

Smarmy little—

'Kate!' boomed Archie.

Kate excused herself and nearly broke into run, she couldn't get out of Tamsin's personal space fast enough.

'So, good weekend?' Archie plumped for his usual opening gambit.

'Yeah, not bad,' came Kate's by now stock reply.

'What about the match, eh? Good start or what?'

'Yeah, great! And how exciting was the atmosphere?! Honestly, it was exactly how I remembered it – like one big love-in, all of us united against a common enemy – every other team! Brilliant.'

Kate perched her bum on the corner of Archie's desk and shook her head slowly, narrowing her eyes and looking out through the wall of window, as if she was a general reminiscing about military glory.

'Yeah, right,' Archie pulled his chin to his chest and gave her a funny look. 'So anyway. I just got a message from Medea Horton, the boss of Medea Media. Apparently she's sent us loads of emails but our system's been down for god knows how long. And the upshot of it all is…' Archie drummed his fingers on the edge of the desk, '…she wants to have a meeting with us. You, me and Tom. To nut out the terms of our apology, she said.'

Kate's heart jumped. She wasn't much of a one for confrontation at the best of times – but with Steve AWOL and her move to Notting Hill imminent, she felt like she had enough to contend with.

'Kate? Are you OK?' Archie asked.

'Fine, fine,' she lied. 'I've just got so much to do and—'

'Any ideas re *Mad Fer It!*?' He cut her off, tapping his fingers impatiently on his lifeless computer keyboard.

'No, not really,' she said, unable to get Steve off her mind.

'Nothing? Not even the germ of an idea? I must say, Kate, I'm a little disappointed in you. You're usually so quick off the mark, so sparky. What's up?'

'Oh, nothing…'

'Kate? This is me you're talking to, go on, tell me all about it.'

Kate looked at him and seriously considered it. He was, apart from Tom and Seamus, her closest work friend after all.

But if she told Archie that she'd been transported from her steamy, chaotic suburban kitchen in 2022 to her old body, job, boyfriend and free, well sleeping, childless state in 1996 – exactly how, she had no idea – and was desperate to get back, what would he say? How would he react?

Imagine she *did* fill Archie in on what had happened in the past week – would he laugh at her? Call her crazy? Slap her cheek and tell her to snap out of it?

Kate decided she couldn't take the risk of telling him about the time travel, but she could let him in on the Steve situation. She took a deep breath and looked him straight in the eye.

'It's just my brother. You know, Steve?' she couldn't remember whether Archie and Steve had ever met. 'I don't understand it entirely, but he's got the right hump with me because I can't afford to pay for his life any more.'

'Right,' Archie nodded sagely. 'And why not?'

'Because I'm moving out of the West Hampstead flat we share with Portia—'

'Ah, the lovely and fragrant Portia,' Archie said, his eyes twinkling.

'…and I'm moving into a flat in Notting Hill. With Tom.'

'You never!'

'Am so.' She smiled for the first time that morning.

'But, Kate – now don't take this the wrong way or anything – and I love Tom, man, you know I do – great bloke to have at a party – but, well, I… you can do so much better than him, that's all.'

'Oh, I agree,' she said, surprising the hell out of Archie and making him sit up that little bit straighter. 'And I will, believe me. Just not yet. Just let me have my last hurrah the way I've dreamed about it for the past twenty-six years.'

'You've wanted to move in with Tom for the past twenty-six years?' Archie looked confused. 'But you only met him when you started to work here... I don't underst—'

'Knock, knock!' Seamus said with a lopsided grin as he rapped his knuckles on Archie's door.

If only Archie knew, thought Kate.

'Ah, Shane,' said Archie, standing up to make way for Seamus to get in front of his computer.

'Seamus,' Kate said, correcting him.

'Sorry, *Seamus*,' Archie said.

'That's quite all right,' said Seamus, who seemed to have gone from nought to sixty in terms of confidence in the last week. 'Now are you sure you've got everything turned on?'

Seamus disappeared under Archie's desk and in a muffled voice said:

'Ah, there's your problem right there. Modem wasn't plugged in.'

'Ah,' Kate and Archie echoed, as if they knew what a modem was.

Seamus reappeared in front of Archie's desk and drew himself up to his full height. And quite impressive he looked, too, Kate couldn't help but note.

'How'd you enjoy the match, Archie?' Seamus asked.

'Fantastic,' Archie replied. 'Aren't you going to ask Kate? She watched it, too...'

'Oh, I know what Kate thought – I was right there, watching it with her,' Seamus said with – what was it

– *pride*? 'How did you go with your idea to save your favourite teen mag, Kate? What did Archie think?'

There was something quite different about Seamus today. And Kate was taken aback by how attractive she found him.

'Kate?' Archie turned to her. 'You said you didn't have anything!'

'Oh!' Kate dragged her eyes away from Seamus. 'It was actually – Seamus' idea, really. Um, how about in a bessie mates special or something, we get the Mirage men in a boxing ring with the Fuzz fellas and get them to fight out their friendship problems – interview them about what annoys them most about each other – and then, in a world first, get them to kiss and make up. Lots of pix of them hugging and messing about in their satin shorts and stuff and—'

'My god, Kate – that is woeful!' Archie laughed.

Seamus looked crushed. So did Kate.

'They'd never do that! Never in a million years! Far too uncool!'

'But… but what if—'

'I must say I expected better from you, Kate,' Archie said as he wiped a tear of mirth from his eye. 'Keep thinking, though – maybe without the aid of alcohol this time.'

'Well, also,' Seamus began diplomatically, changing the subject, 'I wanted to let you know that the IT department is quickly expanding – yay – and I have employed a new member of the team. His name is Kevin—'

'Of course it is!' Archie started laughing again.

'…and he will be starting any day now, so—'

'What is this? Revenge of the fookin' nerds or what?' Archie had to hold onto his stomach, he found himself so hilarious.

Kate had never seen Archie like this before – he was being cruel and unkind and unnecessarily mean.

What was it with everybody lately? Everyone acting out of character, not being the constantly lovely, predictably *nice* people she used to know? Why were they all so different from the way she remembered them?

'Come on, Seamus,' Kate said, steering him out of Archie's office by his elbow. 'Will you tell me if my modem's turned on now, too?'

Kate hooked her arm in Seamus' just as the Mike Flowers Pops version of 'Wonderwall' started playing on the radio outside amongst the cubicles and her laughing colleagues thwacking each other with rulers.

'What would you say to sideburns?' Kate asked Seamus as she watched some young shaggy-haired scamp proudly combing his in a mirror atop a tall, grey steel filing cabinet.

'Um – run them under a cold tap? Call 999? Same as I'd say to front or back burns, I suppose…' Seamus chuckled.

Kate shot him the look she usually reserved for Declan when he was experimenting with jokes and word play – a fond look that said 'not bad, needs work'.

'Side *boards* then,' she giggled, despite herself. 'Like that boy has, over there?'

'Boy? *Man*, more like!' said Seamus with a slight hint of admiration in his voice. 'I've already started thinning out, I doubt whether I'd be *able* to grow anything as impressive as that. But they do look rather good, in a very mod way…'

The pair had reached Kate's desk and she sat down in her swivel chair while Seamus looked around, leaning on her desk one minute, folding his arms across his chest the next and finally running both hands through his hair (ever-so-gently, of course, so as not to cause any unnecessary fall-out) before he curled them into fists and stuck them on his hips.

'So what was it you wanted me to do?' he asked.

'Could you get my modem working again, please? And then can you help me find some search engines? I can't for the life of me remember what they're called and I really want to find out—'

Seamus momentarily put one hand on Kate's thigh as he got down onto his knees and peered into the small dark recess under her desk.

'Oops, sorry about that… just needed something to hold onto…'

'That's OK,' she said softly, realising in that instant that she didn't mind. Didn't mind at all. She watched the top of his head that, she noted, seemed to be thickly thatched and not thinning in the slightest. She remembered that Seamus had always done that – thought he was much balder than he was. It was like her with her weight – she always thought she was about one to two stone heavier than she actually was. It was exactly the same thing, come to think of it. Why do we always do that, she asked herself. Why do we exaggerate and make much worse the thing we're most concerned about? Why are we so mean to ourselves?

She made a mental note to stop that once she got back to 2022. She vowed to be healthy and happy and not obsess about how she looked and how everything was going south – or had already gone south, left ages ago – no! Stop it! There will be no more room left in her fabulously fulfilled, busy, happy life for such negative self-talk, as Portia called it, when she got back.

If she ever got back.

'I've got to know how long I've got left here, Seamus. I simply have to know!'

Seamus, holding onto five thin black wires, backed out from under her desk and sat on his haunches, looking quite pleased with himself.

'The information superhighway is an amazing thing – but no one knows that sort of stuff – that's between you and, er...' Seamus pointed up towards the ceiling.

'Who? Management?' she said, knitting her brow. 'Someone on the fifth floor?'

Seamus leaned towards Kate, saying in a whisper, 'No, no – *your maker*.'

'What *are* you talking about?' Kate was beginning to get a little irritated.

'I could ask you the same thing,' Seamus got up, holding the wires to his chest. He tossed his hair a bit and thrust his chin in the air, looking like he'd just said he didn't want to play any more and he was going home with his ball.

'Urgh,' Kate grunted. 'Just give me the names of some search engines and I'll look it up myself.'

Seamus wrote three names down on the A4 pad sitting at the side of Kate's desk.

'There you go,' he said, dropping the pen on top of the pad and readjusting the wires under his arm as though they were a clutch bag. 'Now when are you going to take me shopping?'

But Kate was already getting busy with her keyboard, typing in 'time travel' and watching her screen, wide-eyed and expectant.

'Argh!' she harrumphed. 'Why does it take so bloody long?'

'Well, technically speaking—'

'And where the hell is Wikipedia?'

'Wiki-*what*?'

'Oh, never mind!' She cut Seamus off. 'I'm going to have to go to the library. Ha! Imagine! Are there any libraries left? God knows, they're shutting them down with such gay abandon these days, is it any wonder we're… all so… computer… obsessed…?'

She glanced up at Seamus, who was looking down at her, an expression of vague concern on his face.

The air between them hung heavily for a few portentous seconds before the rest of the office appeared to melt away and whirl around them at supersonic speed, turning everyone and everything into merely spinning atoms, while the two of them stayed stock still, gazing into each other's eyes.

The moment was loaded – fairly *dripping* with meaning.

'You know, you seem so familiar to me.' Seamus furrowed his brow, his forehead creasing in its usual spot. 'I just can't work out where from.'

Kate nodded encouragingly and stayed silent, wanting to squeeze all possible droplets of romance out of it, like it was a sponge, soaked in the wonderful memories of their relationship.

She took a deep breath as he opened his mouth to speak.

'Maybe I've seen you on the bus… um… do you ever catch the 38 to Clapton Pond?'

Kate shook her head and felt her face forming into that look again, the one she reserved for Declan and his jokes. Because really, was this as good as it was ever going to get with Seamus? Was this the best he could do to sweep her off her feet? Swivel chair, whatever.

Kate willed him on, moving her head back and forth, inching herself ever forward, as though her chair were a rocking horse and she was coming down the straight, winning by a nose in her imaginary race.

Come on, Seamus! You can do it!

'All I know is that I feel somehow safe with you. And that every morning when I wake up, ever since we met, I just can't wait to see you.'

Kate's breath caught in her chest.

That's better… keep going, keep going!

'Weird, eh?' He raised his eyebrows.

The office careening around them slowed down and, within a couple of seconds, came to a standstill.

The air thinned out, 'Return of the Mack' started up on the radio and people carried on exactly as they had before, no one commenting on or in any way acknowledging what had just happened. As though it hadn't.

Seamus said he'd better be going and looked confused as he sloped off down the corridor to The Lift.

Tamsin's annoyingly high, tinny voice got louder in Kate's ear – she was walking towards the reception desk with Lucy, barking orders about some fax or other that Lucy was to send.

And then, when she saw Tom swagger in, singing along with the song, as though he himself *was* the Mack and this was his triumphant return, she sighed.

'All right, babes?' He upped the cockney as he perched on the corner of Kate's desk, chewing gum rapidly and whipping off his Aviators.

Kate smiled the way she would at a puppy's vain attempts at climbing up a couch too tall for him, where no

151

purchase could be found. Because Tom was quite sweet, really – trying so hard to impress and be cool all the time.

'Right. Coupla places to see up West tomorra, which I have 'igh 'opes for. And what's this about a meeting with Medea?'

'Ah – I dunno,' Kate said. 'As far as I know we haven't set a time or place or anything yet—'

'I hope you don't mind,' Tamsin butted in, 'but I took the liberty of organising this meeting for you. Medea Horton – she's the, ah, she's the boss of Medea Media, right?'

Tom and Kate nodded.

'Well, the only time she could make it was this Friday, but I know you're off to Ibiza then, Kate, so I scheduled it in for, um, this afternoon.'

Kate gasped.

'I know it's short notice,' Tamsin said apologetically, 'but that's the only other free slot she had and—'

'Hey, hey,' said Tom, standing up and putting his hands on Tamsin's shoulders. She, in turn, looked up at him with such reverence, it was as though the very hands of God were upon her.

Kate rolled her eyes skywards and mumbled 'Oh, *por favor*!'

'It's all OK,' Tom continued in soothing tones. 'You did the right thing, as it goes. This whole Medea thing's a storm in a tea cup. Or a D-cup, more to the point!'

Tamsin tittered and Tom looked appreciative. Kate couldn't believe the cheesiness of what she was witnessing.

'Anyway, the sooner we get it over with, the sooner we can get back to doing what we do best!'

The radio went off, the shuffling of papers stopped and rulers ceased their incessant thwacking – the atmosphere was so heavy with anticipation, all eyes on Tom, and so quiet, you could hear a spitball drop.

Tom flashed a nervous look at Kate. He desperately needed help here – a prompt.

'Profit, good ti—' she began in a whisper out of the side of her mouth.

'Fuck profit! We want PARTIES, good times and banter!' shouted Tom to rapturous applause from the rest of the office – and a squeak of pure delight from Tamsin.

Kate rolled her eyes, but also couldn't help but grin. Because even if everyone else saw Tom as simply the one-dimensional, drug-addled, boob-obsessed party boy, she knew better. She knew the soft-sided, insecure, bitter-sweet truth about Tom and she actually felt sorry for him.

16

Kate, having reduced Medea to her own prejudiced cultural stereotype in her head, imagined she would be heavy-set with purple DMs, black leggings, floaty purple shirt, a black velvet waistcoat (XL) or shapeless, manly, oversized denim jacket and a buzz cut.

But when Medea Horton walked into the PGT&B offices that afternoon, it was as if she was Charlize Theron in that J'adore ad. Her long, wavy, blonde tresses bounced on her slim shoulders as though she were wading through waist-height wheat on a bright blue-skied, sunny, spring day.

Her cream silk shirt's top button was undone, to a very business-like but human level, her dark-blue suit jacket slung casually over her arm. Her heels sank into the plush pile carpet of the meeting room, but this was nothing Medea couldn't handle.

She smiled a dazzling, straight-toothed, positively *radiant* Hollywood-white smile and extended her beautifully manicured, soft hand to Kate.

Medea's gold watch dangled elegantly on her delicate wrist and when she looked as if she was about to say something, Kate expected a symphony to start up.

'Hello there! I'm Medea. And you must be...?' she said in a heavy Scottish accent.

'Kate,' said Kate, standing up too fast and bashing her knees on the table. 'Um, I'm Kate and this is Tom, Editor of *Lashed* and Archie, head of PR at PGT&B.'

Kate swept her hand in the men's direction, but could detect no movement nor hear any sound from them.

She tore her eyes away from Medea and instantly saw why: both Tom and Archie were slack-jawed and speechless, struck dumb, quite literally, by Medea's stunning beauty. Their eyes were out on stalks. And despite the fact that Tom saw thousands of drop-dead gorgeous women every day as part of his job and Archie was a professional who always remained calm in a crisis, these two were hopelessly, helplessly mesmerised.

'Guys? GUYS!' Kate tried to get their attention with a little light shouting and a knock on the table.

'Yes, yes, of course,' said Archie distractedly, glancing at Kate and spluttering a bit as though he'd just been woken up. 'Ah, yes. Do… ah… take a seat.'

In a rare display of competitive chivalry, Archie and Tom swapped goading glances for a millisecond and then simultaneously shot out of their seats, racing for the chair nearest the door, both fumbling with the back of it and elbowing each other out of the way.

'Pathetic,' said Kate quietly, raising her eyes to the buzzing on/off strip lighting hanging from the ceiling.

Medea laughed.

'It's quite all right, fellas, I can manage to pull my own chair out, thank you.'

Summarily dismissed, the two men backed away, never taking their eyes off her, mumbling apologies and returning to their own chairs.

Bet it happens all the time, thought Kate.

'It happens all the time,' said Medea and smiled at Kate. 'No big deal. So. Shall we get down to business?'

'Yes,' said Kate, surprised by how there was no football talk taking up the whole meeting time, resulting in another meeting having to be planned for the following week – for that's how meetings at PGT&B were notorious for panning out. 'Would you like some water? Coffee? Tea?'

'Beer? Wine? Me?' grinned Tom, getting his mojo back.

'No, no thanks. I'd rather just crack on if we could – I've got back-to-back appointments this afternoon.'

'How about a front-to-front appointment—' Archie whispered to Tom.

'Ah, I think Medea's right—' Kate cut Archie off. 'Let's get on with it.'

'Right,' said Medea, ignoring the leering lads and looking straight at Kate. 'Now, as both magazine publishers and women, we strongly object to the idea that the imagery, tone and blatant male sexual aggression that magazines like *Lashed* perpetrate and purport is acceptable – and, even worse, agreeable – in our society.'

Kate nodded.

'Now hang on a sec,' said Tom, 'what does, er, porpoise? Purr-pot? Purport mean? I am but a poor, illiterate pornographer...'

Archie and Tom exchanged schoolboy sniggers while Medea just ignored them. Kate felt a familiar sinking feeling and wondered whether Tom would ever drop the lager lout act.

'And while we're perfectly open to the ideas you expressed in your fax, Kate, we don't actually believe it in the case of *Lashed* for one cold, hard minute. I mean, how stupid do you think we are?'

'But... I-I,' Kate stammered.

'However. We are *very* interested in doing business with you. Not getting into bed with you, as such...'

Archie and Tom couldn't help themselves when they heard this and, clutching their stomachs, howled with laughter.

'Oh, here we go,' Medea went on. 'Which one of you's Beavis and which one's Butt-Head?'

Kate tittered. Suitably chastised, Tom and Archie coughed and sat up straight, recovering remarkably fast from their little bout of schoolboy hysterics and all three from PGT&B were in Medea's thrall.

'Now. We definitely want to take you up on your offer of free advertising on prominent *Lashed* pages for a year.'

'You do?' Kate was surprised. 'I thought if you wanted to see us in person, you probably weren't going to go for it at all.'

'Well,' said Medea, softening, 'we're only a small business and we are starting to struggle a bit, what with the rise of the lad and so-called irreverent, binge-drinking "ladettes" eclipsing us and our comparatively sober views...'

Kate, Archie and Tom all nodded, willing her on.

'It's a long story,' sighed Medea. 'But suffice it to say, I want us to be a success on our own merits. I set the company up myself and I want to prove that our values and ideals are still relevant today – and are, indeed, crucial to building a decent, fair, nurturing society for all. I know it sounds a bit high-minded and out of step with today's individualistic, hedonistic, party, party, party attitudes, but, well, there we are.'

'Good on you,' Kate said, admiring Medea more and more with every passing moment.

'But the advertising is not all I'm after,' Medea said quickly, sensing her audience was not only captive but even in a bit of a trance and, therefore, totally receptive to anything she had to say. 'I also want a regular, monthly spot – a column or something – in not just *Lashed*, but another of your publications. Any ideas?'

Kate snapped out of her semi-hypnotised state and stood up (for height and authority). 'Yes!'

Everyone looked at her expectantly.

'I think *Mad Fer It!* could really do with something like this – as long as you could dress it up and make it funny and relevant to twelve-year-old girls – you know, focus on pop stars and movie stars and not take yourself too seriously and lean more towards girl power than radical feminism… Don't you think, Archie?'

Archie stroked his chin.

'Oh, come on, Archie!' Kate pleaded. 'Medea'd be a great role model for young girls – she's beautiful and ballsy and cool – and with some help from the *Mad Fer It!* editorial team, we could really produce a ground-breaking, history-changing – I mean, history-*making* – feat, here!'

'I love it!' Medea flashed her mega-watt smile.

'What about me?' Tom pouted.

'What about you?' Archie countered.

'Well, don't I get a say in any of this? I'm only the editor of *Lashed* with a hundred per cent editorial control, you know. It says so in my contract,' said Tom, coming over all Naomi Campbell in a strop.

'Well, go on, then,' Archie said. 'What do you think?'

'I think we should all go to O'Flaherty's to celebrate – and, ah, plan your first column, Medea. Who's with me?'

'Love to – but I've got to run,' said Medea, standing up and pushing her chair out with the backs of her knees. 'Another time, maybe?'

17

'It was as though I was invisible!' Kate moaned to Portia as they waited in the queue to board the plane to Ibiza.

'Well, I hate to say it, Kate, but that's what Tom's like. It's what he's *always* been like. What he always *will be* like.'

'I know, I know,' Kate sighed at the hideous three shades of blue, swirly airport lounge carpet. 'I just thought I'd seen a different side to him, lately, that's all.'

'Well, he's a bastard,' said Portia matter-of-factly. 'He'll never change. And to salivate all over that girl in front of you, well, bah! You know he's beneath you, don't you?'

'Chance'd be a fine thing,' said Kate, a wicked smile creeping onto her face.

'Honestly – what would Medea say?' Portia sniggered.

The pair withdrew back into their own respective head spaces in quiet contemplation of things to come.

Portia had packed several tiny bikinis, and so, in anticipation, had also had everything even remotely resembling hair waxed, plucked or shorn off her body. Despite the fact that the pregnancy hormones racing around her system made her skin so much more sensitive, she was determined to ignore the whole baby thing and carry on as normal. Which is why she even went so far as to have a Brazilian.

'I plumped for a small, but oh-so-sexy landing strip,' she proudly showed Kate the night before. 'Get a load of *this*!'

'Yowch!' Kate recoiled in horror. 'You look like a plucked chicken! With a black go-faster stripe on your... on your... you know, *there*.'

'It'll calm down,' said Portia, pulling her pants up and plonking herself down in front of the telly. 'And when it does, I'm going to look fabulous.'

'To who? Or should that be "whom"?' Kate wondered out loud.

'I don't know, do I?' Portia said tetchily. 'Whosoever gets lucky enough to see me in all my glory, I suppose.'

'Yeah, right,' Kate scoffed. 'Because you're going to be getting so much action in Ibiza in the two days we're there...'

'Well, a girl's got to be prepared,' Portia said. 'And nothing says "prepared" quite like a Brazilian.'

Kate laughed through her nose. It whistled.

'Well, I wouldn't expect a grannie like you to get it,' Portia shook her mane. 'I mean, you're so po-faced and... I dunno... *mumsy*, lately, it's as though you've aged forty years and forgotten how to have fun.'

'Hang on!' said Kate, looking up from her suitcase at Portia. 'I haven't forgotten how to have fun! I love fun! I'm taking off for a quick holiday – that's fun!'

Portia widened her eyes at Kate as if to say, 'Got any more examples of extreme good-time seeking?'

'Um,' Kate stalled for time, 'and I had drinks with you at the football the other day – that was fun!'

'You don't fool me, Kate,' said Portia, getting up off the sofa and looking under cushions for the remote. 'I may have been on one, but that didn't stop me noticing your return to limes and sodas after the match. Honestly – the way you've been behaving lately, anyone'd think *you* were up the duff!'

'Oh, as if!' scoffed Kate, whose hand instinctively sought out her flat tummy to marvel at its tight, smooth, youthful feel. 'I haven't even had sex yet, since I got back—'

'Back? Back from where?' Portia pulled her chin into her neck in disbelief. 'Work this afternoon?'

'No, I mean,' Kate blushed, searching frantically for a way to backpedal out of this one. 'Um, that is to say, we, ah, we never seem to get the chance what with all the big nights Tom has and stress at work...'

'There you go again, sounding old before your time.' Portia sighed. 'You're only turning twenty-nine in two weeks, Kate – not eighty-nine! Now, where's the bloody remote?'

Kate shrugged her shoulders and studied the contents of her suitcase in an effort to look unfussed.

But she was fussed – really fussed.

What *was* wrong with her, she asked herself. If she was so keen to get at it with Tom, which she thought she was, why hadn't she? She'd been through it a million, trillion times in her head – Seamus and the kids would never know and she'd been dreaming about this opportunity for *years*. She had no doubt a big clock was ticking loudly somewhere, counting down the minutes and seconds until her time back in the past was up. And she couldn't bear it if her second chance in 1996 came to an abrupt end and she still hadn't managed to sleep with Tom.

'Not even that lazy sex, when you're still half-asleep and groggy and— Ah! Here it is! It's always the last... place... you look,' Portia said as she lay flat on the floor, coaxing the remote out from under the couch with a squash racket that had been lying around on the designer-distressed coffee table.

'What are you so keen to watch, anyway?' Kate gave a light laugh, relieved the subject was exiting her sexless waters and entering that great leveller, the wonderful world of TV.

'*Top of the Pops*, 'course,' Portia said, sitting herself down and plumping up the cushions behind her back nicely.

'Oh, yay!' Kate couldn't help herself exclaiming. 'Who's going to be on?'

'Dunno,' said Portia through a mouthful of Wotsits. 'I'll just see, then I'll get straight on with packing.'

Kate grabbed the pack of E-numbered madness from Portia and flumped down next to her.

Ooh, this was going to be good, she thought, enthusiastically stuffing her face with God-knows-what chemicals and toxins. She'd missed decent music so much – when the kids were small, she couldn't get kids' TV theme tunes out of her head – *Fireman Sam* and *Fifi and the Flowertots*, not to mention that jaunty Iggle Piggle number – but back in 2022 she had no idea what was in the charts, her knowledge of modern music confined to the Taylor Swift, K-Pop and Doja Cat she heard blaring out from behind Phoebe's bedroom door.

Still, she noted sadly, it seemed that with every passing year, another part of her once quite good voice and diverse musical repertoire disappeared and she sounded more and more like her own mother who was tone deaf – an utterly *atrocious* singer, made fun of by Kate and Steve incessantly. Sort of like Marge's sisters in *The Simpsons*.

Kate's timing was slightly off these days, too – she couldn't quite hit the right notes and – worst of all – she'd mumble the words in the trickier bits of songs she once knew so well and loved so much – usually seconds after turning up the car radio and proclaiming to the kids: 'I love this song! Played it a gazillion times! Know it better than I know myself!'

She would often count herself lucky that she was in the car at these moments and not facing the kids, so they could interpret her mumbling and sudden dips in volume as concentrating hard on driving as opposed to simply being rubbish at singing.

But, of course, the kids didn't notice or care either way. As they got older, it seemed to Kate that they just ignored her most of the time, as though she was an unseen fairy at the bottom of the garden who looked after everyone tirelessly and never expected any acknowledgement or – god forbid – thanks.

Kate wanted to spit the Wotsits out, they tasted so ridiculously plastic and manufactured. But she didn't want to draw any more attention to herself, so she handed the packet back to Portia and wiped her bright-orange-stained fingers on that week's *Radio Times*, a small stack of them sitting underneath the squash racket on the table where she and Portia were both resting their feet.

'Oh no!' she shrieked. 'It's not on tonight – they've switched it to Friday!'

Portia wheeled her torso around in shock.

'They can't do that – Thursday night's *Top Of* is an institution!'

'I seem to remember reading something about it in *Mad Fer It!*' Kate said. 'It's apparently a bid to catch

164

the going-out crowd before they go out, or there's less competition on Friday nights or something...'

Kate picked up the pile of *RT*s and began leafing through them, but Portia was speechless, still staring at Kate in shock.

'It's all right, Porsh, don't be too upset,' said Kate, sounding, just for a split second, as though she was soothing Declan after he'd scraped his knee or had a run-in with the school bully. 'It's not like they've cancelled it altogether. It'll just take some getting used to, that's all.'

'It's all right for you, Gran – you probably *want* to stay in and watch telly on Friday nights, rest your weary bones after the week from hell. It's one thing to love good telly – as we all do – but quite another to be so dull that you'd actually *prefer* to stay in and stare at a screen rather than go out and experience life. Isn't it? Kate? Kate!'

Now it was Kate's turn to be shocked. As she thumbed through the older copies of *The Radio Times*, she saw that the night she'd been transported back in time, the last episode of Series One of *This Life* had been on. So while she was out disgracing herself all over town, she could have been at home drooling over the lovely Jack Davenport.

'Oh, bollocks!' she mumbled.

'Is so! God, you're such an old biddy—'

'No, no,' said Kate, 'although yes, you're right, I probably am old before my time – in so many ways – but we missed the last episode of *This Life* last week. *That's* what I'm saying is bollocks.'

'Oh.' Portia calmed down. 'Don't know what I'm getting so het up about, Kate, sorry.'

'Maybe those pregnancy hormones are—'

'No, no, NO!' Portia covered her face with her hands in frustration. 'Leave it alone, will you?'

Kate bit her lip and extended her hand to Portia's shoulder. She didn't have to say anything, Portia knew this gesture said, *Sorry. I'll shut up now. Promise.*

'That show's crap, anyway,' Portia eventually said through her fingers.

'But you used to love it!'

'What do you mean, "used to"?'

'We got right into watching the trials and tribulations of a share house full of hard-living young lawyers...' Kate read out the *Radio Times*' description. 'And the guy who plays Miles is a bit on the tasty side, isn't he?'

'Not bad,' Portia slowly nodded her head in contemplation. 'I actually don't mind the guy who plays Egg, either, if we're being honest.'

'Which we are,' Kate pulled Portia in to her for a hug.

'Yes, we are. But I still prefer to actually leave the house once in a while and try to *live* this life – instead of watching other people's fictional versions of it...'

Kate thought back to her first night in 1996 the second time around and shuddered.

'Oh, do shut up,' was all Kate could think of to say. 'You've got the waxing done, now get those bikinis packed – you never know who you might meet in Ibiza, do you?'

At this, Portia fairly leaped off the couch to finish packing.

And now, here they were lining up to board the plane that would take them away from all this, give them time to talk and think and take long, soulful walks along warm, perfect beaches. And, Kate hoped, give her the chance to talk Portia out of what she knew would be the most disastrous decision of her life.

'I'll freeze my tits off out there – no way am I taking my jumper off, let alone actually getting in the water!' laughed Portia as she shivered, trying to flick her towel out and get it lying straight and in an orderly fashion on the wind-whipped sand.

Kate threw her head back and guffawed at the sight and sat down on the sand, her only concession to beach wear being that she'd rolled her combats up a bit. She'd taken great delight in seeing how her large loose-knit boat neck cornflower blue jumper hung casually yet sexily on her almost angular frame and when she hugged her knees to her chest, she nearly yelped at how easy it was with no rolls of flesh getting in the way.

'This'll brush the cobwebs away,' she said, squinting as some dried seaweed blew into her face and got tangled up in her hair. 'There's something so much more romantic about a beach in the cold, don't you think?'

'You'll have to speak up!' Portia yelled back. 'I can't hear you over the roar of the force ten hurricane!'

It *was* blowing a gale, Kate had to agree. Not exactly how she'd pictured Ibiza, that's for sure. Maybe global warming had already started to turn temperatures and tides upside down in 1996 – and, like most things from that decade of debauchery, she never noticed.

'I said, DON'T YOU THINK A BEACH IS MORE ROMANTIC IN WINTERY WEATHER? SO MUCH MORE DRAMATIC AND BROODY—'

'For FUCK'S SAKE, Kate – for the last time, I AM NOT BROODY!'

'What?'

'Eh?'

167

As Kate felt the first few drops of rain on her face, she cupped her hand around Portia's ear and shouted:

'Shall we go back to the hotel and watch the football? Have a hot toddy or two?'

'NOW YOU'RE TALKING MY LANGUAGE!' screeched Portia, stuffing her obstreperous towel into her beach bag and scowling as she threw her bottle of Reef Oil on top of it, as though it were her summer holiday accoutrements' fault the weather was so unsuitable for sunbathing.

The match had already started by the time they had got themselves organised at a warm table for two. It wasn't near the throng clustered around the bar loudly watching Scotland v England, so the girls could talk unhampered by football and the inevitable disappointment from lack of goals.

'I'm not really that into all this Euro 96 palaver, anyway,' Portia said, taking great gulps of her drink.

'Oh yeah?' Kate widened her eyes in disbelief. 'You looked like it was a matter of life and death, like your life depended on it last weekend when we were watching it at O'Flaherty's...'

'Well, it did, in a way.' Portia grinned. 'I mean, there was no way I was going to pull that football hooligan if I didn't pretend to be obsessed by the game—'

'Match,' Kate corrected her.

'Whatever. I just feel like ever since Simon dumped me and I've been lumbered with *this*,' she pointed to her tummy, 'I need to sort myself out. And fast.'

'Well, you do.' Kate saw her chance and pounced. 'But you need to be sensible about this. Grown up.'

'Ha!' Portia spluttered, spitting a wee dram of whisky out onto her chest. 'Like you, you mean? Miss Boring

168

1996? I'm surprised you didn't know the weather here was going to be so crap – I mean, I bet you listen to the shipping forecast all the time, for a little excitement, hmmm?'

'Give me a break, Porsh.' Kate sipped her Diet Coke, a tad wounded. 'All that guff about me being old is starting to get a little bit... um... old, now. And anyway, there's really no need to be so nasty. I'm only trying to help.'

The good time in Ibiza Kate had looked forward to so much was turning out to be as much fun as a wet weekend in Whitstable. Without the glitz and glamour.

Kate knew that Portia was capable of being a tad on the tetchy side at the best of times. But woe betide (*woe betide? She really was talking like an OAP!*) anyone who tried to talk to her rationally when she was pregnant – because then she was, apparently, a veritable tempest. Just like the storm brewing outside.

Silence descended upon their table. But at the bar, the cheers and groans of nearly goals and penalties being wrongly awarded carried on apace.

Kate and Portia craned their necks to see what was going on for a few moments and then lapsed back into easy conversation.

'I'm sorry,' Kate offered her apologies first, figuring she might as well, considering she was older, wiser and, obviously a million times more boring.

'Ach,' said Portia, downing her third or fourth whisky and sounding more and more Scottish as a result. 'Never ye mind, lassie, never ye mind.'

Portia's (pretty bad, actually) accent elicited some dirty looks from the men at the bar, but they were soon distracted by great whooping and hollering from the rest of the crowd.

The pair got up and joined the revellers at the bar and were duly enthusiastically informed of what had just happened. One young gun breathlessly told Kate and Portia – who were both genuinely interested and excited by now – that McManaman had passed the ball to Neville who then made an excellent cross to Shearer who, in turn, headed the ball into the net – and pushed England into the lead.

'I knew that McManaman-amanaman was a man… amanaman… one to watch,' Portia swayed, slurring ever-so-slightly.

It was fifty-two minutes into the match. Soon after, Scotland nearly equalised, but the England goalie with the unfortunate surname Kate couldn't help commenting on (because, come on, who could resist taking the piss out of someone called Seaman?) deflected the ball.

The tension was mounting, the taste of victory palpable – and being a part of it, as the curtain rain lashed the hotel's floor-to-ceiling windows, was the best fun Kate had had since… well, since the last time she'd watched these Euro 96 matches the first time round, really.

'Ooh, don't think much of the colour,' Portia whispered loudly to Kate when Paul Gascoigne's shock of lurid blond hair filled the TV screen.

'Brassy, yeah,' Kate nodded. 'He looks like a fat, ugly Yazz. Remember her? From the Eighties? 'The Only Way Is Up'?'

Kate tried to jog her friend's memory with the wrong words accompanying her out of time, out-of-tune version of the old hit.

'Can't say it sounds familiar,' Portia laughed. 'You sure it was the 1980s and not the 1880s? You are a little on the ancient side, remember.'

'Cheeky moo,' Kate muttered and drained her drink, muscling through the scrum of punters standing broad-shoulder-to-broad-shoulder at the bar.

'Are you blind, ref?' the crowd chorused as a penalty was awarded to the Scots.

Seaman turned the nearly goal into a near-miss and then, with eleven minutes to go, Gazza (he of the comedy barnet), kicked the ball, in a rather astonishing, brilliantly executed volley, into the other net.

The 'dentist's chair' celebrations followed, whereby his teammates sprayed water into a prone Gazza's open mouth, mirroring a boozy drinking game the England team had been busted playing a few weeks before. Or so the young football fan hugging Portia and squeezing her tight in his delight informed them.

'Woo-HOO!' Kate joined in as she made her way back to Portia, remarkably not spilling a drop from the four short glasses. 'It's looking good for us now—'

'Don't say that!' Portia and her man said in unison. 'You'll jinx it!'

But she didn't – England practically *romped* home, winning convincingly; 2–nil.

The roar when the whistle blew at full-time was so loud, Kate covered her ears as she jumped up and down with the rest of the gang.

'Loud enough for ya?' Portia bent away from the foot-ball fan's embrace and shouted in Kate's ear.

'All right, all right!' Kate shouted back. 'No need to yell! I'm not deaf, yet, you know. And I do still have all my own teeth!'

But Portia didn't even crack a smile at this. In fact, she suddenly went grey and looked like she was going to hurl.

'I'm not feeling so great, Kate, think I'll… just sit down over there for a minute.'

Portia extricated herself from the over-zealous fan with the incredible wandering hands and staggered to the table they'd been sitting at before, near the window.

Kate followed and plonked herself down in the wicker chair next to Portia's and started the spiel she had so diligently prepared earlier, on the plane the day before.

'I know it doesn't fit into your life right now, no judgement, no judgement at all – but you might want kids later on. And I'm not saying don't *have* the abortion – of course it's a woman's right to choose and you won't believe what's happening in the US at the moment, all I'm saying is just have it somewhere reputable. Just because you don't want it on your medical record with the NHS… Because if you go ahead with… Oh god, I might as well tell you the truth, Porsh.' Kate took a deep breath, about to spill the beans.

Here goes, she thought to herself. The moment when her friend would have no choice but to declare her insane and section her.

'You'll probably think I'm mad, but… Well, the fact is, Porsh, that I'm here from the future – 2022 to be exact – and having lived through all of this before, I know that the backyard, botched abortion you're about to have will render you completely infertile and totally distraught.'

Portia glanced at Kate, her face all screwed up in pain, her complexion ghostly.

'I know, I know! It sounds crazy, but—'

Portia let out a distinctly primal, blood-curdling scream and, clutching her stomach, slumped off her chair onto the floor, curling up in the foetal position and bawling her eyes out.

'Portia!' squealed Kate, darting down to the floor to tend to her best mate. 'Porsh? Can you hear me?'

But all Portia could do was repeatedly stretch her legs out and then bring them back up to her chest quickly, writhing about in excruciating pain.

'Help me,' Portia sobbed weakly, reaching out a hand for Kate.

'AMBULANCE!' Kate's voice went all deep and gravelly and authoritative. Like when she was scolding Rafferty. 'We need an ambulance here NOW!'

Kate placed Portia's head gently on her lap and stroked her hair, trying hard not to look at the bright-red blood pooling on the carpet underneath Portia's backside.

18

'You don't half come out with some tosh sometimes,' Portia said to Kate as she propped herself up in her bed back at home in West Hampstead.

'What was all that "I come to you from the future" crap you were spouting in Ibiza? And do stop fussing, really. I'm fine.'

'Well, just to be sure, take it easy for a few days,' Kate replied, ignoring Portia's remark and smoothing down the Persil-fresh, deep-purple duvet cover she'd just put on. She'd whipped off the all-white linen that had been there only minutes before – that, it seemed to Kate, was just begging for stain-related disaster.

'You're going to make someone a great wife someday,' said Portia softly, 'and when you have kids, they'll be the luckiest little sods alive.'

'You reckon?' Kate scoffed, sitting on the edge of the bed like it was a horse and she was sitting side-saddle. 'Try telling them that!'

Portia looked downcast and smiled unconvincingly.

Kate hadn't seen Portia's miscarriage coming – it wasn't what had happened the first time around, after all – and she felt almost responsible, as if she should have known, been able to forewarn and protect her friend.

Portia rolled her eyes as she studied the bottom corner of her duvet.

'Do you want to talk about it?' Kate asked.

'Not really,' Portia mumbled.

'Oh, come on, Porshie, that's not like you – you always say there's no cure like the talking cure.'

'Do I?' Portia looked up in surprise.

'Yeah!' Kate's eyes scudded away from Portia's, aware she'd wandered into dodgy future time travel waters again. 'I'm sure you do. All the time! Anyway, moving right along...'

Kate coughed and stood up.

'More tea?'

'No thanks, Mum,' Portia smiled. 'I might just see if I can have a little snooze-ette, if you don't mind. You go to work, go on! I'll still be here when you get home. I'm going nowhere... *fast!*'

But Kate couldn't drag herself away. She remembered how knocked about she'd been by the miscarriage she'd suffered six months before she fell pregnant with Phoebe and how alone and unbearably sad it had made her feel. And even though Portia was a totally different kettle of fish, she knew that somewhere, buried deep beneath that tough, unfazed exterior, Portia now felt exactly the same way.

'So, how are you? I mean, really. In yourself,' Kate said in what she hoped was the tone of voice a calm, professional psychologist might use.

'Knackered,' came Portia's reply, as she closed her eyes, rolling onto her side, away from Kate. 'So bugger off!'

Kate was undeterred by Portia's obvious shut-down signals.

'I know when I had my—' She cut herself off and scanned the bedroom for inspiration, something to help her rephrase what she was trying to say. 'In the stuff I've read about miscarriage – women's mag stuff and the odd newspaper article, it seems that no one really wants to talk about it much and, as a result, the emotional trauma continues and escalates, untreated, only to come out in other self-damaging ways.'

An exaggerated, obviously fake snore rattled the walls and rippled the sheets where Portia lay.

'Oh, come on!' Kate playfully slapped Portia's hand.

Portia laughed and rolled onto her back, pushing herself up with her hands, making Kate jump to attention and rearrange the pillows behind her against the wall.

'I'm fine, really,' Portia insisted.

'Really?' Kate didn't buy it.

'I'm more upset about Simon dumping me than losing the baby, if you really want to know.'

Kate did really want to know, she wanted the truth – desperately. But this wasn't anywhere near what she wanted to hear and she couldn't quite believe her ears. It was as though Portia's brutal honesty sharply and swiftly offended Kate's moral code, made a mockery of all she held dear. And she couldn't let it lie.

'I'm not sure I—' Kate began.

'It's quite simple, really,' said Portia, fixing her dark, brooding (though not, obviously, *broody*) eyes on her best friend, 'I'm too young for kids – I don't want them. Not yet. Maybe never. I don't know. Same as you, really – or the same as you *used* to be, at any rate. I don't know why you're having such a hard time with this all of a sudden. Anyone would think you were married and middle-aged and *you'd* had the miscarriage or something.'

Portia inspected her fingernails and decided that chewing the side of her thumb was a pretty good option at this point.

'I just know you,' Kate said softly, tilting her head to the side for added effect, 'and you're not that shallow – not as unaffected by life as you try to make out sometimes.'

'Oh yes I am!' Portia slapped her palms down on the duvet cover. 'I'm deeply shallow, actually, I'll have you know. And I resent any insinuation to the contrary!'

Kate grinned. Somehow in the melee of the past few days, she'd seemed to have forgotten that, at twenty-eight, the pair of them were really only interested in men, shagging, going out, having fun and trying to hold down a decent-enough job that would pay for all of the above (except the sex, neither of them had ever had to pay for that). It was day-to-day living, lurching from one ill-fated affair to the next, recovering unfairly fast from hangovers and giving scant thought to the future and nary a backward glance to the past, because the present was, quite frankly, such a blast.

How could she have, Kate mused to herself? She'd only been dreaming about these comparatively carefree days for most of her life as a mother – how could she so quickly have dismissed her and Portia's favourite pastimes as the folly of youth and somehow invalid? Not real? Unimportant and silly? How had she become so smug and patronising and judgemental? So *old*.

'Kids,' she muttered, answering her own question.

'Oh god – what now?' Portia groaned.

'Ha! I mean, kids, eh? Who needs 'em, right?'

Kate saw a flash of relief in Portia's eyes.

'Thank god you're back.' She wiped some imaginary sweat off her brow. 'That motherly stuff you were doing was really starting to freak me out!'

'Yeah, me too,' Kate chortled. 'Right. So. You stay there, get better, whatever, and I'll, um, leave you to it.'

As if they'd done it a thousand times before and their moves had been honed, carefully choreographed over the years, Kate got off the bed and Portia picked up a dog-eared copy of *Men Are From Mars, Women Are From Venus* from her bedside table.

Kate busied herself about their flat, doing things she knew she was good at, but didn't do too much of in 2022 – taking clothes off the radiators and clothes horses, folding them, putting them away neatly in their own little drawers dedicated to tops or knickers or trousers.

She heard her grandmother's voice in her head saying, 'A place for everything and everything in its place,' and felt a sudden rush of love for her family and an almost overwhelming desire to get back to them.

What were they doing without her, she wondered. The house must be a right tip by now – shit everywhere, greasy washing-up left lying in a sink full of cold, sud-less, grey water... Were they wondering where she'd got to? Had they even noticed she wasn't there? Maybe they were frozen in time and their lives were all on hold, in suspended animation until she got her own little adventure out of the way and came home.

'Home,' Kate said out loud.

When she did get back, she continued asking herself, would she simply land in the fuggy kitchen and pick up where she'd left off? Would everyone just carry on as if nothing had happened? Would the kids be fighting, the porridge burning, Seamus getting more emotionally distant, she, herself, getting more and more frustrated when she thought of all those ambitions going unfulfilled?

And all the while her Marigolds perishing alongside her spirit?

She shook the thought out of her head and instead focused on her (sometime) ability to make a mess tidy, her way with turning chaos into order. Or if not exactly *order*, as such, then a weeny bit *less* mad.

She thought of how she secretly quite liked it when the kids were sick back in the 2020s – she loved giving her soothing, comforting bedside manner a good workout. She never thought she would, being a driven career girl and all, but she really enjoyed helping to make other people feel better, too.

In fact, having given up the idea of ever returning to full-time paid work (at least until the kids had left home), she might say she even *preferred* looking after the kids to working for The Man, dancing to the beat of someone else's drum for a wage. Because as far as job satisfaction goes, she thought, being a full-time mum sure took some beating.

Or, she smiled to herself, being a full-time mum, you sure took a beating.

Kate sighed as she emptied the dishwasher. Whichever way she looked at it now, she couldn't help but come to the conclusion that her life as a wife and mother wasn't so bad, after all.

Of course little improvements could be made to her life in 2022. *Of course* certain, insignificant things that didn't really matter could be altered just a smidge and life as a whole would be more fluid, more relaxed, more enjoyable.

Of fucking course nothing was perfect.

Like Seamus, for example. If only he could be more confident in himself, see how smart and good-looking he really was, maybe then he would realise his dreams and their lives together would be so much more... passionate and exciting and fulfilling.

And the kids. Don't get me wrong, she told herself, they are great, in their own little ways. But it would be nice, sometimes, every now and again, if they didn't fight and they did their homework and cleaned their rooms without being nagged to death about it – and still not doing it. Actually, she sniffed, forget all of that, if they could just show her a bit more respect every now and then, she'd be much happier. And if she had her own PR and advertising agency as well...

'Haven't you got your appraisal today?' Portia bellowed. 'Shouldn't you be pissing off to work?'

Oh god. Kate had forgotten all about that!

Her appraisal. Where she would be hauled over the coals for a) the enormous number of days she'd called in sick (hungover) so far this year and b) never quite reaching the impossibly high goals and targets Archie would always set for her.

The appraisal. Where she would be told she had to go on various grandmother-sucking-eggs training courses to 'up her capacity' as a PR guru.

Or, if she reframed her trauma, as 2022 Portia was always telling her to do, this could be her chance to have *her* say and suggest ways of improving the company's performance for *her* benefit and all the other women working there.

They were so into spin at every possible turn, PGT&B, that even a sacking was called a 'voluntarily exit, swift-style' (if, indeed, it was ever mentioned at all after the fact) and when someone didn't get a promotion or a pay rise (usually the women), it was referred to as 'consolidation and stabilisation of the status quo' – which, of course, was crucial to the smooth running of the operation. And crucial for ensuring that management always got *their* pay rises and bonuses, too. The patriarchy in plain sight.

Kate, like every other minion in the world – *senior* minion, maybe, but minion nonetheless – *dreaded* their appraisal.

Or, at least, she *used* to.

Today, though, she couldn't wait to get her hands on Archie's Fred Perry lapels and tell him exactly what she thought about how the company – and, in particular, her department – was run.

She practically tripped over herself when she broke into a skip in order to get to the bathroom and her make-up bag fast.

Kate sang 'Wonderwall' slightly out of time in her best nasal, Manchester drawl, as she gussied herself up (which, on the cusp of twenty-nine years old, merely meant a few dabs of some wet/dry foundation, a couple of brushes of mascara and a quick slick of lippie (as opposed to being on the cusp of fifty-five, which meant she was seriously considering Botox, fillers and lipo).

The phone rang just as she was on her way out, and once she'd squeezed her arms into her short, tight, faded denim jacket, she picked up the receiver.

'Hey, baby,' came Tom's undeniably sexy voice, 'it's your dream man here…'

'Hi, hi, hi, Tom,' she said, panting a bit, 'I'm just going out the door—'

'Relax, babe – chill,' he said. 'I know I make you breathless… and… and that's why I'm calling, actually.'

'Is it?'

'Yeah. Call off the dogs, the search is over – I've found us the perfect love nest. In Notting Hill. And as soon as you think Porsh can cope without you, you can move on in!'

'Oh, Tom,' Kate said, hoping that Tom didn't pick up on the slightly scared quaver, the trepidatious tone of her voice. 'That's brilliant news! But I'll see you at work – I've got to run, now – got my appraisal in an hour!'

19

'I'll pour,' Kate said, taking charge of the sturdy silver tea pot and two china cups on saucers that were sitting in the middle of Archie's desk. 'Milk in first or last?'

'Last,' Archie said slowly. 'Exactly the same as all right-thinking Englishmen have it.'

He watched her suspiciously as she carefully dropped two sugar cubes into his cup with the mini silver tongs, gave it a quick stir and in one fluid movement, tapped the teaspoon lightly on the rim of the cup, placed said spoon on the saucer and leaned over Archie's desk to place the whole lot in front of him.

'Thank you,' he said, bringing his huge swivel chair closer to the desk. 'I did ask for some Hob Nobs, but they don't seem to have materialised...'

'Oh, that's OK,' Kate said, trying to hide the fact that she was bitterly disappointed by this egregious oversight. She swallowed as quietly as she could, even though her mouth had been watering since she'd spied the biscuit tin.

'I... ah...' Archie faltered.

'That's easy for you to say.' Kate grinned.

'Um, well, actually,' Archie did his best to look deadly serious and carry on. 'I'm not sure how to go about this, Kate. We've been close friends as well as colleagues for quite some time, now...'

Oh god. Like a bolt out of the blue. This is it. He's firing me! Gird your loins, girl, here it comes…

'…but I still haven't got the faintest idea why you're behaving like such… such an old lady, lately.'

'What?' Kate nearly spat out her tea. 'What do you mean, "old lady"?'

'Well, no offence, obviously, but playing mum, pouring the tea, taking time off to tend to your flatmate, seemingly at odds with all of us here – I mean, your ideas are a bit, to put it bluntly, *crap*, lately. And you seem to have forgotten that you're in PR – it's your *job* to party with the best of them – not come over all sensible and opt for Radio 4 and an early night.'

Kate was gobsmacked. Her mouth had fallen open at the start of Archie's little rant and had remained quite plainly agog until its end.

'I… uh…' Now it was Kate's turn to stumble over her words.

'I don't mean to be rude and I'm sure we can talk openly with each other, but I believe it's professionally – and probably morally, too – incumbent on me to bring to your attention exactly how… how…'

Kate arched her eyebrows and willed him on.

'…how unutterably *boring* you've become.'

'Well!' Kate managed, after fighting for a few seconds to get her lips out of the 'agape' position in an effort to form some words. 'I never!'

Archie rolled his eyes to the ceiling.

'See what I mean?' he sounded exasperated. 'You talk like me fookin' granny!'

At this, Kate took a little bit of umbrage. And a speedy good look at herself.

She had been holding her saucer in her lap with one hand, and was hovering her cup over the saucer in her other hand. Her legs were crossed neatly at the ankle and tucked under her chair, to the right. Her back was straight and, at that very moment, she imagined herself looking like the queen, striking a pose favoured by those well over fifty. In 1950. In fact, she thought, the only things missing were a twin set, a pillbox hat and some kid gloves.

She put her tea on Archie's desk, making sure to slosh some into the saucer and slouched down into the back of the chair. She shook her Jennifer Aniston hairdo and gave a small cough.

'Is this my appraisal or are you just having a pop at me as some kind of a warm-up?' she said, her chin jutting out, helping her assume an air of indignation. 'Is this your major criticism of me?'

Archie nodded and smiled with relief.

'Yes, it's your appraisal, yes, it's my main criticism and—'

'Life can't always be one big, long episode of *Men Behaving Badly*, you know, Archie,' Kate said, plonking one ankle onto her opposite knee and sitting in a decidedly male manner.

Regardless of her newly adopted relaxed way of sitting, though, she still sounded a bit school marmy. A fact that hadn't escaped Archie's ears.

'Just listen to yourself, Kate!' he squawked. 'Since when did you get to be so bloody sensible? Honestly, you're like Julie Sodding Andrews in khaki combats!'

Kate glanced at her thin thighs and ludicrous white plastic high-heeled Spice Girls sneakers and tutted.

She allowed her thoughts to go off on a tangent at this point, wishing she had just one ounce of the poise, the warmth and the great fun ideas that Julie seemed to have for all those kids in *The Sound of Music* – and there were seven of them!

Kate felt herself frown when this happy, serene, contented snapshot of caring womanhood and doting children on lush green hills was replaced by her shouting at her kids, crying and terrified in a damp, dull, peeling-lino-floored kitchen. She flinched as she pictured serpents snaking their way through her wild hair and when she felt the crushing weight of that all-too-familiar clenched teeth tension hanging heavily over their home like a big black cloud. She shook her head and swore to herself that when she got back to 2022 – *if* she ever got back to 2022 – she would channel her inner Julie daily and banish her outer Medusa for ever.

Kate confidently placed both feet flat on the floor, sat up and, like every granny who'd ever gone before her, said, 'Good manners cost nothing, Archie. And if being sensible and boring means I'm nice to everyone and take the time to get to know everyone from the receptionist to the new IT guy—'

'Urgh.' Archie looked away, disgusted. 'I was wondering when we'd get to him. Honestly, Katie, I don't know what you see in him.'

Kate stopped short and bent her head so far to the right, her ear almost touched her shoulder.

'What are you talking about?'

'I've seen the way you look at him, Kate. That dweeby guy from the basement who can't put one foot in front of the other without tripping over filing cabinets and leaving carnage in his wake, demolishing everything in his path.'

'You mean Shay… I mean Seamus? I suppose he can be a bit clumsy…' Kate said, surprisingly fondly. 'But his heart's in the right place. And if you weren't so quick to judge, you'd find out he's a pretty nice bloke, too.'

'I don't care about him, whatever-his-name-is—'

'Seamus.' Kate helped him out.

'I *said* I don't care!' Archie's bottom lifted a centimetre or two out of his chair, such was the force of his declaration.

'All right, all right,' said Kate, patting down the air in front of her with her palms, trying to cool him out a bit.

God, she thought. What's with everyone at the moment? Why is everybody acting so strangely? George, Jenny and Steve (who was still MIA) had all been weird, Portia hadn't wanted to bang on about her feelings ad infinitum, Tom actually seeming quite sweet and homemaker-y – or at least not being a *complete* twat (say, eighty to eighty-five per cent, so far) – and even Archie was acting out of character. What on earth was going on?

It was all so odd. Could it possibly be that her little nostalgia problem – if she could call it a *problem*, as such – was to blame? Could it be the fault of those rose-coloured glasses she was so keen on wearing?

Because no one was exactly how she remembered them, let's face it – not even her own good self. And now it was making her feel uneasy. At least in her mind's eye she knew where she stood – the cast of thousands in her past life were one-dimensional and their character traits set in stone.

But here, in reality – if, indeed, that's where she was – things were quite different.

Perhaps her ageing, wearying memory had let her down. She seemed to have forgotten long ago that that most people have several sides to them and aren't always kind or funny or selfish, but more likely a mish-mash of good, bad *and* ugly. Ad without social media documenting and surveiling our every move, it wasn't so easy.

'Earth to Kate? Come in, Kate!' Archie was looking a little worried now.

'Oh, sorry, Archie, I—'

'I don't get it,' he said, slumping back on his chair. 'You have all these early nights, never get caught up in the fun of a big session, never let the partying get the better of you – and yet you look shattered. Is something bothering you? Are you losing sleep or something?'

'Oh no – it's wonderful.' Kate stretched out dreamily, temporarily forgetting herself. 'You have no idea – I've got the double bed to myself, the kids aren't waking me up several times a night, I'm not getting up to wee every two hours – I don't think I've slept this well for, god, at least ten years!'

'The *kids*? You mean Portia and Steve?'

'Er, no… yes, yes!' She backtracked over her own foot and yanked it out of her mouth. 'Always playing loud music and playing drinking games into the wee small hours in the front room—'

'Which is exactly what you should be doing, too! Be honest with me – why aren't you out, making merry with clients more often? We're losing business here!'

Kate considered being truthful with Archie for a nano-second. And then dismissed the idea as preposterous just as quickly. If he only knew what secret she was harbouring, he'd have her carted away by the men in white coats in a flash, for sure.

How could she tell him that she'd travelled back in time and even though she looked like the vivacious, bubbly twenty-eight-year-old fun-loving girl he knew so well, she was actually a knackered, bad-tempered fifty-four-year-old mother of two who even *she* didn't want to know most of the time?

How could she say to him that, sure, her work may be a little on the lacklustre side at the moment, but, on the bright side, at least she was getting all that delicious, much-needed, unbroken sleep?

She couldn't, that's how. She was just going to have to come up with something good. Something believable. Something that Archie would think a twenty-eight-year-old girl like her would be rocked to her very foundations by. A family problem? 'That time of the month' troubles? A hangnail?

As soon as she began racking her brains, searching for a plausible answer to his question, Archie's office door burst open.

'Roll up, roll up!' said Tom in his best circus ring-master's voice, 'Step right this way!'

There he stood, looking rather cute, legs apart, his tight white canvas jeans hugging his muscular thighs nicely and his white cheese-cloth billowy shirt bestowing upon him a decidedly Mr Darcy impression.

Archie looked at Kate and nodded slowly, a smile of sudden realisation and simultaneously satisfaction spreading across his face as if to say: 'A-ha! – it's Tom. *He's* the problem! Can't be easy going out with the Leader of the Lads, I guess.'

'Is it hot in here?' Kate said, fanning herself with her right hand.

'No,' sneered Archie, 'you're probably just having a hot flush.'

Archie looked admiringly back to Tom and said, 'So go on, Tom – what's your latest caper all about, then?'

'We're throwing a party to welcome Medea, our hottest, coolest new columnist to *Lashed*. Dominic Hurtz'll be there – it's in honour of all *enfants terrible* at his fab new gaff in Soho, Quod Libet.'

Silence.

'That's "whatever" in Latin, you bellends!'

What a show-off!

'Thought it'd get us some good publicity, you know? Thought we'd bring the masses to a bit of culture. Know what I mean?'

Now it was Kate's turn to sneer.

'Ooh, no. All those poor cows suspended in formaldehyde—'

'Sounds like some of my ex-girlfriends,' Tom guffawed. 'Sorry, sorry. Kate, I will not take no for an answer – you are coming to this gig. With me. NOW.'

'She likes her men to be forceful,' said Archie, in a strangely sullen manner, Kate thought.

Yes, it was definitely sullen. And sarky. Archie was acting like a sulky teenager and it didn't suit him.

An almighty crash broke Kate's reverie and all three heads turned to Tamsin's desk in the open-plan office.

'I said re-boot it, not put the boot in!' cried Seamus from somewhere under the debris of fallen papers and computer equipment.

Tamsin stood there, eyes huge, her hands up to her mouth, static with shock that she could have killed half of PGT&B's IT Department with just one swift kick from her stiletto-shod foot.

Kate looked at Archie who shook his head and said, 'Typical.'

Her attention was diverted, then, to what appeared to be a cagoule flying past the windows of Archie's office.

'Hang on, mate, I'll get you out! Just don't move, OK?' said the racing cagoule.

'Who's that?' Tom asked no one in particular.

'I'm not sure, but I think it's Kevin. The IT department's newest – and nerdiest – recruit,' said Archie, his top lip curling so hard it was fairly quivering with contempt.

'Ah, they're always called Kevin, aren't they?' chortled Tom. 'I mean, there's always one nerk in every group of guys who's called Kevin, isn't there? Drummers in bands, usually. It's the classic dork's name.'

'Well, I'm in – well up for a night out,' said Archie. 'What's it gonna be, Kate?'

Kate bit her lip.

There was that mum-in-charge side to her which made her straighten up, push her shoulders back and want to say, 'Oh, grow up, Archie – I've got a stack of washing to get through and there's no way I'll cope tomorrow with all you demanding kids on three hours sleep!'

Equally, however, there was the other side to her, that live for today, youthfully exuberant, slim, vital part that wanted to say 'Way-hey – let's go!'

'Not that you've got any choice – you're the head of PR for fook's sake!' Archie said.

But what about that deep, satisfying sleep and those fabulous feature-length dreams? Could she sacrifice eight to ten solid hours in picturesque Noddington for a potentially 'fun' night out? When her idea of the best, most fantastic fun night possible was one of end-on, hard-core, full-on uninterrupted snoozing?

'But it's so nice just to sleep,' she said, her voice taking on a peculiar timbre, a deep growl almost, as she said the word 'sleep'.

She struggled, grappling with her notions of a good time and wrestling with her hopelessly conflicted split personality for, ooh, about four seconds, before Archie made it clear he'd had enough of her dilly-dallying.

'Come on!' He grabbed her elbow. 'You can sleep when you're dead.'

'All right,' she acquiesced, thinking she might as well make the most of looking young, if not feeling it – and prove to Archie, in the process, that she still had what it took to be tops in the PR world.

'That's my girl.' Tom put his arm protectively around her shoulder and the three of them wandered off, doing the Monkees' overlapping knees walk in the direction of The Lift.

So here she was, on the verge of something beyond exciting: a night on the tiles in a premier restaurant, the chance to quaff good wine (in moderation in Kate's case) and the once (or twice, in Kate's case) in a lifetime opportunity to chat to some potentially interesting celebrities. She should be thrilled. Tamsin would have been. *She* wouldn't have been able to wipe the loopy grin off her face. But instead, as they waited for The Lift in silence, Kate's smile quickly faded to be replaced by a grimace.

She felt that gnawing, empty feeling in her stomach again and stroked her flat belly as if trying to rub it out.

'We'll get something to eat there, babes,' said Tom, noticing her slightly pained expression and stomach touching.

'No, I'm not hungry,' said Kate, furrowing her brow. 'Hang on a sec – I'll be right back.'

Tom and Archie watched as Kate disappeared down the hallway, past reception and ran up to Kevin and a dishevelled Seamus.

Panting – because even though she looked trim, she was still a total stranger to a healthy diet and fitness regimen – she said, 'Seamus! Help!'

Seamus, who was trying his best to disentangle himself from a bird's nest of wires and cables that had virtually wrapped him up like a mummy, glanced up. He did a classic double-take when he saw the look of consternation on Kate's face and tried to wriggle free of his cable cocoon. But it was useless – resistance was futile.

'Stop jiggling about,' laughed Kevin, 'you're only making it tighter!'

Tamsin giggled and even Kate wanted to chuckle – he did look ridiculous like that – how did he get himself into such ludicrous scrapes?

'Um,' mumbled Seamus when he noticed everyone in the office laughing at him. 'I'm a bit tied up at the moment. Would you like to make an appointment and I can speak with you later?'

Kate gently pushed Kevin out of the way and wrapped her arm around Seamus' back. She urged him to move forward and slowly shuffled him away from their colleagues' pricked up ears.

'You have GOT to help me get back home… I mean, get me some info for my new mag,' Kate whispered to Seamus out of the side of her mouth.

Seamus jumped like a kangaroo (though not quite as effectively or gracefully) by her side, trying to keep up with her.

'Are you bibbling about time travel again?' he managed to say, even though the wires were getting quite tight around his chest and he was hopping about like a giant mouse stuck in a lasso.

'Yes,' Kate looked over her shoulder and beamed at Tamsin and Kevin, who were standing gormlessly watching Hop-A-Long Seamus make a total tit out of himself. Again.

'I've done some research for you already,' said Seamus, getting breathless. 'And I think I know how it works. It definitely is possible—'

'I know!' squeaked Kate. 'So... shall we meet somewhere? So you can tell me all about it and I can get my pitch straight, promise the great gift of time travel for one lucky reader on our cover every month?'

'Yeah, OK,' said Seamus, a tad wheezily. 'But what about your side of the bargain? When are you going to help me out with clothes? And tell me how to talk to women?'

Kate had forgotten all about that.

'Let's combine the two. We'll go shopping next Saturday. How about that?'

'Next Saturday?' he said, scanning the inside of his eyelids as if that's where he'd stuck his daily planner. 'The twenty-second?'

'Yep,' said Kate, glancing at Tom and Archie who were standing at The Lift craning their necks to see what she was up to.

'It's a date!' said Seamus, brightening up. 'Of sorts... um... we'll need to get an early start, though – it's Spain v England in the afternoon. Kick-off's at three.'

'It's a deal,' said Kate, grabbing some scissors from a nearby desk and snipping Seamus out of his flexy prison and on towards freedom. She darted away from his side and cantered, triumphant, back to The Lift.

'Super gran,' grinned Archie as suddenly The Lift pinged, the doors opened and all three of them nearly snapped their necks in their haste to get into it.

20

Looking around the restaurant, Kate couldn't help but feel completely out of place.

All the other women there, as far as she could see, were outrageously beautiful, statuesque models, tomboy pop stars and/or painfully, achingly cool, fascinating artists.

And all the men completely ignored her. Now this, as a dishevelled woman in her fifties, she was used to. But surely it hadn't been like this when she was twenty-eight the first time around.

It was the kind of do she'd been dreaming about being invited to ever since she left the media whirl way back when – the kind of thing she was used to and thought nothing of once upon a time. But now, in a cruel twist of irony, she found herself wishing she was at home.

I mean, she said to herself, it's all well and good looking fabulous and having sparkling, witty conversations with your intellectual equals, but what's wrong with teaching a toddler to talk? Sure, you babble on endlessly about fire engines and *Dora the Explorer*, granted – but is there anything inherently *bad* about that? *Au contraire*, she said to herself in her best French accent, it's a far, far better thing to do than ponce about getting pissed on expensive bubbly and braying to anyone who'll listen about how wonderful you are, that's for sure.

Yep, youth is definitely wasted on the young, she snorted into her mini bottle of Moët, blowing extra bubbles with the straw.

She never thought it possible, but as she absent-mindedly stroked her tummy, she found herself missing not only the kids and home, but also the flabby, wobbly bits of her old body, too. Because at least you knew where you were with a stomach you had to tuck into your knickers and cellulite that no longer surprised you.

And the pressure on these youngsters! Not only did they have to *look* great all the time, flaunting their flawless skin and tight flesh, but they had to constantly *act* perky, too. What, in all honesty, could possibly be *wrong* with slobbing out in front of the telly in hideously unflattering, threadbare-at-the-thighs leggings?

Kate smiled at the thought and felt a deep yearning, a longing for the sense of freedom, comfort and joy that only an oversized fleece can give.

But it was more than that – more than simply the sartorial expression of contentment that she missed – it was the easy relaxing of tension: the tension to perform like a monkey, to be cute and smart and popular, all the while keeping your tum in trim and being a contender for Rear of the Year contests.

That was it, Kate thought – that was what she'd been searching for back in 1996 – that elusive feeling you get when you know you're happy and you don't have to try so hard any more. The feeling you get when you're *home*.

No wonder she hadn't felt it yet – she was as far away from home as it was possible to be, at Quod Libet with all the bright young things of the day. And to top it all off, all she could think about was ironing and burnt porridge and an oven that was a million light years away from cleaning itself.

She felt like a mousey housewife at her ebullient husband's work do; a perplexed, childless adult at a kid's party – a veritable fish out of water.

She scanned the room and saw Tom, who'd pretty much deserted her the minute they'd arrived. She watched him (in between toilet trips so frequent, Kate almost started to worry for his prostate), as he busied himself schmoozing his way around the room, eventually settling on a slightly less-than-delighted looking Dominic Hurtz.

Tom was talking ten to the dozen and laughing uproariously at yet another of his own jokes. Dominic held his glass aloft in the direction of the waiters as if to say: 'More here, please. QUICK!'

Kate felt dreadfully alone.

She marched purposefully, pretending she was confident, to the bar and tried to look unfazed, as though she came to these sorts of shindigs all the time and found them, quite frankly, to be a bit of a *bore*.

Her heart leaped when she spotted Archie near the windows. She was almost about to join him when she clocked that he was flanked by two Amazonian models on either side.

Kate thought better of it and turned round to face the barman.

'Another one of these, please,' she said to him and he nodded to a tray further down the end of the bar.

Of course, you silly moo! You don't have to order or pay for drinks at events like this!

Embarrassed by her gaffe – even though no one had noticed – she sheepishly wandered towards the tray.

She picked up a mini bottle of Moët, adjusted the straw, took a long sip and meandered over to Tom, who was now standing near the gents with his arm around Lee Callahan. She said her hellos mere seconds before Medea arrived.

'Ah!' said Tom, reeling around to welcome Medea into the fold with outstretched arms. 'Medea, *my de-ah!*'

Medea smiled and kissed an effusive Tom on both cheeks, then did the same to Kate.

'Oi, oi!' piped up Lee. 'Forgetting someone?'

Medea smiled beatifically and turned to face Tom.

'I don't believe you've met Lee ?' Tom said. 'Lee Callahan, lead singer of phenomenally successful popular modern rock band, Mirage. Have you heard of them?'

'Yes,' said Medea. 'Of course I bloody have! I didn't know you were an art fan, Lee. What do you think of the artists here today?'

'Fookin' puffs, the lot of 'em,' said Lee, slowly half-running on the spot, like he was limbering up and about to go on the pitch. ''Cept that Hurtz bloke, he's all right. I'm mad for 'im, me.'

'Ooh!' said Kate. 'Which reminds me. Now, Lee, remember the last time we met, you said you were mad for *me*? Remember saying I was gorgeous and you'd do anything for me?'

Which prompted Tom and Lee to grab hold of each other by the shoulders and sing along with 'You're Gorgeous', the Babybird song which was playing in the background.

Kate was on a roll. She tried to reach up to Lee's shoulder to grab hold of him, so he couldn't get away from her and her cunning plan. But she needn't have bothered – he ably assisted her by sitting down on a chair at a nearby table and pulling her onto his lap.

'Woah, I say!' said a shocked and inexplicably aristocratic-sounding Tom.

'It's OK,' said Kate, relishing the fact that for once she could sit on a man's knee and not worry that she was going to make his legs buckle under her weight. 'It's work, remember?'

Tom shuffled about a bit until Medea slid her arm through his and walked him over to another table, suggesting they discuss in detail her first column for *Lashed*.

'So here it is,' Kate said soberly, knees together, ankles crossed and hands in her lap as she looked down on Lee. 'I will go out with you – wherever you want – if you do me this one small, teensy little favour.'

'I said I'd do anything.' He stared up at her.

Kate had to fight the urge to tickle him behind the ear as one might do to a Labrador puppy and let her gaze linger on his striking bluey-green eyes a little too long.

Misreading the signs of affection for lust, Lee stretched his neck up and moved in for the kill, right hand gently pushing the back of her head down so that their lips could meet.

Kate jumped up.

'Uh-ah-ah,' she said, wagging her finger at him and keeping her cool admirably. 'Favour first.'

Lee, who looked for a micro-second like he was going to lose his famous temper, let a grin wrap itself around his lips and pulled Kate back down onto his lap.

'I only wanted to kiss your cheek,' he said.

So it was Kate who'd misread the signs! She didn't know whether to feel insulted or relieved, so she decided to ignore it and continue on her quest.

'See your friends, Damien and Alastair from Fuzz over there?' Kate pointed at Lee's main rivals who were arguing about something, gesticulating wildly in front of a glass case containing a dead cow.

'Chelsea-loving, mockney art school ponces.'

'That's right,' Kate cut him off before he got too het up. 'I want you and your brother, Nate, to dress up in boxers' satin shorts and tops and get into the ring with them.'

'The only fookin' ring I'm gonna get into—'

'Here's the deal,' Kate sighed, wanting to wrap this up fast. All the smoke was making her dizzy and although he was undeniably good-looking, Lee was so young, he simply wasn't her type any more. 'You and Nate make friends with Damien and Alastair in a mock boxing match. *Mad Fer It!*, everybody's favourite teen mag, will be there to interview you all about your rules of friendship and how sometimes falling out can be the best thing to bring mates back together.'

Lee sniffed loudly and coughed. He stared at Damien and Alastair through his mauve-coloured John Lennon glasses and stroked his stubble.

Kate got up, imagining this was his lesser-spotted pensive look. And even though the thick, swirling smoke of a million cigarettes was making it hard for her to breathe, let alone see, she could tell that he was considering her proposition seriously.

'You do that for me and I'll do whatever you want – within reason, of course – for you.'

Kate couldn't quite believe that Lee seemed to have fixated on her – short, average, girl-next-door her, when he could have all the ridiculously stunning women in the world he wanted. It didn't make sense to her. Nor did it appear to make any sense to a rather miffed-looking Pammy Kendricks who was striding over towards them.

Sensing she might never get the chance again, Kate dared to derail his train of thought slightly and ask him another question.

'Lee, why are you so interested in me?' she said quickly, looking fearfully over her shoulder at a fast-approaching Pammy.

'I like you, that's all.' He smiled softly.

Kate tilted her head to one side and was thinking how adorable he was, really, like Decko when he was five – all rambunctious and lively – but sweet and loving and ready to smother his mother in kisses at a moment's notice, when Lee spoke again.

'You're different. Wise. You remind me of me mam, I suppose – strong and smart. Not in a sick way or nothing – I love my mum. And there's something of her in you, I think. Is that an awful thing to say? Have I insulted you?' He looked more vulnerable than Kate could ever have imagined.

'No!' she squealed. 'It's a compliment! You think your mum's amazing and wonderful, right?'

'I'll fookin' batter anyone who says different,' he said, squaring his shoulders back and jutting his chin out.

'She must be so proud,' Kate said, just in time to see a woman's hand swoop down and softly slap Lee's cheek.

'You flirt!' Pammy shrieked with a half-laugh, as though she was trying to show everyone that she didn't really mind. 'You're *terrible!*'

Kate leaped up and stood, suddenly dwarfed, next to Pammy. Lee looked up at Pammy then down at Kate. Up to Pammy, down to Kate. Pammy, Kate, Pammy, Kate.

Pammy folded her arms across her chest and pursed her lips. Kate put her hands on her hips, to a) prove to herself that they were still virtually non-existent, despite how old she was feeling and b) to adopt a particularly motherly pose as part of her persuasion tactics.

'I'm a dab hand with a roast,' cooed Kate. 'And my Yorkshire puds are second to none...'

'I'll do it!' Lee said, slamming his hands down on the chair's arms and hauling himself up out of his sitting position. 'If our kid's still talking to me, I'll sort it. Now, let's fookin' celebrate!'

Pammy unfolded her arms and dragged his head down to her breast, laughing.

'He's like a big kid, isn't he?' she addressed Kate.

'Yeah,' Kate laughed, relieved things hadn't descended into an unseemly cat fight and Lee had actually agreed to do her bidding.

It took a while to sink in, because she couldn't quite believe that the infamous Battle of Britpop would be fought and won in the pages of *Mad Fer It!* and everyone would be friends again, not fierce rivals wishing AIDS and death upon each other.

Archie was going to fall off his chair when he heard about this! And all because Kate reminded Lee of his mum. Ha!

Now all she needed to do was get Damien and Alastair in on the story and she could go home, a good night's work done and dusted.

Leaving Lee and Pammy to it, Kate headed for Tom and Medea who were engaged in a deep and no doubt meaningful conversation with Damien and Alastair in front of a badger and a hedgehog suspended in a vitrine case full of formaldehyde.

'...more for the nursery, I think – you know, cute, cuddly little animals to keep the baby company at night,' Alastair was saying.

'Or to scare the bejesus out of the poor little babby,' Dámien replied.

'In my experience,' Kate joined in, 'babies don't ever sleep, no matter what you do. So whether you opt for stuffed animals, musical mobiles or even a dead, dissected hamster in a glass cage, you can forget about sleep for approximately five years, give or take a day or two for when your little one's sick and you do the Nurofen/Calpol every-two-hour dance in a last-ditch attempt to save your sanity!'

She reached into their little circle and grabbed a mini vegetarian pizza off a tray, popped it into her mouth and grinned at the taken aback foursome.

'What do you mean, "in your experience"?' asked Tom.

'Do you have younger brothers or sisters?' piped up Medea. 'Did your mother have a menopause baby or something?'

Suddenly Kate felt the confidence drain out of her and she wondered why on earth she had opened up her big mouth.

Still, she reasoned with herself, she had to break into their convo somehow – and this was as good a way as any, considering she now had their full and undivided attention.

'Ah, no, my...' This thinking on her feet, endlessly trying to cover her tracks was really starting to get on her nerves. She couldn't take much more, desperately trying to remember every little lie she came out with. 'My, um, auntie is a midwife and she always says it's futile to think that anything you do has an effect on whether a baby sleeps or not. She says they have minds of their own and will sleep when they want to and not a moment before.'

Damien and Alastair turned back to look at the badger/hedgehog ensemble, as did Medea and Tom.

Kate knew she'd lost her audience. How was she going to ask the Fuzz boys to do the boxing ring thing? And how on earth was she going to convince them to say yes?

'Babes, can I have a quick word?' She jerked her head towards a corner of the room as she tapped Tom on his shoulder.

'All right, love,' said Tom with a wink. 'You just can't wait to get me alone, can you?'

They moved over to a quieter corner and Tom put his arms around Kate's neck and puckered up in preparation for a super-smooch.

'Hang on, hang on,' said Kate, turning her cheek to him and pushing his chest away with her palms. 'I've got a huge favour to ask first.'

'Anything,' gasped Tom.

'OK, well...' Kate took a deep breath. 'I want you to ask Damien and Alastair Fuzz—'

'That's not their last names, you know,' Tom scoffed.

'I know, but that's what *Mad Fer It!* calls them. I *need* you to ask them to agree to be in a photo shoot with Lee and Nate—'

'Mirage?' he smirked.

'No, Lee and Nate *Callahan*, in a boxing ring in satin shorts and tops, burying the hatchet and talking to the features team about mates and falling out and making up again.'

Kate took a noisy, wheezy breath in, lungs desperate for air.

Tom, however, just stared at her.

After a few seconds – which must have seemed like hours to Tom and his addled brain – he started to laugh.

'That's the stupidest thing I've ever heard!' He slapped his knee, cowboy-style, for added emphasis. 'Why didn't I think of it?'

Tom suddenly went all serious and pulled Kate in close to whisper in her ear. 'I will ask them for you, if the *Lashed* team are allowed to be at the shoot, too, and get their own adult, blokey take on the proceedings.'

'Can't see why not,' said Kate. 'Two birds, one stone – it's a yes from me!'

'*And…*' Tom got a glint in his eye. 'you promise to come home with me soon and let me have my wicked way with you. Let's christen our new pad in fine style.'

Kate giggled and nodded a rather effusive 'yes' that took her a bit by surprise.

God, she thought. All this promising favours of a gastronomic or sexual kind just to get a magazine out of trouble? Talk about dedication to the cause – it gave a whole new meaning to the phrase *job satisfaction*.

Still, she figured she might as well do what she'd set out to do – feel young, free and easy again – and sleep with her old boyfriend who had been, quite literally, the man of her dreams.

Medea and Kate made small talk while Tom, Damien and Alastair went off somewhere 'for a private little chat' Tom called it, as he tapped his nose in a nudge, nudge, wink, wink kind of a way.

When they returned, all three of them had contracted a nasty case of the sniffles.

'It's that bloody cold room where Hurtzy stores his carcasses,' smiled Alastair. 'You just go to see an installation and pow! You're struck down with the lurgy!'

'Yes, but is it art?' Damien asked as he stroked his chin.

—

'So?' Kate linked arms with Tom as they wove their way through Soho to get to Tottenham Court Road tube station.

'So…' Tom teased her, withholding the vital information. 'They're in!'

'They are?'

'Yup!'

'Did they take much convincing?' she asked.

'Nothing I couldn't handle,' Tom answered, proudly straightening up his Ben Sherman button-down collar. 'Actually, they were like putty in my hands. Said they were really looking forward to it.'

'That's amazing!' said Kate, truly astounded. 'I'd better organise it as soon as possible – best not give any of them the time to change their minds and pull out.'

'Bet that's never happened to you before,' Tom said, a tad creepily.

Kate bit her lip. She couldn't bring herself to even laugh nervously at his comment – she was too busy being wracked with guilt over the fact she was just about to be unfaithful to 2022 Seamus who, for all she knew, had been electrocuted on the golf course in that torrential storm.

Oh god, oh god, oh. my. god!

This was it, she thought to herself as they snuggled up close together on the packed tube home. She was finally going to get the chance to relive the best sex of her life.

With the best lover she'd ever had. The best *boyfriend* she'd ever had. The one she probably should have married. Or, at least, the one she wished she'd had the opportunity to turn down before he ran off with that Tamsin at her birthday party.

Not that she felt as strongly about that as she used to. Having seen both him and Seamus as their younger selves, she could see why she ended up with Seamus after all. Because now, with her fifty-four-year-old eyes, she was no longer seduced by the trappings of wealth and power and proximity to celebrity – this time, in 1996, she could see what really mattered, what foundation a solid relationship should really be built on: shared, common interests, a good sense of humour and a top drawer full of mobile phone chargers and Allen keys.

Tom was stroking Kate's back as she leaned into him, his back against the glass partitioning the seats from the standing area. Kate closed her eyes and tried to take it all in: she wanted to make sure she remembered everything for posterity – correctly and exactly as it was, this time – completely without any rose-coloured glasses.

His shirt smelled of beer and cigarettes, but underneath that was his signature scent – some expensive eau de cologne Kate could never remember the name of – and it was making her giddy.

'Mmm,' she hmmed, unable to help herself or wipe the smile off her face.

He moved his hand to the back of her head and stroked her hair like it was the ear of a pedigree Afghan hound and she wondered whether her Rachel do would weather the storm of rampant, wanton, most probably *really dirty* sex with Tom.

When they hit the chilly night air, coming up out of Notting Hill Gate underground station, Kate felt light-headed, as though *she* was the one who'd been making surreptitious trips to the loos all evening.

'You don't know how long I've waited for this, Tom,' she said, rubbing her cheek against the scratchy, woollen sleeve of his coat as they walked.

'Oh, I know, babes,' he said. 'The things I'm going to do to you when I get you home... A-ha! And here we are!'

Tom unlocked the front door to the narrowest, most low-ceilinged hallway Kate had ever seen. It was like something out of *Alice In Wonderland*.

'Bit poky this front bit, sorry,' Tom yawned as he apologised.

'No, no – it's great!' Kate lied. 'It's chic, bijou even.'

'That's exactly what I said when I first saw it,' Tom said, looking at Kate with a gleam in his eye she'd long forgotten. 'Come 'ere,' he growled, pushing her up against the wall and kissing her. She felt little sparklers begin to fizz and pop somewhere deep down at her very core and she closed her eyes again, letting the moment take her over.

'Mmmm.' Tom was the first to break away from their hot and hasty embrace. 'But wait, there's more! Wanna see the rest?'

He grabbed her hand and led her up a stairwell so narrow, she was glad she wasn't carrying any excess poundage. When they walked round the bend and got to the top of the stairs, he pushed open the front door to their flat.

'*Et voilà!*' he said.

'Wow,' she replied. 'When did you find the time to do all this?'

The walls were covered in not paint, not wallpaper, but Elmo-from-*Sesame-Street* red fur.

Kate's mouth couldn't help but turn down at the corners as her eyes drank in the ambience of the room. After careful consideration lasting at least three seconds, she concluded it was a tribute to the Playboy mansion, Hugh Hefner-style, Seventies sex. And she didn't mean sex in your seventies.

'One of the girls at work – Tamsin or something – she helped me,' he said, kicking off his Adidas Gazelles and guiding her into the bedroom.

'And now, for the *pièce de résistance*,' he said, making Kate bristle and wonder why he was saying so much in French in his corny accent.

A big, round purple crushed-velvet waterbed took pride of place in the centre of the room. Tom flopped onto it and lay on his back, his body undulating and bobbing about like a tugboat in choppy waves.

'What do you think?' he said, staring at the ceiling.

Kate's eyes followed his and she gasped when she saw what was Blu-Tacked up there – poster overlapping poster of England players. It was like walking into Decko's room, a little boy's safe haven, the walls covered with portraits of his footballing heroes.

Kate kicked off her shoes and tried to stay in the mood, even though seeing those pictures had alerted her to the fact that this coupling was fifty shades of no-freakin'-way.

She slid on the velvet towards Tom and told him she loved what he'd done with the place.

'Yeah, it's great, isn't it? Especially now that Euro 96 is on. I can easily change my Fantasy Football team line-up with a new pic and a quick flick of the old sticky tape, cos the lads at *Back of The Net!* magazine always slip me a complimentary copy of their latest poster mags and…'

Tom was now even *sounding* like a ten-year-old boy, all gushy and over-excited about… *football*.

The more Tom burbled on, the more Kate realised she couldn't go through with it. She just couldn't sleep with this man-child, this immature boy who'd rather talk about the beautiful game than to his beautiful girlfriend.

As he wittered their valuable foreplay time away, Kate grappled with her memory as she tried to locate, in the song words part of her brain, the lyrics to 'Greetings To The New Brunette', a particularly apt Billy Bragg song that came to her mind. She furrowed her brow as she tried to remember that line about lying back and thinking of England, but not having a clue who was in the team. Or something like that, anyway.

She shook her head in irritation. Should she or shouldn't she?

Kate thought hard, looking up to the football-covered ceiling for inspiration and biting the inside of her right cheek.

But as soon as she'd made up her mind to abort her mission, she became aware of the heavy silence filling the room.

When she turned to look at Tom, to nudge him into action, she noticed he wasn't moving.

'Tom?' she said, grabbing hold of the arm nearest her and shaking it. 'Tom? *TOM!*'

Kate sat bolt upright. What was she going to do? Was he dead? Bloody hell! How could he… well, god knows, he'd probably snorted the GDP of a small South American country up his nose in the past couple of hours, so…

But this was no time for moral judgements or amateur forensic science, she scolded herself!

She knelt beside him and fumbled around trying to hold up his arm, feeling for a pulse in his limp wrist.

'Come on, Tom,' she said through clenched teeth. 'Come ON! Breathe, will you?'

She bent down and put her ear to his mouth, not caring that her hairdo was falling all over the place and getting badly out of shape.

Nothing. She couldn't hear a sound. Not a sausage.

Until, suddenly, like someone coming to the surface of a pool after diving in too deep and running out of breath, a gasping, rasping 'Nyeurrrrgh!' came from the corpse.

Kate was catapulted back by fear, falling off the bed and bumping her head against the mirrored built-in wardrobe. Definitely *not* the spot she'd imagined her head to be banging against in the bedroom tonight, she thought, as she rubbed the sore bit and winced.

'What's wrong with you, Gazza?' squeaked a frightened-sounding Tom. 'Hoof it down the pitch! Go on, my son!'

Tom was alive! He'd come back to life!

'Alan? Is that you, Mr Shearer?' Tom said, even more bewildered this time.

'No it most certainly is not,' said Kate, standing up and walking towards him. 'And what the hell do you think you're doing, passing out on me like that? You gave me the fright of my life!'

But Tom simply shut his eyes, fell back on the bed, stuck his thumb in his mouth and proceeded to sleep like a baby.

Or, more accurately, sleep like a heavily intoxicated man, if what Kate's made-up midwife auntie said was true.

21

Kate woke with a start at 5:30 the next morning. She felt extreme discombobulation as she looked around and saw absolutely nothing even remotely familiar.

Tom was snoring his head off next to her and she cursed the body clock that was still somehow running on harried mum time.

She smiled as images of Phoebe and Declan as babies gurgling and gurning happily for the camera came to mind. She wondered, for the millionth time, who they'd both inherited their soft but crazily static, spiky baby hair from. Seamus and Kate often laughed about those shocks of hair and how it made them look like little baby blonde Don Kings.

Speaking (to herself) of famous, mega-rich boxing promoters, she congratulated herself on the coup of the century – if it came off and Lee et al. could all make up and be friends, then she really would have changed history – saved a magazine, proved to Archie that she still had what it took, helped the silly little boys grow up and give her a much-needed confidence boost. Not bad for an old bag.

Tom grunted and spluttered like he was choking and then, as quickly as it had begun, his breathing settled down again into the deep, guttural snore that meant he was, to carry on a theme, out for the count. Totally KO'd.

So much for the amazing sex with Tom she was sure she was going to have last night – and there was no way she was going to move in with him now! Still, she consoled herself, maybe it just wasn't meant to be. Obviously Fate had a different idea about what her trip back in time was all about.

Which was… *what*, exactly?

Clearly it wasn't about hooking up with her old flame and igniting the bed again, so hot were their sex sessions, so legendary in her memory.

But was it really about being any good at her old job? Saving Portia from certain disaster? Having a flat belly?

Had she been sent back to 1996 to ruin Steve's life? She hadn't heard from him for nearly a week now – where *had* he gone?

That old Travis song sprang into her mind and she sang the wrong words, slightly out of time and tune for a few seconds.

'Driftwood,' she said out loud, shaking her head sadly.

Kate threw back the duvet and sat up. She was still wearing her khaki combats (clean on yesterday) and her red and white crop-top faux football shirt. She adjusted the strap of her M&S bra and tried to make the most of that moment, knowing that once she'd had kids, she'd never be an off-the-peg girl again. She looked down and admired her medium-sized chest, proud of its perkiness.

And then she sighed. She hadn't thought she'd ever get sick of seeing herself slim and youthful, but, to be honest, it wasn't all it was cracked up to be. I mean, she thought, all that constant checking yourself out, monitoring yourself and your calorie, booze and cigarette consumption. Exhausting and boring!

She rubbed her belly, which, in her sitting position only had about three half-centimetre-thick folds on it and realised, for the very first time in her life, that she was a bit of a walking cliché.

For she'd often read about women who said they loved their caesarean scars and their flabby, stretch-marked stomachs, because they were a constant reminder of their beautiful babies, their wonderful kids, their fantastic families. She'd thought those stories were all made up, of course – it was those kids' *fault* she was fat, fucked-off and a wrinkly fifty-five. What's to love about that?

And yet, this was exactly how Kate felt right at this moment – her flat, taut tummy meant she didn't have Phoebs or Decko – and her faithful, loving (if not a tad badly dressed and golf-obsessed) husband, who used to always make her laugh was nowhere to be seen, either.

With not so much as a by-your-leave (whatever that was), she jumped out of bed and hopped around the disgusting fur-covered bedroom, pulling on her high-heeled trainers. She threw her mini black leather backpack on and bolted for the front door.

She couldn't wait for Seamus to faff about, getting tangled in wires and dropping modems on his feet in his attempts to help her find a way back to 2022 – as a mother and a wife IRL, she knew that if you wanted to get something done – and get it done properly – you had to do it yourself.

Surely, she reasoned, there'd be some reference books at work – or maybe in the archives of the TV listings mag, *Your Viewing Pleasure*, they'd have some info on Dr Who telling us how he got about in different time/space continuums. Or Catweazle! Now just how did *he* get transported through time from the Middle Ages to the early Seventies?

And there must be *something* about time travel on the internet by now – it wasn't *that* fledgling a thing.

As she ran down the stairs, she did her best to ignore the intense gnawing emptiness that was threatening to eat her up from the inside. It was like full-on period pains and she felt instinctively that something was changing; her internal sands were shifting.

Then again, maybe it was just her sciatica rearing its ugly head.

She was starting to feel a little confused. She couldn't quite believe it herself, but could it be that she, the nostalgia nut, the has-been queen had perhaps had enough of the past now? She couldn't help but think that in comparison to what she had back in 2022, with all its problems, dysfunctionality and hectic mess, being nearly twenty-nine years old in 1996, being free, single and unencumbered by anyone or anything, going out and drinking all the time was, quite frankly, a bit repetitive and dull.

At the bottom of the stairs, Kate tried to force her arms into the sleeves of her tight denim jacket, but they just wouldn't go all the way, only up to her elbow. She quickly tore the jacket off and inspected her arms. Were they a tad *fleshier* than they were yesterday?

She suddenly felt overcome by a profound sense of urgency and leaped out of the flat, ran into the street and sprinted towards Notting Hill Gate tube station.

But in her speed to flee, somehow, the heel of her trainers came unglued from the all-synthetic sole, got caught on a paving stone and she tumbled to the ground, landing on her bony bum.

Bayswater Road was reasonably packed now, with workers off to start their days early and rich trustafarians returning home from their nights out, but not one person stopped to help her. In fact, one or two men in Burberry trench coats actually trod on the straps of her backpack as they stomped past.

'Typical,' she said out loud. London wasn't famous for its overly friendly, helpful citizens, so she pulled herself up and, rubbing her hip and the small of her back, hobbled down into the underground.

Sitting on the train to Tottenham Court Road, she thought of Steve and George and Jenny and wondered what the hell was happening to them. She wished she had her mobile on her now, so she could call them, rally the troops and get them all together. Because then, surely, they'd all be happy again, wouldn't they? One big, happy(ish) family!

Lost in her own inner world, she beamed at the mental picture of everyone clustered around the Christmas tree when she was a kid. Like a human ViewMaster, she flicked over to the next Hallmark card, chocolate-box image of Jenny, George, Steve and Kate all sitting at the dinner table, mugging for and raising their glasses to the camera, their fabulous Sunday lunch spread out as though Nigella herself had set it up.

She felt all warm and gooey inside, like the liquid centre of a Lindt Lindor ball.

'I mean,' she mumbled, 'what can make you happier than home?'

'Chocolate,' said the woman sitting opposite her, with a smile.

'Cider,' piped up a Worzel Gummidge, trampy-looking guy, propping up the glass partition.

'Football,' chorused a boy and a girl sitting down in their posh school uniforms, while their daddy hung on the strap above them.

Now that's more like it, Kate thought – that's the sort of community, spirit of the Blitz Londoners were supposed to pull out of the bag in times of trouble. She couldn't get the surprised look off her face and felt compelled to join in.

'Actually, sleep – *lots of sleep* – would be my number one essential item for guaranteed happiness.' She smiled.

'Health,' a hoarse old man said. 'You've got nothing if you haven't got your health.'

Everyone nodded.

'What about love?' a middle-aged woman with a Jamaican accent asked.

'Nah – money,' a bespectacled, thirty-something City-type said matter-of-factly.

'Time,' the old lady sitting next to Kate said in a husky, barely audible voice as she touched her arm. 'More time.'

And everyone fell silent.

–

It was weird getting to PGT&B so early. For a start, she didn't have to wait long for The Lift at all – within five seconds she heard the PING! and stepped into the mirrored box.

As per usual, she studied her face in the mirrors as she was carried up to the third floor.

It all looked pretty much the same as it did the day before and the day before and the day before *that* – but Kate was sure she could see an ever-so-slight sag around her jawline. No one else would be able to notice – except maybe Portia – but there was definitely some fall going on there.

As she limped into the empty office, rubbing her still-sore bum, and wondering whether she would have to have a hip-replacement operation when she got back to 2022, she saw the same Take That calendar they had at the flat on the wall and it suddenly struck her that it was a week and a half until her birthday.

In just over a week, she would be turning twenty-nine. Or, if she made it back to 2022, fifty-five. Fifty-five. She surprised herself when she realised she wanted it to be the latter.

She picked up her speed and lopsidedly trotted up to her desk. When she pulled her chair out, plonked herself in it and wheeled herself up to the edge of her desk, she let out an eardrum-bursting shriek.

She leaped out of her seat and stumbled backwards towards Lucy's reception desk, saying, 'Don't hurt me, you stay, I'll go. Please don't hurt me!'

As the vaguely familiar figure emerged from under her desk, drawing itself up to its full, dishevelled height, she brought her forearm up to her eyes, like a Fifties schlock film actress, shielding her beautiful face and delicate, porcelain skin from some gruesome monster.

She held her breath for what seemed like ages until it spoke, this creature from the black lagoon (under her desk).

'Calm down, calm down,' it croaked and then cleared its throat. 'It's only me!'

'Steve!' Kate yowled, bringing her arm down as soon as she heard his voice. 'What? How? Why?'

'You forgot where and when,' he yawned, stretching his balled fists towards the ceiling and exposing his hairy tummy. 'Us journalists must always remember those five crucial questions.'

'What do you mean, *us journalists*? And what the *hell* are you doing here?' Kate was sounding more like her old self – and when she said this last part, she placed her hands on her hips, tapping the toes of her right extended foot as if she were wearing a pinny and telling the kids off for traipsing mud through the house or something.

'I've been working as a journo – doing some work for your boyfriend, as it happens,' said Steve. 'He said he saw some potential in me that Sunday lunch at Mum and Dad's and told me to come and see him the next day. I've been working here ever since.'

'Really? He never said anything to me...' Kate furrowed her brow and shook her head. 'God, he really is *sooo* much a nicer guy than my memory gives him credit for.'

'Yeah, he is,' Steve agreed, scratching his stubbly cheek. 'But I had nowhere to kip, so I thought I'd doss down here.'

'Why not under your own desk at *Lashed*? And why didn't you call or leave a message – or just leave me a note on my desk or something?'

'I was embarrassed, wanted to show everyone I could do things on my own first, before I got in contact. But I missed you – hence the sleeping under your desk. And, well, I don't exactly have my own desk,' Steve looked sheepish, 'and I haven't been paid yet, either.'

Kate stood there speechless and let her heart rate get back to normal. Which gave her time to take it all in, figure out a plan and carefully consider her response.

Her chin wobbled and crinkled up for a moment before she burst into tears, flinging herself at her long-lost brother.

Her sobs came thick and fast, as though she was making up for lost time. Steve held his sister close and they stayed like this for ages, until eventually Kate pulled back, wiping her eyes.

'Come back and live with me and Portia – how could I have let you go in the first place?!'

'I dunno,' grinned Steve. 'You weren't always so heartless and selfish.'

'We'll sort the money out as soon as Tom comes in this morning. If he makes it in at all, that is,' smirked Kate. 'Tea?'

The pair meandered over to the small office kitchen and Kate popped the kettle on.

Steve crouched down and bobbed on his haunches while he sniffed the eight open milk cartons languishing in the small bar of the fridge door.

'Cottage cheese.' He grimaced and poured the contents of seven down the sink.

'So what's the story, Stevie?' Kate said bluntly. 'Why did you run off like that at Mum and Dad's?'

'I don't know,' he said, putting the last carton on the kitchen counter. 'It all got too much for me, I suppose.'

'What did?'

'The pathetic games people play.'

'Who?'

'You don't know?' Steve asked.

'No – tell me,' Kate said.

'You really don't know, do you?'

'Steve! Tell me!'

Kate's worry line, the little crevice between her eyebrows, was deepening into more of a crevasse now – like the cracked lino in her 2022 kitchen.

'Here goes,' Steve said slowly. 'Mum's having an affair.'

Kate didn't move.

'Yep.' Steve carried on.

'But—'

'I know, I know.' Steve shook his head sorrowfully.

Kate couldn't really compute all this, her confusion threatening to completely overwhelm her. Not, she thought, totally dissimilar to the way she felt when the kids were born.

She felt almost exactly the same, come to think of it, her heart rate quickly increasing, her breath getting shallow.

'Are you OK?' Steve put his arm around her.

'I-I think I need to sit down,' she stuttered as he helped her to a chair in Archie's office.

'Hang on a sec,' said Steve over his shoulder as he went back into the kitchen. 'I'll get the tea.'

Kate could hear cupboards opening and closing and then Steve saying, 'What? No Hob Nobs? Call yourselves a media company? It's a bloody disgrace!'

Kate half-smiled and rubbed her eyes, her fingers definitely feeling a few crow's feet that weren't there yesterday.

Steve came back into Archie's office with their tea and perched on the edge of the desk in front of Kate.

'You don't look so good, Kate,' he said, genuine concern in his voice.

'Well you don't smell so good,' she said a tad shakily. 'When was the last time you had a bath?'

Steve snorted as he brought his mug of tea up to his lips.

'So,' said Kate. 'We'll get back to Mum and Dad later but, first, I want to know why you're so bloody angry all the time.'

'I don't know,' he said quietly. 'Actually, that's a lie. I've had some time to think about it and I think I do know why.'

Kate noticed Steve's eyes getting watery and wanted to suffocate him with hugs and smother him with kisses. God, she thought, this is *just* like having a baby – the sudden rush of love, the confusion, the pandemonium in your heart, the dizzy, elated way you feel – even long after the morphine's worn off.

'No, no, no,' Steve repelled her advancing arms. 'Just let me get it all out, will you? I've been bottling it up for years, I might as well let it all out now.'

Kate shifted in her seat.

'Sitting comfortably?' Steve asked. 'Then let's begin. As you know, I was born a couple of years after you and that, unfortunately, was my first mistake.'

'What do you mean?'

'I mean that I've always felt like second best, always in your shadow – and not in a wind beneath your wings kind of way.'

They both smiled at this point, sharing the memory of watching *Beaches*, one of Jenny's favourite movies, on video over and over again until they knew all the lines off by heart.

'It's only recently that I've been able to put it into words, but I think I've always had this overriding feeling that, somehow, I was always a great disappointment to Mum and Dad.'

Kate shook her head as if to say 'no, that's not true', but Steve ignored her and carried on.

'It's nothing you did, but all that Sixties bullshit Dad used to come out with about finding himself and not being held back by the restraints of family – that's what made me feel surplus to requirements. That's what made me feel insignificant and insecure and unwanted and unloved.'

'But there's no way he—'

'He may not have *intended* for that to happen,' Steve cut Kate short, 'but that's what *did* happen. And with Mum constantly off at work, always bleating on about independence and freedom, I took it all as a rejection of *me*. Like I was in their way or something.'

Kate wanted to tell him to stop it – stop being so ridiculous and selfish and pathetically childish and me, me, ME! She'd always suspected this was part of Steve's problem – the sibling rivalry, the vying for their parents' attention and approval. And always coming second, always feeling second best – effectively, to his mind, always coming *last*.

She wanted to tell him to grow up and consider someone else for a change. Why, for god's sake, was it so traumatic for him that his mother was a fully formed, well-rounded individual? Wasn't it enough for him to know that she'd sacrificed her career for her children? That she never reached the lofty heights George had because she had to look after her family? Didn't it ever occur to him that, yes, she was their mummy – but she was also a grown-up *person*, one with normal adult needs and desires?

So their mother had sought a life beyond the four confining walls of home – was that so wrong? So she was interested in millions of things other than her kids – wasn't that good? Why did it have to have such an adverse effect on *him*?

Poor old Jenny – she was hardly Mommie Dearest; a schizophrenic, neglectful, nasty, nutty mother. But here was Steve, blaming her for all *his* issues. As always, she sighed, everything is mummy's fault.

On the flip side, though, Kate completely understood how Steve felt. Because even though she didn't like to admit it – even to herself – she, too, had sometimes felt abandoned and nowhere near as important to her mum as her work, her friends or her emotional needs. She shook her head as if to stop her train of thought.

'But just because she's our mum doesn't mean she can't be a whole load of other things too. Does it? I mean, why can't she seek out fulfilment in life in all sorts of different areas?'

'I don't know. Maybe women can't have it all.' Steve stared out of the window at the city skyline. 'Or maybe she just could have made a bit more of a fuss over me. If she hadn't been so busy being frustrated with her lot and yelling at us all the time and going on about what she could be doing if she didn't have us and how she'd made a huge mistake by marrying the wrong guy—'

The hairs on the back of Kate's neck stood up. This was getting too near the knuckle.

'She never said that!'

'Oh yeah? You didn't hear her,' Steve opened his eyes wide and glared at Kate. 'I wasn't supposed to, either, but she said it all right. Loads of times, whenever she and Dad were arguing in their bedroom.'

'I thought they were always fighting about Dad's affairs!'

'They were.' Steve nodded.

'You sneaky little – what else did she say?'

'Nothing much,' Steve said, looking out of the window. 'Just that she married the wrong guy and her life would have been so different and so much better if she'd only stayed with the love of her life, the one she had electrifying sex with before she even met Dad.'

Kate's mouth fell open at this point.

Eventually, after several dry-mouthed swallows, she regained the power of speech.

'When did you hear all this?' she croaked. 'And why didn't you tell me immediately?'

'It was *ages* ago – about eight or nine years,' Steve shrugged. 'You'd gone off to university and were too busy and bohemian to talk to your little brother about family matters, stuff about home any more.'

Kate nodded – Steve was right – that was *precisely* how she'd felt at the time.

She pictured herself and Portia in their trademark stonewashed jeans and jet-black turtle-necks, smoking anything they could get their hands on, listening to The Smiths and downing bottles of red as though they were starving beatnik artists in a Stella Artois ad. Now *there* was a simpler time – why oh why couldn't she have been taken back to 1987?

'Mother's guilt,' Kate suddenly said authoritatively. 'It's not easy juggling a house and kids and a husband who'd rather play golf or watch football than cook dinner, you know. I bet she felt so guilty about harbouring those thoughts, those fantasies about her ex – and she couldn't bear it. That's why she lashed out and that's why she eventually had some tawdry, grotty, ghastly affair with some hideous old man.'

'Sounds like you've thought about it more than I have,' said Steve, picking up their empty tea mugs. 'I've kind of forgiven her and Dad, now, anyway. They were only doing their best, trying to live their lives at the same time as making decent ones for us. How's that Philip Larkin poem go? Something about how your mum and dad don't mean to, but they really fuck you up?'

'Yeah,' smiled Kate. 'Something like that. So what now? Therapy? Prozac?'

She thought about Portia and how she swore by a combination of the two. Then she thought about her own fear of coming off the old Sertraline.

'I dunno.' Steve looked wistful. 'No one knows what the long-term effects of these drugs are, do they? Sure, I've taken my fair share of Es – which, let's face it, is exactly what anti-depressants are – and I've nearly managed to get away with it. So far. I've had some wicked, completely brilliant nights.'

Kate nodded.

'And some horrific comedowns,' Steve went on softly. 'Which brings me to my second confession.'

'But wait!' Kate grinned. 'There's more?'

'There's no easy way to say this, so I'll just come straight out with it. So to speak.'

Steve closed his eyes, put his hands on his hips and adopted a kind of Freddie Mercury feet-apart stage pose. He breathed in deeply through his nose and thrust it in the air, sucking his cheeks in as if summoning all the inner strength he possibly could.

'Kate,' he began ominously, 'promise you won't tell Mum or Dad – they'd go off their faces, but I'm—'

'GAY!' Kate propelled herself out of her chair. 'Of course you are!'

Steve's eyes flipped open dramatically.

'Yes... But why aren't you shocked?' He seemed miffed.

'Because it's not remotely shocking.' she sighed. 'I mean, so you like men? Big whoop.'

'Appalled, then!' he couldn't quite believe what he was hearing.

Kate shook her head no.

'Totally and utterly disgusted?'

'Get over yourself, Steve! It's really no biggie...' She trailed off, forgetting for a second that in 1996, coming out as gay was, in fact, still quite a biggie. She remembered that the hangover from the Eighties AIDS crisis was still prevalent in the Nineties – what with all that casual-but-rampant homophobia. This was her chance to show solidarity. 'I'll tell the olds if you want.'

Steve smiled and nodded, clearly pleasantly surprised and super-relieved.

''Allo, 'allo, 'allo!' Archie interrupted them from the doorway. 'What have we here, then? Taken over my office already, have you, Kate?'

Archie sauntered in and, in a decidedly proprietorial move, threw his bomber jacket over the back of his over-sized chair. It was the sartorial equivalent of peeing on it, Kate thought to herself.

'Sorry, Archie,' Kate began, 'I just wasn't feeling too well and—'

'Yes, yes – I imagine your celebrations with Tom last night did get rather, shall we say, exuberant?'

'Eh?' Kate and Steve grunted in unison.

'I heard about your success with the Britpoppers,' Archie went on. 'But it hasn't happened yet. If – and it's a big if – IF you pull it off, then maybe we'll talk about you having your own office.'

Well whoop-de-doo, Kate said to herself.

'But you've got a long way to go, baby, before you can handle things at my level,' Archie said. 'What are you doing here Steve? Is this a family takeover or something?!'

'I was just leaving,' said Steve, practically running for the door. 'See you soon!'

Archie raised his eyebrows at Kate expectantly as he sat down and rested his Adidas Gazelles on his desk.

'Um, right,' said Kate. 'I'd better be going, too, I suppose. Really start getting to grips with the shoot, set it up for some time this week.'

'Good girl,' Archie said, patronisingly. 'I'm sure you have a lot of work to get on with. Close the door on your way out, would you?'

Kate stood up and turned to leave. But as she reached the door, she stopped and said, 'Archie? Have I done something to upset you?'

'No,' Archie scoffed. 'What makes you say that?'

'Because lately you're being a bit, I dunno, off with me, lately.'

Archie looked perplexed and shook his head.

'You seem annoyed with me, short with me most of the time.'

'I've always been short.' He grinned.

'Are you sure?' she pressed on. 'I mean, you're sure I haven't said or done something to—'

'Yes! I'm sure! Now go on, get out of here – I want you to have set up the shoot of the century before lunchtime!'

'Yes, sir!' She saluted, turned round and marched out of there.

22

'Porsh?' said Kate.

'Here,' yawned Portia. 'Where are you, you dirty stop-out?'

'At work. Stayed at Tom's new place last night and, I, I just don't think it's going to work, you know? I want to come home.'

'You're in luck, lady – I haven't had a chance to rent your room out yet – even though they've been practically *queueing* down the street…'

'Great, brilliant. What about you? How are you feeling?'

'Fantastic. Top of the world. Never felt better in my life.'

'Still crap, then?'

'No, I'm serious. I'm going to go back into work this afternoon. I've completely recovered from my trauma physically, now it's simply a matter of sifting through the emotional detritus.'

'Wow,' said Kate. 'How are you going to do that, then?'

There was a brief pause, and Kate expected Portia to say 'see a psychiatrist for fifteen years and get a permanent prescription for Zoloft', but she didn't.

'Get right back on that horse, get out there again and settle down with a *decent* man.'

'But where are you going to find one of those? Pubs and clubs are full of morons and—'

'I think I may have already found him,' said Portia with a giggle.

'Who?'

'That guy who helped us home that night – the guy who works in your company – the gentlemanly one, you remember!'

Kate tried to picture any decent, gentlemanly men she knew at PGT&B. She drew a blank.

'You know! The speccy, dweeby one! With the Irish name...'

'Seamus?'

'That's the fella!'

'But you can't! I mean—'

'Why not?' Portia sounded offended. 'He did seem interested, a bit, that night...'

'Oh god, Portia! He's only human! But you can't have him, he's taken.'

'He is not!'

'Not yet, maybe – but he will be. Any day now, if my predictions are correct...'

'Yeah! By me!'

'No! That's not fair!'

Kate had lost many a man to the charms of her best friend over the years – but she wasn't prepared to sacrifice this one.

'You have such a massive head-start, such a huge advantage, you with your Beatrice Dalle-ness and everything!'

'OK, OK, calm down,' Portia said, audibly taking a drag on a Marlboro Light. 'You haven't got your eye on him, have you?'

Kate looked furtively over the top of her carrel and checked to see who was around. She wished she had her own office right now, with the door shut, so she could speak freely without all her colleagues hearing her and thinking she was a) mad and b) had shit taste in men.

Her eyes met Tamsin's, who was wriggling her way over to Kate's desk in an impossibly tight, mid-calf length bouclé pencil skirt. That, coupled with her black patent platform pumps, made her look more Minnie Mouse than Marilyn Monroe and instead of looking sexy, Kate thought she looked comical, bordering on the ridiculous.

Then again, she told herself, she would think that, wouldn't she?

Tamsin hovered over her, waving the monthly targets and bonuses for the marketing department in Kate's face and mouthed, 'I'll take them in to Archie first, yeah?'

Kate always used to have a look at how she and the rest of the team were doing before Archie – so she could be prepared for either a pat on the back or a bollocking. But right now she could give precisely zero fucks about those facts and figures – she had to save Seamus from Portia's scarlet-taloned clutches!

'Whatever,' Kate whispered, waving Tamsin away.

'What?' Portia said.

Kate could hear her best friend's eyebrows rising.

'No, not you,' said Kate. 'Just some annoying little… Now, you listen here, Jolene. Keep your hands off Seamus!'

Portia didn't say a word. For about four seconds.

'But he's so clearly not your type,' said Portia, sounding confused.

'Is too!' was all Kate could think of to say.

'Is not!'

'Is too!'

The pair of them continued like this for a while before they broke into a fit of the giggles.

'Anyway,' Kate said, wiping a tear from her eye, 'I didn't ring you so we could fight over boys, I wanted to get some advice.'

'Spill,' said Portia.

'Well...' Kate hunched over her keyboard and cupped her hand around the phone receiver in an attempt at privacy and told her about Jenny.

'And Steve just came out,' she said.

'Of where?'

'The closet!' Kate squealed. 'The closet under my desk as it goes.'

'Big fucking deal,' Portia sounded bored. 'So back to me. Why exactly can't I go for Seamus?'

'You just can't! Um, for the sake of your own happiness! He'd really get on your nerves after a while, once the novelty of going out with a geek wore off. It would be so boring, so predictable, you'd grow to hate his safeness and predictability – it'll drive you mad. Sorry, it *would* drive you mad. Madd-*er*. Trust me on this one.'

'Why should I?'

'Because you just have to! Honestly, you've got to believe me! You don't want him. I just *know* that he can never meet your emotional needs...'

At that moment, Kevin popped his head up over the back of Kate's carrel and waved a tangle of cables at her like he was a deranged octopus.

'I'll just plug one of these in – if I can find the right one – and we'll see if we can get you online without a modem,' he whispered, as though it was some great state secret.

'But I know a man who can,' Kate said slowly, putting the phone down on Portia without even waiting for a reply.

Kate was in an organisational frenzy. It was either feast or famine with her (usually feast, let's face it, especially where Tunnock's tea cakes were concerned), but when she got going on something (except ironing, she could never really get excited about that), she was often an unstoppable tour de force.

She called Lee and checked that Nate had agreed to the shoot – which, quite surprisingly, he had. She got their sizes ('Massively enormous' and 'tiddly' respectively, according to Lee), confirmed with the eager Fuzz fellas' people and called the All Stars Boxing Gym on Harrow Road to set up a time.

She went down a level to the teen floor of PGT&B and chatted to the *Mad Fer It!* team who were, understandably, beside themselves with excitement.

Kate was thrilled, too.

And when she found herself squealing and jumping up and down while spinning around in a ring-a-ring-a-roses kind of a way with everyone who worked on the magazine, she felt young and fresh and vital and truly lost in the moment.

Until her back gave out, that is, and she had to be helped to a swivel chair so she could sit down under the poster-covered Take That RIP memorial wall.

'Even now it's a mug's game,' Kate muttered to herself as she checked out her body's profile in The Lift mirror. 'I should've known better than to look.'

Mere days before, where there had been nothing but tight, smooth flesh, she could now detect the beginnings of a bit of a paunch poking out from the bottom of her crop-top.

Must be all those carb-heavy beers I've been necking, she thought. Even though she had actually been quite abstemious lately – unlike how she obviously was in 1996 the first time round. Honestly, she shook her head, studying the nylon carpet, was that really how we behaved back then? As badly as the men?

She thought of Phoebe and Declan and their comparatively wide-eyed innocence. She thought of the big, bad world out there, lying in wait to corrupt them and steal away what was left of the sweetness that social media hadn't already nicked. She started to well up and felt her panic rise.

What if she never got back to 2022? What if she was stuck in 1996 for-bloody-ever?

'I have GOT to get back!' she declared, just as The Lift pinged and landed with a jolt on the ground floor.

'Calm down, gorgeous,' said Tom, who was standing there with Tamsin. 'Where's the fire?'

Kate looked at both of them and, expecting to be nearly knocked down with righteous indignation and rabid jealousy, surprised herself no end when she felt nothing. Nothing at all. Except a slight rumbling in her tummy. Well, Tamsin *was* clutching a bag full of unbelievably delicious-smelling cakes and assorted goodies from Patisserie Valerie and the buttery, sugary whiff surrounding her was almost intoxicating.

'Oh, ah – I've got to meet Mum – I'm late as usual!' said Kate.

'Hey! Wait!' Tom wheeled around, trying to grab Kate's elbow as she whizzed past. 'What time did you leave this morning?'

'I dunno.' Kate pulled her elbow into her ribs and picked up her pace, shouting over her shoulder. 'Early. I'll see you later, yeah?'

'I really think we need to...' Tom didn't finish his sentence, just sighed and turned away, stepping into The Lift.

Kate stopped, turned around and saw Tamsin batting her eyelashes like mad.

'Talk?' Tamsin purred as the doors began to close. 'Were you going to say "talk"? Because if you ever need a sounding board, Tom, I'll always be there for you.'

That'd be right, Kate snorted to herself as she battled with the early lunchtime crowds in Oxford Street. Tamsin just couldn't *wait* to get her hands on Tom, could she?

Passing through Soho, making her way to Covent Garden, Kate realised she could *understand* why she used to be so crazy about him and how her heart could have been so smashed when he took up with Tamsin all those years ago. But it just wasn't there for her any more, she simply didn't feel it the way she had.

Thank god he *had* passed out last night and been totally incapacitated, unable to perform. Because even though back in 2022 she'd wanted to do nothing BUT get at it with him if she ever got the chance, imagine the guilt her poor fifty-four-year-old mind would be drowning in today if they *had* actually shagged!

Kate smiled thinking of how close she'd come, how narrowly she'd avoided unbearable remorse. And just as she was thinking about how she never thought she'd *ever* be so cool and calm – almost detached – about Tom, Jenny came trotting up to her.

'Darling!' she panted. 'Change of plan – I can't meet you for lunch today.'

'What?' Kate scrunched up her face. She was starting to get really quite annoyed with her mother. 'But you said—'

'I know, I know.' Jenny looked over Kate's shoulder and then behind her own, as if she were a fugitive on the run from the law, a hunted woman. 'But something came up and I just couldn't get out of it.'

Kate scrutinised her mother. She was wearing a cream, layered ensemble of indiscernible lines – like something Dame Judi Dench would wear – sophisticated and flowing, covering a multitude of sins, as Jenny would say, but still looking stylish and expensive.

Her make-up was expertly applied – the perfect shade of foundation with not too powdery a finish, a few subtle yet effective brush strokes of blush to highlight her sharp cheekbones, several coats of strong yet decidedly un-clumpy mascara to bring out and frame her beautiful bluey-green eyes and a glossy lip tint that complemented her colouring perfectly, no doubt with an SPF of 60 in it (Jenny was nothing if not practical, underneath all that glitz and glamour).

She looked comfortable, well-put together, happy and, Kate's breath caught in her throat, *very attractive*.

Kate thought of herself back home when she was happy and comfy and relaxed – and vowed to burn every cheap, nasty and hopelessly uglifying fleece and pair of jogging bottoms she owned when she got back to 2022. Better alert the council, then, she thought – don't want her, no doubt massive, funeral pyre to piss the neighbours off and mess with the air quality. Or maybe she should wait till bonfire night, donating her gargantuan 'joggers' to any Guys needing bottoms. If anyone would accept them.

A jaunty scarf, one Kate had never seen before, was casually draped around Jenny's neck, discreetly concealing the wrinkling skin wrapping itself around her throat. Kate's eyes lingered on it, as she searched for the words to express her disappointment and growing irritation.

'Liberty,' said Jenny, by way of explanation. 'It was a gift.'

Kate's eyes shot up to Jenny's.

'From a… a friend,' she smiled, turning her body half around nervously and then holding onto her daughter's forearms with an urgency Kate found unsettling.

'I bet it was,' Kate sounded miffed.

'Look, I've got to go now, darling. But Sunday lunch? At ours? Bring whoever you like and – have you heard from Steve yet?'

Kate's eyes were inadvertently turning into slits as she looked her mother up and down.

'Yes,' she said curtly, as though she was unsure as to whether it was any of Jenny's business.

'Oh!' Jenny's hands shot up to her mouth, without actually touching her face, lest she muck up her make-up. 'How is he? Where is he? Is he all right?'

Jenny suddenly looked frightened – and it aged her at least ten years.

'Yes, he's fine,' Kate softened a little at this display of motherly concern. 'Don't worry, he's fine.'

She was starting to really understand how her mother must have felt all those years, bringing up two kids with a distant husband and nothing to fall back on when the nest inevitably emptied.

She put her hand on Jenny's shoulder and said, 'You go, Mum, it's OK – I've got plenty of work to do and I'll see you on Sunday. Go on, go!'

She shooed her mother away, watching as she skipped happily into the crowd. But where was she going? And why was she dressed so smartly? Who on earth could she be seeing? Who could *possibly* be more important than her daughter, back from the future, with only limited time to sit and talk and make the most of each other?

Kate instinctively felt it, then – the second best-ness Steve had talked about. Now she really knew how he felt, how awful it was to suspect you were languishing low, lingering somewhere at the bottom of a long list of your parents' priorities.

She felt the irresistible urge to follow and quickly took off after her, like Usain Bolt out of the starting blocks – albeit with a dodgy hip, an aching back and a really sore ankle.

She managed to catch sight of Jenny's scarf, so exquisite was it, flying behind her mother's head as she weaved her way through the throng, and did her level best to hobble faster, the pain visible on her knitted brow, her lips puckered like a cat's arse as if she was continually saying 'ooh, me aching bones!'

When she got to Carluccio's, Kate stared through the plate-glass window at the front of the restaurant and gasped when she saw Jenny smoothing down her hair, passing a hand self-consciously over her linen-trousered bum and hugging the breakfast out of the tanned, grey-haired gent who stood up to greet her.

'That guy again,' Kate muttered. 'Get a room!'

She'd always been a little uncomfortable with PDAs, but now she was positively squirming with the unease of it all.

Because, in this instance, she was the public and her mother was the displayer. And the object of her mother's unseemly display of affection was most definitely not her father.

23

Even though it had been cleared of its usual punters and been closed to the public for the day, All Stars Boxing Gym was a hive of activity.

The air fairly fizzed and popped with excitement as the *Mad Fer It!* team fussed over their favourite pop stars and the *Lashed* lot tried to make out that they couldn't care less.

Medea – who probably really didn't give a toss – had been sent to cover the shoot for her first column. She chatted idly to Damien and Nate respectively, looking more bored than all the rest of them put together until Tom arrived.

'I've brought everything we'll ever need for the best shoot ever,' he announced, wiping his nose.

'Did you bring batteries?' Medea asked him. 'Only I think mine are running out and I'll need my Dictaphone to work without a hitch today – don't want to misquote anyone in my first piece.'

Tom replied in the affirmative, desperately trying to keep the enthusiasm out of his voice. Kate couldn't tell whether he was suppressing the yelps of an excited puppy because of Medea's presence and undeniable beauty – or whether he was simply over the moon to be in the same room as his style and musical heroes.

Either way, she thought, he looked happier than she'd seen him for ages. Now if only she could keep him at arm's length, keep on avoiding having the awful break-up chat that they obviously had to have, everything would be perfect.

Steve wandered over to the tea and biscuits table where Kate was making short work of a packet of Penguins.

'You'd better take it easy with those,' he teased gently. 'You've been stacking it on a bit, lately.'

'How *dare* you?' replied Kate, through a mouthful of chocolatey crumbs.

'I can always go and get some more,' squeaked Tamsin, who seemed to have appeared out of nowhere.

'What are you doing here?' Kate couldn't help but ask.

'Archie sent me,' said Tamsin, smugly. 'He said he wanted me to make sure everything went smoothly until he could get here.'

'Did he now?' Kate raised an eyebrow.

Tamsin nodded superciliously and inched her way between Steve and Kate, pouring herself a brew.

'Is Lucy coming down, too?' Steve asked.

'Who?' Tamsin asked.

'Lucy! The receptionist? With the long, dark hair that looks perfect and smells—'

'A hundred times better than you, Steve,' Kate coughed, exaggerating the effect of the overpowering BO emanating from her brother by holding her screwed-up nose. 'Have you showered yet?'

'Yeah, you're 'angin',' said Lee, bounding over to the group and grinning as he bent down to give Kate a hug.

Tamsin giggled nervously and Steve stared at the Mirage front man in awe.

In the absence of any idea about what to do herself, Kate patted the top of Lee's head. She couldn't have been more patronising if she'd tried and felt the brief hot sting of embarrassment.

'Make-up lady's here, Lee,' shouted the picture editor from *Mad Fer It!* from the dressing rooms, freeing both Kate and the pop star from this uncomfortable, awkward moment.

'Make-up's for—'

'Jessies!' Kate, Steve and Tamsin all said in unison, laughing and hoping that Lee wouldn't take offence and knock their collective blocks off.

'You're learning,' laughed Lee, pointing his finger at the threesome and backing away, long arms swaying and bandy legs bending at the knee, making him look positively simian. 'You're fookin' learning.'

Sitting down on the cream-coloured plastic chairs, Kate noticed Tamsin was carrying what appeared to be a small shoebox. She placed it on the tiny strip of material masquerading as a mini skirt (which barely covered her knickers) when she sat down and stared at it lovingly.

'What *is* that?' asked Kate.

'Oh, this little old thing?' Tamsin's voice went all high and squeaky, like she was an impressionable young country singer being asked what her guitar was by some grizzled, old Nashville record company CEO.

Kate nodded.

'It's the office mobile phone,' Tamsin answered, proudly. 'Archie wanted me to be contactable at all times.'

The shoebox rang.

'Oh!' Tamsin shrieked, jumping up and sending the phone tumbling to the floor. 'Cheeky thing vibrates!'

Steve did the chivalrous thing and picked up the vibrating brick, handing it to Tamsin as he body-popped, pretending he had been given an electric shock by the new-fangled, alien-looking mobile telecommunications device, as Seamus would say.

'Hello? HELLO!' Tamsin yelled into the receiver, once she'd fumbled about with it a bit, got the wrist strap and antenna untangled from her hair and flipped open its retractable mouthpiece.

Archie's voice crackled through the line.

'YES, YES – THEY'RE ALL HERE – YES, EVEN NATE – YES, SHE'S HERE... HANG ON... HE WANTS TO SPEAK TO YOU, KATE!'

'All right, all right – no need to shout,' Kate said extra softly, to highlight how uncool Tamsin's unnecessary decibels were and took the phone from her colleague. With both hands.

'Hiya, Arch,' she said into the phone, nearly toppling over ear first with the weight of the thing.

Much to Tamsin's visible annoyance (she folded her arms across her tight cashmere sweater, looked very cross and actually uttered the famous phrase 'harumph!' as she stamped her high-heeled foot), Kate wandered off towards Tom and Medea sitting outside the dressing room, studying the scuffed lino while she walked.

'No, no, it all seems to be going well, so far, touch wood,' she playfully, lightly knocked on Tom's head as she passed him and Medea, deep in editorial conference. 'No bust-ups whatsoever. All rivalries appear to be in check, so far.'

'But that's exactly what we DON'T want!' Archie barked at her. 'We need drama! We need conflict! Come on, Kate – you've got two of the most volatile, unpredictable personalities in there – make some waves! Wind 'em up! We've got to milk the publicity on this for all it's worth – and then some!'

'But—'

'And if it doesn't kick off, front page of the red tops style, don't bother coming back to work – I'll get Tamsin to clear your desk for you!'

Kate was stunned. Her mouth was moving, but no words came out. She must have looked like a fish out of water, an old trout, landed in a boxing gym, taking great gulps of air in vain.

What *was* wrong with Archie? What had she done to provoke his ire so?

'Archie, I hardly think that's fair—'

Click.

Bloody hell, Kate thought, as she walked back to Tamsin, smiling weakly at Tom and Medea and the outrageously famous pop stars lounging about in the ring, looning about on their guitars with boxing gloves on, waiting for their turn with the make-up and hair artist.

Tamsin looked more smug than usual when she clocked Kate's confused, hurt countenance and snatched the phone from her.

'Cracking the whip a bit too much for you today?' said Tamsin, oozing smarm.

Kate glared at her and was almost relieved that she was still bereft of the power of speech – she felt as though the red mist might descend upon her any minute now, and she wouldn't be responsible for what great vengeance her tongue might unleash on silly little Tamsin. Who was about two feet taller than Kate.

'I don't have to put up with this,' muttered Kate narkily as she swiped her khaki anorak off a chair, folded it over her left forearm, turned tail with her nose and chin in the air and stormed out of the smelly old gym. 'I'm going to give that Archie a piece of my mind.'

But by the time she got back to the office, Archie was nowhere to be found.

'Lucy?' Kate approached the reception desk. 'Have you seen Archie?'

'Hmm?' said Lucy, looking over the top of her magazine. 'Who?'

'Archie! The boss! The Big Cheese! The Big Ka-huna!'

'Oh, ah, have you checked in the—'

'He's not at his desk, not in the tea room, not upstairs in the *Lashed* office – nowhere! Oh, Archie – where are you?'

'Well, he's not in there,' said Seamus as he walked out of the gents doing up his fly. 'What's the panic?'

'Oh, nothing,' Kate breathed hard, steam still coming out of her ears. 'Just a work problem.'

'Maybe he's gone down to the shoot,' offered Lucy.

'But I was just there,' Kate said, trying to calm herself down.

'Lucky you,' Lucy said under her breath. 'How is it all going down there, then?'

'Good, good,' said Kate. 'Too good for Archie, though – not enough drama, no real fisticuffs.'

'So everyone really has kissed and made up?' asked Lucy. 'They're all friends again?'

'So far so good,' Kate smiled at the young girl and remembered what it felt like when your pop star heroes were your whole world, when they mattered to you more than your family, when your whole identity was wrapped up in their personas.

'And who else is there? I mean, who's covering it for, um, *Lashed*?'

'Medea and Steve, I think,' said Kate, who couldn't wait to read their different takes on the same event. 'Tell you what – why don't you go and see for yourself? Go down to the shoot, check it all out first-hand? And if Archie's there, tell him I'm looking for him.'

Lucy didn't need to be asked twice and leaped up, vaulting over the reception desk, bolting past The Lift and taking the fire stairs, two-by-two. She didn't even remember to take her handbag, she was in such a rush.

For some unknown reason – maybe it was a force of habit – when Kate turned around, her eyes were drawn towards Seamus' crotch area, where a big wet patch had taken on an oblong shape. She'd seen it now nigh on a trillion times back in the future and knew exactly what it was, despite Seamus' lame excuses.

Seamus looked down to see what Kate was gawping at and blushed.

'Oh, uh,' he stammered. 'It's the cold tap in those toilets – comes out with such force, it nearly hits you in the eye as it splashes off the basin.'

He laughed nervously and added: 'The *eyes*, I mean, the eyes in your head.'

Kate felt a wave of disappointment wash over her. Twenty years, she thought to herself. Do I have to suffer through *at least* the next twenty years of my life with a man who blames his poor willy-shaking technique on faulty tapware?

At first she thought it vaguely amusing, way back when, but after two kids and being relegated to a tedious existence in the suburbs, Kate had begun to see such sloppy behaviour as merely pathetic.

'You just didn't dry yourself properly,' she said, deadpan, and turned away in disgust.

'Yes I did! Honestly,' protested Seamus, 'it's cold water! From when I was washing my hands! Aren't you pleased I was *washing my hands*? How many blokes do that?'

But Kate dismissed him with a click of her tongue and a mumbled 'whatever' as she tried to make out what kind of alien life force had landed on her desk.

'At least I was washing my hands,' Seamus murmured again, feeling quite sorry for himself at this, as far as he could see, unsolicited attack.

'What's all this?' Kate asked, holding up a black box and a nest of wires.

'Oh, Kev and I are trialling some new equipment on your computer,' Seamus' eyes lit up and he almost skipped to her side. 'That's the old modem which, as you can plainly see, is quite clunky and cumbersome.'

Kate could, indeed, see that. As well as Seamus' obvious passion for all things tech. She softened to him at this point, forgetting all about the wet patch.

'You love it, don't you?' she stated rather than asked.

'Pardon?' he replied, wide-eyed.

'All this new-fangled technological stuff,' she air-typed and jerked her head towards her computer monitor and keyboard.

'Oh! Yes, yes,' he nodded emphatically. 'It's fascinating, really, how...'

Kate didn't hear the rest of Seamus' sentence – she was too busy trying to hold onto the edge of her desk as the world, with Seamus at its centre, started to spin around her.

Bugger, she thought. *I bet this is it – I'm going to be shunted back to 2022 right now and I haven't even managed to sort my career out…*

The spinning slowed down a little, while Seamus continued to burble on in the background, but all Kate could hear were soaring violins. She felt more than heard the vibrations and the hum of his voice and could see him getting more and more animated as he took the top off the computer and showed her the delights it contained.

A creeping sense of sickness started working its way up Kate's body from the tips of her toes to under her arms, making her armpits bristle.

She must be being sent back to the future – unless she was having a particularly violent hot flush. She felt dizzy and discombobulated, so she closed her eyes and held her breath.

Slowly, like she was coming to after being knocked out, Seamus' voice grew louder and she felt the spinning stop.

'…and so, yeah, I suppose it's my dream, now – to start up my own company, make several million, make the most of the internet while I can and use my millions for good, helping other people less fortunate than myself. My philanthropy could really be financed by what I like to call the *"c" full stop, "o" full stop, "u" "k" boom…*'

Kate saw Seamus wriggle his fingers like fuzzy bunny ears at her as he said the last bit and noticed that, for the first time since she'd been back in 1996, Seamus looked quite pleased with himself, like the cat who got the cream, as though there might be some confidence buried deep down in there somewhere. Very deep.

'To coin a phrase!' came Kevin's voice, his face slowly coming into focus for a bleary-eyed Kate.

'Are you all right, Kate?' asked Seamus.

In an unprecedented act of chivalry, Kevin whipped off his cagoule and put it over Kate's shoulders while simultaneously guiding her down into her swivel chair.

'I've got it, I've got it,' said a slightly annoyed Seamus, elbowing Kevin out of the way and trying to pick Kate up. 'Would you like an Irn Bru? Red Bull? Beer?'

He really was as clueless as he looked.

'No, no thanks – I'm fine,' Kate said, rubbing her forehead. 'Just got a bit dizzy, that's all.'

The genuinely concerned Seamus held her as if he were carrying her over the threshold and Kate looked up at him with what felt like new eyes, like she was seeing him – really seeing him – for the first time.

'Have you… erm… I don't really know how to put this, but have you been… ah… scoffing a lot of chocolate lately?' Seamus stuttered.

Kate looked at him and smiled beatifically as she felt warmth flood her veins, making her imagine them with caramel flowing through them, instead of blood.

'Hmmm, caramel, toffee…' she smiled blissfully.

'A-HA! I thought you looked a little bit, I dunno… *chunkier* than when we first met!' declared Seamus, dropping her a bit roughly into her chair. 'So you *have* been getting my little gifts, eh? I hope you realise that not just anyone gets my last Rolo, you know.'

'You really have no idea, do you?' Kate sat up, her interior caramel cooling and hardening rapidly. 'You just don't say *anything* to a woman about how she looks or what she's been eating. Unless it's "wow, have you lost weight?" or "have my chips, I don't mind – honestly, there's nothing of you".'

'But I—'

'Ah, forget it,' Kate heaved a sigh. 'Just the one Rolo, then, was it?'

'Well, no,' said Seamus, looking hurt. 'A whole packet. Every day. Didn't you get them?'

'But I LOVE Rolos!' she said, her legs kicking out like a toddler on a too-tall chair, making something rustle under her desk.

'Steve?' she said, bending down to look.

And there, amongst all the wires and crumbs and empty Pot Noodle cups and sparkling Ribena bottles, were about six Rolo wrappers.

'Steve!' she huffed.

And then she looked up into Seamus' eyes, slowly nodding her head in approval. Because maybe he wasn't so hopeless about women after all.

24

'Oh, come ON!' Kate huffed when she woke up on Saturday morning. 'How can I *still* be here?'

Somehow, with her tummy swelling and her arms puffing up (not to mention her jowls making a re-appearance and her eyelids starting to droop again), she thought she might have woken up in 2022.

But here she was, still in her bedroom of the West Hampstead flat, a clueless Seamus to take shopping in an hour, followed by a football match at smoky, rowdy O'Flaherty's.

To think she would have given her left (podgy) arm for such an experience a few weeks ago – to be right in the thick of it again, footloose and fancy free, with no familial responsibility, no ties that bind to hold her down – who wouldn't be over the moon to have that chance again?

But now, instead of throwing off the shackles of her life as a wife and mother and leaping into the past with gusto, she felt sad to be without her adorable little handbrakes – now she was starting to feel quite uncomfortably *stuck*.

'Chains' by Tina Arena bellowed out of the radio.

'You said it, Teen,' Kate muttered to herself as she slid out from between the sheets.

'Oooh!' she drew a sharp inward breath.

The sciatica at the top of her left buttock was really pinching now – only to be outdone by the sudden searing pain in her right hip. She lay back down, musing about how she supposed the flesh could go back in time, ironing out the wrinkles and disintegrating some unsightly flubber in the process – but the bones, dem bones, dem bones, dem dry bones – there was no way they could ever be twenty-eight again.

Carefully and in slo mo, Kate raised herself up to a sitting position and, from there, managed to push herself up with her arms to a Neanderthal Man hunched over, knuckle dragging standing stance.

She swore she could hear herself creak as she straightened herself out and drew herself up to her full height. She placed her open palms on the curve of her waist and was instantly gratified to find it was still slim. Not as slight as it had been ten days ago, granted, but at least it was still *there*, unlike her waist in 2022, which had vanished, missing in action, sometime around 2006.

And so were her smooth, barely there hips – a million miles away from the dimply shelves they would one day become.

She wondered whether it was glucosamine or cod liver oil that the oldies took for their joints and made a mental note to herself to buy a couple of vats of each when she was in town next, picking up her pensioner's bus pass.

She thought how great it would be to have free off-peak bus travel, actually – just think of all the places she could go! Other towns not within walking distance, London... But then her eyes fell to the floor and she sighed, imagining that the brilliance of the bus pass would be rather cancelled out by the inevitability of having to get up the bus's steps on a zimmer frame – if you managed to remember it as you left the nursing home.

'Getting old is no fun,' she said.

She looked at herself in the long mirror attached to the inside door of her flimsy pine wardrobe.

'And what's so amazing about London, anyway?' she asked her reflection.

It didn't answer her, but she stared at it for ages, just in case.

Her body was still a marked, major improvement on the latter-day version, but she could definitely see the signs pointing to where it was heading: due south, no stopping on the hard (sloping) shoulder.

She stepped closer and scrutinised her face. And for the first time ever, she didn't grimace as she felt the beginnings of her jowls – and she barely flinched as she felt her brow line sagging down, nearly meeting her eyelashes.

In fact, she broke into a grin when she saw that Seamus and Steve were right – her belly was rounding out rather nicely, thank you very much.

She was convinced all this body expansion and face droop meant she was being prepped for being flung back to the future. And this put a spring in her step and a song in her heart as she threw on a way too short, flowery baby doll dress and Doc Martens boots that came up past her thin, bony, but still a little bit sore ankle.

Stylish *and* supportive, she congratulated herself on her wise choice of footwear as she did up the laces. You can't be too careful with dodgy old bones and ankles and metatarsals these days, her inner OAP said prudently.

She'd always longed to have the kind of tall, thin body that could carry off floaty dresses teamed with clunky boots and even make that particular ensemble look *sexy*. She wanted to look like Diane Keaton in *Annie Hall* – all lithe and coltish and limby.

But she was always far too short and chubby for that sort of caper – or, at least, she always *thought* she was.

Today, however, she felt like she could give even Audrey Hepburn a run for her money, because, stop press, she actually looked… quite good!

Go on, say it out loud, like you're talking to your best friend – make yourself really believe it!

'You look great!' she obeyed herself.

Say you're enough, go on! You. Are. Enough!

Back in 2022 she always struggled with this one. But she didn't hesitate now.

'You are enough.' She nodded at herself.

A little bit perplexed by this positive self-talk *sans* snark, she narrowed her eyes, bit the inside of her cheek and wondered fleetingly whether it was her body dysmorphia that was in full swing or whether her eyesight was now officially up the spout.

She had been feeling a little out of focus, a bit blurry, fuzzy, slightly off-kilter lately.

She peered at herself.

'Yep, you look great!' she said again. 'Even though you're porking out, it's now or never to start loving your body – or at least liking it a little bit. No matter how much it makes the ground beneath you shake.'

See what she did there? She couldn't help herself. She wandered cautiously into the kitchen.

'Brave outfit, our kid,' said Steve in a shockingly bad Mancunian accent. 'Do you really think you should wear that?'

'Don't listen to him,' said Portia through a mouthful of toast. 'You look fab. All you need is a hat with a massive flower on it, like Blossom, and you're away!'

255

Kate wasn't sure whether Portia was taking the mickey or not, so she simply worked her lips into what she hoped was an enigmatic smile (although she had no idea how to do this) and sat down on the kitchen bench.

She self-consciously tugged at the hem on her dress, trying to pull it over her plump knees, even though they were out of sight, hidden underneath the heavy oak table.

'Where you off to, anyway?' asked Steve.

'Shopping first, football after,' Kate replied, helping herself to an unfeasibly large bowl of Crunchy Nut Corn Flakes.

'That's not like you,' said Portia, gathering up her thick dark hair into a ponytail and securing it with a fluoro-orange scrunchie.

'Oh!' cried Kate. 'I haven't seen one of those for—'

'Yeah, sorry,' said Portia. 'I raided your supply ages ago – haven't had the time to get any more.'

Kate screwed up her face and stared at Portia. How she could wear neon-coloured hair bands and still look beautiful, was beyond her. The bright colours always clashed with Kate's skin tone whenever she tried for a casual up-do and she invariably ended up looking like some saddo who never got over the Eighties.

'Ahem,' Kate coughed. 'Forget about it – with all these layers, I can't do anything with my hair, except the Rachel.'

'And even that's not going too well, lately, is it?' said Steve as he got up to put his cereal bowl in the sink.

Little wonder, she thought, that she was so insecure about her looks, when those closest to her took pot-shots at her appearance as a matter of course. Thank god for the Kindness Revolution of the twenty-first century!

'What's with you this morning?' Kate said, starting to get a little tired of Steve's verbal assault.

'Oh, nothing, nothing,' he said, frowning. 'I'm sorry. I don't know what's wrong with me – you look fine. Honestly.'

Fine? *Fine?*

'Gorgeous, you mean,' Portia corrected him. 'Fine is for weather, not women.'

Good line, thought Kate. She repeated it in her head three times in an effort to remember it for when Seamus said the exact same, infuriating thing back in 2022.

'You're right, you're right,' said Steve, putting his hands on Kate's shoulders from behind and bending down to kiss her cheek. 'You look gorgeous. I'm just a little tetchy this morning because I've got... a date!'

'A *date*?' the girls chorused.

'Who is she?' Portia asked.

'*He,*' Steve said pointedly.

Bloody hell, Kate thought. Let's not get all hung up on pronouns just yet. We've got ages to go till that becomes a thing!

'Oh yeah, I forgot. About bloody time,' Portia dead-panned and went back to her cereal.

Steve hesitated, surprised that Portia looked so bored by his 'bombshell'. Then he grinned, turned his back and took off.

'See you at O'Flaherty's!' he yelled as the front door slammed heavily behind him.

–

Despite the warm air, Kate shivered a little as she stood in front of Selfridge's, waiting for Seamus.

Her knees hadn't been this exposed for what felt like centuries and the body-loving, confident attitude she had assumed only an hour ago, had all but deserted her as she hugged herself, glad of the last-minute Hennes pin-striped blazer she'd grabbed on her way out of the flat.

Not that she was into or even normally *aware* of labels – unless they were of the Primark or TK Maxx bargainous variety. In fact, she didn't care for shopping much, either, if truth be told.

She was okay shopping for everyone else, but when it came to clothes shopping for *herself*, Kate just couldn't get into it.

Just like her old size 12 jeans.

Perhaps it was the fact that she was entering (or had already entered) that phase of life where comfort was more important to her than being on-trend; for at fifty-four, she wore Fit Flops rather than Havaianas, Hush Puppies as opposed to killer heels and Ann Summers was a shop of the past; M&S being her first choice these days for big knickers, shapewear and anything with an elasticated waist.

Maybe it was because she found the whole depressing experience a colossal waste of time, when nothing ever fitted or looked good on her, she had no idea what was age appropriate and she was constantly shocked by the old woman she saw staring back at her from changing room mirrors.

She much preferred shopping for food, lulling herself into a false sense of domestic goddessery, where she could indulge her fantasies of preparing perfect three-course meals for her wonderfully erudite, Wildean, very-possibly-off-the telly friends as they noshed under fairy lights in her bijou London garden. She often imagined their faces as they took their first bite of her tiramisu, their eyes closing in ecstasy as they lustily declared her dessert 'absolutely heavenly' for the cameras.

She loved food (clearly) and she loved *shopping* for food. Nothing cheered her up more than a fully stocked fridge. But clothes shopping? Meh.

But anyway, she reminded herself, this wasn't about her. This little expedition was all about Seamus. Because not only did she have to secure Seamus' help if she was ever to get back to 2022, it was also the perfect excuse to just spend some time with him, alone together.

She wanted to get to know him again, find out what it was about him that made her fall in love with him in the first place. Assuming she really did, once upon a time.

Given her attitude to clothes shopping, though, how on earth was she going to save Seamus from a life of leisure suits and other trainspottery garb? Particularly when she herself had known some tragic outfits of her own?

She stifled a giggle, remembering the day she'd just bought a pair of pixie boots in Carnaby Street and was wearing them when she met Portia out the front of some shop. When Portia saw that Kate was wearing new boots, and that her old Spice Girls trainers were in a plastic bag, she grabbed the bag and shoved it in a nearby bin, quickly shepherding Kate towards The Sun & 13 Cantons pub, lest she bin-dive to retrieve them.

Still, she reasoned with herself, she *had* to have more innate dress sense than Seamus did. God knows, Timmy Mallet had more taste in his *hat* than Seamus had in his entire wardrobe. All she had to do was remember what passed for cool mens clothes in 1996 – otherwise it could all go horribly Pete Tong.

When he ran up to her (Seamus, that is, not Pete Tong), out of breath and panting, his old-school Adidas tracksuit top flapping about behind him, Kate greeted him with a tentative kiss on the cheek and a quiz.

'First up, let's test your fashion IQ,' she said, wondering for a second whether she had been working with magazines for a bit too long. 'For instance, what do you think of what I'm wearing?'

'Yeah,' he answered distractedly, panting like a dog. 'Yeah, it's fine.'

'Fine?' she shook her head, as though she couldn't quite believe what she was hearing (even though, of course, she'd heard it a million times before from Seamus and had even come to expect it as his stock response to just about any question she threw at him). 'Fine is for weather, not women.'

So proud of herself and her short-term memory, she nodded as if to say: 'Oh yeah, baby, that's how I roll! That's what we're dealing with here; wit *and* repartee!'

'Oh, I didn't mean to sound—'

'Like a typical bloke?' she finished his sentence for him, feeling as sharp as a tack.

'No, I-I actually think it looks fantastic!' Seamus' voice cracked when he said 'fantastic'.

'Oh.' Kate looked down at her spongy knees and put her hands on her hips. 'This old thing?'

'No, not you – your dress!' Seamus tried to elbow her in the ribs, but only made it to her upper arm, such was their height difference.

Kate's arms dropped to her sides and she pulled a pretend offended face.

'Let's head to Topman, see what they can do for you,' she said, steering him towards Oxford Circus.

Not twenty minutes later, Seamus pulled back the changing room curtain for his big reveal. There he was, this six foot two gentle giant in skinny jeans, a white t-shirt with a red-checked lumberjack shirt tied around his waist, Reebok pump high-top sneakers and a baseball cap dangling from his fingers.

'It's just not really me,' he said quietly. 'All feels a bit too East 17 to me. But if you like it...'

And she did. Sort of. She was so used to seeing Seamus as the trainspotter that style forgot, she was desperate to get him into something young and cool while she had the chance.

But even she found Seamus tarted up like he was from One Direction circa 2012 a bit mutton dressed as lamb... if you could say 'mutton' for men.

Kate didn't think you could. And anyway, it sounded like an ad for aftershave, she giggled to herself – Try new Mutton For Men – and have the ladies baa-ing for more/and send the ladies baa-ing mad/and you'll never baa up the wrong tree again/the hottest aftershave known to man – baa none...

Focus, Katie, focus.

But she couldn't. She hadn't thought like this for ages. She used to always be like this, thinking up slogans and soundbites, a frustrated advertising exec with nowhere to go. If only she could get out of PR and into advertising. But more Darren Stevens in *Bewitched* than Don Draper in *Mad Men*, she thought to herself. It had been her dream ever since she was a little kid.

Maybe she meant *rammy* – more rammy than lamby? No, that didn't sound right. Ram dressed as lamb. Yes! That was it.

'Hmmm,' she said, rubbing her slightly less defined chin. 'Bit rammy, you're right. How old are you again?'

'Twenty-eight,' he answered. 'Why?'

Kate shook her head quickly, as though his very question was a massive irritation.

'It's just... why do you insist on looking so old? Way before your time?'

'I didn't think I did,' he replied, sounding a smidge hurt. 'But even if I do, what's wrong with looking old? What's so *bad* about old?'

That shut her up. Kate couldn't find the words to express how she felt about age – especially as she'd done somewhat of a 180 in the past few days where her attitude towards her ageing body was concerned.

'Nothing.' She shrugged as Seamus drew the changing room curtain and got back into his own clothes. 'There's nothing bad about it at all, I s'pose. Beats the alternative, as all the old farts say. I just think that, while you're young, you might as well make the most of it – all that tight skin, all that wrinkle-free flesh...'

At that moment, Seamus emerged, rubbing his just-about-to-start-balding-any-minute pate.

'Ah, it's not all it's cracked up to be,' he grinned, the twinkle in his eye burning bright.

'You see?' said Kate, holding out her hands in exasperation. 'You've got a full head of hair and you're acting as though you're fucking Kojak!'

'All right, all right,' said Seamus, his smile fading and the twinkle dulling. 'Keep *your* hair on!'

'You'll be growing hair out of your ears and nostrils before you know it, your nose getting bigger and more bulbous...'

'And on that bombshell...' Seamus smiled, handing the clothes clothes back to the bored salesgirl at the counter.

As the pair walked out of the youth-crazed shop and meandered up Oxford Street, Kate began her sermon.

'I just think you're really quite good-looking, you know, and you don't do yourself any favours wearing all that boring old nondescript gear,' she explained. 'I mean, as a girl, sorry, a woman, rather, I know that when you think you look good you feel good. Or is it vice versa? Bugger! I can never remember which way round they go! Anyway, the point is, your confidence soars when your outer self is as interesting or as charming or as amusing or as good looking as your inner self and—'

'What a load of old—'

'It's true!'

'So do you think I'm charming and funny, too?'

'Only if you're wearing that football shirt as some sort of a joke.' She smiled up at him.

Seamus stopped mid-lope and held onto Kate's elbows gently, turning her around to face him.

'I've never said this to a girl – *a woman* – before, Kate, but I want you to know that you can always count on me...'

'Yes?' Kate looked past Seamus' nerdy specs, deep into the dark-brown pools that were his eyes.

Here it comes, she thought, his declaration of love, how he's hot but dependable; fun and feisty, desperate to dedicate his life to making her and their kids happy.

Kate drew in a deep breath, nearly paralysed by the potential poignancy of the moment.

His gaze bore into hers, eyes moist with meaning.

'You can always count on me to never, *ever* joke about Liverpool.'

Kate let Seamus keep his cool tracksuit jacket because they saw a couple of the guys from Ocean Colour Scene wearing them as they trawled the shops in Carnaby Street and Seamus convinced her this was proof he was a trend-setter not a trainspotter.

But as they passed a bin on their way to O'Flaherty's, she did a Portia: she wrestled the plastic bag containing his too-tight denim jeans, his ugly boat shoes and his Seventies shirt that was giving off so much static electricity even the hairs on Seamus' arms were standing on end – and chucked them all away.

Before they walked into the pub, Kate admired her handiwork.

'You look great, Seamus,' she reassured him. 'Really good.'

'You sure it's not too try-hard?' his eyes searched hers, uncertainty in his voice.

'Don't be ridiculous.' Kate dismissed his concerns. 'You're just not used to looking so fit. It'll take your brain a while to catch up. In the meantime, I suggest you get some new glasses. Or why not go for contacts?'

Seamus shook his head at this and she realised she was pushing him too far, too fast.

'All in good time,' she smiled, silently encouraging him to trust her, embrace change and make an appointment at Specsavers. He had, after all, gone leaps and bounds in the style stakes today and if he carried on like this, Kate thought, she'd have to beat the competition off with a stick.

Speaking of competition, as they pushed the saloon doors open, Portia bounded up to them.

'A-ha!' she slurred, unsteady on her feet already. 'I KNEW you were up to something, Kate! Knew you wanted him all to yourself!'

Kate directed her best friend away from her husband-to-be and manoeuvred her through the rowdy crowd towards the other end of the bar.

'God!' Kate exclaimed. 'Was it just us or was everyone drinking like fish in 1996?'

'What? Just get me another vodka Red Bull and show me the guy you want to set me up with. You said he worked at PGT&B?'

Kate scanned the pub, standing on the metal pole at the foot of the bar, ike a meerkat looking for safety on the savannah – all rigid of back and jerky of head movement. But she couldn't see Kevin anywhere. Not that that meant anything – due to her restricted height and slightly blurred vision, she couldn't see much at all. Kevin could well be there, it's just that Kate wouldn't know it.

What she did know, though, was that Archie was on her horizon. She could feel it.

Her eyes darted left and right and then BULLSEYE! Her gaze locked onto his and he called her name as he approached.

'Kate!' he yelled, standing on his tiptoes as punters barged into him, lager sloshing out of their pint glasses and splashing onto his shirt.

Pubs where you couldn't get a seat were no place for those shorter in stature, Kate thought to herself as she looked around for a vacant table. When she couldn't see one, and Archie began to close in on her, she fought the almost irresistible urge to flee.

'Kate!' He muscled his way through the burly blokes surrounding the girls and looked up at Portia, as though

265

he'd only just noticed how positively Amazonian she was, compared to his little tiddly self.

This'll be interesting, Kate thought.

'I'm so glad I found you,' he said, short of breath. 'I wanted to apologise, explain why I've been behaving the way I have towards you lately.'

Portia gave Kate an 'I'll get the popcorn' kind of look, shoved a straw into her mouth and sucked the living daylights out of it.

'Could we talk somewhere a little more private?' he asked, looking decidedly awkward.

'Oh! Don't mind me,' said Portia, straw still in her mouth. 'I was leaving, anyway. I believe there's a man somewhere out there with my name on him.'

Kate felt her stomach lurch, hoping against all hope that Portia didn't mean Seamus. Because no man stood a chance against her feminine wiles! Even if said wiles – whatever they were – were a little slow due to their being drenched in vodka.

She took a deep breath through her nose and tried to calm herself, find her centre, as Portia had told her to do so many times when the kids were driving her crazy.

'So, young Archie,' she said, in an only slightly patronising way. 'What have you got to say for yourself, then? You've been really horrible to me lately and—'

'I know, I know.' Archie cut her off. 'But I can explain.'

A space cleared next to Kate and Archie leaped up onto the empty bar stool that was revealed, like a ten-year-old gymnast, straddling the horse.

'I'm listening,' Kate said, trying to fold her arms across her chest, but not being able to, thanks to her bust doubling in size right before her eyes.

Oh lord, Kate said to herself. So they're getting bigger now, too! What's the bet I'll be back in a 38DD and lounging about in 2022 before I've even finished this pint!

'Blimey,' said Archie, unable to tear his gaze away from her bosoms.

'You were saying?' Kate said, taking another mouthful of beer and playing with the condensation on the glass with her fingertips.

'Right, yes, I, ah… I wanted to apologise for acting so weirdly around you lately – it's all my fault, of course.'

'Of course,' Kate echoed.

'I couldn't help it,' Archie carried on. 'I've had a crush on you ever since we met and even though I knew, deep down, that we would never get together, that we weren't actually ever meant to be a couple, that didn't stop me seeing red and getting insanely jealous whenever what's-his-face craned his scrawny neck into your orbit.'

'Who?' Kate took a step back. 'Tom?'

'No! You know,' said Archie, looking to the floor as if he was about to spit in disgust. 'That IT guy, Wayne or Shane or something.'

'*Seamus*, you mean?'

'Something like that,' Archie said quickly, as though he was annoyed for conjuring up the mental image of the very man he wanted Kate to ignore. 'Anyway, he's not important. What is important is that I couldn't handle it every time I thought of you with him and so—'

'And so you acted like a real dick?' Kate helped him out.

'Yes,' said Archie sheepishly. 'Can you ever find it in your heart to forgive me?'

Kate looked off into the middle distance as though she were seriously considering his question.

'Kate?' Archie said after a few minutes. 'Kate, I'm so sorry. Please forgive me.'

'I dunno...' She milked it for all it was worth.

'What if I fixed your contract and you only had to work a four-day week?'

'Hmmm,' hummed Kate, sure she could see some sweat forming on Archie's brow. 'I dunno. That open-plan office is getting me down a bit...'

'You can have your own office! You can have mine! Would that help?'

'Could I WFH?'

'What the fuh—?'

'You know, work from home. Everyone's doing it since the pandemic and it's way more productive and, like, two or three days a week would be perf—'

Archie looked at her as if she was confessing to cannibalism.

'Well, what about my salary then? It's so shit! Barely keeps me in rent and microwave meals for one!'

'Easy, tiger! Now you're just taking the piss!'

But just then she saw something move out of the corner of her eye; something so striking, so compelling, so *gorgeous*, she simply had to ignore everything around her and stare straight at it.

The crowd noise died down to almost nothing and everybody else in the packed pub morphed into one slow-moving mass. And what came into sharp relief, where the spotlight was shining brightest, was on the profile of an impossibly handsome man. A man who was wearing an outfit that would make Paul Weller green with sartorial envy. The crowd parted, the angels sang...

The dashing figure walked straight up to Kate and when their eyes met, she felt her knees buckle.

25

'Halloooo!' George beamed when he opened the front door. 'Come in, come in, come in!'

He ushered Kate, Seamus, Steve and Portia into the front hall of the family home, the intoxicating aroma of Jenny's roast lamb and perfect potatoes filling the air. All four guests swooned simultaneously at this, with Seamus and Portia saying in unison: 'Smells great!'

'Dad,' Kate addressed George solemnly. 'I've got… I need to talk to you.'

'No! Don't!' Steve jumped in between them.

'It's not about you, Steve – not everything's about you, you know,' Kate got a teensy bit narked. 'Anyway, I've already told them you're—'

'Nooooo!' Steve put his head in his hands. 'I knew they'd disown me!'

'No one's disowning anyone, Son,' said George, putting his arm around him. 'We don't care whether you dig men or women – we just want you to be happy. If you're lucky enough to find true love in this crazy old world, grab it with both hands and never let it slip away!'

Steve's chin dimpled.

'Really? Thanks, Dad,' he said, giving George a bear hug.

Kate felt herself welling up.

'Can I have a quick word, Daddy?' she said.

269

'Not you too?!'

'No,' she said, 'not that there's anything wrong with that!'

'Is everything all right then?' He looked worried.

'Everything's grand,' she said, reaching up to rest her hand on George's shoulder and coming over all serious. 'I just wanted to say, while you're here and I've got the chance, that I love you, I miss you and I forgive you.'

'For what?' George looked perplexed.

'We're all human,' Kate continued undeterred, 'and we all make mistakes – some more than others, granted, but it's the way we deal with our failures that really matters.'

'Good grief – is this going to be like one of your mother's interminable lectures?' George laughed.

'I mean, I know it can't have been easy—'

'Come on through, everybody!' Jenny called out from the kitchen. 'I'm just pouring the champagne!'

'Better do as 'er indoors says – you know how she gets.' George kissed Kate on the cheek and trotted off into the kitchen.

'Ooh! Champers!' trilled Portia. 'What are we celebrating?'

'Life!' Jenny chuckled as she turned around from the wall oven and extended her hand to Seamus. 'Kate? Aren't you going to introduce us?'

'Oh! Sorry,' said Kate. 'This is Seamus, my..., my friend, Seamus.'

'Pleased to meet you, Mrs—' Seamus began.

'Jenny, please. Do call me Jenny.'

'Right, right,' said Seamus, ducking his head in deference as Kate gently put her hand on the small of his back.

'But not you,' Jenny said, spying Steve, 'don't you ever call me anything but Mum!'

In the warm kitchen, everyone watched as Jenny hugged Steve for all she was worth.

'You're not getting away this time,' she said, her voice muffled as she squashed her face into his shirt. 'How could you think we'd… that we would ever be anything less than proud… Oh! I refuse to ever let you go!'

'Well, OK, but can you just… loosen your grip… a little bit?' laughed Steve through short breaths. 'I can't breathe!'

'No!' Jenny sniffed. 'Never!'

Mother and son separated, but held each other's gaze.

'Where's my hello?' Portia broke the spell.

'Ah, Portia,' cooed Jenny. 'We haven't seen you for such a long time! How are you, hmm?'

'Good, good,' Portia smiled. 'But absolutely Hank Marvin!'

'Well, sit down,' Jenny tore herself away from Steve shortly after pinching his cheeks puce. 'I thought we could start with soup in the garden, it being such a lovely day – and then migrate inside for the main event.'

Kate drank in the wonderfully warm family scene unfolding before her. She felt like she was having an out-of-body experience, hovering above somebody else's near-perfect, almost-functional family.

Seamus looked at Kate, feeling half like the invisible man, half like the jolly green giant. She turned her attention to the oven, though, a slightly unsettling smile on her face.

'Hmm. Roast,' she said, absent-mindedly licking her lips and giving herself permission to fall right off the vegan wagon.

Seamus shifted about uneasily as Jenny looked him up and down.

'You've got something stuck to your face,' she said.

With the index finger of her right hand outstretched, like ET pointing to the sky, Jenny skipped over to Seamus and tried to pull off the patchy bits of hair covering his cheekbones.

'It's just… a bit… of fluff…'

Seamus pulled away and rubbed his cheek.

'Actually, they're my sidies,' he said sheepishly. 'Or will be, eventually.'

Jenny looked at him, puzzled.

'Sidies? What on earth—'

'Sideburns, Mum,' Kate said. 'You know, mutton chops! Anyway, leave him alone, will you? Can we eat? We're all wasting away here!'

'Hardly,' Jenny raised an eyebrow, pursing her lips as she made a point of glancing southwards at Kate's bum.

'Don't fat shame me.' Kate grinned.

'I beg your pardon?' Jenny looked confused at Kate's decidedly twenty-first century choice of phrase as she herded the group outside.

Once in the garden, the Pimm's and the champagne flowed – for everyone but Kate, that is.

'You know, you lot can really put it away,' she couldn't help but comment, a touch of the school marm to her tone.

'So can you,' Steve retorted. 'Usually you can, anyway.'

'Yeah,' said Portia, putting her glass down for a split second and sparking up a Marlboro Light. 'And she doesn't smoke any more. Maybe that's why she's stacking on the weight.'

'I'll have you know,' said Kate, 'that I am not "stacking on the weight" as you so delicately put it, Portia – I am simply becoming a proper, grown-up woman, getting my

priorities straight, keeping a clear head and along with my
maturity, gaining some lumps and bumps along the way.'

Kate took a sip of her lemonade (home-made – Jenny
was pulling out all the stops on the domestic front today)
and winced as she heard what she'd just said and realised
how boring and old farty she sounded.

'I mean, I might be getting, um, a tad *curvier*,' she went
on, trying to redeem herself, 'but that's what real women
look like as they get older. And there's nothing wrong
with that at all, is there, Mum?'

'Sorry, sweetheart?' Jenny said.

'A lot of men find The Older Woman quite sexy, don't
they, Mother?'

'I'm sorry, but I don't have the faintest idea what you're
talking about,' Jenny said.

Kate leaned in towards her mother, conspiratorially,
but continued talking loudly.

'I saw you with that… that man,' she said. 'At
Carluccio's the other day. Likes a more *mature* woman,
does he? Hmm?'

'Carluccio's… Carluccio's?' Jenny visibly racked her
brains.

'Oh come on!' Steve butted in, pushing himself up by
the arms of his chair and crossing his legs theatrically, like
Kenny Everett used to do on his old video show. 'All this
talk of Carluccio's is killing me! When's lunch, Ma?'

'Ooh! Yes,' Jenny clutched the lapis lazuli beads that
hung around her neck. 'I nearly forgot! George, darling?
Would you get the joint out and wrap it up in tin foil, let
it sit for twenty minutes? And someone get the veg out
and start on the gravy, too, would you? I just want to have
a little word with my devoted daughter here.'

Kate looked at Seamus, almost apologetically, and motioned for him to go inside.

'I'll be in in a sec,' she whispered to him, reassuringly. 'Go on. Portia'll look after you.'

'That's what I'm afraid of,' said Seamus at the same moment as Portia linked her left arm into his right.

'Come on, you great hunk of man,' said Portia, rubbing her right hand up and down what would have been his bicep, if he'd had any muscles.

Jenny busied herself picking up the pitcher of Pimm's and a couple of empty glasses.

'So, dear,' she began. 'You've gone off the booze and fags, there's a, shall we say, a *thickening* around your middle...'

'I wouldn't say thickening,' Kate interrupted, her chin falling to her chest as she inspected her waist.

'Are you pregnant?'

'What?' Kate could hardly believe her ears.

'I beg your pardon, you mean,' her mother corrected her.

'No!' Kate slurped up the last bits of creamy potato and leek soup that Seamus and Portia had left in their respective bowls. 'Of course I'm not!'

Jenny either didn't hear her daughter's response – or flatly didn't believe her, because she carried on regardless.

'And is that nice young man, the one with the hairy face – is he the father? What the hell happened to Tom? And why don't you tell me anything anymore?'

'No!' Kate cried. 'No, I am not pregnant. And no, Seamus isn't the father, either. Not yet, anyw—'

She stopped herself when she heard those words and shuddered to think how close she came to going off with Tom and effectively erasing Seamus from her life. She screwed up her nose, thinking that if she'd ignored Seamus and rid herself of him, then, as a result, Phoebe and Declan would disappear, too.

'And Tom?' Jenny pressed. 'Last I heard you were moving in together – what happened there?'

'Nothing, really,' Kate said, trying hard to remember what had actually happened. 'I think we both realised it wasn't going to work. He's a nice guy and everything—'

'Well, he did save our Steve from rack and ruin.' Jenny looked at Kate with wide eyes.

They both looked over at Steve, who raised his glass at them, wondering what on earth they were talking about.

'I know, it's just…' Kate squirmed and looked over the garden fence. 'I just didn't fancy him in the end.'

Kate dared to look at Jenny, who softened and nodded as she picked up the soup tureen and began to head inside.

'Hmm,' she hummed, dreamily. 'I know exactly what you mean.'

'You do?'

'Yes, darling, I do. Even women of *uncertain age* need to get their rocks off from time to time, you know.'

'So that's what put this rather unseemly spring in your step, is it? You've been *at it*, like a dog in heat, have you? Hmmm?'

'Hardly, sweetheart.' Jenny laughed. 'And a little less of *the dog*, if you don't mind.'

Kate thought of the suave man she'd seen her mum throwing herself at in Carluccio's and felt her face redden.

'Mum! How could you?'

'How could I not?!' Jenny squealed, suddenly looking ten years younger.

'Well, I think it's disgusting,' Kate couldn't hide her displeasure. 'At your age! And what about poor Dad?'

'What do you mean, "at my age"? And "poor Dad"? Poor Dad nothing! He's been up to all manner of extra-curricular activities for... He is just fine about it, thank you very much. More than fine, actually – he's over the moon! Just look at him!'

Kate knitted her eyebrows. Was she missing something here, or was her mother saying that her father approved of her having an affair?

'He's never felt better – no need for a live-in nurse now!'

'Wait a minute.' Kate tugged at her mum's elbow and stopped her in her tracks. 'Are you telling me that Dad's OK with it? Happy about it, even?'

'Of course he is!' Jenny pulled her elbow away from Kate's grasp. 'He's bloody *delirious*, darling!'

'This isn't right,' Kate shook her head, studying the ground at her feet. 'No, no – this is wrong on just about every level!'

'What *are* you on about, Kate?' Jenny said in hushed voice, as though Kate might be losing her marbles – or need a good lie-down, at the very least.

'You can't run off with the first old guy who takes your fancy and start having affairs all over the shop! Not when you've got a husband who loves you like crazy and kids who look up to you and depend on you for... for their moral guidance and everything!'

Jenny took a step back, as though the force of Kate's words was blowing her off her feet.

'Sit down,' she said after a few seconds. 'I think you've got the wrong end of the stick.'

Kate and Jenny put the crockery down on the grass and headed back to the shade of the John Lewis outdoor furniture set, complete with umbrella, that Jenny and George had agonised over buying for years.

Sitting down, visibly shaken, Kate listened to Jenny's side of the story.

'Sweetie pie, I know how hard this must be for you to hear this, but I think it's important you do, so please, bear with me.'

Kate agreed to let her mother speak without interruption.

'While being a wife and mother is wonderful, it's not without its hardships and tough times. As a young mum – which you could still be if you get a wriggle on – you devote all your time and energy to your kids. And it's a privilege to do so. But after a while, you start to realise that a big part of your old self and your old relationship with your man has gone AWOL – and, try as you might, you just can't get it back.'

Jenny studied her wedding and engagement rings.

'The world has changed, hopefully, so have your friends and now you're older, you've got more responsibilities. You can never go back to how it was and thank god, really – when I think about what I used to find fun and important, I almost have to laugh. I mean, what a waste of time!'

Kate smiled at this and knew exactly what her mum meant. Even though she didn't agree with her one hundred per cent (she *had* managed to go back, after all – even though she had no clue exactly how), she could finally see how boring all her drinking and smoking and so-called 'partying' was.

'One day you'll realise that things have changed – and you, yourself have changed – for a pretty good reason.

277

And that good reason is family. It's the most important thing in life, without a doubt.'

'So why—'

'Ah-ah-ah,' Jenny sing-songed, wagging her finger at Kate. 'Let me finish. Now where was I? Um, jeepers, my memory is definitely not what it used to be, that's for – ah! Family, that's right! *Family*. So while family is an important part of a woman's life, it's not the *only* important part. Some women are satisfied with taking care of their family – whether that involves working at a job to bring in money or working tirelessly at domestic duties for no pay at all. But some women – and I am, rightly or wrongly, one of these – need more excitement, more drama, more *danger* in their lives than living vicariously through their husband and kids can bring.'

Kate felt just like she used to as a six-year-old kid when she'd ask her mother what a particular word meant, only to receive a lecture on the word's etymology and modern usage by way of a thousand examples.

Kate wanted to get to the nub of the matter quickly, just as she had way back then – and nodded impatiently, as if the increasing speed of her head movement was going to give Jenny a subliminal message and her mini seminar would wrap up fast as a result.

'Which is why I thought going back to work at uni might be a good idea for your father *and* me. I thought it might help us rekindle the spark, relight the fire, as Lulu sang… with that pop group… what were they called again?'

'Take—'

'Take That!' Jenny jumped up a little bit out of her chair, she was so excited to have remembered something from the recent past with only a teensy bit of prompting. 'Yes, Take That, that's right.'

'YOO-HOO, YOU TWO! COME ON!' George called out from the French doors.

'Won't be a minute,' Jenny yelled back.

Kate hoped she was telling the truth – she was keen to get at one of her mum's roasts while she still had the chance and her mouth started watering at the thought of it.

'Now I've totally lost my train of thought. Where was I?'

'You were relighting your fire. With Dad, I might add!'

'Well who else, darling?'

'I dunno – that tanned silver fox I saw you snogging in Carluccio's the other day?'

'I wasn't snogging any... you mean Harry? The vice chancellor?'

'The nice who-cellar?'

'The vice chancellor! Of King's College!'

'Eh?' Kate put her hand up to her mouth.

'He'd been on at me for ages to go back to lecturing, but when you suggested it to me, you actually gave me the confidence to say yes. I can't tell you how it's rejuvenated me, darling – I feel like a new woman!'

Kate struggled to process this.

'And now with all that creativity coursing through my veins, it's really got my juices flowing again – pun well-intended – and, consequently, as your father was saying just this morning, it's given me a sort of glow, a whole new vibe, that's not only irresistible to him, but... well, something in me has been reawakened, too.'

Jenny paused momentarily.

'It's like we've rediscovered why we fell in love with each other in the first place, all those hundreds of years ago. Me with my energy, him with his manly vigour – we feel like teenagers again!'

Jenny sighed and looked wistfully at the daisies and dandelions not far from her feet. Kate wondered whether this was her chance to jump into the conversation.

It wasn't.

'But anyway, snuggle pot, you don't want to hear about our sex life!'

'No!' said Kate, relieved, starting to get up. 'I bloody don't!'

Kate's tummy rumbled loudly and when she put her hand to it, she felt its fleshy softness, reassuring her in its familiarity. This was how she was used to her stomach feeling to her touch, and she was convinced that every inch she gained on her body now meant she was getting closer to getting home.

'Thing is, darling, you can never go back – not to how *you* were, not to how *things* were. You've got to move, evolve and change with the times. Which is great! It's so exciting! And that's what life's all about, what living is all about – the here and now. Lord knows, life's too short and no one knows what the future will bring.'

But Kate did. And she got a little teary at this, thinking about George and how she wouldn't be able to prevent the massive heart attack that would kill him at the stroke of midnight on New Year's Eve 1999.

'Oh, what's the matter?' Jenny asked, getting up, putting her arm around her daughter's shoulders and pulling her head to her pinny.

Jenny – or, rather, Jenny's pinny – smelled of Comfort fabric conditioner, roast dinners, chocolate chip cookies and bread and butter pudding. Somewhere in that heady mix was the smell of cigarettes and red wine, left over from the days when the whole family indulged their vices a little too enthusiastically. It seemed to Kate, in her upset-but-happy, relieved-yet-anxious state, that the top notes were all about the safety and security of the home, just about managing to contain the unruly, rebellious teen, fags and booze middle and bottom notes.

Kate lost herself in these aromas for a short while, letting her mind swim in the great memories they evoked. Like the kids' birthday parties full of tears and tantrums and bikes and scraped knees; the adults' dinner parties, where Kate and Steve would sneak wine and whisky all night, listening to the grown-ups get sillier and more slurry with each passing course; the camping holidays that went horribly, hopelessly, hilariously wrong and which were the stuff of family legend, now – folklore to be passed down through all subsequent generations.

Kate's thoughts quickly jumped over the family fence and fairly raced back to her own kids. Oh, how she wished she had her iPhone on her now and she could quickly trawl through the million photos of her beautiful bundles. What she wouldn't give to proudly show Jenny the fruits of her and Seamus' loins.

Slowly she became aware of something buzzing around her head. As it got a little louder, it became clear that it was the sound of someone talking. Jenny was still banging on!

'...because the greatest gift of all we can give to our children is the confidence to get out there, keep on moving and always be themselves. If I had to give you one bit of advice that I thought would see you right through life it would be this, darling: happy wife, happy life.

Constantly jabbering on about what's wrong or what used to be is a sure-fire way to guarantee a miserable life. For all the family. Find who you love, someone who makes your knees go weak – you'll know in your heart of hearts when you find him – settle down, have a family, build a bank of wonderful memories together and don't forget to find a little something for yourself, discover something you love doing. Love what you do and you'll never work a day in your life, as they say! And don't ever hold onto the past and the way things were – embrace the future and its amazing possibilities. It's the best recipe I have for a fulfilling life.'

There was a lull as Jenny stopped for breath, and Kate closed her eyes, pondering the wisdom of her mother's words. The sound of loud, comedy snoring suddenly filled the air.

'Kate? Kate! Are you asleep?'

Kate looked up at Jenny and sniggered.

'You little bugger!'

'Just teasing, Ma,' Kate laughed, as the whole family used to after winding poor old Jenny up about something or other.

'Yeah, well,' Jenny grinned. 'I'd better get back inside before Steve gets too jealous because you're getting all my attention.'

The pair got up, and as they got closer to the house, Kate caught sight of Portia tracing Seamus' sideburns with her index finger while Steve and George looked on, understandably agog.

'Think I'd better save Seamus from Portia,' Kate squinted to get a better look. 'And himself.'

26

'You loved it!' Kate elbowed him in the ribs.

'I did *not!*' grinned Seamus. 'You know me – I *hated* it!'

Kate bit her tongue and realised that, yes, she did know him. Pretty well, come to think of it. And he really would have felt intensely uncomfortable when Portia was making her moves, her unwanted advances towards him at lunch on Sunday.

But today was Wednesday – Wednesday, June 26, 1996 – the day the advance copies of the latest issues of both *Mad Fer It!* and *Lashed* came into the office, with the Germany/England semi-final to look forward to later on.

It was a big day, and she had come in early, so as not to miss the initial reactions from everybody and was killing time down in the basement of the PGT&B building, with the whole IT department – both Seamus *and* Kevin.

'So you couldn't help yourself, couldn't keep away any longer, could you? You just had to come and see where the magic happens,' Seamus said when she strolled in. 'The heart of PGT&B's publishing operations, the very *nerve centre*, if you will.'

Or 'nerd centre', as Archie called it.

'The mags will be coming in upstairs any minute – why don't you two come up and see them with me?' Kate said as she flicked through a dog-eared copy of *Back of the Net!*

sitting on Seamus' desk. 'And also, I wanted to invite you two to my birthday party this Saturday.'

'The night before the final on Sunday,' Seamus said.

Kate resisted telling him that England were going to be knocked out of the competition tonight and he might not be as interested in watching the match the next day, if his team weren't playing in it. Then, quick as a flash, she wondered whether she should get down to Ladbroke's and put a bet on tonight's game going to penalties and Gareth Southgate subsequently missing his, effectively costing the country the game and, in turn, the chance to win Euro 96.

As she grappled with the ethics of the monumental cheat she was considering, Seamus spoke.

'I'm in!' he chirruped. 'How old are you turning?'

'Fifty-fi—' Kate stopped herself and, with the aid of her fingers and a chewed Bic biro sitting on top of a scrap of paper (mental arithmetic not being her strongest suit), calculated that in 1996, she turned twenty-nine.

'Twenty-nine,' she said finally, triumphant. 'God! Twenty-nine! Who'd a thought?'

'Getting old there, dear,' said Seamus softly. 'I said: YOU'RE GETTING OLD THERE, DEAR! Any minute now, you'll be thirty and then that's it. It's all over.'

'Doesn't have to be,' said Kate. 'It's all in how you look at it. Perspective is everything.'

Seamus pushed his glasses up with the tip of his middle finger and groaned.

'Next you'll be saying rubbish like "age is just a number" and "life begins at forty" and "you're only as old as the man you feel".'

'Yeah, I know!' Kate laughed at the ridiculousness of it all, wondering whether she had ever, in all sincerity, uttered those sorts of phrases. 'Or "ninety-eight years young" or whatever...'

'Are your parents coming to your birthday bash?' Seamus asked. 'I've got a few questions about my swing I'd like to put to George.'

'No, actually,' Kate sighed. 'No, and I'm a bit disappointed about that, to tell the truth. I thought they might be able to at least drop in and say hi.'

'Got a better offer, did they?'

'Well, yeah. Turns out they're both on a promise – with each other!'

'Urgh,' the men grunted in unison.

'No, I think it's great, actually. Ever since Mum went back to work, they can hardly keep their hands off each other. It's like a new lease of life for them – just when they thought it was all over.'

'It is now!' the boys chorused again.

Kate groaned.

'Actually,' said Seamus, scratching his cheek in a deep-in-thought kind of way (although it's entirely possible that it was more a why-am-I-trying-to-grow-these-ridiculous-sideburns-when-they-make-my-face-so-unbearably-itchy? kind of way). 'That gives me a bit of an idea...'

'What?' asked Kate.

'I've got a feeling the internet is going to be huge and change life as we know it – but if youngsters like us have trouble trying to figure out the new technologies, what hope do OAPS have?'

'And this is relevant because...?' Kate couldn't see it.

'Well, they're going to need to know how to get around the information super-highway and build their own web presence... es...'

Kate smiled. That was her Seamus, that was her man – always looking to the future, never dwelling in the past.

'You're right,' Kevin piped up. 'There's defo something in that.'

Kate's eyes were drawn to the place Kevin's voice had come from, and she could see that he still had his cagoule on, even though he was sitting down in front of his monitor, barely visible amidst the towers of manuals, newspapers, wires and Tamagotchis.

'Yes, I know,' Seamus spoke slowly and confidently. 'Poor old pensioners are going to need to be totally *au fait* with the internet.'

'And if,' Kevin went on, standing up and shedding his geeky coat. 'If, as you predict, the interweb is going to take off in amazing ways, older people and techno-doofuses alike are going to need some help getting to grips with all it has to offer.'

Seamus stuck out his lower jaw and continued clawing at his cheeks.

'And they'll need someone in the know, someone who can speak to them in their language, on their level, to explain it all,' he said, eyes bulging and blinking the more he saw into the bright future. 'Which is exactly where we come in! We'll advise businesses, individuals – anyone who needs our help – and anyone who can pay us hand-somely for it! That's it!'

'What?' Kate blinked, pretending she didn't have a clue what he was on about.

'Don't you see?' Seamus wheeled around, spinning in a semi-circle, his khaki parka flying out behind him like a superhero's cape.

'We'll start up our own web consultancy, bring IT to the masses, debunk the mysteries of the information superhighway!'

'Well, not too much, I hope – don't want to do ourselves out of any business.'

'Oh!' Seamus clapped his big hands together and brought them in to his chest. 'There's no end to what we can do with this! We'll get in on the ground floor – even develop some personal AI...'

He looked at the Tamagotchi in his hand.

'Maybe we could even branch out and create, I dunno, online companions for all the lonely people out there, life-like human robots who can think and feel real emotions...'

Crickets.

''Course, we'll need some good marketing behind us, so people will know we're out there...'

Seamus and Kevin looked at Kate.

'Who? Me?' said Kate. 'Oh, no – you don't want me, I'm too much of a flibberty-gibbet.'

'Flibberty – *what?* You sound like my grandmother! Next thing you know, you'll be knitting me a scratchy jumper and giving me fifty pence for Christmas!' Seamus laughed.

'I'm way too unpredictable, much too unreliable – you never know where you are with a girl like me – I'm here one day, gone the next!'

Kate crossed her fingers behind her back hoping against all hope that this really was the case and, any minute now, some invisible force would fling her straight back into the future.

'Well, either you come into business with us – or some other company benefits from our talent and expertise.'

287

'Not to mention modesty,' Kate muttered, surprised at Seamus' sounding so self-assured all of a sudden.

'But how are we going to get the money together to set ourselves up in business?' Kevin wondered out loud, emerging from the manual and magazine mountain. 'I mean, start-up costs will be through the roof – we'll need equipment, advertising, a premises to rent...'

A silence descended upon the threesome as they thought about this.

'That's assuming we're partners, right, Shay? I mean, we're in this together, right? It'll be half my business, too, yeah?'

'Of course!' said Seamus. 'Fifty-fifty, equals, straight down the middle. Unless Kate wants in, too, then all the colossal profits will be split into thirds. Now, we'll need a name – something catchy that says what we're all about...'

More chin rubbing, cheek scratching and jowl stroking (this was mainly Kate) ensued.

'What about... the it boys?' Kate offered to a sea of blank faces before her. 'You know, like Tara Palmer Thingy and Tamara Beckwith – they're it girls, right?'

Kevin and Seamus swapped glances, not getting where she was going at all.

'But instead of *it*, we cap it up, so it's IT! Geddit?'

'Um,' Seamus and Kevin ummed in unison.

'The I.T. Boys! Like *it boys*, right, but I.T.!' Kate carried on, losing them completely.

'Let's think on,' said Seamus, flashing Kate a sympathetic smile. 'So how are we going to raise the finance? Any ideas? Anyone?'

'No,' said Kate forlornly. 'Anyway, the mags will be arriving right about now upstairs – wanna come with?'

'I think we should stay down here and plot our escape from the corporate jungle,' said Seamus, clearing his desk of all its debris with one sweep of his right arm.

'OK,' said Kate, turning to leave. 'But you are going to come on Saturday, aren't you? To the Bonaparte pub on Chepstow Road. About one o'clock? That means you too, Kevin.'

'Really? Me?' squeaked Kevin. He cleared his throat and took his voice down an octave or two. 'I mean, ah, yeah, cool, whatevs.'

As soon as Kate stepped out of The Lift and into the third floor, she knew the magazines had turned up and that, as a result, some seismic shift had taken place.

The peals of laughter coming from the marketing department – particularly Tamsin – brought to mind Phoebe's squeals when she was three years old and they went on the tea cup ride at Longleat.

Kate felt the knot of excitement in her tummy and couldn't wait to get her hands on the magazines. As she strode over to her desk, Tom jumped out at her.

'I've been looking for you everywhere, but you've been so hard to find,' he said, very possibly quoting lines from an old song, although Kate couldn't be sure. 'Where have you been?'

'At home,' she replied breezily. 'West Hampstead home, I mean.'

'We really need to talk – I've been going out of my mi—'

Never one for confrontation of any sort – particularly the public kind – Kate cut Tom off before he had a chance to finish.

'Ooh, look! There's the latest copy of *Lashed*! It's my favourite magazine, don't you know. Course, I only read it for the articles and comment on current affairs – I find it is brilliant at raising consciousness. And it has some *excellent* columnists writing for it…'

She winked at Steve and picked up the heavy glossy with the boxing ring and all four Britpop boys adorning the cover, Lee's face the biggest, naturally, looking like it was almost about to burst through the expensive paper stock.

Flicking through endless pairs of boobs and oiled-up flat bellies, Kate eventually found Steve's piece about the shoot at the gym and read the intro out loud:

> When we asked the two biggest bands on the planet to stop their sniping and play nice, we didn't even think they'd answer our calls, let alone show up to the shoot. But they did. And so we got bold in this, the coup of the century, and told them to kiss, make up and walk away the best of friends – or else. So did they? Or did they look back in anger? Steve O'Toole finds out…

'Great stuff, Steve!' Kate looked at her brother, blushing in front of her. 'Like your pen name, too – O'Toole!'

'They do it to all the new recruits,' Steve said. 'Make up a surname alluding to your manhood.'

'How grown up of them,' Kate mumbled, holding the magazine in and out in front of her face as the words on the page wobbled about in a fuzzy mess.

'Ah! It's all gone blurry,' Kate said, bringing her fist up to her face to rub her eye, just like Declan did when he was dog-tired. 'I'll read the rest later, when—'

'Here,' came Medea's velvety voice out of nowhere. 'Try my reading glasses – they're not prescription as such, just magnifying glasses really, from Boots.'

Kate reached out and put the old lady link chain over her head and the frames on her face. They fitted rather nicely, she thought to herself, and reasoned that if the stunning Medea wore granny glasses, complete with an ugly plastic chain attached with little black rubber bands to the glasses' arms, then the thought of getting her own pair back in 2022 wasn't so dreadful.

While Kate fiddled with her face furniture, Medea grabbed the magazine, turned to her column in the book and thrust it back at Kate, placing it right under her nose.

Kate looked down and began to read, the words fairly jumping off the page at her. Honestly, she thought, these glasses are incredible – it's like the letters are in HD, they're so crisp and clear!

'Let's see,' she said out loud. 'Our woman with more front than Blackpool—'

'Way-HEY!' came the chorus of twelve-year-old marketing boys in the background.

'...Medea Hor'nbag...'

Kate looked over the top of the magazine and turned her mouth down at Medea who, in turn, winced at the discomfort of her name being bastardised in such a sleazy way.

'...blah-de-blah-de-blah,' Kate continued quickly. '...what really happened when Britpop boys Lee, Damien, Nate and Alastair got together... boxing clever... yermmurmer... rarely if ever has such a revolting display... hang on! Such a revolting display of stags swaggering, rutting and burping as though part of an erotic mating ritual – with each other! Ah... homoerotic...

um… fragile male ego… pathetic posturing, zero intelligence, more artistic integrity in my arse… talentless twerps… chauvinist pigs…'

Kate dropped the magazine down from her face and stared at Medea who was, she noted, in fantastically sharp focus.

She carried on reading.

'Just like the pages of the disgusting rag you're holding… worthless, misogynistic, about as funny as a fart in an elevator, boorish and boring…'

Kate's mouth hung open and she searched Tom's eyes for some sort of ocular explanation.

None was forthcoming – in fact, Tom looked more frightened than in the mood to discuss his editorial decision.

'Are you quite fucking mad?' Kate quizzed him gently.

'But she's right!' Tom whimpered. 'I just couldn't go on living a lie, so I decided to go out with a bang and tell the world what I really think.'

'Using Medea Hor'nbag as your mouthpiece,' Archie joined in, reaching up a little to pat Tom on the back. 'Genius, Tom, genius. It's hilarious! The readers will get it – they're a smart bunch who love nothing more than having a laugh at their own expense! It's brilliant – well done.'

'Have you seen my Ed's Letter?' Tom asked Archie.

Kate flipped back to the front of the magazine and saw, under a picture of Tom giving the camera two fingers, in bold capital letters:

I QUIT!

'Yeah – but why?' Archie whined. 'This is going to fly off the shelves – you're going to be massive!'

Tom shifted about from foot to foot and coughed, clearing his throat in preparation for his speech, unaccustomed as he was.

'I figured that, in the end, domination of the media world isn't going to make me happy. In fact, it's turning me into a bit of an alcoholic, drug-addled twat, to be completely honest,' Tom looked sheepishly at Kate at this revelation. 'I want to have a family one day – one day soon – and I thought if I ended up having a daughter, how could I possibly explain all this to her? I'd be so deeply ashamed, as though I'd betrayed her and her sex before she'd even been given a chance to make her mark in the world.'

He took a breath and turned his gaze from Kate to Medea.

'I want my daughters to know that I'm behind them one hundred per cent. And that being a girl isn't a handicap – or shouldn't be – and that she can do anything she wants to do, regardless of the misogynistic world she lives in. I want her to know that she'll have more than just her looks to offer the world.'

Medea gave him the old thumbs up of approval while Kate nearly passed out from shock.

'And if we have boys, I want them to I want them to be proud of me, too – not embarrassed. And to know, too, how to behave like a decent human being towards the opposite sex as well as their own.'

Kate watched as Tom looked Steve dead in the eye, Steve slowly nodding back, as if silently encouraging him.

'I suppose,' Tom went on, 'something – or someone – has finally made me realise that none of this is me at all – not the real me, anyway. Not the me I actually like. And it's not what I want my life's work to be, not how I want to be remembered, either. So that's it, folks. I'm out.'

He paused and looked at Kate. Kate, in turn, looked bewildered and bemused – what on earth could have brought this on? Or, more accurately, who? This was not the Tom she knew so well, the Tom whose double entendres were so puerile and yet so legendary. She wondered what they'd done with the real Tom. And who was this impostor?

'So long, folks,' he went on, 'and thanks for all the mammaries!'

The crowd cheered, Tamsin tittered.

'Sorry,' Tom guffawed. 'Couldn't help myself.'

27

The big cheeses at PGT&B gave everyone the rest of the day off, so they could celebrate their magazines' reversals of fortune and prepare for the Euro 96 semi-final between England and Germany, starting at 7 p.m.

Of course, for just about every employee of PGT&B, that meant a quick trip to the offie to stock up on fags and then straight down to O'Flaherty's to get a good seat in front of the big screen. And, obviously, get a few bevvies in before kick-off.

The banter and the pints flowed – even Kate managed to gulp down one or two as the excitement and anticipation grew.

Or maybe it was more like three or four pints, Kate couldn't quite remember.

Whatever she'd drunk, though, she placed the blame squarely at the feet of alcohol for what transpired a few hours later.

'It's the best mag in the world – ever!' *The Mad Fer It!* team chanted over and over as they clinked glasses, spilling sticky lager on the pages of the Friendship issue.

'I love the photos of them, looking so scrawny in their satin shorts!' Kate said.

She carried on leafing through her favourite fort-nightly and giggled at the captions accompanying every photo. Not a single opportunity to take the mickey out of pop stars was missed and she was surprised at how near the knuckle some of their comments were. You'd never get away with some of that in 2022, she thought to herself. This funny, ballsy editorial team would have been cancelled yonks ago!

As the whooping and cheering escalated and there was still just over an hour to go before the match began, Kate decided it was time to use her insider knowledge for good and so took her leave, mumbling something about going to see a man about a dog.

When she got back to O'Flaherty's (or O'Farty's as Seamus pronounced it), the tension was palpable. A large table with an excellent view of the screen saw Portia, Steve, Archie, Tom, Tamsin, Lucy, Medea, Seamus and Kevin sat round it. Kate spotted the spare chair in between Portia and Seamus loaded up with bags, light jackets and cardis for if it got a bit chilly later.

'It's such an amazing feeling out there,' she said, scooping the clothes off the chair and carefully placing them by her feet, only for them to be kicked mercilessly under the table during the match that was about to start.

'It's not too bad in here, either,' said Portia casting a lusty glance at all the men present.

'Actually,' said Kate. 'Have you met everyone here?'

'Yep – the lovely Seamus introduced me while you were – where were you just now, anyway?'

'Um,' Kate racked her brains for a plausible excuse for not being in the thick of it for the whole afternoon. 'Just ducked down to the, ah, National Portrait Gallery.'

She didn't know where that came from – somewhere deep down inside her belly full of regrets, she supposed –

visiting the NPG more often was always on her long list of things she wished she'd done more of.

'Ah! A woman after my own heart,' shouted Tom. 'What's on at the mo? Any special exhibitions?'

'Just lots of… um, portraits, really. You know, the usual stuff.'

Tamsin batted her eyelashes at Tom and said, 'Speaking of portraits, we never did get to do that glamour shoot starring, er, *me* – did we? Perhaps we could do some private photos later – I'm sure I have a Polaroid camera at my place…'

Tom shuffled about in his seat and clearly didn't know where to look. Neither did anyone else.

'All right then, everyone,' said Archie, popping the big balloon of unease that hung heavily over the table and turning to face the screen. 'It's about to start.'

'Well, someone's going to have to tell me what's going on,' purred Medea. 'I'm not terribly au fait with soccer, you see.'

'Football!' the table said as one.

'I know a bit,' said Lucy. 'Five brothers will do that to a girl.'

'I can get you up to speed,' Tom trilled. 'I love nothing more than explaining the beautiful game.'

'Except the sound of his own voice,' Portia whispered to Kate.

Kate snorted and looked at Tom fondly. It had surprised her that he'd revealed such well-hidden depths lately – and she couldn't believe how wrong she'd got him in her memory. To her mind, in 2022, Tom was a bit of a one-dimensional figure with an eye for the ladies, a masterful, wildly satisfying sexual technique and a pornographer's attitude towards love and commitment.

But now she realised he was just as insecure and confused as everybody else. Just as desperate to find a real connection and true intimacy as everybody else – and just as cack-handed.

She looked at Seamus crossing his long legs in the chair next to her. This made the cuffs of his well-cut, light-tobacco-coloured cord trousers rise, revealing a black sock festooned with mini Bart Simpsons, grinning his little yellow head off poking out over the top of his desert boots.

Yep, Kate told herself, there is definitely no rhyme or reason to this love game.

'GOAL!' the pub suddenly erupted.

'I say,' said Medea. 'That was quick!'

'Shea-rer, Shea-rer!' chanted Tom, jumping up and down like Declan on the pogo stick Kate had bought him from her favourite online shop, Retro Toys Were Us.

The already-super-charged atmosphere ratcheted up several notches at this early suggestion that England might actually beat Germany and Kate basked in the ambience, remembering how ecstatic everyone had been at this point all those years ago.

She almost couldn't bear to think how devastated everybody in the pub – in the country – would soon be.

She got up to order a lemon, lime and bitters at the bar, figuring there'd be no queue, considering everyone else would be far too busy hugging and crying and generally being jubilant.

But she couldn't battle her way through the crowd. The pub was completely rammed. Getting bumped and jostled about like a pinball, she managed to make her way to the perimeter of the pub and, with her back against the wall, manoeuvred herself to the bar.

By the time she got the Australian barmaid's attention (which took a while), Germany had equalised.

She knew this for sure, because once the unsportsman-like groans of the England fans died down, she heard Tom, in his cockney accent say:

'Ah, now Medea, *me de-ah*,' Kate could hear him smile, 'now we need to get another goal and not let the Germans get any more goals.'

'Der!' cried Lucy and Medea in unison.

'Awight, love. Keep your 'air on!'

Apples and pears, whistle and flute – why did Tom lapse into cockney when excited or upset or being candid? Was it his involuntary way of exposing the real him? The vocal equivalent of shedding his artificial skin and letting us all see his real self via his glottal stop?

'Well, *der* – any fool knows *that*,' Medea piped up. 'I meant I don't get things like the offside rule and penalties and stuff.'

You won't have to wait long for a heated discussion on the merits and disastrous drawbacks of the penalty shoot-out, thought Kate.

But in reality, they did. And after seventy-four more minutes of play and continuous standing at the bar, Kate's feet, adorned by her stiff new all-white Adidas trainers, were killing her.

Then, three minutes into extra time, Kate heard Portia yell, 'Oh, McMan-aman-aman-aman-aman! How *could* you?!'

'If 'e'd'a go' tha' in, we'd a' won,' Tom said, now sounding like he had several missing teeth and a swollen tongue. He must be really nervous, thought Kate. But what could be making him like that? Or, more to the point, *who*? Or should that be *whom*? As Kate grappled with her internal grammatical issues, Germany must have scored, judging by the boos and bitter mutterings from all those of normal height around her.

''Ang on, 'ang on – ah, right – so the ref's not allowing that goal,' explained Tom. 'Foul, apparently.'

'What did he do that was so foul?' Medea and Lucy asked in unison.

'Um,' Tom wasn't interested. 'Now if Gazza can just get… it… DOW!'

The punters roared with disappointment, signalling to Kate that Gazza had, indeed, missed.

'Righ',' said Tom, smacking his lips. 'Now it's a pen-al-ee 'uck-in' shoo' ow.'

'I can't understand a word he's saying!' laughed Portia.

'He said it's a penalty shoot-out,' Kate heard Kevin say. 'It's a bit like tennis when it goes to deuce, you know, forty-all.'

'Oh! Why thank you, kind sir, for explaining it to dumb little old—' said Portia in a Southern belle accent, cutting her own sarcastic self off. 'Well, 'allo,'allo, 'allo! What have we here, then?'

Portia must have turned to face Kevin, because Kate couldn't quite make out what she said next, although it sounded an awful lot like 'Ding dong!'

Kate was convinced she could hear Kevin blush and smiled, picturing him pushing up his foggy glasses, his Adam's apple bobbing up and down and starting to sweat.

Five times the crowd cheered and brayed and five times they ignored the German goals, talking over them, as if they didn't matter and were simply a dull, but necessary formality.

Then it was Gareth Southgate's turn. Kate hid her face with her hands, turning round to the bar.

She desperately wanted to make it back to her table for this bit, be there with her shoulder for Seamus to cry on when it all went so horribly wrong, but she couldn't for the life of her break through the wall of bodies, several layers deep, blocking the way to her table.

So she gave up trying, just as a hush fell on the crowd, breezing through the pub like a silent cumulonimbus, a hazy, cloudy portent of doom. The crowd held their collective breath, Southgate kicked the ball... but German goal-keeper, Andreas Kopke saved it! The crowd whimpered as they exhaled: Southgate had missed.

The sour smell of devastation hung heavily in the air. As the German player approached the ball, even the nervous gulps of a group of people anticipating a crushing defeat stopped.

You could have heard a pin drop — and Tom's aitches, as he continued with his running commentary in Medea's ear.

'So this German fella, *Moller*,' he sneered. 'Just 'as to 'oof it in and crash, bang, wollop! We're out of the competition.'

The faint sound of boot on ball felt like a kick to the nation's collective stomach. And the nation howled in response.

'NO-O-O-O-O-O-O-O!'

The air filled with grief and despair and, just like the first time round, Kate felt like crying.

And as the final whistle blew, the tears, the wailing and the gnashing of teeth reaching fever pitch, Kate slipped out of the pub and headed back into Soho.

28

'So when I got into work on Friday morning,' Seamus said, 'seven a.m., as usual—'

'As you do,' Kate butted in.

'Yes, as I do, every day. Well, every *week* day, of course – I'm not that keen!' Seamus snorted.

They were walking along Bayswater Road, past Hyde Park, on their way to the Prince Bonaparte pub, right down the bottom of the dodgier end of Chepstow Road. If there *was* such a thing as the dodgy end of the street, of course, flanked as it was on either side with outrageously expensive-looking white-stucco Victorian terraces.

'So you got into work at seven,' Kate prompted him, looking behind her for a second, to make sure Portia and Steve and Kevin were still there.

'Yeah – and sitting on my keyboard is a plain A5 envelope with a note in it telling me to look under my desk where there is a large cardboard box.'

'Really? How fascinating!'

'No, listen,' smiled Seamus.

'Is A5 bigger or smaller than A4?' Kate crinkled her nose. 'I can never remember.'

'Smaller,' he said authoritatively. 'The larger the number, the smaller the size. So A1 is bigger than A2. A3 is bigger than A4 and so on and so forth.'

'Yeah, yeah,' said Kate, rolling her eyes and pretending to yawn at Portia who had linked arms with both Steve and Kevin, and was walking ten or so paces behind her and Seamus.

'Well anyway, I opened the box and nearly fell backwards in a crumpled heap—'

'Ooh, make sure you don't – not in that gorgeous brushed cotton parka, anyway – cost a bomb, that did.'

'…because there was a MILLION POUNDS in there!'

'Shhh.' Kate put an index finger to her wonkily-lined lips. Even then, in 1996, she was trying to make her lips look big and plump and bee-stung – despite Portia often pointing out that her efforts merely made her look more Robert Smith than Julia Roberts.

'What's that about a million pounds, Shay?' called Kevin.

'Nothing, nothing,' said Kate.

'Your shout then, Seamus – if you're talking about that kind of dosh!' Steve joined in.

'Yeah, so,' Seamus carried on. 'I thought I'd take it to the police, see if anyone's lost it.'

'You *what*?' Kate stopped dead in her tracks.

'Well, it's not mine and it's an awful lot of money – someone's bound to be missing it…'

Kate felt her frustration levels rise sharply, exactly as she did when Phoebe and Declan ran rings around her, answering back and refusing to do what she asked of them.

She frowned.

Take the money and run, you fool! This could set you up – set us all up – for life!

As they walked, Kate steered Seamus away from every newsagent's sandwich board they passed, so as to avoid the day's headlines screaming at him:

303

BOOKIES BANKRUPT!

said one side.

BIZARRE BET PUTS BOOKIES OUT OF BUSINESS

shouted its other side.

Kate pointed out how pretty the trees were at this time of year and when the pleasant breeze carried a vaguely familiar half-singing/half-yodelling voice to their ears, she knew she'd stumbled upon a big enough distraction.

'Good old Alanis,' she giggled. 'What's she warbling on about now?'

'Irony, most probably,' said Seamus. 'I was actually going to ask you if you wanted to go to the Prince's Trust concert in Hyde Park with me today – as a birthday present – but you got in first with your pub party and... and, anyway, I couldn't get tickets.'

'Oh, that's sweet, Seamus,' she said, looking up at him as they walked. 'Well, now we can hear it for free – and not have to use a Portaloo when we need to spend a penny.'

Spend a penny? Now where the hell did a twee, old-fashioned phrase like that come from? I'm getting older by the second!

'There you go, sounding like my grandmother again,' Seamus grinned, cautiously putting an arm around Kate's shoulders. 'Which is fine by me – I loved my gran. Gutted when she died.'

Kate shook her perfect Rachel do and looked up.

'Was that rain?' she asked, holding her hand, palm-side up to the greying sky.

'Nah, it can't be,' said Seamus. 'I was surfing the net this morning and found a weather site. Pretty amateur it was, but it said London would be dry today – if not bright and sunny.'

Kate could have sworn she'd felt a raindrop and so, keen to avoid frizz and follicular mayhem on her birthday, she pulled Seamus underneath a newsagent's awning.

WAS MATCH FIXED?

asked the sandwich board next to them, with

WE WAS ALL ROBBED!

emblazoned all over its other side.

'Oh yeah,' said Seamus 'did you read about that? How someone won an absolute fortune on Wednesday night's match? It was as if the bloke who put the bet on knew exactly what was going to happen or something.'

'No, no, I hadn't heard,' Kate said quickly. 'Oops, looks like it was a false alarm, no rain here – let's get to the pub. Pronto!'

They picked up the pace and Kate directed the conversation back to Seamus' windfall.

'So what did the note say? You know, the one in the envelope?'

'Just to look under my desk,' he said. 'Nothing else.'

'It didn't have your name on it? In blue pen? With a little love heart next to it?'

Kate was sure she'd addressed said note to him. She distinctly remembered toying with the idea of addressing it to 'The I.T. Boys' but thought it might be too obvious who it was from and really give the game away. Even though she knew that Seamus didn't like the play on words. Or give a damn about It Girls, let alone I.T. boys.

She can't have been that drunk, can she?

'Don't think so,' Seamus answered. 'Hang on, I'll check.'

Kate gasped as Seamus pulled the envelope out of his deep parka pocket and saw that it was stuffed with fifty-pound notes.

'Put it away,' she hissed. 'Put it away!'

He did as he was told and as soon as the envelope was safe, Kate grabbed him by the elbow, looking nervously over both her shoulders.

'What? What's going on?' Seamus' voice cracked.

'Nothing! But, you know – you don't want to be flashing that amount of cash about in the street. You never know who might snatch it off you.'

'Kate, do you know something about this money?' Seamus held her still and locked his eyes onto hers.

This was getting too tricky, she thought. Seamus with his do-goody ideas and lofty morals would never under-stand her reasons for betting. He *might* get that she'd come to the past as a visitor from the future, but gambling? And then using her ill-gotten gains to feather their own nests? When every night on the telly, news of war, poverty, hunger and misery bombarded them?

'Because if no one claims it from the police station, I think I might do something really worthwhile with it – like give it to Great Ormond Street or some needy charity. Hey! Maybe I'll even use the money to start a charity of my own...'

Seamus had a bit of a Mother Theresa thing going sometimes, Kate remembered. Which was another reason she'd fallen for him the first time round.

He'd always been a boy scout in long pants, forever wanting to do the right thing, always being kind and compassionate – exactly the sort of traits that make a man good dad material.

As if to illustrate her point, a beggar on the corner of Westbourne Grove and Chepstow Road mumbled something about food and shelter, holding out his hand to them. The pair suddenly felt painfully bourgeois and middle class as they stood there, about to enjoy an afternoon of drinking alcohol out of a glass, with a greasy, delicious kebab to look forward to on the way home to their safe, warm beds.

Seamus glanced down at the beggar and put his hand in his pocket. Right at that moment, Kate was adamant that from somewhere in the distance, she could hear Alanis singing about putting one hand in *her* pocket…

Don't do it, Shay! Don't do it! Think of the kids! Please don't do it!

'There you go, mate,' said Seamus cheerfully, as he pushed a couple of fifty-pound notes into the beggar's hand. 'Get yourself a nice cup of tea.'

Kate laughed with relief and brought her hand up to her chest.

'I may be kind-hearted,' he gazed at her, bending his head down close to hers. 'But I'm not stupid.'

'My hero,' she whispered, standing on tippy-toes to kiss him full on his plump, juicy lips.

Kate was truly touched to see so many familiar, smiling, friendly faces as she walked through the front door of the Bonaparte, holding Seamus' hand.

'Happy birthday!' Archie, propping up the bar, was looking extremely pleased with himself as he raised his pint to Kate.

She figured he must have finally recovered from his bout of jealousy and come to terms with the very real possibility that faint heart may well have won fair lady this time. If she was to be so bold as to refer to herself as 'fair' – or, indeed, a 'lady'.

As she approached Archie, lips puckered, reaching out for the flesh on his right cheek, Tamsin intercepted. Kate's lips landed square on Tamsin's cheek, much to the amusement of the onlookers.

'Steady on, girls,' laughed Archie. 'There's more than enough of me to go around!'

'Now that's something you don't see every day,' sniggered Seamus. 'Although it might be nice if you did...'

'Urgh!' grunted Kate, resisting the overwhelming temptation to wipe her mouth with the back of her hand, as if to rid herself of Tamsin germs. But she wasn't that childish. Well, she was – just not in public, usually. And anyway, she'd spent ages applying her brown lipliner that morning – carefully colouring in outside her natural lip line, so that everyone would think she had big, beestung lips – and she couldn't bear to smear it off now.

'Way-hey!' Portia, Steve and Kevin cheered in chorus as they bounded up.

'So who's getting some birthday action, eh?' Portia nodded at Seamus and elbowed Kate in the ribs. 'I knew it! I knew you were saving him for yourself!'

'You don't want him, Porsh, really, you don't,' Kate whispered in her ear.

'No, I know,' Portia agreed cheerfully. 'I've got my eye on another prize, as a matter of fact.'

Portia looked wantonly at Kevin. Kate followed her best friend's gaze and felt a twinge of pity for poor Kevin as his Adam's apple bobbed up and down. Portia would, no doubt, eat him alive. He would never know what had hit him.

'Happy birthday, Kate,' came a rather timid female voice behind her.

She turned around and saw Lucy, the receptionist, offering Kate a little ESPA bag.

'Oh, Lucy!' squealed Kate. 'For me? You really shouldn't have – that stuff's way too expensive!'

'Well,' her big blue eyes blinked with shyness, lashes enviably thick and long, 'it's from both of us, actually. Just to say thanks.'

'Thanks?' Kate looked over shoulder to see who Lucy was batting her eyelashes at. 'What for?'

'For bringing us together,' said Medea, stepping into Kate's view and sliding her arm across Lucy's shoulders. 'If it weren't for you, we'd never have met.'

Lucy gazed up at Medea.

'Awww,' Kate cooed, 'thanks, guys!'

Kate suddenly thought of herself, Declan and Seamus from an aerial viewpoint, all snuggled up together, limbs entwined, their breathing in sync with each other... or, at least, Kate and Declan's were – in her mind's eye, Seamus looked like he was about to fall off the bed, his back turned to the cosy wife/son twosome.

Kate frowned. The fact that she and her husband weren't ever in the same room together *alone* anymore – let alone the same time zone – might really have something to do with the fact that they hadn't made love for... ooh, let's see... how long was it again?

'Absolutely yonks,' she said out loud, starting to panic. 'Argh! I'm never going to get back, am I?'

Just then, Tom's beaming face came sharply into focus.

'Ah, well,' he said, scuffing his Cuban heels nervously on the original Edwardian floorboards. 'That's what I've been meaning to talk to you about, Kate. I'm not sure how to say this, but… I don't think we should get back together.'

'And happy birthday to you, too!' Kate grinned, unfazed.

'Yeah, yeah, sorry,' he muttered, kissing her cheek. 'Happy birthday. I just don't think it's going to work between us. I think you're a great girl and so much fun and—'

'Just not *that* great or *that* much fun,' she finished his sentence for him.

'No! Don't be silly! It's me, not you…'

'Ha! That old chestnut!' Kate couldn't believe her ears.

He looked sincere enough, though, Kate thought. And seconds later, she found out why. When a pint of Caffrey's appeared out of nowhere over her shoulder, offering itself to Tom, she turned around to see where it was coming from and locked eyes with Steve's.

'To be perfectly honest,' Tom went on, 'it really *is* actually me, not you. I'm so sorry, but… well, I've met someone else.'

As he said the last bit, he looked longingly into Steve's eyes. Kate could hear their breathing getting shorter and more urgent. Their heads moved closer and closer until they could resist no more and then they proceeded to snog the very faces off each other.

'Blimey,' muttered Kate as she left them to it and made her way over to two leather sofas facing each other, a low coffee table in the middle separating them.

The couch backed up against the wall was packed to capacity and Archie was sitting next to Tamsin. Tamsin was fixated on Archie, hanging on his every word.

Kate wriggled her bum down into the small space between Portia and Seamus, buoyed by how completely painless her break-up with Tom had just been.

'Oops, sorry!' Portia growled as her thigh slammed into Kevin, sitting there quite innocently and unsuspecting at the end of the sofa.

She looked at Kate and said, 'You might want to go easy on the pies, my friend. But in the meantime, what say you and me and Beavis and Butt-head here get totally and utterly wasted?'

Kate drew in a sharp breath and held it. She'd love to really let loose and have a taste of some of the pure, unadulterated fun she used to love so much. But what about her horrible hangovers? That lasted three or four days. ? And what about her waistline – lord knows how many Weight Watchers points are in vodka Red Bulls! And what about the kids?

She chewed the inside of her right cheek, looked out of the Georgian windows and saw dark-grey clouds rapidly rolling across what had, minutes before, been bright-blue sky. The lights inside the pub flickered on and off, making a hissing sound as the first dollops of hard rain forced the punters sitting outside to run for cover.

Lightning streaked across and lit up the sky like spindly, sharp, blindingly white branches of light, threatening to electrocute and disintegrate the chimney pots of Notting Hill.

And then the thunder hit – as loud and as terrifying as though Thor himself had brought his hammer down on the rickety old roof of the Bonaparte.

'Ooh!' Tamsin squealed and leaped into Archie's delighted arms.

The rain pelted down on the pavements, bouncing off the stone slabs like they were mini cement trampolines, the wind howled and raged – and Kate watched it all, transfixed.

But the heavier and more oppressive it became outside, the lighter she felt. It was as though a great weight had been lifted off her shoulders for the first time in a hundred years and she felt not tied, not bound – but deliriously, deliciously *free*.

She quickly reasoned with herself. She was clearly never going to make it back to 2022; she didn't have any kids or job responsibilities to consider and, quite frankly, at this stage in the game, she'd had quite enough of being so prim and proper and old before her time.

'Oh, sod it,' she yelped. 'I'm in. Let's get trolleyed!'

As the rain storm turned into a torrential downpour and the barmaid had to turn 'Champagne Supernova' up to drown out the dreadful roar of the rotten weather, Kate put one arm around Seamus' broad shoulders, the other around Portia's bony back and began to sing her little heart out.

As she caterwauled along to the song, she slowly became aware that hers was a solitary (out-of-tune) voice echoing and bouncing off the grey concrete walls of what looked like the inside of the Blackwall Tunnel whooshing past her.

Suddenly she felt herself falling fast, her Rachel do whipping her face, flying all over the shop, despite her spraying nearly a whole can of Elnett extra hold on it earlier that morning.

And as an almighty crack of thunder frightened the life out of her, making her squeeze her eyes tight shut, she clapped her hands over her ears and screamed.

29

'Oh there you are, darling, where've you been?' Someone who looked a lot like Seamus smiled as he set out cutlery on the huge, long oak dining table.

Kate was staggering out of an enormous tastefull -decorated and beautifully organised Hamptons-style larder.

'I've been looking all over for you. They want you to accept the award for me, considering I'll be in India when they're holding the ceremony.'

Kate brushed a few fine strands of hair from her face and looked around her feverishly, like she'd just been tele-ported back to another time and another place. Which, in actual fact, she had.

She looked behind her, to her left, to her right and she gripped the edge of the luxuriously soft, rich milk chocolate-coloured nubuck leather sofa with her fingers.

An enormous mirror, framed in oak, hung on the wall to her right and she shot up out of her seat and raced up to it, desperate to get a look at herself.

Gone was the Rachel do (which, let's face it, never really worked all that well on her naturally curly hair and was always a total nightmare to maintain) and in its place was a short-ish, sophisticated layered dark-brown bob. Several grey hairs around her temples acted like visual klaxons to her fascinated gaze, but, actually, she quickly thought, they made her look…rather *distinguished*.

She pointed her chin to the ceiling and studied her neck. Yes, it was a teensy bit crêpe-y and, yes, those jowls she so fretted about had definitely reappeared along her jawline. But instead of shock and panic, Kate felt calm and cool.

No matter how tightly she stretched the loose skin up and pulled it behind her ear lobes, when she took her hands away, the sag was swift and inevitable. She did this several times, just to be sure, and felt a strange sense of relief every time, as though this was what she wanted to see, this was how things *should* be.

Her skin felt soft and dry – as opposed to slightly greasy and prone to break-outs – and she noticed that her face powder stuck well as a result and didn't look too caked on.

And even though her upper eyelids drooped a tiny bit lazily over her blue eyes, they still shone brightly back at her, twinkling excitedly, as she saw the reflection of their family planner on the kitchen wall screaming the date at her.

29 JUNE 2022

And underneath that, with lovehearts and balloons obviously drawn by kids, the words that made her heart sing:

MUMMY'S BIRTHDAY!!!!

A satisfied smile curled itself around her lips.

'Oh, here we go – earth to Kate, come in, Kate,' Seamus sighed wearily.

'Hmmm?' She turned around and faced him. And was struck by how handsome he looked.

He was wearing a lightweight cream sweater, the sleeves pushed up to reveal tanned, manly, hairy forearms. His trousers were tobacco-coloured and tapered at the ankle – were they skinny jeans? Her fashion-backward Seamus? Her eyes dropped to his feet and she brought her hand to her chest, taking in a sharp breath, when she saw they were shod in a moccasin-y French-looking loafer – without socks!

'The award? For services to the IT industry?' Seamus sounded a bit bored as he carried on setting the table. 'They want to give me a lifetime achievement for setting up the Institute for the Technologically Challenged. No biggie. But I'll be helping out at our orphanage in Kerala, so I won't be able to pick it up. I know it's a pain – but would you mind accepting it for me? It's your marketing genius that put us on the map, anyway...'

Kate stared. Her mouth dropped open and she felt the flesh between her chin and the base of her throat wobble a bit. Who was he? Who *was* this amazing man?

'Course,' Seamus carried on, 'we never would have been able to do any of it if we hadn't ever had the cash and the *cojones* to set up our own consultancy, all those years ago. It's hard to believe that once upon a time we were trapped in the basement of PGT&B, putting up with abuse from the suits and feeling like second-class citizens.'

He stopped and looked out the wall of glass doors, opening out onto the garden, manicured and lush, complete with trampoline, covered sundeck leading to a... what's that? A small house?

'I'm always a wee bit embarrassed that we profited so hugely from the internet and people's fear of it, to be

316

totally honest,' he went back to laying out the cutlery that looked suspiciously like real silver. 'But, you know, what else could we do?'

Kate couldn't believe her ears. For a start, Seamus was talking like someone who was at home in their own skin – someone who knew his own mind and wasn't backward in coming forward. He sounded so confident, so comfortable. And that small house out the back? Was that her garden office or something? Whatever it was, it fair blew Kate away.

She coughed and steadied herself on her pins, wandering back through the unnecessarily large downstairs open-plan Swedish blonde-wood-floorboarded room to the couch. Curled up on said couch, a stunning Irish Setter half-opened one eye, stirring slightly when she sat down next to him. This wasn't Rafferty, was it? Rafferty who was so big and badly trained he'd jump up on you and knock you down as soon as look at you?

'Rafferty?' She looked closer.

His tail lazily thumped on the couch twice in recognition and then he rolled onto his back, spread his back legs out in typical Setter-style as though he was presenting his fabulous family jewels to the entire world, and fell fast asleep, starting to snore almost instantly.

Charming, Kate thought and smiled. 'And what's this?' she said out loud.

A massive magazine sat on the coffee table, with a pair of pinky-purpley-framed glasses on top of it. She carefully picked up the glasses and placed them gingerly on her face. They were a perfect fit! And, all of a sudden, it was like the world around her had gone 3D, not the slightly fuzzy, blurry blancmange she was used to.

She dragged the magazine off the table – for it weighed a ton – and dropped it on her lap. Detail from *Dejeuner Sur L'herbe* (the naked lady in the foreground) was on the cover and Kate said the mag's title out loud when she read it, all big and bold in confident capital letters.

'FRAME.'

'Yeah – the latest issue from Lucy and Medea,' said Seamus. 'Came in the post this morning. Special birthday issue, apparently.'

'Is it… art?' she said absent-mindedly, flicking through the weighty tome.

Seamus scoffed.

'The eternal question, my love. They said to give you *their* love, of course, and apologies that they couldn't make it today – art fair in Bologna or some such.'

She looked up from the magazine and scratched her head.

'I'm off to St Andrews on Wednesday, too, hon, remember? It's our annual trip.'

'I… I…' Kate stuttered.

'Honestly, Katie,' Seamus looked at her as though she was mad. Or a bit thick. 'Were you on one of your nostalgia road trips when I told you last night? You seem ever so spacey. And I thought you'd sworn off living in the past… anyway…'

At that moment, she became aware of a familiar sound, music not unlike that she'd been hearing in the Bonaparte mere moments before.

'Who's this?' she pointed at the ether.

'What? The music?'

'Yeah.' She tilted her head back, as though the answer might be painted on the ceiling.

'Fuzz-ahhj, of course.' He went to the big double-doored American fridge and took out several bottles of Veuve Clicquot. 'Only the biggest, bestest supergroup since, oh god, I don't know.'

'Fuzz-*ahhj*?' She brought her head back down and squinted at him as though she couldn't be sure that she'd heard him correctly. 'Is that, like, French for bum-fluff or something? Fuzz-ahhhh—'

'Fuzzage! Fuzz and Mirage joined forces, remem— You sure you're OK?'

'Yeah.' She let out a little laugh, as though everything was fine and dandy. Completely normal. Fantastically hunky and totally dory.

'Those crazy guys – still mad fer it after all these years...' Seamus sighed fondly.

'Mu-um!' Declan shouted from somewhere upstairs. 'Where's my iPad?'

Kate's mouth rounded itself into an 'O' when she heard this. Her boy! Her baby boy!

'Don't shout from up there,' Seamus yelled. 'Come down here and talk to your mother like a proper person!'

'Just tell me where it is!' Declan sounded exasperated.

'It'll *be* where you *left* it!' Kate and Seamus said in unison, grinning at each other.

'I'll go.' Kate jumped up, the urge to see her offspring overpowering her.

When she got to the top of the stairs on the *first*-floor landing (there was at least one other storey on top of this one, she was delighted to see), she bit her bottom lip and looked longingly at the name plate on the door to her right that said PHOEBE surrounded by pink roses.

She brought her fist up and was just about to knock on that door, when she heard a decisive BUGGER OFF! from behind it.

'Charming,' Kate said to herself. 'Happy birthday, Mummy.'

She turned around and didn't bother knocking on Declan's door, just barged in.

It was the usual carnage in Declan's room – the toys, the clothes, the books, the unidentifiable chaos and clutter spread across the floor – but there was something different about it. Or, rather, *someone* different about it. Two someones, in fact. And both of them were sitting on Declan's bed.

'Hey, Kate,' said one boy who seemed familiar somehow, without looking up from his phone.

'Yo, Auntie K,' said the other, raising his hand for a high-five.

'Who—'

'Mum!' a jubilant Declan came crashing into view, crunching over the debris separating them. 'Where'd you put my iPad?'

Kate stretched her arms out and felt her face crumple as she dragged him to her.

She inhaled the delicious scent of her son; the hair infused with that heady mix of sweat, Lynx and Eau d'Adolescent, the t-shirt with the merest, lingering whiff of Tesco own-brand fabric conditioner still in its weave and the smooth baby-soft skin of his neck.

'I have missed you SO much, young man,' she sniffed into his shoulder, her embrace tightening.

'Mum,' he tried to push her off, 'you're hurting me! Let... go!'

Reluctantly, she relinquished her grip on Declan and beamed at him, wiping a tear from her cheek.

'What are you crying for?' he said, looking almost unbearably cute and impossibly doe-eyed. 'It's your birthday – you should be happy!'

'Oh, I am, sweetheart,' she laughed. 'I *am* happy. Delirious, even!'

Declan looked perplexed – or was it embarrassed?

'What I mean is, ah, we'll be down in a minute.' He waved his mother away with his hand and sat between the two other boys.

'Right, right,' said Kate. 'And who's "we"?'

Declan rolled his eyes.

'Mum said you were getting to that age,' said the first boy.

'When you start to forget who close friends and family are,' said the second one, nodding.

Kate narrowed her eyes and glared at the boys.

'You're not,' she started, 'you're not my nephews, are you? Has Steve had kids? But how? By what – surrogate?'

Declan tutted.

'Oh, Mum, just stop. Please.'

'Okay, okay,' she said, backing out of the room and closing the door.

She turned to look at Phoebe's door again. She took a deep breath and was just about to close her hand around the door knob when she heard that voice again.

'NO!' Phoebe barked from behind the door.

Kate retracted her hand and started down the stairs.

Some homecoming this turned out to be, she thought, as she schlepped into the open-plan kitchen/dining room/fantastic space.

But it was hard work and, quite frankly, exhausting to feel slobby and disappointed and cynical in this amazing house, so when the video doorbell rang and she looked on the small screen, she gasped.

'Portia!' she squealed, running through the *Good Housekeeping* cover-worthy house, trying to find the front door.

'Let us in!' Portia yelled.

When, finally, Kate did find the front door and put her eye up to the retina sensor so that it would open, she was practically bowled over.

Portia and Kevin threw their arms up in the air.

'HAPPY BIRTHDAY, KATE!' they chorused.

Kate was agog.

'Happy birthday, darling girl,' Portia said, bending down to kiss her best friend a nano-second before she wondered loudly who was playing such rubbish music. 'Can't you put some Haircut 100 on?'

'Happy birthday, Katie,' said Kevin, standing in the doorway, his designer stubble scratching her skin a bit as he kissed her continentally.

Kate was stunned. That Kevin and Portia were clearly a couple was enough to render her speechless. But when the penny dropped and she realised those two boys in Decko's bedroom were obviously the remarkable result of their union of beauty and the geek, it was all nearly too much for her.

'Come on, Porsh,' came Steve's voice from somewhere behind her best friend. 'Give the old girl a peck and let's get this party started!'

The twins and Decko came tumbling down the stairs as Steve, carrying loads of presents, kissed his sister on the cheek.

'Meet the newest members of our fam, Sis.' Steve stepped aside to reveal two beautiful, but painfully shy teenagers behind him.

'Shoosh, everyone!' he yelled, beaming with pride. 'Please put your hands together for Nina and Yosyp!'

Steve wolf-whistled and whooped, clapping his hands like a drunken, deranged performing seal.

The teens looked mortified by all the fanfare and tried to slip inside as surreptitiously as possible.

'Give over, Steve,' came a familiar voice from behind the kids. 'Just let them be.'

That voice. Sounded an awful lot like…

'Tom!' Kate gasped.

'That's my name, don't wear it out,' Tom said as he sauntered up to Kate and pulled her to him.

'Your brother is a NIGHTmare! As if these poor kids haven't suffered enough trauma in Ukraine,' he whispered in her ear.

'Conga!' Steve cried as he grabbed hold of Tom's hips from behind and shunted him into the kitchen.

Kate laughed, her heart nearly melting with all the warmth.

She closed the door and was just about to join the conga line when she heard distinctly belligerent knuckles rapping at the door.

But Phoebe was upstairs in her room, wasn't she?

Kate did the eye thing again and the door slowly swung open. And standing on the doorstep was her mother. Two suitcases by her side.

Here we go, Kate groaned to herself.

'Grannie!' Phoebe shrieked, pushing past Kate to get to her grandmother. 'So you *are* coming to live with us?'

'Wild horses couldn't keep me away,' Jenny said, hugging her granddaughter tight.

Kate had never seen such a display from Phoebe and felt a bit dizzy as a result. If that even *was* Phoebe. Her Phoebe – the one who would brook no quarter if she so much as sniffed a differing opinion? The one who was often seen sneering at home, but pouting on Instagram? The one who didn't give a tinker's toss about Kate?

'I've been fixing up the guest house for you all week,' Phoebe squealed. 'You're gonna love it so much, you'll never want to leave. Come on!'

Phoebe grabbed Jenny's hand and they practically skipped into the main house. As they passed, Kate thought she heard her daughter whisper, 'Happy birthday, bestie!' to her. But that would never happen. So who *was* this kid? And what had they done with her Phoebs?

Puzzled, Kate shook her head and went to join the throng, convinced she had finally snapped and was now officially stark, raving, in-bloody-sane.

At one end of the table, way down the other end of the room, Steve sat chatting to Kevin and Jenny. Right up the other end of the table sat Kate, surveying the celebratory scene before her.

She watched speechless as her family chattered and joked with her friends and laughed – an easy, relaxed laugh – pinching herself on both bingo wings, to check that a) her arms were back to being reassuringly flabby and b) she wasn't dreaming.

She closed her eyes and breathed in the sweet perfume of her favourite flowers. She flipped her eyes open, scanning the electricity sockets for Air Wick plug-ins, but she couldn't see any. Not even any empty, dusty ones! But white and pink lilies were everywhere – on the table, in the kitchen, on the hallstand – and as she let their smell overtake her, she felt an arm slip around her waist.

She immediately stiffened and sat up straight, trying desperately hard to hold her stomach in.

'Ah, it's no use,' she said, exhaling loudly. 'After a couple of kids and countless cupcakes, there haven't been any muscles down there since—'

'Who cares, Kate,' Seamus said, bouncing on his haunches next to her, his shaved head, stylish sideburns and Edwardian beard making him look rather dashing. 'Your body has given us our beautiful kids – why would you want it to look different?'

Kate's eyes searched Seamus for signs that this was an elaborate ruse and he was about to present her with liposuction or a face lift for her birthday.

'What a load of shi—' she started, incredulous. 'Are you serious?'

'Never been more so,' he said, his voice deep and steady.

Kate felt that dizziness descend upon her again and she fanned her face with her right hand.

'Is it getting hot in here?' she asked no one in particular.

'Open your presents! Open your presents!' Declan chanted, making minuscule dents in the table as he banged his knife and fork onto it.

Phoebe copied her little brother and soon the whole table had joined in.

But Kate, although obviously keen to find out what she'd been given for reaching the ripe old age of fifty-five, didn't want to break the spell she was under. And she was rather pleased with herself that she could string a sentence together at all, when she stared into Seamus' eyes and said, 'No matter what's happened in the past and no matter what the future holds, I just want you all to know...' She paused and looked meaningfully into everyone's eyes at this point, her chin dimpling, holding back a veritable flood of tears, 'that *this* is the best present ever.'

Both guests and family groaned in response to Kate's uncharacteristically mushy declaration, but Seamus simply cupped her cheek (and jowl) in his hand and let his gaze fall softly, intensely upon her own.

She felt sweat bead on her upper lip and something flip in her stomach again, as if trapped butterflies were flitting about in her belly. And, at that moment, everything except Seamus disappeared from focus, becoming one big, shapeless, amorphous mass rolling around her head like fog.

But she didn't wonder what on earth was going on. She didn't ask herself whether she was having a hot flush or coming over all unnecessary and lusty – nor did she entertain the possibility that she was even the slightest bit inebriated.

This time there was no doubt in her mind as to what this feeling was. She closed her eyes and let it wash warmly and deliciously over her, as though she was lying under a chocolate fountain with her mouth wide open on a guilt-free designated diet-break day.

It felt good. It tasted sweet.

And, this time, she knew it was love.

'So Tamsin and Archie have invited everyone over to the OFC,' Seamus said, standing up and walking back to the other end of the table.

'Is that some kind of boring football club?' Kate asked.

'No,' he grinned. 'It's their social club! Opened last week? You know! It stands for Old Farts Club – a club for the local over-fifties who are too old for nightclubs, but too young for lawn bowls.'

'Watch it,' Jenny warned.

'Yeah,' said Kevin. 'It's like a virtual chat room, but *actually* IRL. And way better.'

'They play banging Eighties and Nineties tunes,' Seamus piped up again. 'Not too loud, mind,' Jenny joined in. 'And you can get afternoon tea with scones and cream and play Scrabble if you want or—'

'Are we in an ad for it?!' Kate looked around for the cameras.

'Or you can just settle down on their couches for a good long chat with old friends,' Portia raised her glass.

'What a great idea,' Kate was impressed.

'So,' Seamus looked up. 'You want to go there, then?'

Kate's thin, wonkily-over-lined, Robert Smith lips twitched.

'Nah,' she smiled. 'Think I'd rather just be here, now.'

A letter from Mink

Ahoy there fellow menopausal mom-com fans!

I first started thinking about time travelling back to simpler, more carefree days when my wonderful kids were still very little. The Groundhog Day-ness, the chaos and the clutter would sometimes get me down if I ever got a moment to think about it. And then, one day, I was having one of those rare moments, having a shower during a Sydney storm – you know, rolling thunder, eyeball-meltingly bright lightning, hail stones the size of tennis balls – when I thought, wouldn't it be great if I got struck by a shard of lightning and was transported back to a time in my life when all I had to worry about was myself and making sure that when I left the flat I had two full packs of Marlboro Lights, a couple of lighters and enough cash for booze and taxi fare home in my bag? I answered myself out loud in the affirmative: 'Yes! It would be bloody amazing!'

Obviously, I realised it was never going to happen IRL, so I lived out my sci-fi fantasy on a Word document instead. I wrote about a dissatisfied, frustrated nostalgia-mad suburban mum who stumbles upon a time portal in her pantry that whisks her back to London at the height of her heyday, 1996, where she gets a once in a wife time second chance to make some tiny tweaks to her relationships and hedonistic outlook so that she can reap the benefits in the present, if she ever gets back to the future... And breathe.

With the invaluable help of my then-husband, I self-published *A Mother Dimension* to, quite literally, absolutely NO fanfare in 2013. I think I sold about 11 or 12 copies in the end. And I bought five of them.

Fast forward nine years and my brilliant publisher, Keshini Naidoo of Hera, told me she was looking for something about an older woman – and I am NOTHING if not an older woman – so would I mind refreshing *A Mother Dimension* for a 2022 audience? Would I mind?! Just try and stop me!

But so much has changed – thank God – and the casual but rampant sexism, racism, misogyny and homophobia of the Nineties looked bad in 2013, but it's a world, a universe, a veritable galaxy away from where we are now. Looking at the Nineties through the 2020s lens was like #metoo had never happened! Oh, wait...

Remembering those old days, those internet and social-media-free days – when no one knew or cared what you had for dinner and if, in the unlikely event you did take a photo of your meal, you had to wait at least two weeks to get the pix back from Snappy Snaps – did make me smile, though.

And as I re-wrote, I began to realise that in order to be present in the, um, present, you really do have to exorcise those demons of the past. To put it like an inspirational quote, you can't go forwards if you're always looking backwards. Or my new literary, book-based fave: you'll never start a new chapter if you keep re-reading the old one. So, so true!

I guess what I'm trying to say is I learned two big things on my trip down memory lane:

1. The past isn't all it's cracked up to be and
2. The present isn't all that bad, you know

Not that it's about learning or anything… but if you're confused and feeling somewhat at odds with the modern world, unsure whether you have a place in it; if you don't quite recognise yourself when you look in the mirror anymore; if talking to your kids makes you wonder whether you're living in a parallel universe… welcome to *The Glory Years*!

So here's to you, here's to putting your past behind you and here's to the future. Enjoy!

Lots of love,

Mink Xxx

Oh, and PS: So the fellas couldn't quite manage it in 1996, but thanks to those fantastic Lionesses, football finally came home in 2022. Proof, if proof were needed, that we are women, hear us roaaar! X

Acknowledgments

First of all, I'd like to thank the brilliant Keshini Naidoo, publisher/editor/person extraordinaire, for without her tenacity and foresight, *The Glory Years* would still be languishing about in a dark, damp long- forgotten, seldom-seen corner of the internet. I will be forever grateful for all your help, encouragement and enthusiasm, so here's to you, Kesh, you total ledge!

Speaking of legends, I'd also like to acknowledge, thank and completely out of time/tune sing the praises of my wonderful mum. Your optimism, grace and courage under fire inspire me daily and I'm so lucky to have you in my life.

And brilliant Dad – you're not the wind beneath my wings, you are my wings.

Ma-HOO-sive thanks also to Rolls, The Kezer, The Emster, The Deanster and Jaxie Jax for all your support – you put up with a lot and it can't be easy, let's face it! Lastly, thanks to Cucullain (Cooks) for never letting your beautiful sleeping self lie and barking at me incessantly to take you out from 6am–9pm on the daily. Yeah. Thanks a bunch.